# THE Fairest BEAUTY

*Other books by*
*Melanie Dickerson*

*The Healer's Apprentice*
*The Merchant's Daughter*

# THE Fairest BEAUTY

# MELANIE DICKERSON

ZONDERVAN®

ZONDERVAN

*The Fairest Beauty*
Copyright © 2012 by Melanie Dickerson

This title is also available as a Zondervan ebook.
Visit www.zondervan.com/ebooks.

Requests for information should be addressed to:
Zondervan, 3900 Sparks Dr. SE, Grand Rapids, Michigan 49546

ISBN 978-0-310-72439-1

All Scripture quotations, unless otherwise indicated, are paraphrased from The
Holy Bible, *New International Version®, NIV®.* Copyright © 1973, 1978, 1984, 2011
by Biblica, Inc.™ Used by permission. All rights reserved worldwide.

Any Internet addresses (websites, blogs, etc.) and telephone numbers in this
book are offered as a resource. They are not intended in any way to be or imply
an endorsement by Zondervan, nor does Zondervan vouch for the content of
these sites and numbers for the life of this book.

Published in association with the Books & Such Literary Agency, 52 Mission Circle,
Suite 122, PMB 170, Santa Rosa, CA 95409-5370, www.booksandsuch.com.

*Cover design and photography: Mike Heath/Magnus Creative*
*Interior design: Publication Services, Inc. and Greg Johnson/Textbook Perfect*

*Printed in the United States of America*

HB 08.05.2021

# Prologue

*Pinnosa passed through the town square and* the cobblestone *Marktplatz*. Hagenheim Castle loomed straight ahead. Once she passed the guard at the gatehouse, she would need to find her way to the young lord.

A chill passed over her thin, old shoulders. This fever, brought on by rain and exhaustion, would probably kill her, but if she could only make it to the castle, could only tell them that Sophie was still alive, Pinnosa's life would not have been in vain. Perhaps God would forgive her for helping the duchess perpetuate so many lies.

She plodded forward, wanting to hurry, but she could only force her swollen feet to take slow, mincing steps. Sweat dripped from her eyebrows even as she shivered and fought the urge to drop to the ground, close her eyes, and sleep.

"Who goes there?"

Pinnosa stopped, then leaned her head back as far as she could. When she parted her cracked lips, no sound came out. The guard's face began to blur, her knees trembled, and the ground quickly came up to meet her. Strange how she didn't ... even ... feel it.

# *Chapter*
# 1

Sophie kept her head bowed as she waited for the duchess to speak. She started to clasp her hands together but stopped. Clasped hands presented an image of idleness, the duchess often said, and the gesture sent her into a rage every time. Sophie let her arms hang limply at her sides.

Carefully, she peeked through her lashes at Duchess Ermengard. The woman's skin was unnaturally white, her hair dyed ebony using black hickory hulls. Her lips were stained red from berries, and her teeth were so white they made Sophie want to shade her eyes. Did the duchess ever think of anything besides beauty? The irony was that she was naturally beautiful and would look better without all the powder and dye.

The duchess stood unmoving, not making a sound. The silence began to crowd against Sophie's ears. Duchess Ermengard liked to draw out the waiting, knowing it only increased her victims' apprehension. Having to stand and wait to hear what her punishment would be was perhaps the worst part.

At long last, when the duchess addressed Sophie, her hoarse voice sent a chill down Sophie's spine.

"So this is how you repay my kindness to you? You, an orphan, and a girl at that. I could have let you starve by the roadside. Others would have done so in my place."

*No one but you would be so cruel.* Sophie's breaths came

faster—she was dangerously close to speaking—but she forced the words down.

"How could you be so audacious as to think … when I rightfully punish one of my servants … No. No, I want you to confess what you have done. You seem to enjoy prayer. Surely you enjoy confession as well. Now confess." Sophie's skin crawled as the duchess's voice lowered to a slow, quiet whisper. "What … did … you … do?"

Sophie almost wished the duchess would scream instead. A dark feeling of oppression, of an evil presence in the room, came over her, as it often did when the duchess was interrogating her. *Jesus, help me. Take away my anger.*

The oppressive feeling subsided.

Following the rote formula required by the duchess, Sophie began, "Duchess Ermengard, your servant Sophie confesses to sneaking food to your servant Roslind while Roslind was being punished in the dungeon." Sophie curtsied humbly. *Oh, God, please, please, please let it be enough. Let my confession be enough to appease her. And let me appear meek before her.*

Silence. Again. With a churning stomach, Sophie waited for the duchess to speak. Her hands trembled but she dared not hide them behind her back. The duchess had a rule against that as well.

Sophie waited so long for the duchess's next words that her mind began to wander, imagining what her friends, the other servants, would be doing now. But she pulled herself back, bracing herself for what the duchess would say or do next.

"You confess as though you're not truly sorry for what you did."

"Please forgive me, Duchess Ermengard." Sophie suppressed a shudder. This was not going well. It was no longer a matter of if she'd be punished, but how severely. She bowed her head lower, hoping to appear truly repentant. Even though she wasn't.

"And there is more, isn't there?" Once again, the duchess let the silence linger.

What would the duchess accuse her of now? Sophie searched her mind for things she had done that the duchess may have uncovered. She had given food to some starving children who had come begging at the kitchen door, but that had been days ago. She searched her memory for something else ...

Then she remembered. Yesterday she had followed a guard into the woods, and after he'd heaved a sack of squirming puppies into the river, against her better judgment, Sophie had dived in after them. Dragging the heavy cloth bag from the bottom of the shallow river, she'd dumped out all five creatures on the riverbank, wet but alive. Someone must have seen her and told the duchess. She couldn't read minds, could she?

"Nothing to say? You know what you did. You defied me." The duchess's voice sounded like the hiss of a snake. "You followed the guard to the river in order to save those worthless, mongrel puppies. You are a disobedient, deceitful, horrible little wretch." She spat out the words as if they were venom.

Sophie's mouth went dry. Duchess Ermengard hated dogs, especially lap dogs. Anything small and helpless incited her hatred. And these puppies would never grow anywhere close to the size of hunting dogs, which the duchess gave to Lorencz the huntsman to use in his deer hunts.

"I expect my orders to be obeyed. I don't expect my scullery maid to defy them." She said the words *scullery maid* the way she always did, as though they were a curse.

Sophie thought about the tiny dogs she'd saved and remembered their soft fur and the way they'd whimpered and licked her hand. For a moment she could almost feel the little brown-and-white one snuggled against her cheek. The feel of his furry little face against her skin had made her feel loved, as if he knew she'd saved him.

"You are a wicked ..." The cold, hard edge of the duchess's voice tore Sophie out of her pleasant memory.

Sophie closed her eyes. *I will not listen. I will not listen . . .*

". . . rebellious, disrespectful girl. You will learn to respect me. You were nothing, a changeling orphan, an ugly child. You wouldn't even be alive if it weren't for me."

*I am not wicked. I am not ugly.*

The duchess was snarling now, her voice growing louder. "You will learn not to treat my rules with contempt. You will be disciplined."

Sophie didn't have to open her eyes to see the malicious glint in the duchess's eyes or to see her lips pressed into that tiny, pinched, cold smile, the smile she always wore when doling out punishment.

*I am not wicked. I am not rebellious . . .*

Sophie longed to touch the wooden cross that hung from her neck, to squeeze it and feel comforted by the thought of her Savior's suffering, his compassion and forgiveness. But she didn't dare. If the duchess found the cross that was hidden under her dress, she would tear it away from Sophie and destroy it.

"For your wickedness," the duchess went on, slowly, as though savoring each word, "you shall spend the next two days and nights in the dungeon with no food or water."

Two days and nights. Sophie's heart seemed to stop beating. But at least, maybe, the duchess was finished with her.

Sophie curtsied, keeping her head low. She focused on replying according to the duchess's rules. "Let it be as you say, Duchess Ermengard. I am your servant Sophie."

Two soldiers came forward and grabbed her by her arms.

Just as she relaxed slightly, Sophie heard, "Wait! Bring her here."

Sophie's stomach dropped. What would the duchess do now? Sophie determined not to show panic as the two guards dragged her forward. Any expression of fear would only make things worse.

"Look at me," the duchess ordered.

Sophie lifted her face, preparing herself for the black emptiness of the duchess's eyes.

As soon as their gaze met, the duchess lifted her hand and slapped Sophie across the face.

Stunned, Sophie closed her eyes against the sting, tasting blood on her teeth. Her eyes watered but she refused to cry. She took deep, slow breaths to drive away the tears as the duchess kept up her cold stare. *I mustn't show weakness.*

Time and silence hung heavy in the air. Then Duchess Ermengard ordered, "Take her away."

The guards pulled Sophie, stumbling, across the stone floor toward the dungeon.

Gabehart hurried down the corridor with his father, Duke Wilhelm. The slap of their boots on the flagstones echoed against the walls. An old woman had been brought in the day before, feverish and unconscious. Gabe had paid the visitor little mind until their healer, Frau Lena, sent for him and his father, saying the woman had awakened and was telling a tale they needed to hear firsthand to believe.

Of course, if his older brother Valten hadn't broken his leg a few days ago, keeping him confined to his chamber, she wouldn't have sent for Gabe at all.

Gabe and his father entered the healer's tower and strode across the room to the sickbed. The mysterious traveler lay still, her white hair plastered to her head, her wrinkled eyelids closed. Her lips were white and her cheeks gray. *Is she already dead?*

Frau Lena, their tall, red-haired healer, curtsied to Duke Wilhelm. "Your Grace"—a nod to Gabe—"my lord. Thank you for coming."

"Are we too late?" Gabe glanced from the healer to the old woman on the bed.

Frau Lena smiled. "She's only sleeping." The healer's expression grew thoughtful as she stared down at her. "She'd been mumbling since she was brought in, but her words made no sense—something about saving someone before the evil one kills her." Frau Lena shrugged. "She was so feverish I didn't pay attention. But this morning, she awoke. Her fever had lessened, and she begged me to send for 'the young lord who is betrothed to Duke Baldewin's daughter.'"

*What?* Gabe glanced at his father. Duke Wilhelm's forehead creased.

"Go on," Duke Wilhelm said.

"When I told her Duke Baldewin's daughter died as a small child many years ago, she said, 'No, it's a lie. She lives. Tell the young lord to go to her, posthaste, and save her from …'" Frau Lena hesitated.

"From?" Gabe found himself leaning toward the healer.

Frau Lena let out a deep breath, then whispered, "From Duchess Ermengard."

Gabe sank back on his heels. Visiting merchants often told stories about the queenly duchess, claiming she never left her castle in Hohendorf, dabbled in black magic to the extent of placing curses on those who crossed her, and even poisoned people. But Gabe had never seen her. Rumors said she never left her castle.

If Duke Baldewin's daughter *were* still alive, it made sense that she could be in danger from the shadowy Ermengard; Duke Baldewin's daughter would be sixteen, maybe seventeen years old, making her a threat to the duchess's rule. Though surely someone would have corrected the erroneous report of her demise by now. The truth would surely have leaked out and spread to Hagenheim. Or so one would think.

And if Duke Baldewin's daughter were still alive, that would mean Valten was still betrothed. His brother was going to be awfully surprised to find out he had a bride.

A strangled croaking sound came from the bed. The old woman's faded blue eyes opened and locked on Gabe's face. She lifted an emaciated hand toward him, beckoning him closer with a crooked, skeletal finger.

"Come here."

He looked back at his father, who nodded, so Gabe stepped forward and dropped to one knee by her bedside.

He was handsome, though he looked quite young. There was something so pleasing in his features. Such gentleness, an earnest look in his eyes. If only he were strong enough, clever enough … *God, help him.*

Pinnosa's voice was weak, along with the rest of her, and she willed her words to reach the young man's ears. He was Sophie's only hope. "My lord, I am an old woman, soon to look my last on this earth." She paused to breathe. She was here. The one she had journeyed to find knelt before her, and she would soon impart her secret to him. If she weren't so feeble, she'd laugh with joy.

The man picked up her limp hand and pressed it gently. Such kindness to a poor, old woman on her deathbed.

"And you are Duke Wilhelm's son?"

"I am."

"The secret I have to tell you has cost the lives of more than one person." Pinnosa spoke haltingly, stopping frequently to draw in another shallow breath. "You must be brave, strong, and highly favored by God to escape the same fate. Are you willing to hear my tale?"

"Aye, frau. Proceed."

"I was a servant in Duke Baldewin's castle when his daughter was born. The poor mother died, and His Grace was heartbroken. His wife had been exceedingly fair—her skin, pure and perfect as new-fallen snow; her eyes, the bluest blue; and her hair, black as ebony and silky as a waterfall. The baby girl was the very image of her."

Pinnosa closed her eyes to rest for a moment. Her strength seemed to be ebbing away with every word she spoke. She must impart only the most pertinent information. After managing to take in a little air, she opened her eyes and continued.

"The duke remarried. His new wife was beautiful, but heartless and cold. I believe she killed the duke."

Shock flickered over the young lord's face. He was sheltered and seemed inexperienced, but at least the surprise was quickly replaced by anger. *Stoke that fire inside him, that sense of outraged justice I see in his eyes.*

"People would tell me I shouldn't say such things. But I am old. It doesn't matter what happens to me if I can save Sophie."

"Did you walk all the way from Hohendorf?"

Pinnosa tried to laugh, but all she could manage was a wheeze. "You can look at my feet and legs if you don't believe me." They were swollen to twice their normal size. "I would walk much farther for Sophie."

The only way she'd been able to get away without raising the duchess's suspicions was by faking her own death. She'd taken a bit of one of the duchess's sleeping potions, which slowed her heart and breathing until people thought she was dead. She had bribed the mute son of a farmer to dig her back up after dark. It had been risky and terrifying to be buried alive beneath the cold earth, but if Pinnosa had left the castle any other way, the duchess would have sent her men after her to kill her. Duchess Ermengard was too powerful, too clever. Pinnosa was one of only two people still alive who knew that Duchess Ermengard had faked the death of her stepdaughter. The duchess had long ago killed everyone else who could have revealed this secret.

"Who is Sophie?" the young lord asked.

"Sophie is a servant in Duchess Ermengard's service. A scullery maid. But the truth is she is the duke's daughter." Pinnosa managed to squeeze his hand. "I saw in a dream that the duchess will kill her soon if someone doesn't intercede. Please ... save her. If you don't hurry, Duchess Ermengard will destroy her. She delights in tormenting her. Sophie ... so kind and gentle ... may God ... watch ... over her."

It was done. Now she could sleep.

# Chapter 2

*The moment the woman stopped talking, her* hand went limp in his. Gabe waited as Frau Lena examined her. After a few minutes, Frau Lena shook her head.

"Her heart has stopped. She's gone."

A chill passed over Gabe's shoulders and he shuddered. What if it were true? A beautiful girl, born to be a duchess but being used as a scullery maid, tormented by her own stepmother. How would he feel if such a thing happened to one of his sisters? His chest tightened at the cruel injustice.

He couldn't stop staring at the old woman's body, trying to divine the truth from her features. But what reason did she have to lie? Someone had to at least investigate the old woman's claims and attempt to help this Sophie.

Valten should save her. His brother Valten was the warrior, always excelling in tourneys, in jousting and sword fighting with the best knights of the Holy Roman Empire and beyond. But right now, Valten couldn't even walk without help.

"Gabe." His father touched his shoulder, pulling his gaze away from the face of the dead woman. "Come. We must discuss this with Valten."

Gabe followed his father through the castle corridor to Valten's chamber. What would his brother think of this woman's claim? Would he believe it? And who would their father send to uncover the truth in Hohendorf?

Gabe should go. His father had too many concerns and duties at home to go cantering off on a wild chase after a kitchen maid who may or may not be a dead duke's daughter. And Gabe couldn't imagine his father sending one of the knights out to handle something so intimately connected to their family.

He also had to admit that the thought of saving this girl himself was strangely appealing. No one thought of Gabe as a warrior. He was a rambler, a fun-loving friend, but certainly not a knight. He had never cared for fighting or jousting and left the tournaments to his older brother and his father's knights. As the second son, Gabe *should* have trained as a knight or applied himself to a trade such as a master mason or even joined the church. But none of those things appealed to him—a life of chastity least of all. He preferred roaming the countryside with his friends, sometimes drinking too much and doing other activities he was glad his parents knew nothing of. His few skills included flirting with fair maidens, playing the lute, and archery. In fact, archery was the only war sport in which he could best Valten.

If Gabe rescued his brother's betrothed while Valten lay helpless in bed with a broken leg, it would be perfectly ironic. Valten traveled the world entering tournaments and winning glory and gold. But Gabe could do one better—rescue a girl from a terrible fate, thwart an evil ruler, and complete a quest that should have been Valten's.

Perhaps Gabe wasn't as tall or as muscular as his brother, had not the sheer girth or physical power his brother possessed. But here was his opportunity to impress his parents, his brother, and even Brittola, the girl he was expected to marry.

Gabe followed close behind as his father entered Valten's bedchamber. The heir to the duchy of Hagenheim was propped up by pillows and reading a book.

"Thank God you've come." Valten closed the tome with a loud snap. "I was about to come out of my skin from boredom."

Valten was indeed pitiable in his forced confinement to his room. With all his purpose and energy and strength, the passivity of healing didn't fit him very well.

Gabe hung back as his father approached Valten's bed and began relating the story of the old woman who had just died in the healer's chambers and the tale she had told. Gabe watched closely as astonishment and something akin to disbelief clouded his brother's eyes.

Several moments passed while they waited for Valten to absorb the information. He seemed to be concentrating on the cover of the book in his lap, his eyebrows scrunched. Gabe had the strangest feeling that his future depended on what his brother would say.

When he finally spoke, Valten's voice was low. "Probably just an old woman's senile ramblings." He glanced up and met his father's eyes. "But we must find out."

Duchess Ermengard stared into her mirror. During the past year, tiny lines had appeared around her eyes. The white powder hid them. Mostly.

Sophie had no wrinkles or even a blemish. Ermengard's lip curled as she thought about the girl's pale, perfect skin and the natural red of her lips, her thick black eyelashes and brows. The way Lorencz the huntsman's eyes lingered on the girl made Ermengard's blood boil. Did he think the little chit was fairer than Ermengard? While two days in the dungeon should take some of that rosy glow out of the girl's cheeks, the duchess had started to question if she should keep that wretched child around. Ermengard enjoyed forcing her to work as a scullery maid, making her do her bidding. Inwardly she gloated over Duke Baldewin and imagined his pain; if he only knew what his only *beloved* daughter was suffering. But watching her capture the attention of Lorencz … it was time to get rid of either her or Lorencz—or both.

She gazed into the mirror, studying her face more closely. Was her skin starting to sag beneath her chin? Perhaps if she cut off a fold of skin just below her jawline it would be tighter when it grew back together. She couldn't abide sagging jowls. She wouldn't allow them.

A knock sounded at the door. "Come in."

Lorencz entered and bowed low. She extended her hand and he kissed it, lingering long enough to make her smirk at him. *You'd* better *endear yourself to me …*

"You wanted to see me?"

"Yes. I need you to do something."

"Anything, Your Grace."

Perhaps she should insist he call her something besides "Your Grace." That sounded too formal. Her husband had called Sophie "my precious," never noticing the seething rage it caused in her, his wife. He never called Ermengard sweet endearments like that. She could order Lorencz to call her that … No. He wouldn't mean it.

What did everyone see in Sophie? It seemed as though her fellow servants couldn't do enough for her. They all flocked to her, wanting to help her. It was sickening.

"I want you to kill someone for me."

Lorencz did not look away from her direct gaze, a quality she admired in a man. "Did someone try to run away again? One of the servants?"

"No." But if they had, the penalty was death. The duchess couldn't afford to have anyone leaking her secrets. If the king knew of the people she had killed or of Sophie or of what had become of Duke Baldewin … "I have just sent the scullery maid, Sophie, to the dungeon. I want you to gain her trust. Then, when she gets out, I want you to take her somewhere in the woods and kill her."

There, the look on his face ... was that disgust? Or merely distaste? Her huntsman wasn't going soft on her, was he?

"Take her some food or some wine, maybe. I want you to kill her without a struggle, without anyone knowing. No screams. I want her to simply ... disappear." She allowed a smile, imagining the girl's pain when Lorencz betrayed her, when he thrust his knife through her heart.

"You will have to bury her afterward. I don't want anyone finding her body. We'll say she ran away, and no one will be the wiser." *And no one will ever know who she truly is.*

Unless she was mistaken, Lorencz had turned a shade paler. "It shall be done as you say, Duchess Ermengard."

"Do not fail me. Now go."

Sophie held her wooden cross against her cheek. She had whittled it herself from a piece of cedar and wore it tied to a strip of leather around her neck. It was rather large and somewhat thick, and she had to be careful to keep it hidden down the front of her dress. Feeling the smooth wood against her skin, she whispered her prayers as she paced back and forth across the hard, earthen floor of the dungeon. Staying in constant motion kept the rats away. She couldn't continue pacing all night, but she wasn't tired enough to stop—yet.

As she was being dragged away to the dungeon, Sophie had glimpsed Lorencz entering the duchess's chamber. Were the rumors about him and the duchess true?

The huntsman had arrived at Hohendorf a few years before. He was handsome—even Sophie thought so—with his wavy brown hair and daring smile. And he had seen much more of the world than anyone else she knew. All the female servants sighed over him, giggling and whispering whenever he came into view. His confident swagger differed greatly from the bent-over, bow-legged shuffle of most of the men in the village, and his bright-green leather jerkin, brown-leather knee boots, and jaunty cap were a stark contrast to the dull-brown woolen tunics, loose hose, and hoods with long, floppy tippets the servants and poor villagers wore. Compared to them, Lorencz was almost a different creature.

But it was no business of Sophie's what the huntsman and the duchess did together. She wouldn't waste time thinking about them.

She shivered as the shadows deepened outside the high, grated window, located at eye level. The early spring air still wielded a sharp chill. Despite the breeze, the small dungeon chamber reeked of human waste, proof it hadn't been cleaned since the last person spent time here, but she was already growing used to the smell. Stench was the least of her troubles.

As Sophie paced the dungeon cell, she prayed for Duchess Ermengard, since the book of Saint Luke told her to love her enemies. It was a difficult task, she had to admit. But the verses also said that God would someday put her enemies under her feet. She supposed she needed to be righteous for God to do that, so she continued praying for her enemy.

Duchess Ermengard was an unhappy person, given to vengeful speeches and angry outbursts, and Sophie shuddered to think how the duchess would be punished if the injustices perpetrated by her—especially all the cruel things she had done to the innocent people who served her—were discovered. Trying to kill defenseless puppies was the least of her offenses. Sophie had heard whisperings of people the duchess had murdered over the years, often with poison the duchess concocted herself. And she had killed at least one servant Sophie knew of, a servant who had attempted to leave Hohendorf without the duchess's permission.

The duchess's sins spread yet farther. She had destroyed the castle's chapel when Sophie was only seven years old, and she'd done away with the village priest. Sophie wasn't sure if the duchess had killed him, but she must have, or he would have told someone what she'd done. The church in Hohendorf had been vandalized and looted, but many people, including Sophie, still went there to pray. She could still see the young priest's face, could still recall his reverent look when he spoke of Jesus the Christ and his love for mankind, his sacrificial suffering.

One of the maids had rescued an illuminated, transcribed portion of the Holy Writ that had been destroyed when the duchess burned the chapel. The rescued pages contained the book of Saint Luke, or most of it. Sophie had kept this precious portion of the Bible hidden ever since, and only took it out when she was certain none of the duchess's spies were about. She wished she had it now so she could read it. In truth, she practically had the whole portion memorized.

The familiarity had come in part because she often had to read it aloud to the other servants, as she was the only one who could decipher its words. The priest had secretly begun teaching her Latin when she was five years old, claiming it was because she was the last surviving member of a noble family, though she still didn't know what he'd meant by that or who her parents were. She had long ago decided the priest must have been mistaken—what noble parents would leave their daughter in such a dreary and hopeless demesne, and as the lowest servant of such an evil duchess?

Facing the small window, Sophie let her mind travel. She was standing in the middle of a sunlight-drenched meadow, situated in a safe, spacious, warm land far away from the duchess and her evil intentions. She was free. No one was yelling at her or belittling her or locking her in a dungeon.

Sophie wasn't sure if she had dreamed the vision of her standing in the sunny meadow, or if it was a vision from God. All her life, as far back as she could remember, she had lived on the hill of Hohendorf, at Hohendorf Castle, where the dense forest surrounded the stone castle and blocked out the sun. Sophie had never experienced an open field. Each day was dominated by the gloom and shadow of the forest. In fact, when Sophie felt oppressed by her surroundings, she recalled the time she had been allowed into an upper tower to help clean. There, through one of the windows, she had seen the village below, at the base of the castle hill, and had gotten a far-off glimpse of a sun-soaked meadow. For a moment, in front of the window, she had felt the sun flooding her from head to toe. It had seemed like heaven, and she had wanted to experience that again.

Of course, as a servant, it was a sin to run away from one's mistress. But would Sophie not actually be saving the duchess by escaping? By leaving the duchess's service, she was keeping the duchess from further sin — the mistreatment of an innocent person. And Sophie *was* innocent, for she had always tried to be a good servant to the duchess. No, that wasn't true. She had sometimes done things she knew the duchess wouldn't like. Things that had led to her standing in this cell now — saving the drowning puppies and sneaking food to Roslind when she was in the dungeon.

When Sophie was younger, she'd thought if she were good enough and behaved well enough, the duchess would come to love her, or at least treat her better. But she had eventually come to realize that her efforts were wasted on the duchess.

Still, because of what the Bible said and what the priest had told her, Sophie stopped herself from taking petty revenge on the duchess like some of the servants did when they spit in her food or spoke hate-filled curses against her under their breath. The priest had once told her — this she remembered clearly — that God loved the merciful and pure of heart. The priest had also said that she must never hate anyone. Hate was of the devil, and love was of God. So even though the duchess had locked Sophie in this horrid dungeon with the rats and the filth—all because she had saved some puppies—and punished her for every perceived slight, Sophie must not hate her. And, Sophie reasoned, since she was the servant the duchess hated the most, leaving the duchess's service was the greatest gift of mercy she could bestow on her mistress.

"Jesus," she whispered. Just saying his name comforted her as she came to accept that she was going to be locked in for two days and nights. Two days was a long time to go without food or water, so daunting a thought Sophie had to clutch the cross to her chest and pray more fervently.

"Sophie."

She looked up, squinting at the window. A hand was there, holding an apple. She hurried over and found Roslind kneeling on the ground outside, which was level with the window.

"You shouldn't be here!" Sophie grabbed the apple through the bars. "Make haste! Get away before the guards see you. I couldn't bear for you to get in trouble."

"No one is around." Roslind peered in through the bars. "Your lip looks swollen. Did someone hit you?"

"It is nothing. It barely hurts." Further evidence of the duchess's sins. "I'm glad you came and am thankful for the apple, but you really must go unless you want to join me in here."

"All right, Sophie. I'll be praying for you."

Sophie smiled at her and waved at her to go.

Roslind smiled back and called, "Good-bye, sister!" as she ran off.

Both Sophie and Roslind were orphans and had no siblings that they knew of, but they and the other servants were their own family.

Sophie bit into the apple, hoping to eat it before the rats smelled food.

The apple tasted sweet, though it was a trifle shriveled, left over from the previous autumn. Sophie wrapped her arm around herself while she ate the entire thing, then threw the stem and core out the window.

She stared out at the trees that shielded the setting sun, and a chill that had little to do with the cool air nipped at her heart. Her constant prayer was that God would provide a way of escape. Somehow, some way, she would have to flee, and she sensed it would be soon. She was old enough, a grown woman at seventeen years old. It was time she attempted what no one as yet had ever accomplished—escape from Duchess Ermengard and Hohendorf Castle.

She hated to leave behind her "family," the other servants she loved. Sophie often daydreamed ways to save them all. Sometimes she thought of ideas that seemed almost possible, and other times her ideas were farfetched—finding a magic pond that granted wishes, or encountering a brave knight who offered to save her and her friends from the duchess.

But daydreaming would do her no good. She must start planning.

If she were to marry a free man, her husband could take her away. But the duchess would never allow that. Could she hide amidst the traveling merchants' wares? No, guards searched each cart as it left the Hohendorf gates.

As she pondered each potential mode of escape, the rats became bolder, skittering out of the dark corners of the dungeon and watching her, their beady eyes shining in the dark room. Sophie forced herself to ignore them.

As the sun began to set, she noticed someone else approaching her window. "Mama Petra!"

The cook, Petra, lifted her skirt and ran the rest of the way, falling to her knees by the window.

"Here, Sophie. Some bread and cheese for you. Eat it quickly. And a stick to keep the rats away."

Petra shoved the things at her through the bars. Sophie grabbed the food but couldn't catch the stick before it clattered to the stone floor. She almost laughed.

"Oh, Petra, you mustn't be seen! I couldn't bear it if you were punished for helping me."

"Nonsense, child." Petra stuffed her hand through the bars and squeezed Sophie's arm. "I would do much more for you, my dear."

Sophie saw tears in Petra's eyes as her bottom lip quivered. Then Petra jumped to her feet and hurried away.

"Thank you, God," Sophie whispered. "Thank you for Mama Petra and Roslind."

She set about to eat her food as quickly as she could. If she got rid of the evidence, perhaps her friends wouldn't get caught and punished for helping her. Although it seemed as if Duchess Ermengard had eyes everywhere and could see through the very walls.

The sound of a key grating in the door lock made her jerk away from the window. She shrank into the dark corner, clutching the half-eaten food to her chest.

The door creaked open and something came sailing through it, landing on the floor. Then the door slammed shut again, the key grating once more.

Sophie crept over to see what had been thrown in.

A blanket of gray wool. She picked it up. It smelled clean, so she wrapped it around her shoulders, unable to hold back the smile on her face. "Who could have done this?" she whispered to herself. Most likely, the old guard Walther. Sophie had helped care for his sick child when everyone else was too afraid to come near, frightened of catching the strange fever that had been accompanied by a rash. Sophie suspected he had a soft heart for her because of it.

The scratching of the rats came closer, reminding her to eat. She bit into the hunk of cheese, then her bread. It was still fresh and soft. She sighed as she chewed.

"Sophie." This time a large, dark form knelt at the window. *Lorencz.* Her heart skipped a beat as she recognized him. He'd paid a lot of attention to her lately, and she couldn't help but wonder why.

And now he was kneeling by the dungeon window, calling her name.

Ever on her guard around anyone connected to Duchess Ermengard, Sophie asked stiffly, "What do you want?"

She heard a confidant laugh. "Come and see."

Slowly, Sophie stepped closer, dropping the blanket to the floor and flipping her apron up over her food to hide it.

As he watched her, she studied his face, which was hard and flinty, with sharp angles. A short, stubbly, light-colored beard covered his chin and jaw, and a small scar cut a line under one eye. But he was undeniably handsome, especially a moment later when he flashed his smile, showing perfect, white teeth.

"See what I brought you?" He held out a flask.

"What is it?" She shouldn't let him think she trusted him.

"Some wine. I heard you were here and thought you may need the refreshment. I know the duchess forbid you to have water, but she never said anything about other ways to quench your thirst."

Sophie stared at the flask. She had no desire to indebt herself to him by accepting his gift, but two days and nights without anything to drink was a dreadful thought. Still, she made no move to receive it. She wasn't dying of thirst yet.

"Perhaps I can convince the duchess to let you out after one day instead of two." He quirked his eyebrows up.

Sophie chewed her lip. Why was he being kind to her and offering to help? Or was he pretending? Sophie had learned early in life that she was unprotected in this cruel world, and the way to survive was to be suspicious of everyone's motives and intentions until proven otherwise, especially if they had more power and freedom than she had.

"Will you accept my gift?" He held the wine flask up to the bars.

Sophie hesitated. She reasoned that perhaps this was God's way of providing. Perhaps God had sent him. She would like to believe this man was the answer to her prayers. But she didn't dare; a deep part of her warned that his gift came from an ulterior motive.

Then she remembered the pain of thirst, the sharp, raw ache in her throat after one day without water, the horror and desperation of the second day.

Sophie slowly reached her hand toward the window. Lorencz slipped the flask through the bars into her open palm.

"Thank you."

"It is my pleasure. Have I told you how comely you are?"

"Once or twice." She forced a hard, sarcastic edge into her voice.

"You should go for a picnic with me tomorrow."

"Even if I were to agree, that would be impossible. I will still be in this dungeon tomorrow." She tapped one of the bars for emphasis.

"Not if I get you released early."

"How do you plan to manage that?"

"I have my ways." His eyes flashed mischieviously.

"A personal favorite of the duchess, are you?"

"You might say that." His voice was deep and smooth.

"I see."

"I like you, Sophie. You're not like the other servant girls."

"You're wrong. I am exactly like the other servant girls." Poor, orphaned, and powerless against her mistress.

"No, there's something special about you." He leaned his

shoulder against the stone casing around the window, giving her a lopsided grin, his eyes focused on her face. "You have" — he sighed — "a beauty that is quite rare. Any man would be proud to have you for a wife."

Sophie snorted and was glad she had allowed the rude sound to come forth. She wanted him to know she didn't trust him, that she believed his mention of marriage was a ruse. He was hoping to fool her into trusting him.

"Why don't you trust me, Sophie? Don't you believe that I like you? That you've stirred this hard heart of mine?"

*So he admits his heart is hard.* "Maybe I don't trust you because I've heard it all before. Maybe you're not the first to lie to me . . . to attempt to lead me astray."

Lorencz laughed out loud. Sophie resisted the urge to shush him. She supposed it wouldn't matter if he did get caught, seeing as he was immune to the duchess's rules and above punishment. Still chuckling, his gaze returned to her face, and she tried hard to find sincerity in his expression. Was it possible that he was willing to help free her from Duchess Ermengard's clutches? Unfortunately, there was a wily, secretive glint in his eyes that made such hopes seem foolish.

Still, it was tempting to throw off caution and tell him she'd love to go on a picnic with him, just so he would get her out of her cell. Perhaps she should agree. Why not?

*Why not? For many reasons.*

Though his laughter had ceased completely, he continued to smile at her in a way that made her feel funny inside. His half grin, his confident look, and the obvious strength in his broad chest and shoulders appealed to her much more than they should have. If anyone could help her escape the duchess, it was surely this man.

He leaned into the bars, only a foot away from her. She took a half step back.

"Come with me," he whispered, his brown eyes mesmer-izing her, like an invisible string holding her to him. "I promise not to lead you astray on our first picnic together." His mouth twisted in a grin.

Sophie's heart thumped hard against her chest. He was handsome, yes, and he had singled her out, but he was danger-ous. She had to keep telling herself that.

"Very well, then. If you can get me out, I'll go with you."

Sophie immediately regretted her words.

Lorencz jumped to his feet. He swept the leather cap from his head and bowed low. "Fare well, then, my lady."

He was mocking her now. He chuckled as he strode away.

She shuddered at the commitment she now couldn't rescind, even as a surge of hope rose inside her.

# Chapter
## 3

*Valten had stared down the tip of a lance and* had been confronted with broadsword and battle-ax, but those tournament games seemed like a child's playacting. His betrothed alive? And in danger? If there were any small possibility that she was his betrothed, he had to go and rescue her. But how? He couldn't go anywhere with a broken leg.

"We must find out if this Sophie is Duke Baldewin's daughter. It wouldn't be right to ignore the woman's claims." Valten clenched his hand into a fist and met his father's gaze. "I would leave today if I could sit a horse."

"I know, son." His father thoughtfully rubbed his jaw.

Valten glanced at Gabe, who stood in the background, looking as deep in thought as Valten felt. Surely Gabe wasn't concerned with this business? Valten felt a twinge of resentment at his little brother even being allowed in on the discussion. After all, Gabe was no warrior. What could he do? And it wasn't *his* betrothed in question. It was Valten's. Or, rather, she might be.

"I would go and take a few knights with me," Duke Wilhelm said, "but I have that emissary coming from King Sigismund in two days. It is too late to put him off."

Gabe stared steadily at Valten, then at his father. Valten knew that look. His little brother was about to propose something thing foolhardy.

"You must send me, Father. I can find the girl." Gabe was twenty years old, only two years younger than Valten, but in Valten's eyes Gabe was still a mere boy—an irresponsible, reckless boy who often overestimated his charm and the trouble it could get him out of.

Valten stifled a laugh, which came out as a snort. "Come now, Gabe. You know ..." Valten shook his head at him.

"What? You can't go, Father can't go, but I can."

Valten raised himself higher, pulling himself up with his arms until he felt a stab of pain in his leg. His face grew hot at hearing his brother state the obvious.

"Do you think you can save a duke's daughter from an evil and powerful duchess? Do you fancy yourself a fierce knight bent on rescuing the damsel in distress?" Valten knew he was being unkind to his little brother, but Gabe needed to come to his senses. "You only like the idea of playing the hero and saving *my betrothed.*"

Gabe glared back, holding his brother's gaze without blinking.

Valten folded his arms across his chest and turned to the man he knew would support his argument. "Father, you're not thinking of letting him go, are you?"

His father raised his brows and took a deep breath. He turned to Gabe. "Son, I'm glad you are willing to go, but I'm afraid it's just too dangerous for you to venture alone. When Valten is well again, we can travel to Hohendorf. Besides, the old woman's claims will most likely turn out to be false. We may learn there is no Sophie, and the duke's daughter is dead, as we have all believed for the past fifteen years. And even if there is a Sophie who turns out to be the duke's daughter, she will be safe until we are all able to journey there."

Gabe shrugged and looked at the floor. "As you say, Father."

He was giving up too easily, which was a sign that Gabe had

an idea—a dangerous idea. Gabe had better not be planning to take on the rescue alone, because Duchess Ermengard had a very alarming reputation, and Gabe was just a thoughtless boy.

Just as Sophie's eyes closed and her body and mind threatened to relax enough to let her fall asleep, the scurry of tiny claws against the hard dirt floor forced them open again. She lifted the stick and brought it down with a whack. It missed the rat's head by a whisker and violently jarred her arm all the way to her shoulder. Sophie stifled a moan and sighed instead.

She'd hardly slept all night. As soon as she felt herself dozing, another rat would scuttle close. One had even run across her foot just before daybreak. She shivered at the memory. A scar on her wrist was all the reminder she needed that rats had sharp teeth and assumed everything was food until proven otherwise.

A gray light showed itself at the window. The night was over. Her arms trembled as she pulled the blanket tighter about her, and she drew her knees up to her chest. "God, please save me from this place," she rasped. But she refused to pity herself. Pity would only make her cry, and crying was worse than useless; it would give her a headache.

She might as well drink the last of the watered-down wine, especially as she needed to get rid of the flask before any of the guards found it. No doubt the duchess would lengthen her stay in the dungeon by another day or two if she knew Sophie had been given food and drink. Her bread and cheese had long since been eaten—so as not to send the rodents into a frenzy, driving them with more desperation toward her.

Uncorking the flask, Sophie said a quick prayer of thanks, thinking of Lorencz the huntsman, and drank the last of it. Then she hid it under a loose rock in the farthest corner.

And not a moment too soon, as she heard the sound of

metal scraping metal—a key in the lock. The door creaked open with agonizing slowness.

Sophie waited to see who was there and what they wanted before expending the energy to stand.

"Come," a gruff voice ordered. "Time to go."

Sophie scrambled to her feet, dropping the blanket—too late to try to hide it. Walking as though in a daze, she climbed the steps and passed through the doorway while the guard held the door. Could Lorencz truly have secured her release after only one night?

A terrible thought entered her mind. Perhaps the guard was letting her out so he could take her to the duchess for more railings, and so the duchess could strike her again.

Sophie looked at the guard, waiting for his orders, but the man only walked away. Within moments, other footsteps sounded down the corridor, growing louder as they came closer. Should she run before the person saw her? Maybe the guard had let her out by mistake, a mistake that would be remedied by the person stalking toward her.

But as the nearby wall torch illuminated the man's face, Lorencz's features came into view.

He smiled. "Little Sophie. You survived the night."

She felt a surge of gratitude that made her knees sag. He stepped forward and reached out to her, as if he thought she was falling.

Sophie warded him off by raising her hands. "I am quite dirty."

He looked slightly affronted but recovered his smile quickly. "I shall come for you at midday for our picnic, then, after you've had time to bathe. Shall I meet you at the back door of the kitchen?"

Sophie blinked at him, unable to make sense of his words. Ah, yes. She had almost forgotten her promise to spend a meal with the huntsman.

"I am sorry, but I have work to do. The cook needs my help."

"Then I shall speak to the cook. Surely she can spare you for one hour."

"You may speak to her, but Petra can get very angry, and I am certain she will not allow me to go with you." That much was true, but only if Sophie could get to her first and warn her not to say yes to the huntsman's request. "Petra keeps me quite busy." *And I will make sure she continues to need my service during every meal.*

"Don't use me ill. You will dine with me as soon as I can free you from the kitchen?"

Sophie nodded. "I shall."

He winked, then turned and walked back the way he had come.

She couldn't hold him off forever, though. Eventually, she would have to keep her word and go on that picnic with him.

Gabe strode down the corridor to his bedchamber and began gathering up some clothes and supplies, shoving them into a bag he could attach to his saddle. His brother had been right about one thing during his puffed-up tirade—Gabe did want to "play the hero" and save Valten's betrothed. Admittedly, he had not yet done anything heroic in his life, but how hard could it be to outwit a secluded duchess and rescue a servant girl?

This was his chance to show that he was just as brave as Valten, as well as have the adventure of rescuing this seventeen-year-old maiden from her dire circumstances.

Minstrels would write songs about him that would be sung through every demesne. He might even help them craft a line or two.

Best of all, Valten would be furious that his younger brother had gone on a quest that was rightfully his.

But it was much more than that. Gabe felt a yearning inside him to go and rescue this girl, a compulsion so strong it almost overpowered him. He wasn't even sure why a strange maiden would affect him so much.

Then he remembered his little sister and how he had let her drown. Gabe hung his head as a sudden rush of memories flooded him. Gabe had felt such a heavy weight of guilt — and still did. If he could save this Sophie, it wouldn't bring Elsebeth back, he knew, but ... he suddenly wanted to save this other girl so much it caused an ache in his chest.

At dinner that night, Gabe listened as his father and mother discussed the news that Valten's betrothed might still be alive, and discussed when Valten and Duke Wilhelm would be able to make the trip to Hohendorf. As if their next-eldest, healthy, brave, and willing son wasn't even an afterthought.

Gabe chewed his food slowly, plotting his own trip. He would sneak away during the night with plenty of provisions and borrow some old clothes from a servant so he could pass himself off as a poor pilgrim on his way to some cathedral or other. He was thinking through his plan, mentally gathering the things he would need, when his mother spoke up.

"Gabehart, you look so lost in thought. What are you thinking of?"

Gabe knew he shouldn't reveal anything, but he couldn't resist finding out just how much his parents believed he was capable of. "Mother, what if I went to Hohendorf to find out if this story is true, if Duke Baldewin's daughter is truly alive and being mistreated by her stepmother? I would be more than willing to do so."

"My son," his mother said, looking alarmed, "how could you think about doing such a dangerous thing?"

"Mother, I'm not exactly a child." She had no issue with the dangerous things Valten did — his broken leg was proof.

"I am glad you want to help this girl. I think it's very noble of you. But instead of thinking about saving Valten's betrothed, you should be thinking of Count Waldomar's daughter, Brittola." Her voice was gentle, more pleading than chastising. "Don't forget, you've agreed to marry her. She's the perfect wife for you ... quiet, sweet, raised in a sheltered, peaceful home. And her father will gift you a large estate adjoining his own."

Gabe stared into his goblet of wine. His mother meant well, after all. He felt a pang of conscience when he imagined how worried she would be when it was discovered he was gone. He should not grieve his parents. The saints above knew they both had experienced more than their fair share of grief already.

His mother and father were good parents who loved their children and each other. They rarely disagreed, and they smiled at each other more often than any two people he'd ever seen. He'd realized that not all married couples were so happy when he started observing some of his friends' parents. He'd even seen his friend Otto's mother clobber her husband over the head with a small barrel of vinegar, smashing it and soaking the man, then screaming that it was probably the first bath he'd ever had. He couldn't imagine his own mother doing such a thing.

As for his mother encouraging him to marry the count's daughter, Brittola ... he had every intention of marrying her. It was a profitable marriage for Gabe, since, as a younger son, he would inherit little from his parents. And she was pretty.

"What does Brittola have to do with this?" he asked.

"I'm not sure how Brittola would feel if she heard you had gone to Hohendorf to save a young, beautiful maiden."

"Mother, you can't think I have designs on Valten's betrothed." He raised his eyebrows at her. "This girl may not even be his future wife, but if she is, I hardly want to take her away from my brother. I just don't see why I can't go and simply look into this old woman's claims."

"You can. When your brother's leg is healed and your father's duties allow him to leave, you can go with them."

Gabe swallowed his pride and the angry retort that was on the tip of his tongue and instead hung his head. He could pretend compliance. After all, he didn't want her to guess what he was planning. "Yes, Mother." *Whatever you say.*

# Chapter
## 4

*Gabe headed south for seven days, the last* few without encountering a single village or inn. He was counting on his father not sending soldiers after him. After all, Gabe often went on adventures without telling others where he was going.

On the seventh day, when he realized he was nearing Duchess Ermengard's castle, he backtracked into the forest and discovered an abandoned cottage, its roof caving in. One corner of the dilapidated house still seemed well sheltered from rain, and that is where he stowed his weapon—his crossbow and arrows—and also his regular clothes. He exchanged his comfortable, fine linen shirt for a rough woolen tunic he'd brought along to disguise himself and filled a leather bag with items needed to convince the duchess he was a poor traveler. His horse and saddle could still give him away, but that couldn't be helped. He couldn't leave Gingerbread in the woods to fend for himself. Especially since Gabe didn't know when he'd be able to come back.

And now that he thought about it, he should change his horse's name to something more warlike than Gingerbread.

Gabe already envisioned his success; he would rescue Duke Baldewin's daughter from being mistreated as the duchess's servant—a fate worse than death—and restore her to her rightful position. Then he'd take Duchess Ermengard to the king to stand trial for her misdeeds. Poets would immortalize him, the whole countryside would sing of his valiant deeds, and beautiful maidens would throw their scarves at him whenever he rode down the street.

Even Valten would be impressed. He would take back all the abuse about Gabe being a weakling and show him respect for the first time since they were young children.

Gabe held his head high as he led the horse through the village of Hohendorf on his way to the castle, until he reminded himself to try and look more humble, to keep his head down and stop thinking about his future triumphs. But as he looked around at the townspeople going about their day's work, he realized he could not have come close to looking as humble as they did in their tattered and stained clothing. Most of them were gaunt, appearing half starved, their clothing hanging off their sharp, angular shoulders and hips.

No one smiled. People stared at him as if his face had turned purple and horns had sprouted from his head. One carter was bent over, picking up the handles of his cart, when his gaze landed on Gabe and his horse. The man jerked back, his eyes round. Gabe stared back at him until the man seemed to collect himself and nodded a simple greeting.

Gabe nodded back and said, "*Guten Morgen.*"

The man mumbled, "Good morning."

Why were the people so startled to see him? Was the presence of a stranger such an odd occurrence in this town? Did he look so out of place? Or was something else amiss?

He looked around for a shop of some kind where he might find someone loitering, or a group of people talking and passing the time. But there were no clusters of people anywhere on the street. He kept walking until he came to a baker's shop. He flung Gingerbread's reins over a post and stepped inside.

His eyes slowly adjusted to the dimmer light. The shop

seemed deserted. There were no cakes or fruit pasties for sale, only a few round loaves of coarse bread.

A man entered the room from behind a curtain in the back, rubbing his hands on his apron. His step stuttered a bit when he saw Gabe, and his eyes narrowed.

"*Guten Morgen*," Gabe greeted.

The baker nodded his acknowledgment. "Some bread for you?"

Gabe nodded toward a loaf and handed the man a coin. The baker took it and handed the bread to Gabe.

"I am new to this village and was wondering if you think Her Grace, Duchess Ermengard, would be interested in hearing my music. I play the lute and write song—"

"Your music won't be welcome here." The man's eyes had grown quite large while Gabe was speaking, and his voice was gruff. "You'd best leave here and go elsewhere."

"The duchess doesn't like music?"

"She don't like strangers. Nor music."

"How long have you lived here?" Gabe decided to try a different tact. Perhaps the man would open up and give him some information.

The man narrowed his eyes.

"Were you here when Duke Baldewin was alive?"

The man brought his fist down hard on the heavy wooden counter and leaned toward Gabe. "Hist, stranger. You are barking down the wrong trail. This is no place for you. If you want to see the morrow, I suggest you depart forthwith."

Gabe stared at the baker until he turned and left the same way he had come.

Walking back out into the street, Gabe retrieved his horse and continued through the village. The few people he saw stared at him until he tried to make eye contact, then they invariably looked down. Should he try to talk to someone, try to get lodging for the night in the village, and try to find someone who would answer his questions about a girl named Sophie? If no one was any friendlier than the baker, he would be wasting his time.

Hohendorf Castle stood above the village, on a forbidding hill overlooking the valley inhabitants and surrounded by a dense forest of evergreen trees. Even though the winding road that led up the hill to the castle looked steep and long, Gabe felt a thrill of boldness stiffen his spine and make him walk faster. He was almost there, and he suddenly felt very close to what he was looking for.

At the top of the castle mount, he came around a bend in the road and found himself in the rear courtyard of the castle. He entered the copse of trees that surrounded the road and courtyard and tied Gingerbread to a tree.

Several yards away, a woman stirred a large black pot over a fire. She wore similar clothes to the women in the village, with a stained apron covering her front. As he moved closer, two maidens stepped through the kitchen door into the courtyard.

Gabe hid behind a tree to watch. It was probably best to find out as much as he could before he incited anyone's curiosity.

The maidens were giggling, until the woman stirring the pot shushed them. She pointed to what appeared to be a heap of clothing resting against the wall.

"Quiet, now. Sophie's asleep."

*Sophie!* He'd only just arrived and had found the girl already. *I may be able to leave this place before sunrise tomorrow.* He hadn't proven she was Duke Baldewin's daughter, however. That would no doubt take quite a bit more time.

As the two maidens hurried off down a worn path into the woods, the woman left off stirring the pot and went toward the heap. Carefully, she peeled back an apron that was on top, revealing the face of a young maiden. After watching her for a moment, the woman left the girl's face uncovered and went inside the kitchen.

Finding himself alone with the sleeping girl, Gabe crept toward her, keeping just inside the cover of the trees and bushes. When he was barely twenty paces from her, he stopped and studied her.

She lay curled into a ball, her head pressed against the hard stone wall. Her face was relaxed, her eyes closed, and he was sure she was the most strikingly beautiful girl he had ever seen. Her skin was pale and flawless, her lips a dark rose color, and her hair a glossy black. The girl's eyebrows and lashes, the same black as her hair, stood out against her pale skin.

Was this Duke Baldewin's daughter? His heart seemed to press painfully against his chest as he felt a deep yearning to protect her, to save her and fight for her.

This girl could be Valten's betrothed and the daughter of a duke. But other than her extraordinary beauty, there was no outward sign she was more than a common servant. If the old woman, Pinnosa, had simply been senile, then this girl was no more a duke's daughter than those people he had just seen in the village below.

What should he do now? As Gabe weighed his options, he heard breaking twigs and rustling leaves, the unmistakable sound of someone walking toward him.

A guard appeared around the side of the castle, a sword hanging down from his belt and bumping his leg with every step.

The man was enormous, and as he came around the corner, his eyes went straight to Sophie. He halted a few steps away from her, grunted, and then muttered angrily. Like a territorial bull, he lumbered forward, and Gabe held his breath again. If the man intended to harm Sophie ...

Gabe crept out of the trees, trying to stay quiet, his eyes glued to the huge guard's back. The guard went straight up to Sophie and drew his foot back to kick her.

"Halt!" Gabe leaped toward him.

The guard spun around with a fierce growl. His hand hovered menacingly over his sword hilt.

Gabe faced him down, even though he had no weapon except a dagger concealed in his boot. He wasn't used to having to look up at anyone, since he was taller than most men. But the guard was even taller than Gabe, and his girth would make two of him, maybe three.

This giant could crush him with a few blows of his immense fists. Not to mention his sword could slash Gabe to death in the blink of an eye. But Gabe couldn't back down like a coward, and he couldn't let the brute kick Sophie while she lay there asleep, looking defenseless.

The enormous man's eyes grew wide, his face turned red, and he roared, "Who are you?"

Out of the corner of his eye, Gabe saw Sophie sit straight up, then scramble to her feet.

A woman's voice sounded behind the giant, getting closer as she ran toward them. "Who's there? What is it? Sophie, are you all right?"

Gabe decided to change his story, since the one about being a troubadour hadn't gone over very well. He turned to address the guard. "I am but a poor pilgrim on my way to see the relics at Aachen Cathedral."

The giant guard snorted and glanced over his shoulder. When he saw Sophie standing there, he stuttered. "S-Sophie, is this man bothering you?"

Her eyes were wide — the brightest blue eyes he'd ever seen. She rubbed her cheek as she spoke. "No, I've never seen him before."

The guard turned back and shoved Gabe's shoulder, knocking him off balance. "Don't stare at Sophie!" he roared — the only tone of voice he possessed, apparently.

"You were about to kick her," Gabe accused the giant.

The servant, a slightly plump woman who had run up behind the giant, gasped and put her arm around Sophie.

The giant looked sheepish as he glanced back at the two women. "I didn't know it was Sophie. I couldn't see her face from where I was standing. You know I would never hurt Sophie." He turned back to Gabe, anger returning to his face. He flexed his massive arms by his sides and leaned down over Gabe. "I'm not done with you, stranger. Who are you and what are you doing here?"

Gabe resisted the urge to turn his head and cough, as the man smelled like he'd been eating raw onions and garlic.

After catching his breath, he said, "I told you. I'm a pilgrim from Hungary on my way to Aachen Cathedral." He reminded himself to try and look humble, like the villagers he'd just seen. "My name is Gabe, and I'm also a musician." Should he have chosen a different name? Though who would be looking for him here?

"A musician?" The man grunted in disgust.

"I was just traveling through this region—"

"Why did you come up here? The castle mount is hardly on your way."

Gabe had no idea how to answer that question and realized he should be acting more afraid of this man.

"I came to seek an audience with Duchess Ermengard. I thought perhaps she might enjoy my lute playing for a season and would send me on my pilgrimage with her blessing."

"If you're looking for work of that kind, you won't find it here. The duchess doesn't like music. Or musicians."

Gabe thought about telling the man that he preferred to ask the duchess himself what she liked and disliked, but he held his tongue. Instead, he bowed humbly and said, "You are wise, I am sure."

The giant frowned and shook his head.

Who did this man—very handsome and not much older than she was—think he was fooling? He was no poor pilgrim from Hungary.

Sophie studied him from where she stood by the fire, dipping candles in the black iron cauldron, taking over the job from Petra, who had been helping her so Sophie could rest. She'd been awake most of the night nursing a sick maid. The young man sat on a stool against the wall, drinking the watered-down wine she'd given him. Walther had taken his horse, with its expensive-looking saddle, to the stable while the man stayed with Sophie.

The stranger's boots were some of the finest she'd ever seen, the kind worn by noblemen. Few enough noblemen came round their castle, but Sophie had seen a pair just like them on a margrave who'd called on Duchess Ermengard a couple of weeks before. And this "pilgrim" had obviously forgotten to take off his gold ring, with a large ruby in the center, when he'd donned his poor-man's disguise.

Besides, he didn't have the visage of a pilgrim. He lacked the sun-beaten, haggard, shuffling look of someone who'd been traveling for weeks over mountains and dusty roads. Instead, he had the distinct look of the rich and privileged, with his high cheekbones, straight nose, and well-groomed hair and fingernails. But more than anything else, it was his tranquil demeanor that set him apart.

He was obviously lying.

Roslind, who had been scrubbing the front steps of the castle, came around the side and threw her arms around Sophie's neck. "I thought you'd be picnicking by now!" Sophie tried not to cringe at the reminder—for a week she'd been putting off her promise of a midday meal with Lorencz, and she'd run out of excuses. Today he'd been making a show of ordering various foodstuffs from the kitchen.

Not that Sophie could be angry with her friend for her excitement about the huntsman wanting to take her on a picnic. Roslind was sweet, with her wide-set brown eyes and pretty, childlike face that looked much younger than her sixteen years. In her innocence, she likely assumed the time with Lorencz would be enjoyable. Sophie loved and protected her like Roslind was her own little sister, but it was the truth that the girl's head was as empty as a day-old sparrow's. Most people realized this right away, and Sophie was always interested to see how they then treated her.

Roslind turned toward the "traveler," and Sophie watched the interaction between her and their guest as she continued her work of dipping candles.

Roslind chattered away at him, innocently inquiring, "Where are you going to? We almost never see strangers here. Are you lost?"

The stranger, who called himself Gabe, smiled. "No, I'm on my way to Aachen Cathedral."

"Where is Aachen Cathedral? Is it very near?"

"It's many days' ride from here, to the northwest."

"Where do you come from? Have you seen much of the world? I have heard there are large waters a long way from here—waters so big that you can't see the other side of them. Have you been there?"

She continued to ask him lots of questions, and he patiently supplied answers.

The stranger had a gentle, though guarded, expression, and he was obviously being evasive with Roslind. He might fool Roslind, but he wasn't likely to fool the other servants or Duchess Ermengard. And it was a dangerous thing to try to fool the duchess. The last person who'd tried had ended up buried behind the old cemetery in an unmarked grave.

Gabe simply didn't know who he was dealing with, and someone needed to warn him.

Roslind went inside the kitchen to help Petra prepare the midday meal, leaving Sophie alone again with the stranger. She approached him as he sat on his stool, still drinking the tankard of wine she'd given him. He looked up, much too boldly for a poor pilgrim, and met her gaze with the warmest brown eyes she'd ever seen. For a moment she felt a bit startled and almost forgot what she was about to say. She cleared her throat.

"I would advise you to not approach Duchess Ermengard with any requests. Our mistress, the duchess, isn't given to hospitality."

He smiled at her, and she had to remind herself to breathe. She wasn't sure she had ever seen anyone with such an unworried look on his face. It was quite a contrast to her fellow servants, who looked out of hunted, desperate, bloodshot eyes more often than not, their teeth stained and uncared for. But his teeth were even more perfect than the huntsman's.

He was more handsome than Lorencz too, and he completely lacked the hardened expression Lorencz often wore.

She glared at him, uncomfortable with her own reaction to this stranger. But she must make him see the danger he was in. It would be tragic indeed if this handsome young nobleman ran afoul of the duchess. He wouldn't even live long enough to rue it.

"You must be careful," Sophie said in an urgent whisper.

"Careful? Of course. I am always careful."

His lack of fear frightened her. How could she impress upon him the need to hurry on his way?

He had found her. There could hardly be another servant here named Sophie with such black hair, fair skin, and rose-red lips. He was not sorry at all that he'd come on this quest. He had the oddest impression that he was exactly where he was supposed to be, that his whole life had been preparing him for this.

Sophie's eyes were a deep blue, framed by the longest, blackest lashes he'd ever seen, making her Brittola's exact opposite. She wore a tattered dress and an even-more-tattered apron, but the state of her dress didn't seem to diminish her loveliness. Her movements were captivating—even the simple act of rubbing the sleep from her eyes before going straight to work dipping candles.

He could see that he would do well to bring Brittola to mind from time to time.

The other servants—the cook and the large, burly guard—had warned him that their mistress the duchess would not tolerate being disturbed at this time of day. If he was determined to speak to her, the best time was just before the evening meal. So here he waited, alone with Sophie.

Using a stick to hold the candles, which dangled from one long wick, a candle on each end, Sophie lowered the candles into the hot beeswax in the pot over the fire. Two by two she dipped the candles, then hung them over a piece of twine that stretched across the back courtyard. Each time she dipped a pair of candles in the hot wax, she let the excess drip back into the cauldron before hanging the candles back over the line to cool and harden. It was a long process to form a good-sized candle, but each time the candles were dipped, it formed another thin layer of wax.

Her hands were red from touching the hot wax. Gabe imagined how rough and callused her hands would be if he were to turn them over and examine them. The hands of a servant, not a noblewoman.

Again, he wondered if the old woman had told the truth.

Was Sophie actually the daughter of Duke Baldewin? For some inexplicable reason, he believed it.

Abruptly, Sophie stopped her work and looked around shrewdly, then lowered her voice to a whisper. "Duchess Ermengard doesn't like strangers. She is not a person to trifle with. You should leave while you have the chance."

"Don't I look like a man who can take care of himself?" He smiled and lifted his eyebrows at her in a way that always made young maidens blush and giggle.

But Sophie placed her hand on her hip, cocked her head to the side, and said, "I am not seduced by your *charm*"—she said the word as if it were a disease—"and flirting. You're lying about who you are. I'm no fool, and neither is Duchess Ermengard, so if you are wise you will leave now."

He may not have charmed her, but he was beguiled by her flashing blue eyes and lovely face. He tried again to make himself look humble, then took a different approach. "You are obviously a maiden not to be trifled with. I was hoping to ask the duchess for work. I can play the lute and sing." He patted the bag that was slung over his shoulder, out of which protruded the handle of what Sophie assumed was a lute.

"Oh no. That is not a good idea." She looked over her shoulder and shuddered.

"Why not?"

"Walther already told you—the duchess doesn't like music or musicians."

"It's hard to imagine someone who doesn't like music."

Sophie shrugged. "Strange, but it is indeed true."

He'd finished his wine and set the tankard down on the ground.

"So you are leaving now? You should not tarry."

Her eyes became hopeful, anticipating his imminent departure. Was she really that concerned? Or did she only want to get rid of him? Sophie had no idea she was the whole reason he was here. Not that he would tell her yet. He had to focus on his next course of action — finding out if Sophie truly was the duke's daughter and learning why the duchess was keeping her existence a secret.

He stepped toward her until they were face-to-face, only an arm's length from each other. He lowered his voice. "Do you know who your parents were?"

She narrowed her eyes, obviously suspicious. "Why do you ask about my parents?"

He was as subtle as an ox. But perhaps it was better to go ahead and tell her the truth. "Did you know a woman named Pinnosa?"

"I know only one Pinnosa, and she died a few weeks ago. She was buried beside her husband in the churchyard."

"Was she a servant here in the duchess's castle?"

Sophie stood silent and unmoving. Finally, in a soft voice, she answered, "Yes. She helped Petra, our cook, in the kitchen." Her expression turned defensive. "What do you know about me? About Pinnosa?"

"She told me you were in danger."

"Ridiculous. She's dead, and you're the one who's in danger."

Why was she being so stubborn? He was here to rescue her. The least she could do was give him a chance to prove himself. "Is it so strange that I would come here to help you?"

She looked him straight in the eye. "Yes."

"You're the one who's being ridiculous."

"Am I? I'm a servant, while you are clearly not from Hohendorf and are lying about being a poor pilgrim." She sneered when she said those last two words. "Now you tell me a dead woman told you I was in danger."

This was not going as he'd hoped. He needed to gain her trust, and he'd done just the opposite. But she was not even giving him a chance. She didn't even appreciate his smiles and attention. Why was this girl so distrustful? Well, she wanted the truth. He'd give her the truth.

"Pinnosa did not die a few weeks ago, and she's not buried in the churchyard."

"Is that so?"

"She only pretended to be dead."

"You've lost your senses."

"I know it sounds farfetched, but she walked all the way to Hagenheim to tell us that you are in danger. I've come here to help you."

Sophie spun around on her heel, picked up her stick, and resumed dipping candles. "You're the one who needs help. I can take care of myself. Besides, who goes around thinking they can save servants from their cruel mistresses?" She shook her head and refused to look at him.

He'd imagined her heaping thanks on him for going to so much trouble and endangering himself to save her. Instead, she didn't even believe him. Didn't trust him one whit. *Ungrateful girl.* Perhaps she wasn't Duke Baldewin's daughter after all.

~❦~

She was only a servant. Why would he ask about her parents? This stranger was behaving very suspiciously. And this story about Pinnosa only pretending to be dead ... Sophie had seen them close the coffin. She had seen it lowered into the ground. But now that she thought about it ... some of the maids had been whispering the following day about the grave being disturbed and how strange it was that grave robbers would have bothered to dig up a penniless old woman.

Could Gabe—if that was his real name—truly have spoken to Pinnosa? But his story was ridiculous. Pinnosa, faking her own death ... it was preposterous. Pinnosa was a common-enough name. But why? Why was this man making up these strange stories?

He ran his hand through his hair and frowned. "The truth is," he went on, "I only met Pinnosa briefly, but she was adamant that you were in danger."

He hesitated, watching her closely, as though trying to read her thoughts. His intense brown eyes and good looks made her heart beat faster. She would have to be extra cautious with this man. He was much too handsome and flirtatious to be trusted.

Besides, Sophie already knew she was in danger. Anyone the duchess hated—and she certainly hated Sophie—was in danger. But this stranger could no more protect Sophie from the duchess than he could have saved himself from the beating Walther almost gave him.

At least Sophie knew what to expect from Duchess Ermengard. This stranger had no idea.

"What did she look like, this Pinnosa? And what did she say?"

"She was very old," he replied. "She was hunched and had a mole below her left eye. Her hair was white and her eyes were faded blue."

It certainly sounded like Pinnosa. Sophie turned away from him, trying to collect her thoughts.

"And what did Pinnosa tell you?" she asked again.

He stared hard at her. "She said you were Duke Baldewin's daughter."

Sophie returned his stare. He looked perfectly sane and serious. Her mind went back to when she was a little girl: The priest singling her out to teach her to read. Pinnosa and Petra whispering in the kitchen. Sophie had heard her name and the name of Duke Baldewin, but when the two cooks had perceived her standing behind them, they abruptly stopped talking.

Could it be true? Was she Duke Baldewin's daughter? The

duchess's hatred of her would make sense, as the duke's widow wouldn't want to share Hohendorf with anyone. She wouldn't want the king to learn of an heir's existence either. King Sigismund might want to marry Sophie off to someone, after which she could safely reveal all the duchess's evil secrets, including the fact that the duchess dabbled in magic and created potions and poisons.

But perhaps this was all a trap. The man could be lying. He could have been sent by the duchess to trick her. It was the sort of entrapment the duchess delighted in.

She turned away from him, as though the conversation were a waste of her time, and went on with her task of dipping candles. She pretended to ignore him while her mind raced. If this man knew she was the duke's daughter, and if he forced the duchess's hand, Ermengard would kill them both. It seemed so terrible, especially when she probably *wasn't* the duke's daughter.

Why would he come here, alone, to tell her this? Perhaps he was crazed, daft. After all, who else but a madman would climb the castle mount to Duchess Ermengard's castle claiming to be a musician, wanting to play for her? And she was even dafter for thinking, even if it was only for a moment, that this inexperienced son of a rich man could help her. Could he defend her against the duchess's entire guard?

She sent him a quick glare. "You shouldn't have come here. You are in terrible danger." She spoke carefully, pronouncing each syllable slowly. "Duchess Ermengard will kill you. She doesn't like strangers entering her realm. And if she finds out you think I'm the duke's daughter ... you'll find yourself dead before you even finish such a declaration."

"But what if you are the duke's daughter?"

Sophie pondered this. "I can't prove that I am or am not. I never knew my parents, and the duchess claims I was an orphan she took in. Unless you can prove I am Duke Baldewin's daughter ... You were foolish to come here." She had to be practical. She couldn't let herself hope.

As she continued with the monotonous task of taking cooled candles from the line, dipping them in hot wax, and hanging them back on the line, she could feel him watching her. She turned and stared at him.

"Why would Pinnosa tell you about me? Why would you care?"

"Sophie." He took a step closer to her, his voice a deep whisper. "I know you have no reason to trust me, but I'm here to find out if you are truly Duke Baldewin's daughter. And if you are, I want to take you back to Hagenheim."

Sophie turned her back on him. Against her better judgment, optimism rose up inside her. Her heartbeat quickened as something inside her told her he might be telling the truth. Again, she remembered whispers that stopped when she came into the room, the duchess's special hatred of her, almost as if she were jealous. Something inside Sophie had always wondered if her parents were more than servants, were people who had enraged the duchess so much she was taking out her wrath on their daughter.

*But how can I ever know for sure?* "So you have no proof that I'm Duke Baldewin's daughter?"

"No, I don't. Do you know anyone who might know? Someone who knew the duke or his first wife? Which servants have been here the longest?"

Petra. She had come after the first duchess had died but before the duke had passed away—almost sixteen years ago. When Sophie was younger, Petra would sometimes tell her stories of the duke and how much he had loved his little daughter.

*Oh.* The hair on the back of her neck seemed to stand on end. "Petra would know." Her voice sounded hoarse. She cleared her throat. "But why do you care?"

"Because if you are Duke Baldewin's daughter, you are betrothed."

"Betrothed?"

"To my brother Valten Gerstenberg, the Earl of Hamlin, who will someday be the Duke of Hagenheim."

Sophie felt as if the world had gone quite still.

"Duke Baldewin and my parents were friends, and they arranged the marriage when Duke Baldewin's daughter was only a baby. After the duke remarried, the duke and the new duchess only met once with my parents, and that was to sign the betrothal agreement. My brother was only six years old, but he remembers."

Sophie watched the stranger's mouth as he spoke, as if seeing the words forming on his lips as well as hearing them would help her make sense of everything he said. Was she Duke Baldewin's daughter? Was she betrothed? It was too strange to comprehend.

"If I am to marry your brother, why are you here? Why didn't *he* come to take me away from the duchess?" The thought — that she belonged to someone who would care for her and save her from the duchess — was so beguiling that it frightened her. Such things didn't happen, and if she started to believe in them, her disappointment would crush her.

"My brother wanted to come as soon as he heard you might be alive. But he broke his leg in a tournament less than a week before."

"So he sent you. Alone."

"Well, he didn't *send* me." Gabe rubbed his chin and shifted his feet, a wry half smile on his face. "My brother and father wanted me to wait until they could come with me, but I came without their permission."

"Why?"

"Pinnosa said you were in danger." He bent to pick up a stick and appeared to be examining it, turning it between his fingers. "I didn't want anything to happen to you while my brother's leg healed."

Again, she wondered if he was telling the truth. But if it was all a lie, why wouldn't he simply say that *he* was her betrothed? If he wanted to take advantage of her, why make up the story about his brother? They stood with nothing to break the silence except a bird cawing in the distance and the occasional muffled banging of a pot in the kitchen nearby. Finally Sophie turned and began dipping candles again. Her thoughts echoed around in her head, confusing her.

"I've only known you an hour and already you've lied repeatedly. Why should I believe you?"

He let out an exasperated breath behind her. He was angry. Good. Maybe he would let the truth slip from his lying lips.

"I don't even know if you are the duke's daughter. If you are, then I'm here to help you. If you don't believe me . . ." He let his voice trail off.

"If I did believe you — which would be the height of foolishness — can you explain how you plan to get away from the duchess without her killing us both?" The awful truth was Sophie desperately wanted to believe him. To be wanted, to belong to someone, to be betrothed . . . it filled her chest with the most delightful warmth and light.

*And to be proven a fool will only lead to coldness and pain.*

She hung another candle on the line. Gabe grabbed her hand and stood in front of her, compelling her to look into his eyes. She took a step back.

"Take me to this servant, Petra. We will ask her together if you are Duke Baldewin's daughter."

She closed her mouth and tried to veil her expression so he wouldn't know how his words filled her with hope and joy, how the thought that he believed it was possible she wasn't simply a poor servant encouraged her. To show emotion was to become vulnerable. And Sophie should never allow herself to become vulnerable to anyone who had the power to hurt her.

She was almost afraid to ask Petra, to find out the truth. After all, would Gabe's brother still want her after he saw how untaught she was in the ways and manners of noble society? When he saw that she had no idea how to behave like a proper duchess? When he realized she was awkward and clumsy, as the duchess was always telling her, that she was ugly and too wicked for anybody to ever care for?

But Petra told her she shouldn't believe any of those things the duchess said about her.

And if Petra told her she wasn't the duke's daughter ...

The crackle of breaking twigs drew Sophie's gaze to the forest at the edge of the courtyard. Lorencz emerged from the shadow of the trees. *Another man I know better than to trust.* His eyes were focused on Sophie and Gabe as he strode toward them. He stopped and stared, then called out a cautiously friendly, "Ho, there."

Gabe nodded, meeting Lorencz's stare. *"Guten Morgen."*

The scar above the huntsman's cheek seemed to stand out. The two stared at each other until Sophie broke the silence.

"Lorencz, this is Gabe, a pilgrim from Hungary. Gabe, this is Lorencz the huntsman."

They appeared to be sizing each other up. The stranger was not as brawny as Lorencz, but he was just as tall and held his head high. He couldn't have looked less like a humble traveler.

Finally, Lorencz nodded, as though dismissing Gabe, then turned to Sophie and eyed her in a way that made her wary. "Are you ready for our picnic?"

# Chapter
## 5

*The huntsman had come at a very inopportune* time, and it didn't seem to Gabe as if Sophie wanted to go with him.

"I'll fetch our food." Lorencz seemed oblivious to her strained smile and stiff posture.

As soon as the overconfident lout disappeared inside the kitchen, Gabe turned to Sophie. "Are you sure it's safe for you to be alone with him? You could turn him away."

"I know that." She tried to look stern, but her eyebrows came together and her expression gradually changed. She hesitated, then whispered, "Since you are determined not to leave, I only ask that you don't confront Duchess Ermengard just yet. Wait until I return, and I will tell you how you must approach her and what you must say if she summons you. There are rules you must follow if you hope not to incite her wrath. You have no idea how quickly she can become enraged."

Sophie appeared more worried about him than about herself.

"Don't worry. I won't say anything to provoke her."

"It may not seem provoking—"

The huntsman came out of the kitchen carrying a large basket and walked past Gabe as though he were a tree stump. Gabe didn't trust him.

Sophie started out beside Lorencz, turned, and gave Gabe a pointed look. He winked at her.

She frowned and turned away.

Gabe waited until they were out of sight, then followed.

⁓⁓

Sophie wasn't sure she could trust Lorencz, but she always carried a small knife on her person. She'd only had to use the eating utensil as a weapon once, but at least she knew she was capable of defending herself.

"Isn't this far enough?" Sophie halted in a clearing near the stream bank.

Lorencz smiled. "Don't you trust me?"

"No, not particularly."

He ignored her comment and said, "I had a more beautiful spot in mind, with wildflowers and forest strawberries ..."

"I'd rather stop here." *Best to stand my ground with him.*

He frowned, but only for a moment. He stooped to set down the basket and pull out a blanket, which he handed to Sophie to spread on the ground.

She helped him set out the food—more than Sophie ate in three whole days—and was careful not to let even her fingers touch his as he handed her the cheese, loaf of bread, dried fruit, fried pies, cold meat, and wine skin.

Sophie's stomach growled.

Lorencz laughed. "Hungry?" He gave her a wolfish smile.

She blushed but didn't say anything.

He lifted the hunk of bread toward his mouth.

"Stop!" She'd uttered it automatically and could feel her blush deepen.

He halted, his mouth open, just as he was about to bite.

"We must first thank God for the food."

He raised his eyebrows at her and frowned.

Ignoring him, Sophie bowed her head and clasped her hands. "We thank you, O Lord, for this food, and we bless it for your name's sake. Grant that all who partake of it may obtain health of body and safety of soul. Through Christ our Lord. Amen."

When she looked up, Lorencz was staring at her with a slightly bemused look.

"Don't you pray?" she asked.

"No."

Her distaste must have shown on her face, because he cleared his throat and said, "But I have never known how. Perhaps you could teach me."

His words and sly stare didn't exactly evoke any belief in his sincerity. She wanted to believe she could trust the man ... unfortunately, she could not summon any.

But he was asking her to teach him. It would be wrong to refuse, even if he wasn't earnest.

"Praying is simple." Faintly, she remembered the words of the young priest who had taught her so many years ago. "You must do four things. You must tell God that you are thankful, ask his blessing, acknowledge that he is God, and pray through Jesus."

"And say 'amen' at the end?"

Sophie nodded.

"Sounds easy enough." He smiled at her and once again raised the piece of bread to his lips. His eyes never left her face.

Sophie bit into her bread and chewed. She had missed breakfast that morning, since she had slept late after her long night of nursing, but it was hard to eat with Lorencz staring at her. *O God, what are his intentions? Would he help me get away from here?* She stared back at him, trying to read his thoughts and his character.

Lorencz offered her more food, giving her portions of everything he had brought. Before she had even tasted it all, her stomach was full.

"Try this," he urged. "You're too thin. You need to eat more."

Sophie shook her head and ignored the way he was pointing at the food in front of her. She didn't like him saying she was too thin. No man wanted a skinny wife. *Will the stranger's brother think I am too skinny?*

She was being silly. He probably didn't even have a brother.

She let down her guard a bit and stretched her arm behind her, leaning back on her hand. Her eyelids were heavy. If she closed her eyes she would go right to sleep.

"Tired?"

She snapped her eyes open. "I am well." *What came over me?* She had to keep herself alert.

"You're a very beautiful young woman, Sophie." Lorencz had moved closer to her while her eyes had been closed. Now he sat close enough to put his arm around her.

Sophie sat up straight, smoothing her skirt and making sure her ankles were covered. Her thin shoes had slipped off her feet, and she fumbled to put them back on again. When she looked up, Lorencz was leaning so close his face was only a handbreadth away.

Her heart thumped wildly at his nearness—not because she was excited to be near him, she realized, but because she was afraid of what he intended to do next. *Please, God, don't let him be about to try to take advantage of me. I would hate to have to cut him.*

His hand was suddenly touching her cheek. She scooted away, out of his reach, and he let his hand fall.

"I don't mean to frighten you." He lifted his hand again. "You are so beautiful."

This time she slapped his hand away and stood up. The pained look on his face almost made her pity him. But that was a foolish sentiment that would get her in trouble. He'd only take advantage of her pity.

"It's time we were getting back." Sophie shot him a warning glare. "I have my work to do, and you undoubtedly have yours." She bent to pick up their picnic leavings from the blanket, tossing them into the basket.

Lorencz took a step toward her, but Sophie looked him in the eye. "If you have impure ideas about me, *Herr* Huntsman, I'm afraid I shall be forced to frustrate you in your purpose." She injected forceful coldness into her voice.

"It is you who are mistaken, *Fraulein* Sophie. I have nothing but the utmost respect for you."

"If you respected me, you would keep your hands to yourself." She gave him a piercing look before snatching up the blanket and quickly folding it.

Instead of looking angry, he laughed. He picked up the basket as she was reaching for it, so Sophie let him have it, turning and heading back through the dense forest of evergreens and beech trees.

They walked along in silence for a few moments. Then Lorencz said in a deep, low voice, "Sophie? Don't you like me?" He walked so close to her side that his right arm brushed her left.

Sophie drew back from the contact. "I hardly know you."

Lorencz said nothing. They were almost back to the castle, though still in the cover of the trees, when Lorencz grabbed her arm and spun her to face him, pulling her against his chest. Sophie clutched the blanket, which served as a shield between them.

"I can take you away from this demesne. If we leave now, we might be able to get away from her."

"Why should I trust you?" She leaned her body as far away from him as she could, searching his eyes.

"I will marry you. We'll go so far away she'll never find us."

He put his arms around her, pulling her more firmly against his torso — and the blanket.

"I don't believe you."

65

"Think about this when you're deciding whether to believe me." He kissed her so hard and so suddenly she didn't have time to react.

The moment he relaxed his hold on her, she stumbled backward and stared at him, still holding the blanket up in front of her. He stared back at her.

Sophie's cheeks heated. *How dare he kiss me!* "Try that again," she said, her breath coming fast in her fury, "and you'll get a bleeding even a barber cannot mend."

He'd forced a kiss on her, and she hadn't even been able to reach for her knife. Was the large meal slowing her down and fogging her brain? She was still alert enough to wonder if he would truly marry her and take her away from here. Hadn't she thought just last week, when he visited her in the dungeon, that if anyone could help her escape it was Lorencz? But could she trust him to marry her? Besides, she wasn't sure she wanted to spend the rest of her life with him.

And there was the stranger, Gabe. What if he was telling the truth? She had to talk to Petra.

Lorencz smirked at her. "Meet me tonight, in the courtyard, and we'll go for a walk."

"No."

"Then meet me tomorrow morning."

"I have work to do."

"Before breakfast, then, at daybreak."

"Why?"

The skin around Lorencz's scar turned a dark red. He closed his eyes for a moment and took a deep breath. "Plenty of other maidens would eagerly accept the chance to walk with me tonight. If you don't come, perhaps I will ask someone else."

"I think that's a splendid idea."

"How will you ever learn to trust me if you don't spend time with me?"

"It is a problem, but it is not mine to solve."

Someone was nearby, and they both turned their heads toward the noise of rustling leaves and cracking twigs. The stranger, Gabe, emerged into view.

"Pardon me," he apologized. "Were you two conversing?"

"What are you doing?" Lorencz asked irritably.

"Taking a walk."

Lorencz looked him up and down. "You say you are a pilgrim, but you don't have the look of a pilgrim." The huntsman's voice was impatient. "Your boots are too fine, your hands too soft looking. You'd be wise to get yourself back to wherever you came from. Go back to your easy life."

"Whatever my life was before I came here is not your concern." Gabe's voice was quiet but thick with warning. "And I don't take orders from huntsmen."

"Who do you take orders from, then? What is your business here?" Lorencz narrowed his eyes dangerously. Without giving Gabe a chance to answer, he went on. "See that you stay out of my way. This *huntsman* doesn't play games with *pilgrims*." He brushed past the stranger, knocking him sideways with his shoulder.

Gabe watched him go, wishing he could punch that oaf for kissing Sophie.

Gabe turned to Sophie. "You know that man is trying to seduce you, don't you?"

"I don't answer to you. I have work—"

"I thought you were going to help me plan what to say to Duchess Ermengard."

"I was." Sophie moved past him on her way into the courtyard, and Gabe followed several feet behind.

She hesitated as Lorencz came out of the kitchen, waiting

until he walked away before dashing through the door he'd just exited. She came back minutes later without the blanket and glared at Gabe, as if he were to blame for all her life's ills. He waited for her to speak, hoping he could convince her he was nothing like the huntsman and thus worthy of her trust.

She crossed her arms and seemed to be looking him over and thinking. "You need to have a plan. If the duchess becomes aware of your presence, she'll want to know what you're doing here and why." She frowned. "You must decide now what you will say."

"I'll ask her if I can stay for a few days and play my lute for her."

"Why?"

"I'll say I want to earn some money before going on with my pilgrimage."

"Oh no. That will not do." Sophie clasped her hands together and stared at the ground. She whispered, "You have to make it sound like you're doing something nice for her, that you admire her so deeply you can't help but play music for her. And you certainly don't expect payment."

"Very well. I can do that." He tried not to smile at the extreme concern she was displaying.

"Let her know you don't expect her to provide your meal tonight or your bed. She doesn't like it when unexpected visitors arrive and ask to bed down anywhere on the castle knoll, even in the stable or with the servants. Tell her you have a place to sleep in the village."

He nodded, although he was a little skeptical, after his cold reception, that he could find a place in the village to bed down. But perhaps, if he tried again, he could find people willing to speak about Sophie—or Duke Baldewin and his daughter.

She went on, still whispering as she stoked up the fire under the large kettle in the center of the courtyard and added more wood. "Pay her several compliments. She expects it. But be tactful. And remember, you don't expect any reward." She paused a moment to stare vacantly into the trees.

"And you probably shouldn't say you're a pilgrim." She grabbed a long wooden spoon and began to stir the hot wax. "No, you're a troubadour on your way to the fair. You heard of her beauty and wished to come and admire her and write songs about her. That should do it, as long as Lorencz and Walther don't say anything to contradict you." Her satisfied look changed into a frown. "But do take that ring off your finger. You're trying to look poor, not like a rich man playing at being a vagabond."

Gabe wrenched the ring off, feeling foolish for having forgotten such an obvious thing, and thrust it into his pocket.

She pointed at his feet. "And your shoes. They're much too fine for a troubadour."

He bent down and smeared mud on his boots so that it was difficult to see what material they were made of, then he looked down at himself—he didn't see anything else that would betray his true status. He thrust his hands, mud and all, into his hair and mussed it, rubbing the dirt into the strands until they were surely sticking out everywhere.

"Yes, I think you might just live to tell the tale, if you keep a glib tongue in your head." She glanced up at him and flashed a smile.

Pinnosa hadn't exaggerated her beauty. *God, help me save her. Help me discover the truth.*

"If you're still alive after you talk to the duchess, you are welcome to share the servants' fare tonight. It isn't fancy, but it's filling. Or perhaps you can pay for your food in the village. Either way, your presence, wherever you go, will stir a lot of talk and interest. The people of Hohendorf aren't used to strangers coming around."

That was an understatement, considering the way people had stared at him when he passed through the village.

"When will you ask Petra what she knows about your identity?"

She pursed her lips. "Tonight, when no one can overhear us."

As she continued with her task, a comfortable silence settled between them. He tried not to watch her, but his gaze flicked repeatedly in Sophie's direction, especially as she rolled up her sleeves to her elbows, lifting her arms to hang each wick over the line. Though he'd observed her doing the very same task all morning, he couldn't seem to stop noticing her graceful motions. A thought flitted through his mind that she would look beautiful dancing the bassadanza, moving to the music, her hair decorated with flowers and a silk skirt swishing around her ankles. Of course, to fit into the scene perfectly she would need to gain some flesh and not appear so emaciated. He imagined her arms slightly plump, the dark smudges gone from under her eyes, and a joyful smile on her face.

He was enjoying the image a little too much.

After several minutes of silence, Gabe said, "I know you think you can take care of yourself, but I do hope you will be wary of that huntsman. Men like him ... they should be kept at a distance."

"I suppose you think I should keep you close instead." Sophie *humphed* as she looked away from him. She continued with her task but looked ill at ease. He began to think she wasn't going to say anything more.

She sighed and peered up at him. "I believe your counsel is kindly meant. But I can take care of myself—it is something I've done all of my life. I am well aware that men are not to be trusted, whether they be huntsmen, servants, or ... traveling noblemen."

He couldn't help but smile. When he had followed her and Lorencz into the woods for their picnic and eavesdropped, he had seen and heard how well she dealt with the man's forwardness. She was obviously a maiden of personal honor, but the huntsman possessed a smooth tongue. The only question seemed to be whether she would allow the huntsman to marry her in order to get away from the duchess. Or would she entrust her fate to Gabe?

How alone she was. Sophie, whether she was Duke Baldewin's daughter or not, was an orphan, without family connections, without any family at all. Brittola, on the other hand, had brothers and sisters. Her father and mother were still alive and in good health and lavished her with loving words and caresses. No man, whether wealthy or poor, would be allowed near Brittola, especially to try to win her affections, without the expressed permission of her father. But Sophie had no one but herself to prevent ill-intentioned men from taking advantage of her.

The thought stirred something inside him. Even if she was only a poor maiden, she needed ... someone.

Gabe stood, picked up a stick, and started helping Sophie dip the endless row of candles into the hot cauldron of wax. She lifted her eyebrows at him quizzically.

He shrugged. "I have nothing else to do."

She shook her head but said nothing.

They worked together for a long while, until Gabe's arms began to ache from the unaccustomed motion of lifting them over and over again to hang the candles on the line. He thought about Sophie lying asleep on the ground when he'd arrived that morning. The cook had seemed very protective of her, and the guard also, once he found out it was Sophie and not some other maiden. He'd heard the cook say Sophie often spent nights in the dungeon at the duchess's command. Surely the girl hadn't done anything to deserve such punishment. And dungeons were generally filled with all manner of filth and vermin. If the duchess was as cruel as the rumors said she was, and if what Pinnosa had told him was true, Sophie had been mistreated like this all of her life.

Sophie's experiences were so different from any other woman's he'd ever encountered. He tried to imagine his sisters enduring Duchess Ermengard's treatment and shuddered.

He wondered what his family was doing right now. His mother had started a school for poor children in the walled town of Hagenheim. Perhaps she and his sisters would go there today and bring sweet cakes and fruit for the children, or new books or other supplies. Valten was probably chafing at his own inactivity, lying in bed and cursing his brother because Gabe was out doing what Valten could not.

That thought made Gabe smile.

He turned around to dip more candles in the hot wax and found Sophie staring at him.

"Thank you for your help ... Gabe." She seemed to find it amusing to speak his name. "Is it a custom of yours to search out scullery maids and help them with their work?"

Gabe pretended not to notice her teasing tone. "Does it seem strange to you that I would help?"

"I must admit, there have been times a man has offered to help me with my work, but they've always expected something in return." She eyed him critically.

"I assure you, Sophie," Gabe said, gentling his voice and meeting her gaze, "I don't expect anything from you." No, that wasn't exactly true. "I only hope to learn the truth of your identity and gain your trust."

"Trust is something that must be earned." Her eyes widened slightly, and she quickly turned her back to him. "But I hope you will remember my advice about what to say to the duchess. You have a kind face, and I would hate for you to become another of her victims."

Suddenly, they were surrounded by guards, each one armed with a sword. Rough hands grabbed Gabe around the neck and by his upper arms and began dragging him toward the castle.

# Chapter 6

*Sophie followed the guards who were dragging* Gabe away. Walther was with them, and she hurried to his side.

"What is amiss? Where are you taking him?" she demanded.

Walther frowned sympathetically. "Nothing for you to worry about, Sophie. The duchess got word of this stranger being here. We are fetching him on her orders. You'd best turn back before she asks what you have to do with this fellow."

Gabe turned his head and looked at her, even though the guards had his hands pinned behind his back. "Don't worry, Sophie. I'll remember what you said." Then he winked, a confident glint in his eyes. He grew more sober as he said, "Don't forget to ask Petra." One thing was sure: The man was brave. Or just plain foolish. Or he still didn't realize what the duchess was capable of. Probably all three.

She grabbed Walther's arm. "Don't let her hurt him. Please."

The burly guard looked suspicious. "Does he mean something to you?"

"I just don't want him to get hurt." She tempered her words cautiously. "He's innocent, and ... he has a family who will be asking questions if any harm comes to him. Make sure the duchess knows that."

"Now how would I be making sure the duchess knows that? She doesn't exactly ask me how she should conduct her affairs."

Sophie must have looked as upset as she felt, because Walther's voice softened and he said, "I'll do my best."

After they dragged Gabe away, Sophie collected herself and hurried to the kitchen. Inside she found Petra pulling some bread from the oven. Miraculously, no one else was around.

"Petra, I have something to ask you."

"Yes, my dear?" Petra placed the bread on the wooden table and wiped her hands on her apron. "What is it?"

Sophie looked into the blue-gray eyes that were starting to crinkle at the outside corners. Mama Petra was still beautiful, with her kind face and pink cheeks. Could she have kept the truth from Sophie all these years?

"Mama Petra, you were here before Duke Baldewin died, weren't you?"

"Yes, my dear." A sober look came over her.

"You were here when Duke Baldewin's baby daughter died?"

Petra's mouth went slack but she didn't speak.

"The stranger who came here this morning seems to think that I may be Duke Baldewin's daughter, that she didn't die after all."

Petra expelled an audible breath and looked away.

"Mama Petra? Is it true?"

"Yes," she whispered. "It's true. I wanted to tell you, but I wasn't sure it would help for you to know. If the duchess found out you knew, she'd kill you. And she'd kill me as well.

"I've been trying for years to get word out to someone—I've sent word by a few visitors, but I don't think they believed what I told them. Leastways, nothing ever came of it. So few people ever come here and even fewer leave. The duchess watches them all so closely that any letters I send will be read by her, I am certain. I have received a few letters from my brother, and the duchess reads those too. I haven't yet risked telling anyone in writing. I was planning to tell this new stranger, to beg him to tell anyone he knew who could get word to the king. But now I hear he has been taken away by the guards." Petra bit her lip and grabbed Sophie's hand. "Can you forgive me for not telling you?"

Sophie felt as if she'd fallen out of a tree and had the breath knocked out of her lungs. But seeing Petra's stricken expression, she answered, "Of course I forgive you. But are you sure?"

"Yes, my dear. You are the whole reason I am still here. I knew you needed a person who cared about you, and I couldn't bear to leave Duke Baldewin's baby—" Petra's words were cut short by a sudden sob. She quickly took a deep lungful of air and went on. "Forgive me. It is a relief to speak of it after all these years. Poor Pinnosa and I were the last ones who knew."

"What happened to my father?"

"I don't know. Most of the servants believe the duchess killed him. Either way, he is gone these fifteen years." Petra lowered her voice even more.

"Why didn't she kill me too?"

"I think she gets a perverse pleasure out of tormenting you, out of knowing that she's turned the duke's beloved daughter into a common scullery maid."

*The duke's beloved daughter.* Sophie allowed herself to dwell on that. Her father, the duke, had loved her. She was loved. Once upon a time.

Gabe tried not to worry too much about what was about to happen. He'd charmed his way out of predicaments before; maybe none quite like this, but if he kept his head, all would turn out well. After all, what could the duchess do to him besides throw him in the dungeon? If she did, his father's knights would eventually come for him.

Although he didn't relish sitting in a dungeon for days and weeks, or even months.

That is, if the duchess didn't have him killed.

The guards pulled him into the deep recesses of the castle, and if he had his bearings right, they were ascending the stairs of the center keep where the duchess's private chambers would likely be, especially if she were as paranoid for her own safety as he'd heard.

The guards came to a door. They opened it and pushed him inside. Before Gabe could fully regain his balance, he heard the door close behind him and two of the guards moved to stand on either side of him, hands on their sword hilts.

A woman sat motionless on a huge thronelike chair in the back of the large chamber, her hands steepled in front of her. Her face was oddly pale, her lips painted red and her eyelids black, and her fingernails were so long they curled under. He'd never seen anyone so garish. He was no longer surprised at the rumors she was a witch. But she did possess a commanding type of beauty. She was tall, although it was hard to tell her exact height since she was sitting down. She had a long graceful neck and a curvaceous figure with a tiny waist.

"I have a trespasser, do I?" Her lips curled in a way that made his blood turn cold. "It isn't often someone comes to visit me uninvited. You did come all this way to see me, I hope?" She lifted her thin, sculpted eyebrows.

"Yes, Your Grace. Whom else would I be coming to see?"

"I don't know. You seemed to be talking a great deal to one of my scullery maids. What is it you want with her? Do you find her pretty?"

The look in her eyes sent a chill down Gabe's spine. The only sound in the room was the *tick-tick-tick* of her inordinately long fingernails clicking against each other as she waited.

"I came to see you, Your Grace, to be inspired by your great beauty. I had heard of your loveliness and have now found that it was not exaggerated." *God, forgive me for my lies.* The success of his quest, not to mention a young maiden's life, was at stake.

The duchess eyed him in a way that made him think she didn't believe him for one moment.

"I am but a humble troubadour, and it would be my privilege to play for you, to compose a song about your beauty and grace and ... mercy." He threw that last word in for his own sake. "Of course, I ask for nothing in return. It shall be enough that I have feasted upon your beauty. And I shall find my own place to sleep, in the village."

"No," she said quickly. "You shall sleep here, in the castle." She grinned like a cat about to devour the prey within her claws, then crossed her arms, resting her long fingernails prominently on her velvet sleeves.

"Yes, Your Grace. Let it be as you wish." His blood felt cold in his veins as he realized she knew he was lying. Why else would she be so quick to have him sleep at the castle?

She stared at him, unblinking. He had the distinct urge to squirm under her gaze, but forced himself to remain perfectly still.

"Where are you from?" she demanded.

"Hungary, but I have been a wanderer most of my life." That was true enough. He'd wandered all over the Hagenheim region.

"Play something for me."

"It shall be my pleasure to play for you." Gabe took the large leather bag from where he'd slung it over his back and carefully unwrapped his lute. His hands shook a bit, but he felt confident. After all, things were going just as he'd hoped; he was here with the duchess and she was asking him to play.

He began to play a lively tune his father had taught him, one his father had played for Gabe's mother before they were married, when she was giving a dance lesson for their friends Gunther and Hildy.

Now Gabe was playing it for the Wicked Witch of Bavaria, with her creepy white face and hawkish talons.

Gabe concentrated on getting all the notes right, keeping his eyes on the strings of the lute. When he finished the song, the duchess was staring at him coldly, as if completely unmoved by the music.

"You play very well," she said slowly, her eyes half closed. "Play another song."

Gabe began another dance tune, longer than the one before, and then decided to play another, to keep playing until she stopped him. After the third song, she said, "That is enough." She steepled her fingers again, clicking her nails together. "It is my wish that you stay the night and play for me again this evening. But you must stay here, on the castle mount, and not go into the village. Guards, take him to his room."

The guards didn't put their hands on him this time, merely waited for him to precede them out of the room.

When he reached the door, he turned and bowed to Duchess Ermengard. "Until tonight."

She nodded, the eerie smile returning to her face.

After exploring his room, which was adequate though by no means luxurious, he set out to write a song for the duchess. He tried to think of words to praise her beauty, but nothing came to mind. When he finally started writing on a piece of parchment from his bag, scratching with a quill and ink he found in the room, the words flowed through his mind and onto the page as if by magic. Only after the third line did he realize he wasn't thinking about the duchess at all, but about Sophie. Her black hair, her beautiful skin, thick lashes, and blue eyes pierced his consciousness like a sword of inspiration. He would have to be careful to make it sound like he was writing and singing about the duchess. He couldn't let her know his song was actually in praise of her servant.

Did the duchess hate Sophie because she was so beautiful? Or was it because Sophie was the daughter of her dead husband,

Duke Baldewin, and the rightful heir of Hohendorf Castle and all its demesne, and thus the perfect toy to torment?

He continued to pour out the song. Then he took up his lute and picked out a tune fit to accompany the words.

Sophie'd had to stop dipping candles to help Petra prepare the evening meal. After two additional maids had come in to help, Sophie and Petra were no longer able to speak about Sophie's true identity, or about the fact that Sophie was betrothed to Gabe's brother. Nor were they able to talk about Gabe's chances of getting away from the duchess. Sophie prayed for him while she continued with her work. Had he been taken to the dungeon?

As she walked down the cool corridor toward the entrance to the inner courtyard in order to draw water for cooking, Sophie heard the faint sounds of music. She stopped and listened. It was coming from one of the rarely used guest chambers farther down the corridor. But it sounded like someone who was just learning to play, the way the song stopped, then started, over and over.

Or maybe it was someone learning a new song. Or writing one. It had to be Gabe. But was the duchess truly allowing him to stay in the castle?

At least he hadn't been sent to the dungeon. Not yet, anyway.

That night, as the servants were eating in the kitchen, Sophie sat between Petra and Roslind and talked quietly about the stranger.

"He has such kind eyes," Petra said. "Even if he is the son of a nobleman, I like him."

"Yes," Roslind said, taking a bite of her stewed apples. "He seems very kind. And very handsome too. Don't you think so, Sophie? He might even be a brother." Roslind's eyes grew wide with excitement, clearly believing Gabe was nice enough to join their servant "family."

"I don't think we know him well enough for *that*, Roslind." Sophie thought how pitiful she and Roslind were, so desperate for love they created imaginary kinships. The longing to belong had haunted Sophie all her life. She wasn't sure how she would ever be able to stop looking for those kindships, or that she even wished to. It soothed the ache in her heart to call Roslind *sister* and Petra *mama*.

Her thoughts went back to what Gabe had said earlier, that he had come here to help Sophie because Pinnosa had said she was in danger. He must have been telling her the truth after all. She hated to admit it, even to herself, but the thought that he had come here just for her gave her a thrill of hope. Hope that she was not worthless. Hope that someone might love her enough to want to save her from this dark place.

And Gabe had said she was betrothed to his brother. *Betrothed.* The very word meant she belonged to someone. And if she married his brother, then Gabe *would* be her brother. It was a beautiful thought.

Sophie looked up and found herself staring into Gabe's brown eyes.

Petra jumped up from the bench and insisted Gabe sit down in her place, opposite Sophie. She quickly put some stewed pork and vegetables on a trencher and placed it before him.

"Thank you," he said politely, then winked at Sophie. "The duchess said I could eat with the servants."

Sophie nodded and gave him a half smile. With all his bravado and ease at playing a traveler, he seemed too good to be true, as did his story about his brother being her betrothed. Or maybe Gabe's brother was so hideously ugly—rabbit teeth, hairy moles all over his face, and a nose like a hooked beak—that his family had been happy to foist him off on anyone, even a girl who knew more about how to wash a pot than eat at a duke's table.

"I've been writing a song for her. I hope she will let me perform it for her tonight."

"Good." Sophie nodded again.

All the servants stood and began to leave. Sophie looked around her, appalled to see them all glancing slyly at her and Gabe. What were they thinking?

"Will you stay and talk with me?" Gabe asked, placing his hand over hers on the rough wooden table.

A pleasant tingle crept from her hand up her arm. She stared down at his hand on hers, unable to look him in the eye.

"Of course," she said gruffly, then cleared her throat and moved her hand away from his.

Gabe began to eat as everyone disappeared, leaving the two of them alone. "Were you able to talk to Petra?" he said softly.

"Yes," Sophie whispered back. The seriousness of their conversation and all its consequences seemed to fall heavily on her shoulders.

"What did she say?" His eyes were wide as he met her gaze.

"She says ..." Sophie glanced around the room. "She says I am Duke Baldewin's daughter. She apologized for not telling me sooner."

Gabe stared at her a moment longer, then went back to eating. "I will come up with a plan to get you out of here," he said between bites.

"*You* won't be leaving if the duchess finds out why you're here."

He swallowed and winked at her. "Stop worrying."

Sophie slowly shook her head at him.

When he had almost finished his food, he said, "Tell me about your childhood."

"Are you sure you want to know about my childhood?"

He nodded.

She might as well tell him. "I have vague memories of feeling happy. I remember the priest teaching me to read. I can read." She may not know anything about how a noblewoman behaved, but she was very happy that she could at least boast that much knowledge. "I remember the priest telling me things about God. I have a memory of standing in an open meadow with the sun on my face … but I'm not sure if that's a memory or a dream."

"You mean you've never been outside the forest?"

Sophie felt uncomfortable at his obvious horror. "Is that so unusual? This is Bavaria. We—we are a heavily forested land. Everyone knows that."

"Go on. Tell me more."

"My memory is nearly blank for a few years," she continued to whisper. "Duchess Ermengard forced the priest to leave—at least I hope he left, instead of meeting a worse fate at her hands—and she attempted to burn down the chapel. I don't remember very much after that." Sophie felt uncomfortable again. The things that she did remember were so painful she didn't want to share them with Gabe … with anyone.

He was nearly finished eating, having wolfed down his food while she talked. He picked up his tankard and tipped it back.

A longing rose up inside her to hear about a loving family. What had it been like to grow up with two parents, with brothers and sisters? Surprising herself with how much she wanted to know, she asked him, "Will you tell me about your childhood? About your family?"

"My mother and father are wonderful, truly. They punished us if we misbehaved, but they talked to us, helped us, read to us. We would sit around the fire at night and my father would play the lute and sing, and my brothers and sisters and I would dance and play games like shatranj, blind man's buff, and backgammon. Sometimes my mother would read to us or tell us stories that she made up. She was brilliant at inventing stories."

Sophie's heart beat faster as she tried to imagine the scene. When Gabe paused, she urged him on. "Tell me more. How many brothers and sisters do you have?"

"I have three brothers and three sisters. I had four sisters, but ... one of them died." He paused to clear his throat. "I am the second oldest, and my brother Valten, your betrothed, is the oldest."

"Are you and your brother Valten great friends?"

"No," he seemed to say reluctantly.

"Why ever not?" she cried, then wished she hadn't sounded so horrified, as a sheepish look came over Gabe's face.

"You know how boys are."

She didn't.

He began to turn the empty tankard around, twisting it on the wooden table. "We were always competing with each other. I wanted to be stronger and faster and better than my brother, but unfortunately he bested me in nearly everything. Although I am better looking than he is." He raised his eyebrows and smiled. "I remember once"—he chuckled—"I was helping Valten practice for the tourneys. He knocked me from my horse, his lance grazed my head, and I hit the ground and was unconscious for a few minutes." He laughed again, as though he were telling a funny joke instead of relating a terrible accident. "That's how I got this scar." He brushed his hair back, and she saw a pale line on his forehead next to his hairline.

She gasped in horror. "But you are his younger brother. How could he treat you so carelessly?"

"It was only an accident."

"Is he bigger than you?"

"A bit."

"He sounds like a bully." *And I am meant to marry him.*

"No, no. Valten is a good man and will be a good husband. We haven't always gotten along, but ..." He rubbed his chin.

"We're older now and better friends than we were. But I'm sure my brother is quite angry with me right now." He didn't seem sorry. In fact, he seemed rather to relish the idea.

"Why is that?"

"I defied him and my father when I came here to find you."

"Did they not want you to find me?" Was she not wanted after all?

"They wanted to come themselves. Valten was greatly frustrated because he couldn't come right away himself to find you."

Her heart lifted.

"He broke his leg in a recent tourney. Our healer won't allow him out of bed for at least four weeks."

He had told her that already. What Sophie really wanted to know was, *Do you think your brother will like me?* Instead, she asked, "Do you think your ... parents ... will approve of me?"

"They will love you. My mother will smother you with hugs and kisses. She'll make such a fuss over you, you'll wish you had stayed away."

Sophie's heart seemed to swell inside her chest as she imagined Gabe's mother embracing and kissing her. The longing inside her was so great, she was sure Gabe could see it on her face. To belong to Gabe's family ... to have a mother who would show her true affection ... the thought was complete joy. How could Gabe possibly think she would not want that? Would wish to stay away? She was ready to go home with him this very moment!

He glanced around the kitchen before whispering, "I wish we could leave tonight," as though he had read her mind.

She almost leaped at his words.

"But the duchess probably wouldn't let us get far. She's expecting me to play for her tonight."

"No." Sophie came back down to earth. "She wouldn't let us get far." She'd send her guards to haul them both back to the castle and lock them in the dungeon or kill them. Besides, the woods were full of wolves that hunted in packs at night.

Perhaps she shouldn't trust him enough to run away with him. But what if Gabe was her only chance to get away and find out what it was like to be loved?

"Tell me more about your family. What do you do at Christmastime? Who taught you to play the lute? Does your family eat dinner together?"

She was asking about his family again. Gabe noticed that she got a strange look on her face, a look of longing, as if she enjoyed imagining what it was like.

Soon, as soon as he was able to plan their escape, he would take her to his family, and she'd be accepted and loved like she never had before.

"My father is a good musician, and we're all great singers. Except Valten. He sings like a crow." He laughed, then sobered. "Sorry. I shouldn't say bad things about your betrothed. Anyway, we sometimes sit around the fire and sing until the little ones fall asleep in our laps. My little sister Adela always wants to sit with me. I've put her to bed more times than I can count."

"What does she look like?"

"Blue eyes and blonde hair, although it's starting to turn brown now. And dimples in her cheeks. She's two. I have another sister, Margaretha, who's fifteen, and Kirstyn is twelve. Besides Valten and me, there's Steffan, who's ten, and Wolfhart, who's seven. It's always noisy. Someone's always laughing—or singing."

Sophie, who was staring at the table as though she were watching a miracle play, suddenly sighed.

He couldn't wait to take her home.

Just then, the huntsman strode in. He looked first at Sophie, then at Gabe. His jaw twitched, as though he were clenching his teeth. Then his face relaxed as he focused on Sophie. "Go for a walk with me?"

He actually said it politely, and Gabe held his breath as he and Lorencz both waited for her answer.

"No, I'm sorry. I don't take walks after dark." She folded her hands primly on the rough table.

The huntsman clenched his teeth, then composed himself again, making his voice smooth. "I won't let any harm come to you, Sophie. You are safe with me." He smiled, reminding Gabe of a fox eyeing a mouse.

"I cannot."

"Cannot or will not? Sophie, please come with me." His voice was more commanding now. He stepped toward her.

"She doesn't wish to go with you." Gabe rose to his feet and looked Lorencz in the eye. "Stop harassing her."

"I'm not harassing her, and it's none of your business. Sophie"—he turned back to her now, leaning over the table—"you aren't letting this fellow influence you, are you? Come. Take a walk with me."

"Gabe is not influencing me. I told you earlier that I wouldn't take a walk with you, and I have not changed my mind."

Gabe stifled a cheer.

"If you don't go," Lorencz said, his voice quiet but with a menacing undertone, "I may just find someone else to walk with me."

"As I told you before, I think that is a splendid idea."

Gabe waited tensely, watching the huntsman as he glared at Sophie. Finally, Lorencz straightened and then strode out of the room, his boots clomping loudly on the stone floor.

Sophie exhaled. "You should go. The duchess is probably waiting for you. Good night, Gabe."

"Good night, Sophie."

Sophie was helping Petra in the kitchen the next morning when Darla walked in with a big smirk on her face. Sophie always did her best not to detest the maid and prayed for her whenever she thought about the times Darla's tale-telling had gotten Sophie sent to the dungeon.

"*Guten Morgen*, Sophie," Darla said, lifting her nose into the air and breaking into an outright grin.

"*Guten Morgen*, Darla."

Darla sat down on a stool and crossed her legs, staring down at her fingernails. "Guess who asked me to go for a walk with him last night."

Sophie forced herself not to look up from the bread dough she was kneading. "I'm sure I don't know, but you are very popular, Darla, so it could have been anyone." Sophie airily turned away from her as she placed the dough on a flat board and shoved it into the crackling oven.

"Lorencz the huntsman."

"Is that so? I'm so glad he finally found someone to walk with him."

Sophie chanced a glimpse at Darla, who squinted her eyes a moment before breaking out in another sly grin. "We had a very good time."

"I'm sure you did. Walking helps balance the humors."

"We weren't walking the whole time. And we had a very . . . good time." She raised her eyebrows and smoothed her hands suggestively down her hips.

"Did you, now? I'm not surprised." Sophie forced a smile at Darla. The girl was so bold. It gave Sophie a sick feeling, in spite of her efforts to remain indifferent. But Sophie was glad she hadn't gone with Lorencz. She certainly would never trust him now.

"Lorencz said he asked you to stroll with him. But he says he won't be asking you anymore. Only me from now on."

"I'm so happy to hear it, Darla, because I can't stand the man myself." *The low, vile, stinking weasel.* "He is such a bore." Sophie scolded herself as soon as the words were out of her mouth, but the look on Darla's face was worth it.

"You're the one who's a *bore*, Sophie. You're just scared and weak and … and … alone. And you'll always be alone."

Sophie held the bread dough she was kneading in both hands, her teeth clamping tighter as Darla went on.

"The duchess hates you, and you'll never be anything but a sad, lowly scullery maid. You'll probably never marry or bear chil—"

The ball of dough in Sophie's hands hurtled through the air. It was almost as if she were watching someone else throw it. The floury dough hit Darla smack in the face, then it fell on the floor with a dull splat.

Darla's face was smudged with flour. She let out a strangled cry and lunged toward Sophie. Sophie turned and ducked behind Petra's slightly rotund body. Darla grabbed at Sophie's hair, but Sophie slapped her hand back. Darla lunged again and Petra grabbed Darla's face in a pinching grip.

"Get out of here with your disgusting boasts and mean talk." Petra shoved Darla's head backward, forcing her to stumble back.

In spite of the flour covering Darla's face, Sophie could see she was turning red, her eyes glinting dangerously. She turned and stalked out of the room.

Sophie felt triumphant for a moment, but then tears pricked her eyes, though she wasn't sure why. They seemed to be tears of pity. Perhaps Darla only behaved the way she did because, just like Sophie, she only wanted love. But the way she was going about it, she didn't seem likely to get it.

# Chapter

## 7

*Duchess Ermengard seemed very impressed* with the song Gabe had sung for her the previous night. He'd played his admiring troubadour role well, he knew, and it was now clear to him he had won her confidence with each warbled note.

Now he only had to figure out a way to steal Sophie away from the duchess. If he kept plying Sophie with stories of his family, she would surely go with him. But how could he keep the duchess from sending her guards once they'd escaped? Now that he'd seen the number of men she had and how powerful they were, he knew it was too risky to try to hold off the entire battalion by himself. He should go home, tell his father Sophie was the duke's daughter, then come back with a contingent of his father's soldiers to force Duchess Ermengard to let them take Sophie. But he just couldn't bear the thought of leaving her, even for one day, much less for the two weeks it would take him to go to Hagenheim and return. What would stop the duchess from killing her stepdaughter and commanding all the other servants to deny there ever was a servant girl named Sophie?

Gabe walked down the stone corridor, having been summoned to play for the duchess yet again. He had been working on another song. It wasn't finished, but he thought he would play a bit of it for her anyway.

He opened the door, and there she was, sitting on her imposing chair, flashing the same creepy smile. He gave her a few compliments as he took out his lute and prepared to play. *This ruse is becoming easier by the minute.*

He began singing the song he'd written late last night and into the morning. He extolled her silky black hair, red lips, and blue eyes and sang some verses about her virtue and generosity that he knew weren't true, but he had been thinking about Sophie again when he wrote it.

When he glanced up, she was staring at him as though he had turned into an offensive bug and she was contemplating how to crush him. Her face had turned even whiter, if that were possible, or more of a grayish color, actually. Her lips had also turned bloodless under their red stain. What had he said?

Then it hit him.

The duchess had green eyes.

He was caught. The song he'd sung for her yesterday had extolled their emerald hue, so he couldn't pretend he hadn't noticed.

"Who is this song about?" she hissed.

"Why, y-you, of course. Of course, Your Grace." *I'm a dead man.*

"You were talking with that scullery maid last night during the evening meal, were you not?"

He tried to swallow, but there seemed to be a ball of wool caught in his throat. *O God, save me. I'm doomed.*

He nodded.

She stood to her full height—at least as tall as Gabe—and walked across the room to the window. She simply stared out at the gloomy, half-lit forest. The only thing that moved was her lips as she pursed them tighter and tighter.

"Your Grace, forgive me for the oversight. I am still working on the song. Let me perfect it and play it for you tonight." He smiled, hoping he looked confident and casual, while inwardly he was flaying himself.

But she didn't look as though she were listening to him, and her face became more and more thunderous, as though the cloud that was hanging over her was turning black before it unleashed its torrent.

*She will murder me where I stand.*

Finally, she turned to him. That disturbing half smile, more frightening than her menacing grin, was on her face again as she took a step toward him. "You have come here to spy on me, haven't you?"

Had he? No. He had come to rescue Sophie.

"No, Your Grace. Of course not."

She took another step. He forced himself not to back away from her.

"Who are you?"

"I am Gabe, Your Grace."

"Perhaps you think you know who Sophie is. Who told you?"

She stepped closer.

"Told me what, Your Grace?"

"That she is Duke Baldewin's only daughter."

The back of his neck tingled. If she was telling him this, she must have decided to kill him. "Everyone knows Duke Baldewin's daughter is dead. Sophie is only a scullery maid."

"Oh no," Duchess Ermengard crooned in a silky, low voice as she slowly walked toward him. "She is Sophia Breitenbach, daughter of Baldewin Breitenbach, Duke of Hohendorf, and the fairest beauty in the Holy Roman Empire. Is she not?" She stopped only two feet in front of him, her white teeth glowing between her unnaturally red lips.

It was no good to lie. Besides, if he was going to die, he wanted to be right with God.

"Sophie is very beautiful, it is true."

"The *most* beautiful. Admit it!" Her voice rose in both pitch and intensity. "You think she's more beautiful than I am!"

Her eyes were two glowing green orbs. Her expression was one of outraged discovery.

"And you are no lowly peasant." Her voice lowered once again and her eyes narrowed. "I do believe Duke Wilhelm had a son ... a son named Gabehart. But Gabehart was not betrothed to a duke's daughter. No, no. As I recall, his older brother, Valten, was to marry Duke Baldewin's only child. So which one are you? Are you Valten, assuming your brother's name? Or are you actually stupid enough to be Gabehart?"

Her evil catlike eyes seemed to bore into his soul, like a wild animal surveying her prey. Gabe shuddered.

"And if you are Gabehart, why did not Valten, Sophie's betrothed, come to rescue her?"

Gabe cast about in his mind for a strategy, a way of escape from this room and this woman. But the windows were shut and bolted. He could possibly unbolt one and jump out the window, if he took everyone by complete surprise, although he was so high in her tower room he'd probably break something when he hit the ground. The only other option was to physically overpower her, which also appeared to be a gamble. For now, he would tell the truth in an effort to keep her from becoming enraged again. The moment she called for her guards, his lot was hopeless.

"I am Gabehart, second son of Duke Wilhelm of Hagenheim. You are right, Your Grace. I was wrong to try to fool you. Valten couldn't come because of a broken leg. But I am here only to see if what an old woman said was true. About Sophie." As he spoke, he tried to think of a way to overpower her. She was almost close enough that he could grab her. But perhaps it wouldn't be necessary. Perhaps she would let him leave.

She stepped around him, getting between him and the door leading to the corridor.

Duchess Ermengard opened the door while keeping her eyes on Gabe. She screamed, "Guards!"

Gabe ran toward the window, but before he could even get it unbolted, guards rushed into the room, the sharp swish of their swords being drawn from their scabbards, their boots pounding on the flagstone floor. He struggled with the rusty bolt, and just as he shoved it free and threw open the window, two burly men grabbed Gabe's shoulder. They threw him to the floor. He hit the flagstone with the side of his face. As the darkness started closing in on him, the last thing he heard was a crazed, high-pitched cackling.

When she saw that Gabe was unconscious, Duchess Ermengard pointed a finger at the closest guard. "Get Lorencz."

As she waited, she envisioned ways she could dispose of the foolhardy boy laid out before her feet. The only question was how long to draw out his pain.

Once the huntsman arrived, Gabe was taken away to the dungeon on her order, leaving her alone with Lorencz.

He reached out to take her hand and kiss it, but his eyes gave away his fear. She ground her teeth. "How dare you think that girl is more beautiful than I am."

"Your Grace, I —"

"Don't speak! You have become enamored with her too." That useful girl Darla had told her everything, from how Lorencz had failed to get Sophie to trust him enough to take a walk with him, to being so heartbroken he got drunk with Darla instead. "I shall kill this silly, interfering Gabehart of Hagenheim for thinking she is the fairest. Though what shall I do to you? I already asked you to kill her. Why haven't you, pray tell?"

"Your Grace, I simply haven't had many opportunities. In

fact, I was finally able to get her alone just yesterday, but that—that *boy* was skulking about, and even intruded upon us in the woods. You didn't want any witnesses, as I recall."

She gave Lorencz her coldest smile.

"Your Grace, you can't think the girl means anything to me. The only woman with whom I am enamored is you."

She detected fear in the way his scar turned pale. "Good. But your punishment for letting your eye wander is ..." She leaned closer. "Why is it that everyone seems to like her?" She tapped her fingernail against her chin, deliberately drawing out the moment to see if he would squirm. Instead, he kept his face impassive. The only indication of his distress was the barely detectable rapid rise and fall of his chest as his breathing quickened. He knew full well what she was capable of.

"She is an insipid little creature. I could break her in half with my bare hands. What do you see in her, dear huntsman?"

"Not me, Your Grace." Lorencz smiled and shook his head, an attempt to look unconcerned. "She is nothing to me. You are the woman I think about, the one I dream about."

"Very good." She stepped forward and placed her hand under his chin, letting her fingernails glide along his skin, forcing him to look her in the eyes. "I am pleased to hear that. And now I have one thing I want you to do for me."

"Anything, Your Grace."

"As I told you before, I want you to kill Sophie. And I want you to do it *today*."

He blinked several times, as if trying to hide his feelings and not look horrified, but she saw his repulsion. *Weakling*.

"Of course. How?"

She took her time answering him, savoring how his expression twisted with each moment. She had misjudged him. He had more of a conscience than she had given him credit for.

It was a pity.

There was no purpose in thinking up creative ways to kill the girl, as enjoyable as that would be. Now that it was time for Sophie to die, it would be done expediently.

"Take her into the woods. Tie her up and plunge a dagger into her heart. I don't really care how you do it, just make sure it's done without witnesses. Then bury her in the ground where no one can find her." She poked him in the throat with her fingernail as she emphasized, "No one must find her."

Lorencz's Adam's apple bobbed as he swallowed. "Yes, Your Grace."

She studied him, trying to see into his thoughts. She must have proof the girl was dead, but it had to be something no one else would recognize as belonging to Sophie. Duke Wilhelm would surely come digging around, and if he could find definitive proof of Gabe or the girl's death, it would ruin everything.

She smiled at Lorencz and pressed all five fingernails of her right hand into his chest. "You will kill her ... and you will bring back her heart ... to me. If you fail me, you will die. Is that understood?"

"Yes, Your Grace."

"You may go." She raised her brows and flicked her wrist at him.

Lorencz bowed his head and left.

Once she had evidence of the girl's demise in her hands, she would taunt Gabe with it. Seeing how he was infatuated with her, it would be the perfect mode of torture, outdoing anything she'd previously imagined. Once he was sufficiently broken, she would poison him and let him die a slow, agonizing death as he realized the fairest beauty in the Holy Roman Empire, the girl he'd written songs about, was dead. And Duchess Ermengard would remind him it was because he'd thought Sophie was more beautiful than she. It was *all his fault*. Because he'd come snooping around when he should have stayed home.

She walked over to the mirror on the wall and stared at herself. She imagined Sophie standing beside her. The girl was younger, her skin was smoother, her smile more sincere, her eyes larger and brighter. Then she imagined Sophie's eyes closed in death, her skin growing dark gray, then falling away until there was nothing left but a skull.

She laughed. No one could love the girl if she was dead—not Lorencz, not the servants, not even Duke Baldewin.

Sophie would no longer be the fairest.

As soon as Gabe woke up, he knew where he was. The smell of human waste and the damp, cold stone against his body made it quite clear.

His head throbbed. He touched his cheek and looked at his hand. Only a little blood. He pressed on his swollen cheekbone gingerly. He didn't think the bone was broken.

He groaned as he sat up, resting his head in his hands. How would he get out of this?

*God, have I already ruined everything? I've barely been here a day and look at me.*

His mother always said his lack of caution would lead to trouble. It seemed she was more right than she knew. Sophie had warned him as well, but he'd thought she was overstating the duchess's dangerous nature and volatility. After all, what reason did that woman have to imprison him?

Cruelty. Jealousy. She didn't need a reason. She was insane.

The worst thing was that he could no longer help Sophie. How would he rescue her now?

He thought of his mother again and felt a stab of guilt, thinking about how sick with worry she must be. *God, please get me out of this.*

He was the irresponsible son, the one who sneaked away

with his friends when he was supposed to be studying. While Valten was practicing jousting and sword fighting, Gabe was pulling pranks on the old stable master, switching the horses in their stalls and painting white stars on all their foreheads. No wonder Valten's gifts and standing so surpassed his own. *God, forgive me for grieving my mother.*

Guilt used to assault him every time his mother looked at him with concern—and sometimes disappointment—in her eyes. But he'd continued with his foolish behavior. The guilt hadn't been enough to stop him.

He still remembered how devastated his mother had been when his sister Elsebeth drowned at three years old. They'd all been distraught, but his mother had cried for days without stopping. Her eyes, her whole face, became so puffy Gabe almost hadn't recognized her. He'd been frightened by the depth of her grief, and he'd wondered if she would die too.

Gabe didn't like remembering his sister's death. He'd been playing nearby when she'd fallen into the lake. Elsebeth had been splashing at the edge of the water, and he'd assumed she was enjoying herself on the bank. He hadn't even noticed when the splashing stopped. The rest of the day was fuzzy; only bits and pieces stuck in his memory. He'd been very young, only six years old, but he recalled the heavy weight inside him, a feeling he now knew was guilt. At the time he'd felt as if he'd been bad, as if Elsebeth's death was his fault. After all, he was her older brother. He should have watched out for her, protected her, saved her.

And he felt the same way now about Sophie. Sophie needed him. He was supposed to keep her from danger. He should have been wise enough and cautious enough not to get thrown into the dungeon. *I've failed everyone.*

He looked around at the bare, cold dungeon and imagined Sophie spending days and nights here. The unfairness of her being locked in this awful place made him burn to exact justice on her behalf, made him long to put his hands around the duchess's neck and choke her. But here he was, completely helpless to rescue himself, much less Sophie.

The poor girl had been subjected to the horrors of living under the duchess's thumb her whole life. He wanted to see her rescued from this place, living a happy life in freedom. *God, don't let me fail!*

Would Valten appreciate her? Would he cherish her, understand what she'd been through? Gabe would make sure Valten treated her right.

If he got out of this alive.

Right now he wasn't exactly in a position to make anyone do anything. Sophie might never meet any of Gabe's family unless he escaped from this dungeon.

Gabe went over to the one window, which was at eye level, and took hold of the bars. He yanked and tugged, hoping to feel them give a little, but the bars didn't budge. He tugged again. Same result.

*One more time, God.* He rubbed his hands together. He spit on them and rubbed again. He grabbed the bars, took a deep breath and—*Give me the strength*—pushed, then pulled, with all his might.

He wanted to believe he'd felt them give way just a tiny bit. But he couldn't lie to himself. They hadn't budged at all.

"The duchess threw Gabe in the dungeon!"

Sophie stared at Petra, who had just burst into the kitchen, her eyes big and round. Sophie sat down heavily on a stool near the stove.

She would have to save him. She needed Gabe to help her get to Valten, who may not believe she was his betrothed if she simply showed up at his castle declaring she was Duke

Baldwin's daughter. Besides, Gabe had done nothing worthy of death, and Sophie refused to allow the duchess to kill another innocent man. But she'd have to make her escape at the same time. If Sophie helped Gabe escape, the duchess would find out it was her and kill her. It was now or never. The only problem was how to steal the key to the dungeon.

Sophie stood and hurried toward the corridor—and almost ran face-first into Lorencz.

Something about the look on his face—sober and cool, his eyes vacant but intent—made the skin on the back of her neck tingle. She took a step back.

"Sophie. I need you to help me with something." There was no sign of flirtation in his tone, and his face wore a blank expression.

"What?"

"There's a dog, a puppy, trapped in the woods. I need you to help me rescue him."

"Why don't you rescue him?"

"Because I'm too big to crawl into the hole after him."

"I don't believe you." Besides, she remembered the kiss the huntsman had forced on her, remembered what Darla had boasted about, and knew she'd be a fool to go with him.

The set of his jaw let her know he was angry. "Very well, then. The puppy can stay trapped and starve." He turned to leave.

"Why don't you ask Darla to help you?"

He practically sneered. "Jealous, are you?"

*I don't have time for this!* "What is it you really want?"

"If you come with me, I will help Gabe escape from the dungeon."

"Why would you do that?"

"Oh, would you?" Petra spoke up, clasping her hands and looking pleadingly at Lorencz. "I am afraid the duchess will kill the poor boy if you don't help him."

"Exactly. She will kill him. But I will let him out—if you come with me."

"How do I know I can trust you?"

"Have I ever harmed you, little Sophie?" He raised his brows and held out his hand to her. She stared at it.

"When have you ever cared about a puppy?"

He took a deep breath, his chest slowly moving up, then down. He shrugged. "I admit, I don't care that much. But I had promised the puppy to a child in the village who asked for a pet."

"You don't care about the village children."

"How do you know that? I have a sister who lives in the village. She has three children, and her children have friends. Why would I not care? Will you help me or not? Gabe is in the dungeon, bleeding and in need of care, and you are wasting time."

She ignored his hand and gave him a curt nod. He turned and headed out the door, and she followed him out of the castle and into the woods. She felt for her knife, always in her dress pocket, and clasped the handle.

Sophie felt more and more uneasy the farther they walked. She had finally decided to turn back when Lorencz stopped. They were at the clearing where they'd had their picnic.

"The puppy's over here, on the other side of this tree."

The cold look on Lorencz's face made Sophie's stomach sink. Something was definitely wrong. She clutched the handle of her knife as Lorencz turned away. He took two more steps, but she didn't follow, only watched as the huntsman walked just past a large tree and fell to his knees.

"Here it is." He motioned with his hand, staring down at the ground.

*He does seem to be peering into a hole.* Sophie stepped closer. Lorencz stood and slowly turned to her. A hairbreadth of a second later, his hand flew out and grabbed her throat. She drew the knife out of her pocket and slashed at his arm, but Lorencz blocked it with a blow to her wrist.

"I have no choice," Lorencz said through clenched teeth. "The duchess will kill me if I don't do as she commanded."

Sophie struggled, clawing at the hand that was choking her. Her heart slammed against her ribs. *God, don't let me die. I have to save Gabe. Don't let me die.*

Lorencz grabbed her wrists in one of his enormous hands. She had to get away. She struck at him with her knee, hitting his groin.

Lorencz roared, his eyes wild, his teeth bared. He roared again as he slammed her head against the tree trunk behind her.

*No, God,* was the only thing she could think to pray before her world went black.

Duchess Ermengard felt a tingle of excitement all the way down to her toes when Lorencz walked into her private chamber. He carried a small bundle wrapped in a dark cloth. The day she had dreamed about had finally come. Why had she kept Sophie alive so long? Her husband was never coming back — the coward — so it wasn't as if she needed to keep Sophie as a bargaining tool. He couldn't take Hohendorf away from her any longer.

"What do you have for me?" A gleeful giggle escaped her. She clasped her hands to her throat as Lorencz came closer and extended the cloth bundle toward her. She felt like a girl at Christmastime.

"Your Grace, I have brought you the girl's heart." Lorencz looked flushed. His eyelashes were wet and his green eyes glittered.

The man was pathetic. She'd thought he was of harder stock than that. He quickly bowed his head, no doubt to hide his unmanly weakness.

She took the bundle in her hands and unwrapped it. It was still warm and wet. Perhaps she could have it dried, like a piece of fruit, and keep it in a prominent place. Maybe in a decorative box on a shelf. Or if that didn't work, she could burn it and keep the ashes. She'd also heard of barbarians who ate their enemies' hearts, believing it would give them their enemies' strengths.

Not that Sophie had any strength for Ermengard to inherit, but still, she would think about it.

"Thank you, Huntsman. You may go."

"As you wish, Your Grace." He bowed out of the room.

Duchess Ermengard walked over to her looking glass hanging on the wall, still holding the heart in her hand. She stared at her reflection, admiring her own beauty. Each feature was perfectly symmetrical and proportionate. Her nose was small but strong. Her lips were plump and red, her teeth straight and white, her eyelashes stained black, and her face and neck powdered a fashionable white. She was beautiful. And there was no one anywhere — not anymore — who rivaled her beauty.

Perhaps she would rid herself of the huntsman now that he had done something he so obviously detested. Besides, he was straying. He had been with that tart Darla. The duchess couldn't have that. Yes, she would find a new ... huntsman. Someone younger and more exciting. After all, the most beautiful woman in the region deserved the best.

Later, after she'd had her meal and her wine, she would tell Gabe of Sophie's death. She would taunt him and laugh at him and show him the proof that Sophie was dead, that he hadn't been able to save her. How would that make him feel? Would he cry like a baby? And eventually, she would kill him too, of course. But for now she needed to rest and build up her strength. It was going to be a full day and night.

# *Chapter*
## 8

*God, please get me out of here.* *Gabe pressed* his forehead against the wall as he prayed. His arms ached from tugging on the bars of the window, and his shoulder throbbed from throwing himself against the solid wood door. *If you give me another chance, I vow I will not fail Sophie again. I'll get her out of here and get her safely to Hagenheim. Please help me.*

Metal scraped metal on the other side of the door to the dungeon, then the hinges squealed as the door opened.

*Thank you!* Gabe sprinted toward the door. When he saw Lorencz, he hesitated. Would he need to fight this man to get out? Whatever he had to do, he would do it. And now. This might be his only chance. He prepared to lunge at the huntsman.

To his surprise, Lorencz's face was flushed. Gabe had never seen him looking so agitated.

"Well?" Lorencz barked. "Come on, man, make haste."

Gabe took the steps two at a time and leaped out the door, holding up his fists, ready to fight. But Lorencz was already preceding him down the passageway that led out of the castle. Gabe ran after him.

"What is happening?" Gabe asked.

Lorencz didn't answer until they were outside. Gingerbread was already saddled and standing nearby, placidly grazing beside a second horse, a black stallion he presumed was Lorencz's.

"I don't have time to explain everything. Sophie is in danger. If you don't get to her now, the duchess will kill her."

"Where is she?"

"You should know the area well, seeing as you likely followed us there when Sophie and I picnicked." Lorencz raised one eyebrow. "She's tied to a tree in the clearing."

"What do you mean, 'she's tied to a tree'?" Gabe grabbed the front of Lorencz's tunic and clenched his fist.

Lorencz pushed him away, and Gabe stumbled back into his horse, who whinnied and tried to nip his shoulder.

"The duchess ordered me to kill her, but I didn't. Now get on your horse, untie Sophie, and ride as fast and as far from this place as you can."

"I need to get a horse for Sophie."

"No." Lorencz seized his shoulder roughly and turned him around. "Get on your horse and set off. Now. You can't go near the stable without being seen, not with all the guards milling around there. And as soon as Duchess Ermengard finds out you're not in the dungeon and Sophie's not dead, they'll be hunting you. You have to get Sophie to safety."

Lorencz practically shoved him into the saddle, then mounted his own black horse.

Gabe caught his eye. "Thank you. For your help."

Lorencz looked back at him grimly. Gabe wondered where the huntsman would go, with just his horse and the clothes on his back.

As Gabe was turning his horse around, Petra came running out of the kitchen.

"Wait!" She thrust a cloth bag into Gabe's hand. "If you run into trouble, there is a safe place you can go. It's about three days' ride from here, to the north. Locals call it the Cottage of the Seven. It's in a glen on the east side of the river."

Gabe nodded.

"Ask for Dominyk the Wise and the Cottage of the Seven if you get lost."

Gabe was already riding across the yard and into the woods. Her words followed him away from the castle.

In a few moments he was at the clearing.

Was this a trap? Or had the huntsman actually set him free from the dungeon in hopes he'd rescue Sophie? God answered prayers in the strangest ways sometimes.

But there was no scullary maid tied to a tree in the clearing. The only sign that Lorencz may have been telling the truth were ropes at the base of a large tree.

"Sophie?" he called quietly, keeping alert in case the duchess had planned an ambush. "Sophie, where are you?"

*Now that you've given me another chance, God, please don't let me fail. I can't fail again.*

Sophie trembled from behind the tree as she watched Gabe frantically searching the clearing and calling for her. Until his intentions were clear, she intended to stay put.

Her head still hurt from where Lorencz had slammed her against the tree trunk. She had wakened to find herself tied up and him holding his knife against her throat. The huntsman's eyes had held the same darkness she'd seen on Duchess Ermengard's face so many times before, and she was sure he would kill her.

But then Lorencz dropped the knife. He looked at her as if she'd suddenly grown wings and feathers, backing away from her slowly and shaking his head. "I can't do it," he whispered. "Oh, God, I can't do it." Then he'd turned and stumbled away into the trees.

When her vision stopped spinning, she squatted down, stretched her arm, and managed to reach his knife with one of her fingers. Slowly, she nudged the handle close enough to grasp it. She'd freed herself from the ropes just as she heard a horse's hooves approaching, and she ran into the woods. When she saw it was Gabe, she'd been relieved—but only for a moment.

What was he doing out of the dungeon? Had he been sent to lure her into the open? She had never imagined Lorencz would slam her head against a tree, tie her up, and hold a knife on her—her mind was still reeling with the thought that he'd actually intended to kill her—so how did she know she could trust Gabe? His kind words and incredible promises could easily be a ruse.

Gabe dismounted from his horse and knelt to examine the ropes. Sophie turned and ran, still clutching the knife. She sprinted as fast as she could, bushes snatching at her clothes, limbs slapping her in the face, leaves temporarily blinding her.

Her foot caught on a root and she fell headlong to the ground, flinging Lorencz's knife in front of her.

"Sophie, stop! It's me, Gabe!"

She heard his horse's hooves pounding toward her. She'd never be able to escape him on foot. She jumped up and whirled to face him, grabbing the knife off the ground, ready to defend herself however was necessary.

"Sophie, it's all right. I'm here to help you." He looked bewildered. "I won't hurt you."

She wanted to believe him, but her heart pounded in disagreement. The thought of Gabe turning against her, trying to kill her, was even worse than Lorencz's attempt.

Although that had been enough of a shock.

Gabe leaned toward her from the back of his enormous horse. Then she noticed his cheekbone. It was bruised, scraped raw, and swollen. "When the duchess finds out that I escaped and that you're still alive, she will kill us both. We have to make haste."

His warm brown eyes looked so sincere, Sophie decided to

take the risk. She put the knife into her pocket and placed her hand in his.

Gabe hauled her up in front of him. To remain stable, she was forced to sit astraddle like Gabe. It wasn't proper, but it was better than getting herself and Gabe killed, and her skirt was full enough that it hid most of her legs. She adjusted it slightly just to be sure.

He slapped the reins and the horse leaped forward. The saddle was roomy, but Sophie was still practically sitting in Gabe's lap.

"Where are we going? Where will you take me?"

"To Hagenheim, to my family." His prickly chin brushed her cheek as he bent to speak next to her ear.

"Wait!" Her heart seized at the thought of leaving behind her beloved Gospel of Saint Luke. "I have to get something!" She looked up into his brown eyes. "Please. I need it. We have to go back."

"We have no time as it is." After a moment's pause, he asked, "What is this thing you're willing to get us killed for?"

"It's a piece of the Bible, a section from the book of Saint Luke."

"If we make it to Hagenheim, you can have the entire Bible. I will personally get one for you. But you won't need the book of Saint Luke if you're not alive to read it."

He was right, of course. It made her ache to think of losing her precious book, the words that had comforted her through the past ten years of her life, but not enough for Gabe to lose his life retrieving it.

She turned her head and looked up at him. There was a serious look on his face, which softened when he looked into her eyes. "I'm sorry, Sophie."

She shook her head, hoping he understood the gesture meant it didn't matter. She was afraid if she spoke, she might choke on the words.

The bruise on his cheek was quite prominent. She wished she could hurt whoever had hurt him, wished she could command he be thrown in the worst dungeon and locked away for as long as Gabe's bruise remained visible.

She sighed. It was a silly thought. She'd never have that kind of power. Besides, her former priest would scold her if he knew she was wishing for revenge.

As the trail grew more rugged, Sophie was thrown back into Gabe's chest by the sudden upward charge of the horse. The spot on the back of her head where Lorencz had slammed her into the tree hit Gabe's breastbone, sending a sharp, shooting pain through her skull. Gabe wrapped an arm around her waist, holding her snugly, and gripped the reins with his other hand. She turned her neck slightly and rested against him.

They were both silent as Gabe guided the huge horse through the dense trees.

"Are you hurt?" Gabe spoke the words by her ear, his deep voice surprising her, his warm breath like a feather against her ear.

"You don't need to worry about me. I am well."

"Are you sure? I can't imagine how Lorencz managed to tie you to a tree. Did you let him do that to you?"

"Of course not." Sophie bristled. "I was unconscious. My head hit the tree, and I blacked out."

"You hit your head? Where?" The hand that had been around her waist was now on her head, rubbing, his fingers probing.

"Stop that." But she couldn't get away from his examination.

He found her injury, and she winced at the pain his touch caused.

"That's a bad bump. It's bloody too. Are you sure you're well?"

It was strange he should ask, because at that moment she felt as though her last meal was trying to come back up. She closed her eyes and took deep breaths as Gabe's arm circled her waist again. The horse's gait jarred her head and every joint in her body. She hung her head.

"Sophie?"

His voice was so kind and gentle. *Will Valten's voice be as gentle as Gabe's?* She rested her head against Gabe's chest again and breathed deliberately and slowly. Gradually the sick feeling in her stomach subsided. But she didn't lift her head from his chest. It was too hard to try to hold herself steady against the horse's jolting gait.

Gabe had said he was taking her to his home, to his family. As she rested against him, holding her hand over the wooden cross around her neck, a sense of joy and peace bloomed inside her. If they were able to escape the duchess's guards, she would be free from Duchess Ermengard. She would see the sun and feel it on her skin, have the freedom she'd always lacked. Her dream was coming true. And Gabe was taking her to her betrothed. She would marry Gabe's brother and then they would be family.

"I've never had a brother before."

Gabe tightened his grip around her waist. He seemed so intent on getting them as far away from the castle as quickly as he could, she wasn't sure if he'd even heard what she'd said. But then he pulled on the big horse's reins and stopped.

"Sorry, but I have to let you down for a moment. Can you stand?"

She nodded.

He let Sophie slip off the saddle, then he dismounted and stepped toward a half-fallen-down wooden structure amongst the trees. Sophie watched curiously as he went inside then came back out with a large leather pouch and a crossbow he slung over his back by a strap around his shoulder.

Tall, with his head high and a grim, determined glint in his eye, he looked quite capable of keeping her safe.

He strapped the leather pouch tightly to the back of the saddle, next to a cloth bundle she hadn't noticed earlier. "Where did you get that?"

"The cook handed it to me as I was leaving. I hope it's full of food." He helped Sophie back on to the horse, then hauled himself up to sit behind her once more.

Knowing Petra, the bundle *was* filled with food, the kind that would not spoil on a long journey. Petra always did like to show her love by feeding people.

They pressed onward once more. She was nestled against Gabe's chest again—not an unpleasant place to be at all, she discovered. With his arm circling her waist, she felt safe.

"Gabe, does the duchess know you're helping me? Will her guards be after us?"

"I hope she thinks I'm still in her dungeon, and that you're dead. It could buy us some time, because as soon as she finds me gone, she'll send her guards. And she may wonder if you're still alive when she discovers Lorencz has disappeared."

"Did he leave?"

"Yes. The way he took off, I don't think he'll be back."

"Good. I never want to see him again." Sophie suppressed a shudder as she pictured his face again just before he smashed her head against the tree. "How did you get out of the dungeon?"

"Lorencz. He let me out."

"Oh." Perhaps Lorencz was repentant. She hoped so. For his sake.

They'd been traveling since before midday, and the sun had already sunk behind a peak at his left shoulder. Gabe pushed Gingerbread to get as far away from Hohendorf as possible before nightfall. The duchess had probably discovered him missing by now. If so, her guards could easily catch up to them at any minute. Then again, they would probably have some trouble tracking them, since Gabe and Sophie hadn't followed a trail, just headed in a general northerly direction. Every so often they encountered the small river that wound north and south through the mountains and forests. Whenever Gabe saw it, he knew he was going in the right direction.

Gabe was all too aware of the way Sophie felt in his arms. He kept reminding himself that she belonged to Valten, and he conjured up Brittola's face often—as often as he started enjoying the trusting way Sophie leaned her head against his chest, the silkiness of her hair brushing his chin.

But she thought of him as a brother. And that's just what he was, for she and Valten would be married as soon as he could get her back to Hagenheim.

It was a long way to Hagenheim, about seven days. His heart sank a bit as he thought about just how far it was. Petra had said the "Cottage of the Seven" was three days' ride to the north. He wasn't sure what this cottage was, but she had said it was a safe place. In three days, they would probably be in desperate need of food and a comfortable place to sleep. Sophie surely wasn't used to sleeping outdoors, and he had precious few supplies with him. Although he doubted Sophie would complain. She had lived too hard a life to bemoan a few days of living off the land.

She was different from any other girl he had ever met.

But he couldn't let his thoughts about Sophie distract him from his purpose, which was to keep her alive and deliver her to Valten, her betrothed. With two people on one horse, the going was slow, and if he didn't focus, they might end up back in Hohendorf—or dead.

The terrain was getting rougher. They would have to pass through some mountains in order to get to Lower Saxony and Hagenheim. They were now on a narrow trail that led them through a valley that had fewer trees than the mountainside and was parallel to another valley where a river lay. They had only stopped briefly to let the horse rest and get a drink of water, but they hadn't eaten, and Gabe knew they would have to soon. Sophie must be as exhausted as he was, but she hadn't said a word. Neither of them had spoken much, in fact.

A forest-covered mountain lay just ahead, and the trail was already ascending again. They couldn't camp here in the open expanse of the valley where there was almost no foliage. It was too dangerous. Perhaps after they got to the other side of the mountain they would find a sheltered spot. It would be a cool night, unfortunately, but they would have to do without a fire. With all the wolves around, he would try to sleep sitting up, with his crossbow in his lap.

Sophie had gone limp, her head bobbing on his chest. She must have fallen asleep. He forced himself to focus on the trail, which had grown slippery with wet, moldy leaves that covered the path as it grew steeper. Gingerbread was surefooted for such a big beast, but he was slipping more often than not, and Gabe hoped the trail would soon level off.

Just then, Gabe heard a crisp *whoosh* and felt something hit, hard, against the crossbow strapped across his back.

He turned his head and saw the butt of an arrow sticking out behind him.

If not for the heavy wood and iron of his crossbow, the arrow would have gone right through his body.

# *Chapter*
## 9

*Gabe kicked his heels into his horse's sides as* he turned his head again and saw his foe. Through a break in the trees, a man on horseback raced across the valley they had just left. He would close in on them in no time.

Gabe urged Gingerbread to hurry, but speed only seemed to make his hooves slip even more on the steep hillside.

If the man following them was using a crossbow, he'd have to stop to reload. But if he was firing at them with a longbow, he could keep shooting. Gabe couldn't risk looking behind again, but he'd soon know.

Another arrow whooshed by his ear. *Longbow. God help us.* Gabe leaned lower, pressing Sophie securely between his arms as he held onto the reins with both hands. She lifted her head and looked up at him, wide awake now. She leaned her head to one side to look behind him, but he pushed her back in front of him. "Someone's shooting at us. You'd better move your arms."

Another arrow whistled by. Sophie jerked her left arm and gasped. She tucked her arm against her stomach, a flash of bright red on her torn sleeve.

They had to get out of the valley, had to find cover, or they would be dead in a matter of minutes. Not to mention that their pursuer could hit Gingerbread, may have already wounded him.

Gabe prodded Gingerbread off the trail, and they plunged

between trees, dodging limbs. Gabe kept Sophie snug between his body and the horse's neck.

He sensed the animal's nervousness at their breakneck speed between dangerously close tree trunks. They continued their climb up the mountain, but at a more managable angle. Gingerbread was slipping less now, but sometimes the tree limbs were coming at him so fast Gabe couldn't see where they were going.

*God, please guide this horse.*

They were crashing through the woods with such noise, their pursuer couldn't fail to hear exactly where they were if he stopped to listen. But it couldn't be helped. Until Gabe could find a likely place for them to hide.

He glanced down at Sophie's arm. The red stain was growing bigger, but there was no arrow sticking out of the wound. That was good. Perhaps it had only grazed her.

Gabe glanced around, frantically looking for someplace they could take refuge. He tried to listen, to detect how far behind them their attacker was—or attackers, since he wasn't sure how many there were—but he couldn't hear anything except Gingerbread's crashing hooves as he smashed through dead limbs. Green boughs were pushed aside by the horse's powerful shoulders. Gabe was thankful he had taken Gingerbread, his destrier, rather than the smaller gelding in his father's stable who would have tired much more easily with two riders on his back.

Just in front of him, Gabe glimpsed a ravine. He couldn't see the bottom of it, and it pitched almost straight down, but it might be their only escape.

He steered the horse toward the edge. Gingerbread hesitated only a moment, then stepped off. Immediately his hooves began to slide. Had Gabe made a mistake? Gabe and Sophie leaned to the left as the horse's body leaned precariously to the right. All four of his hooves were sliding down the steep, leaf-covered embankment. The horse began to fight for footing. Gabe let go of the reins and wrapped both his arms around Sophie as the horse began to topple over.

Gabe yanked his right leg up and pulled Sophie with him to the left, barely escaping being pinned underneath the huge horse. Gabe's feet hit the ground, almost gently, as the horse came out from under him and slid helplessly down the steep bank, struggling to get to his feet all the while.

Gabe set Sophie on her feet, not aware that he had been holding her completely off the ground until that moment. She clung to his neck, her eyes wide. Then Gabe grabbed her hand and they headed down into the deep ravine, into darkness, after his tumbling horse.

Sophie held tight to Gabe's hand as they hurried down the steep hill, their feet slipping and sliding. Sophie fell to one hip but jumped back to her feet, following Gabe down into the dark ravine.

*God, please help us escape.* She knew Gabe was hoping their attacker wouldn't realize they'd come down this way, and it did seem like a good place to hide. But it also seemed a likely place for a bear's den or a wolf's lair. Only God knew what they would find at the bottom.

Below them, Gabe's horse was finally able to halt his fall and scramble to his feet. He stood shaking his big head, his mane flopping around his massive neck. Gabe pulled Sophie down the hill and around the other side of the horse, putting the animal's body between them and the top of the ravine and their would-be killer. Then he let go of her hand and smoothly pulled his crossbow over his shoulder. He yanked out the arrow that was stuck in the wood stock and threw it to the ground. Then he opened the pack that was strapped to the back of the horse's saddle, which had miraculously not been lost in the fall, and slipped out an arrow. He stepped on the drawstring of the bow and fitted the arrow into place. Lifting the crossbow to his shoulder, and using the horse as a shield, he peered over the horse's back and up to the top of the ravine.

Sophie looked up, but they had gone so far down, she couldn't quite make it out in the descending darkness of twilight.

Something tickled her arm. She looked down and realized it was a trickle of blood running down and dripping off her elbow. She would examine the wound later.

Gabe was staring up, an intent look on his face, as he kept his finger on the trigger of his crossbow. Sophie knew, if ever there were a time to pray, it was now. *God, please let the man — or men — pass us by. Help us stay hidden.*

Gabe rested the crossbow on the horse's back while he waited. Sophie held her breath. Then she heard the sound of horse's hooves on leaves and sticks, the rustle of branches. It came closer, sounding as if it were just above them, just out of her vision. Then she saw movement, at the top of the ravine, though it was too dark to tell who or what caused it. Gabe held the crossbow up and stared down the stock of the partly wood-partly metal contraption. A deadly looking metal projectile was ready to fire at their enemy.

Gabe's horse sidestepped nervously, so Sophie rubbed his neck and softly hummed. She didn't dare speak aloud.

Gradually, the noise of what she assumed was a horse and rider became fainter and fainter. He hadn't seen them in the ravine. They were safe — at least for the moment.

Gabe eased the crossbow away from his shoulder, turned, and looked at Sophie. "Are you all right?" he whispered. "Let me see your arm." He set the crossbow down on the ground. With one step, he closed the gap between them and took her arm in his hands.

"We need to find water."

"Water?"

He nodded. "Gingerbread needs water, and this wound needs to be washed and covered."

He held her arm close to his face, examining it, but it was so covered in blood, and the ravine was so dark, she doubted he could see the actual wound. He pulled a knife from his belt, which he had retrieved earlier from his saddlebag, and cut off her sleeve where it had been torn by the arrow, at her elbow. Then, with a grim look, he wrapped the scrap of sleeve tightly around her bloody forearm. It had hurt before, but now it throbbed.

She thought it strange that he was concerned about washing the wound, but she didn't ask him about it.

"We need to go," he said brusquely, seeming somehow older than he had when she met him yesterday, and certainly more grim. He went to place his hands on her waist to lift her up, but she stepped back, bumping into the horse.

"Wait. First I need to ..."

They had drunk the last of the water in Gabe's flask an hour or two before, and now she needed some privacy for a few moments.

Understanding dawned on his face. He simply nodded and pointed to the nearest tree. "I won't look." He turned his back to her.

Sophie hurried to hide herself behind the tree and some bushes. When she was done, a growling sound just behind her made the hair on the back of her neck stand up. She froze in place, wishing she had imagined the sound, but then it came again.

She itched to turn around and see what was behind her, but she doubted that was wise. Slowly, she put one foot in front of the other and walked back toward Gabe, who was facing her with his crossbow aimed and ready.

"Is that a wolf I hear?"

Sophie nodded, still walking slowly. Where there was one wolf, there was sure to be more. Everyone knew wolves traveled in packs.

Gabe caught sight of the glowing yellow eyes of a wolf stalking Sophie, sending a coldness through his limbs. He lifted the crossbow and aimed for the wolf's head, right between its eyes. The wolf crouched, then launched itself toward Sophie.

Gabe squeezed the metal trigger and the arrow found its mark, slamming the wolf's head back as it seemed to fall to the ground in slow motion.

Sophie ran toward Gingerbread and pulled herself onto the saddle as he slung his crossbow over his shoulder. Gabe mounted up behind her. "There will be more of them," she said. "They probably smelled the blood on my arm. I'm sorry, Gabe."

"Don't be ridiculous. It's not your fault." Gabe's voice sounded gruff to his own ears, but he was shaken to the core that Sophie had come so close to being mauled by a wolf. And they were still in danger. A pack of wolves could pull them from Gingerbread's back and kill them both in a matter of seconds. And he couldn't reload his crossbow while on horseback.

He turned his horse around and headed—where? If they went back up the incline they might meet the man who'd been shooting at them. But if they stayed in the ravine, they might come across the wolf pack's den.

He had no choice. Gabe urged the horse into a gallop to the bottom of the ravine, heading north. He hoped to get to the other side of this mountain and back to the river they had been following. There was always a risk the unknown archer would find them again, but the immediate need was to put more distance between them and the wolves. Gabe had hoped to find a place to bed down for the night, but that didn't seem likely any time soon.

He resisted the urge to look behind him as he forced Gingerbread to keep up the breakneck speed. He wasn't sure just how long the horse could continue running, especially after an already long, hard day of riding.

Then he heard the wolves howl.

The sound came from behind them, not very far away. Their only hope was that they were far enough ahead of the wolves that they could outlast them.

The wolves howled again, and Sophie shuddered against him.

The moon and stars were covered by clouds, making Gabe's eyes burn as he strained to see through the darkness. Though the terrain was treacherous, and Gabe's aching shoulders made him weary to his bones, he didn't dare stop.

The ravine was fairly easy to traverse; rocky, but mostly covered in leaves, with trees widely spaced. They were able to make good time, and the next time the wolves howled, they sounded farther away. *Thank you, God.*

He continued listening for the sound of the wolves' howls to gauge how far away from them they were. And by the way Sophie was sitting, he could tell she was listening as well. She was depending on him to take care of her. Would his brother be thankful that Gabe had protected his betrothed and brought her to him?

He didn't care if Valten was thankful or not. Gabe cared about Sophie and would protect her and get her safely to Hagenheim or die trying. It didn't matter what Valten thought anymore.

After riding for another hour or so, Gabe began searching the terrain for a sheltered spot where they could stop and rest. He hadn't heard the wolves for a while. He found the river and followed it until he saw a large overhanging rock near the bank. It was sheltered on three sides by trees and was tall enough for Gingerbread to stand under. Gabe gratefully steered the horse toward it.

When he stopped, Sophie lifted her head and turned to look at him. Her hair had come loose from its braid and was tousled, and she had a streak of dried blood, probably from her arm, on her chin. But she was still beautiful, looking up at him with something like surprise and trust in the clear blue depths of her eyes.

His stomach twisted and he forced himself to look away. "We'll stop here for the night."

Gabe dismounted and helped Sophie slide to the ground. Then he began unsaddling Gingerbread. Sophie helped, then rubbed the horse's face, talking softly to Gingerbread all the while. He heard her tell the big animal, "Thank you for carrying us so far today. You were magnificent."

Gabe had never felt jealous of his horse, until now. He deserved her praise too, didn't he? He'd risked his life for her, and she wasn't even his betrothed.

But these thoughts were stupid. He was so tired he was going daft. After rescuing a damsel who would surely have been killed if he hadn't, being chased and having arrows shot at him, and keeping his wits about him while saving Sophie from a pack of wolves . . . he'd never felt so alive.

Once Gingerbread was taken care of and set free to drink and graze on the new grass on the river bank, Gabe turned to Sophie.

"Take off that bandage and wash your arm." He'd never get away with barking orders to his sisters that way, but he imagined Sophie understood.

"What about you?" She stepped up to him.

"Me?"

"Your face." She reached out and ran her fingertips along the edge of his bruised cheekbone.

Her feather-light touch created a tingling sensation that spread down to his stomach. He swallowed and drew in a shallow breath. "It's nothing." He turned away from her to his saddlebag and found the roll of clean bandages he'd brought. He yanked out a blanket—the only blanket he'd brought with him besides the sweaty horse blanket that had been under Gingerbread's saddle. When he turned around again, Sophie was gone.

He spread the horse blanket on the ground to dry, as far under the rock outcropping as he could get. Then he loaded his crossbow with another bolt.

Looking around, he saw Gingerbread, calmly grazing. And he barely made out the edge of the river. But he didn't see Sophie anywhere. The only sound was his horse cropping the shoots of grass a few feet away. Where was she? *God, let her be all right.*

# Chapter
## 10

*Sophie bent, dipping her hand in the stream* for a drink. The water was cold and tasted good.

Poor Gabe. How tired he must be after all he'd been through today. She wanted to apologize to him for what he'd suffered to save her. He had barely spoken all day, although it had been hard to talk while riding. But since the archer had shot at them and chased them into the ravine, he'd been very short with her. Perhaps he was only tired and focused on getting to safety. Or perhaps he was angry about all the trouble she'd caused him.

She hoped he didn't resent her. Brothers didn't mind risking their lives for their sisters, did they?

Although at times she didn't feel very sisterly toward him. Today, he had pulled her up into the saddle and taken her away from the duchess, he had taken care of her when the archer was shooting at them, he had saved her from the wolf ... He made her feel so safe, so protected, in a way she'd never felt before. And he was so handsome, the way his brown hair lay thick across his forehead. Once or twice she'd looked back at him and seen such a look of compassion in his brown eyes it had made her heart flop around like a fish on dry land.

In those moments, she did not feel what a sister would feel for a brother. But that would no doubt pass. She would simply ignore the fact that sometimes when he looked into her eyes, her breath left her and she felt a bit weak in the knees. She could never admit those feelings, and if she continued to ignore them, they would go away. She would pretend she had only sisterly thoughts about him. Just as she pretended to Duchess Ermengard that she wasn't afraid. Just as she pretended she didn't mind spending time in the dungeon, that she didn't hate the duchess. Ignoring her pain had made her life bearable.

Grateful to be off the horse's back and on firm ground, she sank her hands into the water and brought them up to scrub her face. The coolness in the air chilled her wet skin and made her shiver. She still wore her apron, and she lifted it to dry her face. Next, she obediently untied the makeshift bandage and dipped her arm into the cold water up to her elbow. The wound began to throb again, but she ignored it as she held it underwater and smoothed away the dried blood with her fingers. When she finally got it clean, she held it up to the moonlight. The arrow had sliced from her elbow to her wrist, but it didn't look terribly deep.

She dried her arm on her apron, then dipped the bloody bandage in the cold water. As she wrung it out, a movement caught her eye. Someone was walking toward her. The figure was tall, but she could only make out the outline. She held her breath until she recognized Gabe.

"Sophie."

She stood and moved toward him.

"I was worried when I didn't see you." His voice was barely a whisper.

"I went to wash my arm."

He reached for her arm. His hand warmed her cold skin as he studied the cut. "Does it hurt very much?"

"No. Not very much."

"I'll wrap it. Come."

She followed him back to the rocky overhang. His crossbow, loaded and cocked, lay on the ground.

"We had better try to make it through the night without a fire," he said as he motioned for her to sit down. Then he knelt beside her, took a roll of cloth, and wrapped the cloth tightly around her arm several times. "Our healer, Lena, says that cleaning a wound with water and then keeping it bandaged makes it less likely to turn deadly."

"Oh. I never heard that."

She couldn't stop staring at his hands as he cared for her arm, the gentle way he touched her.

"Our healer studied under Frau Geruscha, who'd trained my mother once. In a way, I guess you could say I'm from Frau Geruscha's line of apprentices." He tied the bandage snugly and cut off the extra cloth. "And sometimes the training comes in handy."

When he finished, she whispered, "Thank you."

There was a bit of dried blood on his cheekbone. She remembered the cold, wet cloth in her hand and lifted it toward Gabe's face. He looked uncertain. "I just want to clean it," she said.

He kept still while she gently dabbed at his scraped skin. It was badly bruised, so she applied only the slightest pressure as she repeatedly touched the cloth to his face. Then she dabbed at it one last time.

"Ow."

Perhaps a little too hard. "Sorry. But you will heal. Not much blood at all." A self-consciousness came over her but she stifled it. There was nothing wrong with her trying to care for his injury.

He picked up the bag that had been tied to the back of Gingerbread's saddle and opened it. "Now let's see what your cook packed us."

Sophie forgot about awkwardness as they happily perused the contents of Petra's bundle. Inside lay bread and cheese and some dried fruit. Gabe broke off a piece of bread and handed it to her, then did the same with the large wedge of cheese. They ate silently. Sophie hadn't eaten since breakfast, and the food made her feel better, but also sleepier.

Gabe picked up his crossbow and sat near the horse blanket, bracing himself against the rock. He set the weapon by his leg and handed her a dry, clean blanket. "Let's try to get some rest."

The blanket was not very large. Sophie hesitated.

"I can sleep sitting up." He demonstrated by leaning his back against the rock. "I'm sorry I only have the one blanket."

It was spring but the night was cold. She was even shivering a bit. Gabe was only being chivalrous by offering her the only blanket. He needed it as much as she did; neither of them was wearing very warm clothes.

"We can share it." Sophie shook out the fabric. It was made of wool and would be very warm. She spread it over Gabe's lap, then lay down with her feet next to him, her head toward the river. Lying this way, they were both covered.

"Good night, Sophie."

She could just make out his smile in the dim light. Then she remembered the apology she wanted to make to him. "I'm very sorry for all the trouble I've caused you. You were almost killed more than once today, because of me."

"Sophie." He stopped and sighed.

She waited for him to go on. Would he say he was sorry he had ever left his comfortable home to come and find her? That he hadn't expected this to be so difficult? That he wished he had let his brother come for her?

He shook his head. "I want you to stop thinking like that. This is the most adventure I've ever had in my life. Can you truly think I wouldn't want to be right here, slaying wolves and evading evil henchmen?" His perfect white teeth showed in what little light there was. "I've enjoyed rescuing you more than anything I've ever done. And I can rub it in Valten's face that I saved his betrothed." He chuckled softly.

It occurred to Sophie that he was only saying these things to put her mind at ease, but since it *did* ease her mind, she accepted it. Besides, perhaps what he said was true. Men were such strange creatures. Perhaps getting shot at and defending a woman against wild animals and evil archers truly was his idea of enjoyment.

Sophie knew she should try to go to sleep, but her mind was churning. "So Valten was betrothed to me when he was very young?"

"Yes. Our fathers signed the document."

"But everyone thought I was dead. Why didn't Valten marry someone else?"

Gabe shrugged. "My parents decided to let him choose a wife for himself. Our region is at peace and we have no pressing need to make powerful alliances."

"Are you betrothed as well?"

He hesitated for a moment. "No one is as concerned about securing a suitable wife for a second son. But yes, I am considered betrothed, though no ceremony was performed and no documents were signed."

"Who is she?" Sophie suddenly wanted to know all about Gabe's future bride.

"Her name is Brittola. She is the daughter of a count. When she and her father came for a visit, I liked her right away, and so it seemed a suitable match. Our parents agreed."

"When did you last see her?"

"Almost a year ago."

"So you like her?"

"She is a sweet girl."

Is that what men liked? Sweet? No matter. She was happy that Gabe had someone to love and marry. Sophie would marry Valten, and she intended to be happy with him—she wanted Gabe to be happily married as well. And now she should let him sleep.

"Good night, Gabe."

"Good night, Sophie."

Sophie awoke in the night, and it took her a moment to figure out where she was. When she saw Gabe slumped against the rock at her feet, it all came flooding back—Gabe's eyes begging her to trust him when he came searching for her after Lorencz left her tied to a tree. Gabe wrapping her bleeding arm, his face intent and serious. Gabe grimly shooting the wolf as it leaped toward her. Gabe smiling as he told her he was having the time of his life. But none of that meant that he cared about her. He was only doing it for the glory and to make his brother angry. It was a competition between them, as Gabe had said. Sophie would do well to remember that. He was not rescuing her for unselfish reasons. Besides, she would marry Valten, and she would belong to him and to his family, and they were all going to love her. Because she would do whatever it took to make him and his family love her.

When she woke up again, dawn was turning the world gray. Gabe was gone.

Sophie sat up and looked around. She eventually spotted him squatting by the river, filling his water flask. Gingerbread was grazing nearby. Sophie rubbed her cheek, then folded the blanket that had covered them. She tucked it under her arm and yanked up the horse blanket lying nearby. After shaking it out, she started toward Gingerbread.

Gabe started for the horse at the same time.

As he came closer she noticed the stubble on his face made him look rugged and achingly handsome. His boyishness was gone, replaced by an older, wiser look. His cheek was no longer swollen, but the bruising and scraped skin made her want to reach out and touch him, to soothe the hurt.

"Did you sleep well?" She tried to ignore her sudden confusion and the way her heart fluttered at the sight of him. He'd said Valten wasn't as handsome as he was. She believed him. She couldn't imagine anyone more handsome.

"I did. Did you?"

"Yes, thank you." They were whispering. No need to alert anyone who might be nearby of their presence. It was a reminder that they weren't out of danger yet. *God, protect us today.*

He carried his crossbow over his shoulder at all times now, his arrows within easy reach. He looked very different from when she'd first seen him. Then he had been clean shaven, and his eyes had been bright and well-rested. He'd had an unworried look about him. Now he had slight shadows under his eyes, and his soft linen shirt was wrinkled and askew at the neckline, revealing a bit of his collarbone and the hollow of his throat.

He was very easy to look at.

And even if he did have some wrong motives, she was thankful for him. *Thank you, God, for freeing us and keeping us safe.*

She may have a murderous archer chasing her, but, at least for the moment, she was free. She had finally escaped the duchess. She'd never been this far from Hohendorf. And she hoped she never went back.

If it turned out that she wasn't betrothed to Valten, if for some reason he rejected her or didn't believe she was Duke Baldewin's daughter, then perhaps she could find someone to work for. She had heard that sometimes, in large towns, women worked as shopkeepers or sold their own goods in the marketplaces. How she would love to see those places and meet those women. Perhaps she could get a job in a town, maybe even Hagenheim, cleaning for someone who paid her money. It didn't matter what she did, as long as she was away from Duchess Ermengard.

Even if she died here in the forest, at least she could say she was free for one, two, or however many days God gave her. And she had to agree, at least partially, with Gabe. This had been the best time of her life.

As Gabe tied their bags to the saddle, he couldn't help but keep glancing up at Sophie. "We're still about six days from Hagenheim, but your cook friend, Petra, said we could go to the Cottage of the Seven, about two days from here. Do you know what she was talking about?"

Sophie's hair hung down around her shoulders, the black tresses brushing her cheeks. She normally kept it braided and knotted at the back of her head. Now was the first time he'd seen it completely down, and he couldn't help noticing the way her black hair moved in the breeze. He blinked hard, then forced himself to concentrate on what she was saying.

"Petra used to tell me that if I ever escaped from the duchess and left Hohendorf, I would be safe at the Cottage of the Seven. She never explained who the Seven were, but she said I should ask for Dominyk the Wise. Petra is trustworthy. If she says we'd be safe there, then we'll be safe."

"If we need help, we will search out this Dominyk and his cottage. Perhaps he can offer us a knight to go with us the rest of the way to Hagenheim."

He gestured for Sophie to mount up. She stepped closer and Gabe wrapped his hands around her waist. She looked away from him, as if shy about being so close to him. He boosted her up quickly and she kept her eyes averted.

She truly was a virtuous maiden, not flirtatious like some, nor selfish, nor anxious to put herself forward. She would make a wonderful wife for Valten.

Why did that thought make Gabe feel unsettled? Like he'd

fallen on his back and had gotten the breath knocked out of him? Was he so undisciplined that he would covet his brother's betrothed?

Gabe mounted behind Sophie and took the reins firmly in hand. He urged Gingerbread forward and then nudged the horse to go faster. The sooner they reached Hagenheim, the better.

# Chapter 11

*After riding hard for a couple of hours, Sophie* was grateful when Gabe stopped in a small glade to let the horse drink, which also allowed them to stand and eat some more of their bread and cheese, as well as some raisins, dried apricots, and walnuts.

Gabe kept watch all around them, carefully searching the trees across the river while Gingerbread drank his fill. He passed the bundle of food to Sophie. Her fingers brushed his and she pretended not to notice how warm his hand felt.

Sophie finished eating, then drank from the cold, sparkling river. She needed a few moments of privacy so she gestured toward the forest. Gabe hooked his thumb in the opposite direction, and they went their separate ways.

After returning, they mounted up. Sophie noticed that Gabe washed his hands in the river as often as she did, and he splashed water on his face morning and night. He wasn't like most of the men Sophie had grown up with — servants who rarely bathed and smelled like it. Gabe, she couldn't help but notice, smelled … quite pleasant.

But she was tired of thinking about him, and she knew something that would distract them both.

"I have most of the book of Saint Luke memorized. Would you like me to recite it to you?"

"Of course," he said. "That would be good."

Sophie began reciting Jesus's parable:

"A certain man was preparing a great banquet and invited many guests. At the time of the banquet he sent his servant to tell those who had been invited, 'Come, for everything is now ready.'"

"But they all alike began to make excuses. The first said, 'I have just bought a field and I must go and see it. Please excuse me.'"

She glanced up at Gabe. He appeared to be listening, his brows drawn together as he watched the trail ahead. She went on.

"Another said, 'I have just bought five yoke of oxen, and I'm on my way to try them out. Please excuse me.'"

"Still another said, 'I just got married, so I can't come.'"

*Married.* Sophie's mind went immediately to Valten. What would it be like to be married to him? And why would a man say he couldn't come to a banquet because he just got married? Sophie felt herself blush as she pondered what it meant to be wed.

She continued reciting. The parable ended with the poor and lame and blind being compelled to come to the feast, while the rich and those who had refused the invitation were excluded.

*I will prepare a feast for you in the presence of your enemies.*

Sophie listened, and the words came to her again. *I will prepare a feast for you in the presence of your enemies.*

Sophie prayed, *God, I believe you will protect me from Duchess Ermengard, my enemy, and bless me in spite of the duchess's efforts to destroy me. You will prepare a feast for me in the presence of my enemy.*

Gabe hadn't said anything while Sophie kept her eyes closed, listening, praying, and thinking.

She began to recite again, and she came to the parable of the lost sheep. Jesus spoke of the man who left his ninety-nine sheep to go out and search for the one that was lost. That made Sophie think of Gabe, leaving his comfortable home to come and find her. When she came to the end of the chapter, she asked, "Are you rich, Gabe?"

Gabe looked down at her, his brows raised. "My family is wealthy. But I'm the second son. Valten will inherit the wealth, as well as the right to rule." He shook his head and smiled faintly. "Although I am rich compared to some, second sons aren't rich."

"How then will you live?"

"I will marry Brittola. Her father has promised an estate to her and her husband. But I've always expected to have to make my own way. I once fancied becoming a builder, perhaps a master mason, but I haven't applied myself to my studies as I ought. Up until now, I'm afraid I've behaved rather irresponsibly."

At least he was honest. "Planning and overseeing the building of things. Is this what a master mason does?"

He nodded.

Was he thinking of Brittola, his intended bride? Sophie changed the topic of conversation.

"What do you think will happen to Petra and Roslind?" She hoped the duchess wouldn't mistreat them even more because she no longer had Sophie to take out her wrath on.

"I don't know." Gabe was quiet for a moment, then said softly, "Perhaps Valten will come back for them, if you wish it."

"Oh yes! Do you think he would?"

"I think he would."

Sophie thought for a moment. "Valten must be brave then. And kind."

Gabe was quiet, so she glanced up at him. He didn't meet her eye. "He is. He is very brave and strong and capable of rescuing your friends. And I imagine the king will have something to say about the way Duchess Ermengard has treated you after Valten informs him."

Sophie decided to change the subject again. "Tell me more about your family and your life as a child."

He gave her a crooked smile. "Do you truly like hearing about it so much?"

"Yes! It fascinates me." She liked to imagine what it was like to have a real family, and he could tell her. Besides, she wanted to know more about the family she was marrying into, more about her husband to be, and most of all, more about the mother of this family.

Gabe told her stories about all six of his brothers and sisters, but he didn't mention the sister who died.

"Will your mother have more children?"

He shrugged. "It's possible, I suppose." He smiled down at her. "Now it's your turn, little sister."

"What do you mean?"

"You have to tell me some stories about you when you were a child."

Sophie shook her head. "My stories aren't as interesting as yours."

"Come now. I've told you all my family's funniest quirks and antics. You must entertain me for a while."

It was true that she felt she knew his family pretty well now. She even felt she knew Valten. He sounded like a serious child, but even he had had his share of boyish adventures. Any maiden would want to marry him, no doubt. He had everything: wealth, power, fame—especially fame, since he was a tournament champion—a wonderful family, and he would one day be Duke of Hagenheim. He was in a position to make his wife famous as well. But those things weren't what Sophie had dreamed of. She did not want wealth or fame or power, but simply to be loved, to be cherished, to feel safe, cared for, and protected. She wanted someone to be kind to her and love her.

But a person didn't always get what they wanted. Sophie knew that all too well. Would Valten love her and cherish her?

"My stories are mostly sad ... things you wouldn't want to hear."

"No putting me off," Gabe said as he guided Gingerbread up yet another mountain trail. "We have nothing else to occupy us, and I can handle sad. So start talking."

Sophie couldn't help smiling. "Very well. You asked for it." She would soften her stories as best she could, especially the parts about being hated and mistreated by Duchess Ermengard. Instead, she'd try to mostly talk about the happier stories of Mama Petra and her "sisters," the other maids.

Gabe listened while Sophie told of climbing trees and swinging on vines while the duchess was having her afternoon nap. She told of one of the stable men falling and breaking his leg and how Sophie, an eleven-year-old girl at the time, had set the bone with two sticks. The man had immediately asked her to marry him. Sophie laughed when she told the story, but she wasn't laughing at the time, she said. Instead, she had shaken her fist at him and dared him to come near her with such talk, warning him that she would break his other leg if he did so.

She told of rescuing a maiden who'd fallen into an old, dry well. The maiden was unharmed, but the duchess had refused to send a guard to help get her out. So Sophie and another servant had sneaked some rope out of the stable and pulled her up. The duchess had locked Sophie in the dungeon for a day and a night for that.

Sophie certainly had courage. But the duchess locked her in the dungeon for the merest infractions. The duchess's every whim controlled the castle, and although Sophie had defied her many times, it also sounded as if Sophie had also tried her best to appease her.

She described a time when, at thirteen years old, her long black hair had been cut up to her ears, because the duchess had flown into a rage. She told about keeping her precious portion of the Bible hidden until the duchess was asleep, only taking it out at night and reading it to the other maids that slept with her in the small chamber off the kitchen. She told about diving into the river to save a sackful of puppies the duchess had ordered destroyed. That was what had gotten her thrown into the dungeon the week before Gabe came.

Her face got sadder as she continued to talk. Perhaps it hadn't been a good idea to make her talk about her childhood, but he felt a desire to know all about her, all her stories, no matter how sad they were.

"You must hate the duchess. I know I hate her right now."

"Oh, no!" Sophie got a grave look on her face. She turned and stared at him in a way that forced him to stare back into her blue, blue eyes. "I don't hate the duchess. I feel sad for her. She is a very miserable person. You mustn't hate her, either. You mustn't hate anyone. God says we must love our enemies. The priest said so."

"Can you honestly say you don't hate the duchess, after all she's done to you?"

"I don't. I won't let myself. I mustn't." She pursed her lips into a grim line.

His heart ached for her. She was so strong and brave, all alone in the world with no one to protect her. No one but God, apparently.

He couldn't imagine anyone God would want to protect more.

"Promise me," she said. "Promise you won't hate the duchess. Tell God you forgive her."

Gabe took a deep breath and looked into her eyes again. Was she so concerned about his soul? "I promise." He closed his eyes. Gingerbread was going along an easy trail. "God, I forgive her for all her cruelty, but I know you will make it right in the end. '"Vengeance is mine," says the Lord,'" he quoted.

Sophie frowned. "That doesn't sound so forgiving."

"That's the best I can do, I'm afraid." He saw she was still worried, so he smiled and said, "Don't worry, Sophie. It's human nature to be angry at someone who's been as cruel to you as the duchess has. You should forgive her, but you should forgive yourself too, if you feel angry and unforgiving sometimes. God understands. He'll help you."

She stared down at the ground. When she looked up, her expression was such a mixture of doubt and hope. "What makes you think so?"

"The Bible says, 'There is now no condemnation for those who are in Christ Jesus.'"

"Oh. I guess I never had that part. What else does it say?"

He chuckled. "A lot of things. It says if we confess our sins, God will forgive us."

She got quiet again. They headed up a steeper part of the path, and he leaned forward. Sophie leaned too, and held on to the pommel of the saddle to keep herself steady. Her head was pressed against his chest and her silky hair brushed his chin. He couldn't help his arms brushing hers as he held the reins and guided the horse up the rocky trail.

Gabe was flirting with disaster. At least that's what his father had once told him about spending time with a woman he knew he couldn't marry. His father had also said that Gabe should never, even under the most innocent circumstances, spend the night with a woman. He'd broken that rule last night.

And now Gabe understood why his father had warned him. He felt himself on the verge of thoughts and feelings that should never be, of being as irresponsible as everyone believed him to be.

Should Gabe have waited and let Valten come to find Sophie when his leg was healed? If Valten and his father and several knights had come, they could have rescued not only Sophie, but Petra and Roslind as well. Had it been against God's will for Gabe to come? Was Gabe creating a problem for Sophie? Everyone would hear about them being alone together. Would it cause Sophie's reputation to be disparaged? Reproach that could have been avoided if he'd listened to his father?

Gabe thought back to the day he decided to come search for Sophie himself. He'd felt such an urgency, a lack of peace whenever he thought about waiting, but in truth, he hadn't worried about whether he was doing the right thing when he left. He hadn't sought God's will like he should have. And some of his motives weren't exactly pure.

In his defense, though, the old woman, Pinnosa, had said it was urgent, that Sophie was in great danger. And now he knew it was true. In fact, the duchess had ordered Lorencz to kill her. If Gabe had waited and let Valten come to rescue her, she might be dead now.

But perhaps the duchess had decided to kill her because of him, because she discovered he was the son of Duke Wilhelm and realized the duke would be coming for her himself.

That thought made him sick. His haste and irresponsibility had put Sophie in danger.

What if it hadn't been God's will for him to come? What if it had been Gabe's impatience, his not caring if it was right, his simply wanting to go off on his own quest to prove himself?

*God, forgive me for wanting to be the one to rescue her.* But if Valten made one single disparaging remark about Sophie … *God, I'm sorry. Please don't let Sophie get hurt.*

As they came down the other side of the mountain, Sophie caught her breath at the sight before her, at the treeless, wide-open space, an entire mountainside covered in wildflowers. She had never seen anything like it. The only flowers she'd ever seen in her life were small forest flowers, mostly tiny white ones. She'd never seen anything like these red-orange blossoms that carpeted the ground in front of her.

Just then, the sun came out from behind a cloud and shone on the beautiful, grassy, flower-covered meadow, lighting the red blossoms and setting them afire.

Sophie tilted her head up to catch the rays on her face. Her eyes closed, she realized she was revisiting her dream. Maybe she *was* dreaming.

"These flowers are so beautiful," she breathed. "What are they called?"

"*Mohnblumen.* You've never seen wild poppies before?" His voice conveyed surprise.

He let the horse amble slowly. She breathed in the warm air, thanking God for the sun, for the warmth, for this moment of exquisite freedom. Then she stared down at the flowers below them, so close and yet too far to reach.

"Would you like to stop and pick some?" he asked gently.

He helped her dismount, and she knelt reverently toward a flower and placed her fingers on the surprisingly tiny stem. She picked it, then held it up to her face. The petals were almost transparent. How wonderful that such a delicate thing could provide such vivid color. Sophie studied it, breathing deeply, and reveling in the manifestation of her dream. She closed her eyes and let her mind empty itself of all thought except for this beautiful meadow, her dream come true.

When she opened her eyes, Gabe was standing a few feet

away, his fist full of the red flowers. Her gaze met his and she read understanding in his face. But how could he understand how she felt? He'd experienced freedom his entire life. He'd known what it was like to ride out on his horse and discover meadows and wildflowers and feel the sun on his face. But he knew the things she had gone through, even knew of her hopes and dreams. His expression was sympathetic, and it made her heart ache with some new emotion, pleasant and painful at the same time. It became hard to breathe, and she both wished he would close the gap between them, and feared it at the same time.

A feeling of guilt hit her. She turned away from Gabe's eyes and started for the horse, who had dropped his head to graze.

"We'd better go. I don't want to delay us with my foolishness." She reached up and grabbed the pommel of the saddle, and suddenly Gabe was standing beside her.

He held the flowers out to her.

The air felt thick between them. She was afraid to look him in the eye but couldn't resist. His look was serious and compelling, as if he wanted to tell her something. Her heart was beating so hard it seemed to vibrate her chest.

Why was she being so foolish? It was very unlikely that Gabe was feeling anything like what she was feeling. And she wouldn't want him to. She was betrothed to Valten.

She took the flowers from his hand and he lifted her by her waist to set her in the saddle.

Gabe took the reins and hoisted himself up, then set Gingerbread in motion. "There are a lot more meadows like this."

Sophie stared down at the flowers Gabe had picked for her. Gradually, her heart slowed. She kept herself from looking up at Gabe. The motion of the horse, the warmth of the sun, the sight of the beautiful flowers in her hand, and the brush of his arms around her, holding on to the reins, comforted her into a sense of peace and contentment.

Her brother. Gabe was her brother. He was taking her to Hagenheim and safety. That's all.

They continued through the meadow and Gabe picked up the pace, now that they were on more level ground. They could hear the river to their west but couldn't see it, as it was surrounded by trees. Sophie looked all around her at the beautiful trees — such variety compared to Hohendorf — the green grass, and more wildflowers of purple, pink, and yellow.

"Let me know if you need to stop," Gabe said.

"I am well," she murmured.

"I'm thinking of hunting a hare for our dinner."

Sophie was glad. They had precious little left of the bundle Petra had supplied.

Sophie fingered the bouquet and regretted the feelings she'd had for Gabe when he'd picked it for her. Those feelings were only foolishness brought on by her gratitude to Gabe for saving her from the duchess, and because they were alone together. "We haven't seen any houses or people. Aren't there any villages or towns around here?"

"Not many. We'll see more when we get closer to Hagenheim."

She asked more questions about his siblings. His family was always a safe subject, and he always seemed to have more to tell her. Soon they were laughing companionably. She even grew comfortable enough to ask about Brittola. "What does Brittola look like?"

"She has blonde hair and green eyes."

"Is she tall?"

"About your height, I suppose. Although she may have grown since I saw her."

"Does she write letters to you?"

"Rarely. She wrote a few times after our visit a year ago, but I haven't heard from her in months."

*If you were my betrothed, I'd write to you every day.* Sophie was glad she hadn't said that aloud. What an awkward silence *that* would have resulted in.

"Perhaps she doesn't like to write."

"She told me as much."

"Do you write to her?"

"Whenever she writes to me, I always answer. I'm afraid I haven't been any better a correspondent than she has."

"I suppose Brittola had tutors and learned to read and write, everything a well-bred lady should."

"I suppose. Although she did tell me that she wasn't a very good student and often pretended to be sick or ignored her tutor. Which surprised me, because she seemed so docile and meek when she visited Hagenheim."

"It is easy to pretend sometimes," Sophie murmured, thinking of her own pretending. But other times, it was quite hard. "I am sure she must have learned to dance as well." Sophie had always wanted to learn how to dance. Not that she'd ever had the occasion to do it, but she'd dreamed of having many opportunities once she was able to get away from the duchess.

"Yes, she knows all the dances."

They were silent for a few moments. Finally, Sophie said, "It will be embarrassing for your brother if his betrothed does not know how to dance."

"We'll teach you. My family knows how to play the songs and can teach you all of the necessary steps in only a day or two."

Sophie felt herself blush with pleasure. She imagined learning to dance with her betrothed's family looking on, swirling around the floor holding Gabe's—

No, of course not Gabe's hand. She would learn holding Valten's hand.

Learning to dance would be enjoyable. And by the time she became a duke's wife, she would know how to dance very well and he would not have to be ashamed of her. She hoped.

# Chapter
## 12

*Gabe looked up at the sun, high overhead.* Almost time to stop and let Gingerbread rest so they all could get a drink. They hadn't seen any sign of the duchess's guards or the murderous archer from the day before. But they could catch up to Gabe and Sophie at any time. Best to keep their times of rest as short as possible.

He turned his horse toward the river and went down the slight hill into the trees.

Gabe pulled on the reins and stopped Gingerbread. By the river's edge, a large brown rabbit stood nibbling the grass.

He quietly helped Sophie down, then he slowly dismounted. He pulled his crossbow from his back, loaded it, and as the arrow clicked into place, the rabbit lifted its head, suddenly alert. Gabe aimed carefully. He pulled the trigger to release the arrow. It found its mark, right into the hare's skull, knocking it over.

"That was a perfect shot."

Her words warmed him. Valten probably wouldn't have been able to hit the animal, especially from that distance. Gabe always had been a better shot.

He chided himself for his pride and for having such unkind thoughts about his brother. But he was still proud he could provide meat for them both.

He hurriedly skinned the hare while Sophie built a fire.

"We can't take any with us, so we need to eat it all now."

They roasted the meat and Sophie ate almost as much as he did. He wanted to compliment her good appetite, but from his experiences with his sisters, he was relatively sure that would be a bad idea.

He and Sophie covered their fire with dirt, then poured water over it from the river. They climbed back on Gingerbread and headed away from their midday camp.

If they continued to travel hard and fast, they should be close to the Cottage of the Seven by tomorrow afternoon. It would be a good place to spend the night after sleeping outside for two nights. And he hoped to find someone at the Cottage who would travel with them, which would also help preserve Sophie's reputation.

As night fell, Sophie relaxed against his chest, apparently asleep. He should start looking for a place for them to settle for the night, but he wanted to travel as far as he could, as long as he could still see several feet in front of him.

Perhaps he shouldn't have come alone to rescue Sophie. But he *was* taking care of her. God willing, he would get her safely to Hagenheim. For once, everyone would be patting *him* on the back instead of Valten.

But somehow, that didn't matter so much to him anymore. He no longer relished the thought of Valten's envy and anger at Gabe rescuing his betrothed. And the praise he would get wasn't as important to him as he had thought it would be. In fact, he would do it all again even if no one else knew, because he was doing it for Sophie. He wanted to take care of her and keep her safe just because ... she was kind and unselfish and smart and beautiful.

And she thought of him as a brother.

Where were these thoughts about Sophie taking him? Even thinking the wrong thoughts about one's brother's wife was a sin.

Valten wasn't married to Sophie, and he had not been the one to pledge himself to her, but Gabe needed to look at her as if she was Valten's beloved.

Gabe realized he was tired, and exhaustion was weakening his defenses. He had to find a place for them to shelter for the night. Anyway, it was almost dark.

Last night, he had found a perfect place for them to sleep, and prayed they'd find another place just as perfectly situated. He moved through the trees, searching for a sheltered spot.

Gingerbread stumbled on a rock, and Gabe instinctively wrapped his arm around Sophie's middle to keep her from falling. She woke up and glanced around.

"You're just in time to help find a place to stop for the night. It looks like we could all use the rest," Gabe said.

She mumbled her agreement and rubbed her cheek, pulling away from him a bit.

This area wasn't nearly as rocky as the surrounding terrain, so it looked as if the best shelter they would get was in the midst of trees and bushes.

But then Gabe came upon a small stream that fed into the river. The stream trickled down a hill. On a hunch, he followed it a short way and, on the other side of the hill, found a sheer rock floor that was sheltered on two sides by trees.

They both dismounted. When his feet touched the ground, Gabe's knees buckled and he almost went down. Sleeping lightly and traveling hard was taking a toll.

Sophie walked to the stream while he finished seeing to Gingerbread. The moon glowed just enough so that he could keep a subtle eye on her, and see the area around them. Sophie came back and together they spread out the blanket in the sheltered spot.

"You sleep here," Gabe said. His voice sounded stilted, even to his ears. "I'll sleep over there, by one of the trees."

Sophie scrunched her eyes at him, as if confused.

It didn't matter if she was confused. Even if he hurt her feelings, he felt the need to keep his distance.

Gabe heard the crack of a breaking tree limb and looked up. Across the river, fifty feet away, a man was aiming an arrow straight at Sophie.

Gabe didn't have time to grab his crossbow. Instead, he leaped in front of Sophie, putting his body between her and the man.

The next instant, he felt a sharp, searing pain. A glance to his left revealed an arrow shaft sticking out of his shoulder.

# Chapter
## 13

### He dropped to his knees as Sophie screamed.

"Get down! Behind me," Gabe yelled. He grabbed the crossbow still at his feet, but because of the arrow in his shoulder, had a hard time lifting it up high enough to aim it. The man across the river was setting another arrow to his longbow.

"No!" Sophie screamed again.

Gabe heard the faint *whoosh* of an arrow, but the man across the river was still aiming in their direction. He seemed frozen. Then, slowly, he fell face forward into the river, an arrow sticking out of his back.

A big, barrel-shaped man emerged from the forest behind the fallen archer.

Sophie turned to Gabe and threw her arms around him just as he sank to his side on the ground.

⁂

Sophie fell to the ground beside Gabe. She recognized the big man who had shot and killed the archer trying to ambush them. *Walther. Thank you, God.*

Convinced they were now safe, she turned all her focus on Gabe. The hideous sight of the arrow sticking out of his shoulder, its head sticking out his back, made her shake her head in disbelief. Why did he do it? He'd deliberately stepped in front of her so the arrow would strike him and not her. Why? He was only rescuing her to irritate his brother. She felt so sick, she wondered if she was about to throw up.

She had to help Gabe. He was shot ... with an arrow ... an arrow that was meant for her.

His face was contorted in pain, his eyes closed.

"Oh, why did you have to get yourself shot?" She examined where the arrow had gone in. "Don't worry," she tried to reassure Gabe, who was gasping in pain. "You'll be all right. I'll take care of you." *Please, God, help me know what to do. Don't let him die.*

The arrow should have pierced her heart. It was meant for her, not Gabe. She stared at the shaft, dripping with blood where it met his body. She would have to break it off and then pull it out. It should be done quickly, before she had time to get squeamish about it. She braced herself and, with both hands, grasped the end of the arrow sticking out the front of his shoulder. Without allowing herself time to think, she broke it.

Gabe let out a howl of pain.

"I'm sorry. I'm so sorry." Sophie touched his face, laying her palm against his cheek.

"It's all right," he said through clenched teeth. "Just pull it out."

She looked at the metal head of the arrow sticking out the back of his shoulder. It was covered in blood. Sophie had seen blood before, had never been bothered by it in the past, but this was *Gabe's* blood. A wave of weakness came over her. The thought of pulling that arrow the rest of the way through his flesh ... she wasn't sure she could do it.

*I have to do it. For Gabe.*

Suddenly, a huge man was towering over them.

"Walther. I thank God you're here."

"As soon as I heard what had happened back at the castle, I knew I had to find you. I couldn't let anyone hurt our little

Sophie." Walther knelt behind Gabe. "Go get a blanket or something to press against the wound."

Sophie ran and got the blanket she'd slept under last night. She ran back on shaky legs and sank to her knees beside Walther. The big man grabbed the arrow and yanked it out.

Gabe's body went limp, his head sinking to the ground.

She held part of the blanket to the back of his shoulder with one hand and pressed the other half of the blanket over the entry wound at the front of his shoulder.

"You'll have to push harder than that. I'll do it." Walther nudged her aside.

Sophie moved aside. She lifted Gabe's head and right shoulder and placed them in her lap. Tenderly, she brushed the hair from his forehead.

"Gabe? Are you all right?" He must have fainted from the pain. She hovered over him, watching for any flicker of movement. Finally, he groaned. Then his eyes opened.

Walther was still pressing hard on both sides of his shoulder.

Gabe grunted. "I'm sorry I failed you, Sophie."

"You didn't fail me. You saved me." She touched his forehead again, brushing his hair back and letting her hand linger. "You are so brave." She still couldn't believe the sacrifice he'd made. Her eyes filled with tears and one spilled onto Gabe's shirt. She wanted to tell him he was the bravest man she knew, that he was her rescuer and she would never forget what he'd done for her. But she knew she wouldn't be able to get it all out. She would choke on her own tears before she'd said two words of it.

"I should have seen him coming," Gabe said softly. "I should have heard him. I should never have let him get so close."

Sophie shook her head as more tears dripped from her eyes. Finally, she controlled herself enough to rasp out, "Don't talk like that."

His eyes were closed again. She took several deep breaths to calm herself and make the tears go away. If she didn't, she feared his whole shirt would be wet, from her tears and his blood.

"Thank you for coming to our aid, Walther," Sophie said.

Walther grunted, still pressing the blanket to Gabe's wounds. "I couldn't let that foul man kill our little Sophie. The duchess, she ordered all of us guards to find you both and kill you. I convinced some of them to leave with their families under cover of night instead—after I told them what she was planning to do to our Sophie, they were happy to leave the duchess's service no matter what the risk. Lorencz had already gone, and I was able to thwart most of the other guards before they got too far from the castle. But there was one man determined to do her bidding, and that was Malger. After I sent my family to safety, I came after him."

It had become so dark Sophie could barely see Walther's face.

"I don't think we would still be alive if you hadn't found us when you did."

"I don't like to think about it myself."

"Yes, thank you," Gabe said. "I owe you my life."

*And I owe my life to both of you.*

The three of them stayed unmoving and silent for several more minutes while Walther continued to apply pressure to Gabe's wound. Had the bleeding stopped?

In her mind, Sophie listed all the things Gabe would need. They had to find him water, food, bandages to cover the wound, and a warm blanket, now that his was soaked in blood. He would also need to relieve himself, since they'd been riding for some time.

*Walther will have to help him with that.*

"I'll stand guard tonight," Walther said, shifting his weight to his other knee, still pressing Gabe's shoulder and the blanket between his hands. "There may be wolves in the area. They'll smell blood and come hunting."

"You need sleep. I'll stand guard." Sophie had seen Gabe shoot his crossbow and was sure she could do it.

Walther grunted as he shifted his weight again. "No maiden is going to watch over me while I sleep." His voice sounded angry so she didn't argue. "Besides, old men like me hardly need any rest."

Sophie stared down into Gabe's face. She could see it was scrunched in pain, but he didn't move or open his eyes. "Gabe?"

He emitted a small sound from his throat.

She wanted to say she was sorry—sorry for getting him shot, sorry for causing him pain. It was all her fault. Instead, she said, "Is there anything I can get for you? Can I get you some water?"

"When he stops crushing my shoulder," Gabe rasped.

"I'm only trying to stop the bleeding," Walther said peevishly. "Let's have a look." Walther sat back and lifted the blanket from the front of Gabe's shoulder. He leaned close, and Sophie tried to see too. All she could see was the dark spot on Gabe's shoulder where the arrow had gone in and the stain on his shirt around it. She watched and waited for the blood to start seeping out, but it didn't come.

"Praise God and all his saints," Walther said. "Help him sit up. Slowly, now. Don't want to jostle his shoulder too much."

Sophie helped push Gabe into a half-sitting position. "Should we wrap it?"

Gabe winced and nodded.

Sophie hurried to his bag, which contained the roll of bandages he had used to wrap her arm. When she got back, Walther was helping Gabe remove his shirt.

Sophie tried not to look at his naked chest—not that she hadn't seen a man's torso before. The men servants often stripped down to their waists when they were working outside during the summer months. She'd always thought it was disgusting. But somehow, it was different with Gabe—not disgusting at all.

Forcing herself to concentrate on her task, Sophie knelt beside him and started wrapping the bandage around his shoulder so that the cloth covered the entry wound in front and the exit wound in back. She wrapped it over his shoulder and under his arm several times. Then she tied it securely in place.

"Thank you," he whispered. She looked into his eyes. His face was mere inches from hers.

"You're welcome," she whispered back. "I'll go get you some water." Sophie jumped up, but then realized he was sitting there without a shirt, and the night air was cool. She retrieved his shirt from the ground and pulled it over his head. She helped him put his right hand through the sleeve, then moved to his other side, noting the way his shoulder muscles bulged and rippled with his every movement. Pulling her mind, and her eyes, away from his bare shoulders, she tugged the shirt over his injured shoulder, letting the sleeve dangle. Gabe groaned. "Sorry." She pulled the shirt the rest of the way down.

He must be in terrible pain. Instead of complaining, he whispered, *"Danke."*

*"Bitte."* His lips were so close . . . but she shouldn't be looking at his lips. She jumped up again and ran back to his saddlebag, grabbing a cup she knew he stored there, then hurried to the river. Making sure to get the water upstream from where their attacker had fallen in, Sophie hurried back with the full cup.

Walther helped Gabe to his feet, careful not to jostle his left arm, which was pressed against his side under his shirt.

"Here's your water."

Gabe took it from her hand and drank. His throat bobbed three times, she noted in fascination, as he swallowed. His chest filled out his shirt in a very appealing way, and she recalled how he had looked without it.

*Stop being ridiculous,* she scolded herself, taking the cup from him. The man had nearly been killed protecting her — she still could hardly believe what he had done—and she shouldn't be ogling him. She was behaving like Darla, who ogled every man under fifty who still had most of his teeth.

"We'll be back, Sophie," Walther said, as he and Gabe walked away, heading to the trees.

Sophie busied herself with building a fire. Unless Walther had brought supplies, they would all have to sleep on the ground. She picked up Gabe's crossbow, checked to make sure it was loaded, and set it down where she planned to sleep. If danger lurked, she would be ready.

When the two men came back, the three of them sat around the fire and ate. Walther shared some bread, which he toasted over the fire, and some nuts, apples, and strips of dried venison. Sophie's eyes stayed on Gabe nearly the whole meal. She watched how much he ate—which was very little—how he moved, and when he flinched or winced, and she felt wretched about the sacrifice he had made for her. Thinking about it stirred up something inside of her she was terrified to examine.

She got him more water when they finished eating, then he curled up next to the fire.

Walther patted Sophie's head as if she were a small child. "Don't you worry about him, Sophie. He's young and strong. He'll be fine. I'll keep watch and let you both get some sleep, and he'll be as good as new in a few days ... or weeks." He scratched his head as he turned away, then mumbled, "If he doesn't catch the fever and the wound doesn't putrify."

Sophie felt the blood drain from her face. Putrify? Fever? When she was younger, a fellow servant had had a deep gash that had become horribly infected. He'd burned with fever for several days, his knee oozing foul-smelling pus. And then he'd died.

*God, please protect Gabe. Please don't let him die.*

She lifted the wooden cross that hung around her neck and held it against her lips while she silently prayed.

After pleading with God to heal Gabe, Sophie walked over and sat beside him. "Are you cold? I can ask Walther if he has another blanket."

Walther came up beside her and handed her a blanket. "Take mine," he said gruffly. "I don't need it."

She spread it over Gabe before sitting by him again.

"You need to lie down and sleep too, Sophie," Gabe said. "You take the blanket."

"I'll sleep over there on the ground. I'm not cold."

Walther was back again, hovering over them. "We'll all stay close tonight. Sophie, you share the blanket with Gabe. He's a duke's son, isn't he? Petra said he was."

Sophie stared at Gabe, wondering if he would tell the truth.

After a moment's hesitation, he said, "I am."

"Good." Walther nodded. "Sophie is a duke's daughter. You can marry her when this is all over." He turned and stalked toward his horse, as if he'd just settled an argument.

⁓

Gabe stared after Walther's retreating back, and Sophie gazed at Gabe with her mouth open and her eyes wide.

Seconds passed and she didn't say a word. Neither did he.

Gabe should probably tell Walther that Sophie couldn't marry him, but Sophie was in no danger from him tonight. He couldn't even move without the excruciating pain in his shoulder intensifying like a red-hot knife stabbing him. And to be honest, he was cold and wanted Sophie near.

Sophie lay down next to him, the crossbow beside her.

"Planning to use that?"

"Only if we're threatened." She had a plucky, defiant look on her face that made respect well up inside him.

"Do you know how?" he goaded her.

"Yes, I do." She pulled the weapon around to show him.

"I have to press this metal thing here to shoot the arrow. And I have more arrows right here. If I need to reload, I step on this to put in the arrow." She showed him that she had retrieved his leather quiver.

"I have no doubt that you can defend us all."

"I can." She seemed to think he was teasing her.

"I believe you."

She looked satisfied and placed the crossbow and quiver of bolts back on the ground on her other side.

They lay on their sides, facing each other in silence. Gabe wasn't sure of Walther's exact whereabouts, but he was probably close enough he could hear their every word. *See, God? We have our own personal guard. There's no impropriety.*

She broke the silence by whispering, "Are you in very much pain?"

"I would like to lie and say no, not very much."

"I'm sorry," she whispered. "It's all because of me. I'm so sorry."

"Don't say that, Sophie." He could barely see her face, but he had too many sisters not to know that she was crying. There was the telltale hitching breaths and slight sniffling. A bit of starlight reflected off the wetness on her cheeks.

"You never should have taken that arrow for me," she said fiercely. "You should have let it strike me instead."

He snorted. "Don't be silly. I would never have done that."

She sniffed.

"Sophie, please don't cry." He wanted so badly to comfort her, to comfort her as he would his sisters. What could be wrong with that? He reached out with his left hand—which hurt less than he thought it would—and wiped the tears from under her eyes with his thumb. "I'd do it over again. I'd take a hundred arrows for you." His chest expanded at the truth in his words.

"But why? I'm just a servant girl."

"You're not just a servant girl. It would have hurt me far more if the arrow had struck you."

"Because of your manly pride."

"Because you're worth protecting, Sophie. So worth it." *God help me.*

She made a small sound, like her breath catching in her throat, and closed her eyes.

He should shut up before he said something irresponsible. Pain was clouding his judgment. He'd think more clearly in the morning. Besides, her betrothal to Valten was legally binding, and he couldn't betray his own brother.

# Chapter
## 14

*You're worth protecting. Gabe's words sank* into Sophie's heart. That he would take an arrow for her and then say that he would do it again, that she was worth it ... Then he had wiped the tears from her eyes.

She tried to stop crying and calm herself, to think of how she should behave. What would Petra say?

Petra was always telling Sophie how a lady should conduct herself. Apparently Petra had lived in the homes of wealthy nobility—although she never spoke of her life before she came to Hohendorf. Petra would probably tell Sophie to pretend she wasn't crying, pretend she didn't want to put her arms around him. Pretend she felt what she was supposed to feel, and then the proper feeling would follow.

Petra would certainly tell her that she should pretend her heart didn't feel as if it were breaking. How could she possibly pretend she only felt what a sister would feel for her wounded brother? "I'm sorry," she said yet again.

"Please stop saying that. You didn't do anything to apologize for."

She mustn't have feelings for Gabe. He cared about her as a brother would a sister, and she would think of him as a brother and no more.

"I shall tell your family of your bravery. They will be so proud of you." There. Her voice sounded perfectly calm.

"And they will love you, Sophie. You'll never feel unloved again."

Did he know that to have a real family that loved her was her greatest longing? His words made the tears come back, but she didn't want to cry again. So she closed her eyes and said, "Good night, Gabe."

"Good night, Sophie."

Sophie woke up just as the sky was lightening with the coming dawn. She looked at Gabe, who appeared to be sleeping, although she knew he hadn't slept well. She had woken several times during the night and had seen that he was awake. Once she'd heard him mumbling in his sleep. His shoulder must have been paining him severely. And now his cheeks looked flushed.

She reached over and laid her hand against his forehead. His skin was unnaturally hot.

*Fever.*

She got up and retrieved his cup and what was left of his bandages. She ran to the river, dipped both the cup and the cloth in the cold water, then ran back. She sank down beside him.

He blinked up at her.

"Drink this. Then I'm going to bathe your face," she explained, "to try to bring down your fever." She had cared for many adults and children with fevers. But she'd never felt quite so desperate before.

He didn't say anything, only used his right arm to push himself into a sitting position. Then he took the cup from her and drank. Walther was watching them from where he stood saddling the horses.

Sophie began to wipe Gabe's forehead and cheeks with the

cloth. He closed his eyes, and she could tell he was not well. *O God, please don't let him die.* Her stomach clenched in fear. Was his fever a precursor?

She applied the wet cloth to his stubbly jaw as Walther walked up beside them.

"Fever, eh? It won't likely turn putrid for a few days yet."

*A few days? Is that all the time he had?* But perhaps it wouldn't become diseased at all. Sophie held on to that hope.

"Are you able to ride?" Walther asked Gabe.

"Of course. I am well." To prove it, Gabe stood up on his own.

Sophie hovered close beside him in case he needed any help.

He glanced down at her and gave her a slight smile. "Thank you."

She pretended not to notice the warmth she felt at his smile and busied herself with folding the blanket and packing everything away so they could get back on the trail.

"Where are we headed?" Walther asked.

Gabe's voice sounded a bit strained. "Hagenheim, straight north."

"Petra said there was a safe place about a day's ride from here, called the Cottage of the Seven."

"She told us the same."

"She gave me some idea as to how to get there. You'll need to rest there until you're well again."

Walther came toward Gabe and Sophie, who were standing next to Gingerbread. Sophie was about to ask Gabe if he needed help mounting his horse, but she didn't want to insult him. He looked pale, though his cheeks were flushed.

Walther didn't hesitate, merely knotting his fingers to offer Gabe a step up while saying, "Up you go." He grunted as he gave Gabe a helpful boost into the saddle. Next, he did the same for her, saying, "Pardon me, Little Sophie," as he grabbed her about the waist to lift her.

"Thank you," Sophie said, feeling grim as she settled into the saddle in front of Gabe. Since Gabe only had use of one arm, she held the reins for him. "Are you all right?" she whispered, while staring up at him.

"I've felt better, but I'm well, Sophie. Or should I call you *Little Sophie?*" He grinned at her, seeming more like himself.

"I know you don't feel well. A fever, along with having an arrow go all the way through your shoulder, does not make for a pleasant morning."

"Oh, I don't know. At least I have pleasant company."

She shook her head at his humor and didn't dare to peek at him again, afraid of what she would see—or not see—in his eyes.

They traveled through more rough terrain, interspersed with flat valleys and meadows. It was cloudy all morning, and Sophie shuddered at the thought of rain.

She paid close attention to Gabe. His head hung lower than normal, almost resting on her. Extra heat radiated from his body, but he didn't complain. He held on to Sophie with his right hand and held his left hand against his body. Fortunately for Sophie, Gingerbread didn't seem to need much guidance.

She wanted so much to help Gabe, but she didn't know how. He'd insisted on strapping the crossbow to his back.

When Sophie glanced back at him at midday, his eyelids were drooping and his face was red. She reached back and touched his forehead, then his cheek. His skin was hot, much warmer than the last time she'd checked.

"Are you feeling very bad?"

"I am well. But I forgot to check your arm this morning." He spoke haltingly, pausing to take quick breaths. "You probably need ... a new bandage. Let me see."

"My arm is fine." But she obediently held it up so he could see that there was no blood seeping through the bandage.

"At least it's not ... bleeding."

"Do you think yours is bleeding again?" He didn't answer, so she added, "What would your healer say? Would she have stitched the wound closed?" Sophie knew people also sometimes cauterized wounds, using a piece of metal heated in the fire to burn the wound, creating a scar that would close it up and keep it from bleeding. She shuddered inwardly at the thought of such painful treatment.

"I don't know ... Possibly."

She tried to sound courageous for him. "If there's anything you need me to do, I will do it." She remembered how she had hesitated to pull the arrow from his shoulder. But if Walther had not been there, she was sure she could have done that for Gabe. God would have given her the strength.

She pulled out her wooden cross and clutched it tightly in her hand. She prayed silently for God's mercy on Gabe, that God would heal him as he had healed those who had touched the hem of Jesus's garment. If God could heal a man born blind, he could heal Gabe's fever and wound.

She was still praying when Walther stopped, and they all dismounted for their early afternoon meal. Gabe was the last to dismount, and even though Sophie was helping him, he still stumbled. Sophie put her arms around him and let him lean on her.

Even Walther had a worried look on his face as she kept her arm around Gabe and helped him walk away from the horses and sit on the ground. He closed his eyes and lowered himself the rest of the way down to lie on the grass. "I just need ... to lie here ... for a little ... Not hungry."

Sophie sank down beside him and stroked his feverish forehead, brushing back his hair.

*O God, please help us. Please provide a safe place to stop and a healer who can help Gabe. Help us find the Cottage of the Seven and Dominyk the Wise, and please make him able to help us.*

She glanced up at the darkening sky. *And please let it not rain on us.*

Gabe lay on the ground, grateful for the grass underneath him. He knew he was frightening Sophie, but it couldn't be helped. If he could just rest for a few moments, he felt he could go on and ride the rest of the day, at least until they found the Cottage of the Seven or a place to camp for the night.

Sophie was beside him again, bathing his face. Her gentle touch and the cold water soothed him. He opened his eyes a tiny slit. She hovered above him, and there seemed to be an aura around her, like an angel illuminated by the cloudy sky behind her.

He closed his eyes and drifted to sleep.

Sophie stroked Gabe's forehead until she realized he was asleep.

"Sophie," Walther said, nudging her arm as he handed her a strip of dried deer meat. "Eat."

She took the food he offered and ate while she watched Gabe, not tasting a thing. She sent up desperate prayers with each slight rise and fall of his chest. They let Gabe rest after they finished eating, Walther stretching out on the grass himself. But finally, he got up and started tying his bag to his saddle. "I could ride ahead and try to find this Cottage of the Seven myself. Then I could come back for you and Gabe."

Sophie bit her lip. She hated to wake Gabe, but the sooner they left, the sooner they would find help for him and a bed in a warm, sheltered house. She was sure it was about to rain, and she couldn't let Gabe stay out in that.

She touched Gabe's face, careful to avoid his bruised cheekbone. He didn't wake. She glanced behind her and saw that

Walther had gone to relieve himself behind a tree. She bent down and whispered, "Gabe? Can you travel? Or should we send Walther ahead to find the Cottage of the Seven?" Gabe opened his eyes and stared up at her. He raised his hand and caressed her jawline, sending ripples of warmth all through her. *He doesn't know what he's doing.*

"Can you travel?" There was no real shelter for them here, and if they could only get to the Cottage—

"I can travel. I can do anything for you, Sophie."

It was the fever talking. He was half out of his mind with pain. That was why he was looking up at her that way, making her heart ache. "Let's go, then. Before we get drenched." She got behind his good shoulder and pushed him into a sitting position, then she helped him the rest of the way to his feet. Walther came and helped them both onto Gingerbread's back.

As they started on their way, Sophie took the reins again and tugged Gabe's right arm around her, urging him to relax and lean on her for support. He rested his cheek against the top of her head as Gingerbread followed Walther's horse.

She felt a few sprinkles around mid-afternoon, but then the rain stopped. She breathed a sigh of relief. But an hour later, the sky let go of the heavy raindrops it had been holding back. Gabe lifted his head and looked down at her. He gave her a lopsided smile when she turned to peer up at him. "It's raining."

Even when his eyes were bright with fever, he took her breath away. She lifted her hand to feel his forehead. He didn't feel as warm as before, but it may have only been because of the cold rain falling on their heads. She was at least encouraged by his smile.

She noticed he was staring at her lips. She turned back around and bowed her head, wrapping his arms more tightly around her. This way she couldn't see his face and neither of them could do anything foolish.

The rain was coming down steadily as they continued their trek through the heavily forested river valley. Walther didn't slow their pace for the rain and Gingerbread continued to follow Walther's black gelding.

Soon Sophie was soaked through. Her hair was plastered to her head and rain ran down her neck, over her face, everywhere. It was getting darker and colder. She wasn't sure, but Gabe's fever seemed to have lessened. He wasn't radiating heat like he had been earlier this morning.

After riding in the rain for at least an hour, they came to the first house they'd seen in days. It was large—two stories—plastered white and painted all over with colorful flowers. The thatched roof looked dense enough to keep out the hardest rain.

Walther turned in his saddle and shouted, "I think this is it!" Rain dripped off his nose and slung off the ends of his hair when he turned.

If indeed this was the Cottage of the Seven, which Sophie prayed it was, it was very large. She hadn't realized how tired she was, how much her shoulders ached and how miserable her cold, wet clothes felt until she anticipated having a safe place to stop and rest.

Behind her, Gabe began to shiver uncontrollably. Waves of shudders passed through his body.

*O God, please let this be the place Petra told us about. Please let them invite us in. And please let there be someone here who will know what to do for Gabe.*

They dismounted and Sophie helped Gabe walk to the door. He was shaking violently, and instead of looking flushed, he now looked pale. Walther knocked.

The door creaked open, but Sophie couldn't see around Walther's huge bulk.

"We're looking for Dominyk the Wise and the Cottage of the Seven."

"You've found both," the gruff voice answered. "Who sent you? Why are you here?"

The voice seemed to be coming from down low, as if the person were squatting while he talked. Sophie tried to peer around Walther but couldn't if she wanted to continue supporting Gabe.

"We were sent by Petra at Hohendorf Castle. She said you could offer us a safe place to sleep." Walther stepped back and gestured toward Gabe. "This is Duke Wilhelm's son Gabe. He's injured and needs help."

Sophie finally saw who had opened the door. It was a man, but he was shorter than any man she had ever seen. She was fairly certain she had heard stories of men like him, who were called dwarfs. He seemed to be about middle age, and he stared up at Walther with a crusty look on his face.

"Petra? How do you know her?"

"She is the cook for Duchess Ermengard of Hohendorf. She and this girl, Sophie, work together."

The man scowled, then shifted his gaze to Sophie and Gabe. His harsh demeanor softened as he stared at them. "Very well." He stepped back. "You may come in."

# Chapter
## 15

*Gabe leaned heavily on Sophie as they walked* inside. Sophie breathed a sigh of relief at the sight of the cheerful room and the roaring fire in the large stone fireplace.

Then she realized the room was positively filled with men of all heights, ranging from Dominyk's, who stood only as tall as Sophie's waist, to a shaggy-haired giant standing at the rear of the room with his mouth open.

The men all stared at them. Then Dominyk barked out, "Siggy, Vincz, take this man"—Dominyk pointed at Gabe— "to the west room and give him dry clothes and put him to bed."

Two average-sized men came toward them and, nudging her out of the way, half carried Gabe, one on each side, up the stairs at the left end of the large room.

Sophie watched them go, taking a step as if to follow them, unsure what to do. "His left shoulder is injured," she called after them. One of the men turned back and stared at her. Then he turned around and continued up the steps with Gabe.

Another man, who wore a rough woolen tunic that went all the way to his ankles, similar to a monk's garb, bowed his head and followed after them. His gait seemed unusual, and when Sophie looked down at his feet, the sight almost didn't make sense to her. His feet were bare and misshapen, turned inward in such a way that he had to walk on the sides of his feet as if he were on stilts or clubs. He didn't look up at her, and she was glad, since she was rudely staring.

"Bartel will see to his injury," Dominyk said.

After the three men went upstairs with Gabe, the four that were left stood staring at Sophie and Walther. She sensed in her heart that these seven were good men and would treat Gabe kindly. Tears of relief and gratitude pricked her eyelids. *Thank you, God.*

Dominyk, who was obviously their leader, turned to a man with a massive scar on the side of his head where no hair grew. "Gotfrid. You and Dolf go and prepare a bath for the lady." He made some hand signals to the young man with neat brown hair and a kind face, who hurried out of the room. Gotfrid, his scalp shining in the firelight, scowled and grumbled under his breath as he followed Dolf out of a door at the back of the room.

Sophie would be so thankful for a bath. She hadn't had one since before she and Gabe had escaped from Hohendorf. *Was that only three days ago?* It seemed like months.

She wrapped her arms around herself as she was beginning to tremble with cold and fatigue. Now Sophie and Walther were alone with Dominyk and one last man—the shaggy-haired giant who was standing behind the much-smaller Dominyk. Dominyk turned to him.

"Heinric, go get some rags to clean up the water they're dripping on the floor. Go. Rags."

Smiling ear to ear, Heinric ran out the back doorway, then came running back in, his arms full of cloths.

Sophie looked down at her feet and saw that she and Walther were making a mess, dripping water on the floor. Heinric came toward them, grinning at her, and fell to his knees at her feet.

"I'm so sorry about the mess," Sophie said.

Heinric grinned up at her as he wiped up the water on the floor. Then he started wiping her feet. And she was sure he would have gone on to wipe her legs too, but Dominyk said firmly, "That's enough, Heinric."

Heinric stopped and looked back at his short leader. "Enough?"

"Yes, Heinric, enough. Very good. Now wipe the floor—only the floor—at the man's feet."

Heinric moved over to Walther and began wiping the floor around his feet.

"I believe we have some clothes that will fit you," Dominyk said, addressing Walther. "Go upstairs and into the first room on the right. You'll find clean clothes and a basin to wash in. We will have supper in an hour, when you and the young maiden are ready."

She and Walther exchanged glances, then Walther went upstairs, Heinric watching him go and saying, "*Bis bald. Bis bald.* Bye-bye. Bye-bye."

Dominyk gestured to Sophie, as if he didn't notice Heinric's behavior was somewhat strange. "Come into the kitchen, my dear. Gotfrid and Dolf will have your bath ready."

Sophie followed him meekly, not sure what to think about having strange men serve her in this way, but she sensed that these men were trustworthy. Besides, Petra wouldn't have taken the time to tell all three of them—Sophie, Gabe, and Walther—to come here if she wasn't absolutely sure it was a safe place.

"You seem to know Petra, but she hasn't told me anything about you."

Dominyk looked up at her from beneath bushy gray eyebrows that grew all the way across, like one giant, hairy caterpillar. "Petra and I must be careful what we say to and about each other. The duchess has ears and eyes everywhere."

Before she could question what he meant by this, he went through the door into the smoky semidarkness of the stone kitchen. Gotfrid and Dolf were busy pouring water from a giant iron kettle into a large metal basin, large enough for Sophie to sit in and be covered up to her shoulders. After pouring hot water into the basin from the steaming kettle, they poured cooler water in from a bucket on the floor. Then, after Dominyk instructed them to put up a blanket that hung from a rope to partition off the corner of the room, they left her.

Sophie checked to make sure the blanket was secure and the room was completely empty before taking off her clothes and the bandage on her arm. She sank into the warm water and could hardly believe how good it felt. Until the water touched the cut on her arm; she jerked her arm out at the burning sensation it caused.

A bar of soap lay on the side of the tub. She picked it up and sniffed it. *Heavenly!* Instead of the stinky soap she and the other servants made out of ashes and lard at the castle, this soap smelled of lavender and something else she couldn't quite name, something fresh and clean and wonderful, like fresh air and flowers. Sophie quickly rubbed it all over herself, being careful to be gentle with the long cut on her arm, and then scrubbed herself with a cloth. She washed her hair as well, rubbing her scalp with her fingers, then dunking her head in the water.

She hated to leave the relaxing haven of the water, but she was also afraid to linger. It made her nervous to be so vulnerable, even if she did *mostly* trust the seven strange men. Besides, she wanted to check on Gabe, to see if the terrible shivering had stopped once he had gotten out of the wet clothes. She hoped that Bartel would know what to do to make him well.

Suddenly, she realized she had no dry clothes to put on, as what she had worn into the cottage was still soaked. She began drying herself with the towels the men had left for her while she debated what to do.

A knock at the door sent a jolt through her. She was safely behind the curtain, but she held the towel in front of her like a shield. The knock came again.

"Yes?" Sophie called.

"I am putting some dry clothes by the door," Dominyk's voice called out on the other side of the door. The door creaked open, then shut again.

Sophie cautiously peeked around the curtain and saw the pile of clothing. She grabbed them before retreating behind the curtain.

A long shirt, some hose, and a rope for a belt. *Men's clothes.* Her heart sank. To wear men's clothing in front of men? Petra would certainly disapprove.

She dressed quickly and then, after finding a pile of clean cloths nearby, rewrapped the ugly wound on her arm. She also paused long enough to stir the pot of stew that was bubbling over the fire.

As Sophie reentered the main room, two men were coming down the stairs. When they finished descending the stairs, they bowed respectfully. One of them came toward her.

Sophie nodded back. "*Guten Tag.* I am Sophie."

"*G-g-guten . . . Tag.* I am . . . S-s-siggy," the tall, slender, handsome blond man said.

"Hello, Siggy." She smiled, grateful for a kind face.

The second man came toward her and bowed as well. "Fraulein Sophie, I am Vincz." He was shorter than Siggy, with dark hair and dark eyes framed by droopy eyelids. "Bartel is still upstairs with Gabe. He wanted me to tell you that Gabe has been asking for you, and that he is well. The fever is probably caused by the wound, which is usually a bad sign—"

Sophie inhaled audibly and then pressed her lips together, hard.

"But he is well," Vincz rushed on, obviously trying to reassure her. "His heart is strong and the wound is not in a life-threatening place. The arrow missed any vital parts of the body. As I said, the fever is sometimes a bad sign, but Bartel says he sees no sign of sepsis in the wound. Perhaps now that Gabe is able to rest, the fever will go away."

Sophie breathed a sigh of relief. "Thank you. Is Bartel a healer?"

"He learned the healing arts from the brothers — he lived in a monastery."

"May I see Gabe?"

Vincz and Siggy led her up the stairs and stopped in front of one of the doors.

At that moment, Sophie heard Gabe's muffled voice calling her name from inside the room. "Thank you," she said over her shoulder as she quickly turned the knob.

The room was lit by a fire in a fireplace and a candle by the bedside. Bartel was leaning over Gabe, but he stepped back when Sophie entered the room.

Sophie hurried to the bed where Gabe lay with his head and shoulders propped up on pillows.

"Where's Sophie?" Gabe's eyes were closed as she approached the bed.

"I'm here, Gabe. It's Sophie. I'm here." She picked up his hand, which was lying on the blanket, and squeezed it gently.

His eyes flickered open and fastened on Sophie's face. "I didn't know where you were."

"All is well. Don't worry. We are safe here," she said soothingly, bending low to look into his eyes. "These men are good. They will help you get well." As she spoke, she laid her hand on his forehead to check his fever. Still warm.

Bartel held a cup of something toward her. "He needs to drink this. Healing herbs and wine."

Sophie took the mixture from Bartel, and with his help, propped Gabe up straighter. When Sophie held the cup to his lips, Gabe drank it all in three swallows.

"Now he needs to sleep," Bartel said quietly.

She handed the cup back to Bartel and helped Gabe lay back down, taking away some of the pillows so he could lie flat. His feverish eyes stared up at her, his eyelids drifting shut.

"Sleep now and get well," she said softly in a crooning voice. "You will feel better tomorrow."

Gabe squeezed her hand, then closed his eyes.

She lightly stroked his forehead, watching his face relax and his chest rise and fall rhythmically. Relief swept over her at seeing him asleep and safe and comfortable.

She turned and addressed Bartel. "Thank you so much for all you've done for him."

Bartel, who was probably twenty years older than Sophie, nodded but wouldn't meet her gaze.

He stepped toward the door and Sophie followed him, closing the door silently behind her.

When they were in the corridor outside Gabe's room, where it was too dark for her to see his face, Bartel began to speak quietly. "I have treated his wound with some medicinal leaves. He simply needs to rest now. He is young, so the wound should heal quickly. If the fever goes away, he may be able to ride in two weeks."

Sophie felt oddly relieved that they wouldn't be going to Hagenheim right away, and she didn't want to ask herself why.

"I see you have an injury to your arm. Take off the bandage, please, and come with me downstairs so that I may examine it."

Sophie swallowed, not relishing having a strange man look at the cut on her arm. But she turned to follow him downstairs while she undid the makeshift dressing.

Sophie sat in a chair while all seven of the men, plus Walther, stared curiously at her. She felt herself blush from the sudden attention. Bartel came close and instructed Sophie to hold her arm near the candles beside her. After a few moments' scrutiny, he said, "I can sew it up for you, or you can leave it as it is and hope it heals properly."

Sophie didn't like the idea of this man touching her arm and certainly didn't like the idea of him sewing her flesh.

"I appreciate your offer, Bartel, but I think it will be well to let it heal on its own."

He didn't say anything, only produced a linen bandage from his copious sleeve. He wrapped the bandage tightly around her arm, then tied it in place.

"I will want to check it in the morning," Bartel said.

"Thank you."

After Bartel stood and excused himself from the room, each of the cottage men exchanged a playful look and nodded. Dominyk moved a drum from the corner and sat behind it, while Siggy reached for a lute very much like the one Gabe had had with him in Hohendorf. Gotfrid, meanwhile, sat with his arms crossed in front of his chest, a hat now partially covering the bald spot and massive scar on the side of his head. Heinric sat smiling with his entire face — his entire body, it seemed — as he squirmed in his seat and clapped his hands. Beside him, Dolf leaned forward, as if anticipating something wonderful but willing to wait patiently for it. Vincz sat in a chair, his head drooping to one side, obviously falling asleep with his mouth hanging open.

Dominyk began beating the drum rhythmically with his hands, and after three beats, Siggy strummed the strings of the lute, causing Vincz to jolt upright and his eyes to open.

As a song began to emerge, Dominyk looked over to Sophie. "The men asked if we could play something for you before dinner. I hope you enjoy it."

Walther motioned with his hand for Sophie to sit in the wood chair next to him. She did so, and smiled at Dominyk in thanks for the festivities, but worried that the men's music might disturb Gabe. What Bartel had given him to drink would, she hoped, keep him asleep.

Heinric erupted in happy gurgling noises and bounced up and down in his chair when Siggy began to sing. Siggy's voice flowed effortlessly, even though he had hardly been able to string two words together without stuttering a few minutes before.

Gotfrid continued sitting with his arms folded, a grumpy scowl still on his face. Sophie might be imagining it, but Gotfrid seemed to relax a bit when the music started. He seemed to be pretending to scowl, as if he didn't want anyone to know he was enjoying himself.

Vincz's eyelids were almost closed again. Soon they fell shut and his head drifted down onto his shoulder as he fell asleep again.

Dolf sat between the two music makers, one of his big hands on the back of each of their chairs. He was patting his foot in rhythm with Dominyk's drumming.

Walther was tapping his foot as well, a slight smile on his weathered face. She only wished Gabe were well enough to join the band. She would love to hear him play and sing along with these woodsmen. That was what she decided to call them for that was how they were dressed, in tough leather breeches and thick woolens.

After the first song, Siggy and Dominyk stopped playing and Siggy stood up. He opened his mouth to say something, but—after obvious effort during which he looked like he was going to sneeze—he closed his mouth and hooked his thumb over his shoulder toward the kitchen, looking sheepish. Then he turned and went through the kitchen door.

Next, Heinric stood up, his face bright and smiling, as he made happy grunting sounds. He was staring right at Sophie, and he flung his arms out in front of him and started toward her. Immediately Dolf jumped up and met Heinric halfway across the floor. He shook his head at Heinric and blocked him forcefully with his body.

Heinric's grunts turned angry, but Dolf simply shook his head.

"No, Heinric," Dominyk said firmly. "No hugging. Don't hug the girl. She does not know you."

Heinric's face scrunched up like a child about to cry. "Girl!"

"The girl does not want you to hug her." Dominyk added, pronouncing the words carefully, "Girl, no hug."

"Girl ... no hug," Heinric whimpered.

"Now go into the kitchen with Dolf."

Dolf was already herding Heinric toward the kitchen door, patting the giant man on the shoulder.

Dominyk looked up at Sophie. "He may still try to hug you, but don't let him. He doesn't know his own strength."

Sophie nodded.

Gotfrid nudged Vincz's shoulder with his fist, waking him again, and they both followed Dolf and Heinric into the kitchen as well.

Dominyk and Walther began discussing the weather. After exhausting that fascinating topic, Walther began to relay the events that led to Gabe getting shot. Sophie cringed as he told the part where Gabe jumped in front of her.

"I saw him aiming straight for Little Sophie. Before I could place arrow to bowstring, he let his arrow fly. Gabe jumped in front of Sophie without hesitation, taking the arrow in the shoulder, or it would have hit her square in the chest. That villainous ruffian was getting ready to aim again when I managed to shoot him in the back. He tumbled forward into the river. I'm only sorry I hadn't gotten there a few minutes sooner."

Sophie felt a bit dizzy and weak in the knees at the vivid reminder of what had occured, and how close both she and Gabe had come to being viciously slain. She was glad Walther and Dominyk weren't paying attention to her at the moment. She took a deep breath and blew it out slowly, but she still couldn't get Gabe out of her mind, his face tense with pain and pale from loss of blood.

Had she thanked Gabe for saving her life? She wasn't sure she had.

She would check on him again the first chance she got. Would he be all right?

The kitchen door burst open and Siggy stuck his head out. "S-s-s-s-s." He stopped and tried again, closing his eyes and re-opening them. "S-s-s-s ... supper is-s-s ... ready."

Sophie smiled at him, wanting to tell him that he was doing well, but she didn't want to embarrass him. His face was already beet red.

Walther and Dominyk let Sophie go first, and she walked into the kitchen. After they all sat down at the long, rough-hewn table, Dominyk commanded, "We shall all formally introduce ourselves to the lady."

They went around the table, nodding respectfully at her as they said their names.

The last man, with neat brown hair and a kind face, held up two fingers and drew them across his forehead and down his cheek.

"Th-that means *Dolf*," Siggy said, and repeated the action with his own hand.

Sophie nodded back at them, smiling. "And I am Sophie. I am very happy to meet you all, and I thank you for your kindness and hospitality."

They nodded, several murmuring, "*Bitte schöen.*"

Supper was venison stew, which didn't taste bad, though it also didn't taste as good as it could have. A few herbs and spices would have livened up the flavor considerably. The bread was also lacking, as it was doughy and flat. Glancing around at the dust and cobwebs in every nook and corner, the house didn't look like it had had a good cleaning in months. *Perhaps I can help the men with a few things before I leave.*

They started their meal in silence, as if the men were afraid of disturbing her. They all had good manners, much better than the servants Sophie was used to eating with. After a few minutes, some quiet conversation began. The men, including Walther, discussed the advantages and disadvantages of crossbows and longbows, which only caused Sophie's thoughts to wander back to Gabe. Everyone spoke politely, except Heinric, who didn't seem to follow the conversation at all but interrupted several times to ask for more food or drink. The others served him, and he smiled, even while he ate, chewing happily while bits of food fell from his overflowing mouth.

Dolf's hands and fingers moved in deliberate precision, accompanied by soft grunting noises, prompting Siggy or Bartel to speak aloud for him. Other than to interpret for Dolf, Bartel did not speak.

Vincz kept nodding off to sleep. Sophie watched, fascinated, as his head sank toward the table and his half-eaten food. He would jerk his head up, but a few seconds later, it would start to fall forward, dipping lower and lower. Just as his forehead neared his plate, his head would come back up again, as if pulled by a puppeteer's string.

Gotfrid argued with almost everyone else's opinions. But other than Gotfrid and his scowls, everyone seemed to be enjoying the camaraderie — even Walther, who joined in as if he'd always known the Seven.

When everyone finished eating, Siggy and Dolf began clearing the table. Sophie stood and began to help them.

"You don't have to do that," Vincz said, jumping up to help. Then they all starting helping, and in no time, the table was clean and everything had been put away.

Sophie turned around and found all seven men, plus Walther, staring at her. She smiled at them. "Thank you. Thank you all for everything. If you will allow me, I would be happy to cook breakfast tomorrow. I learned to bake in the kitchen of Hohendorf Castle."

Their faces all lit up, except for Gotfrid's. Sophie wasn't sure Gotfrid was even capable of smiling. He seemed to wear a perpetual scowl to match the curved scar on the side of his head.

"Can you make fried apple pies?" Vincz asked.

"And p-p-plum c-c-custard?" Siggy said.

Dolf made some motions with his hands and Vincz interpreted, "And stuffed dates fried in honey?"

"I can make fried apple pies and plum custard. I've never made stuffed dates fried in honey, but I can certainly try."

The men shouted and danced around like little boys. Heinric came toward her with his arms outstretched again, but the men intercepted, and he ended up hugging them instead.

Sophie laughed at their enthusiasm.

They all made their way to the large hall at the front of the cottage, and Siggy again played the lute and sang while Dominyk played the drum. Sophie slipped away and hurried up the stairs to Gabe's room. She opened the door to find Gabe still asleep. She tiptoed over to him and carefully laid her hand on his forehead. It didn't seem as hot as the last time she was in here. She watched his chest rise and fall beneath the blanket. She longed to bend down and kiss his cheek, but she had better not.

With a deep sigh, Sophie turned and left the room.

# *Chapter*
## 16

*Sophie awoke in a room by herself, though* there were two more beds beside hers. She had obviously displaced three of the men from their normal sleeping quarters.

The sun was still not up, but tentative rays of light were showing through the window. Sophie got out of bed and dressed in her new makeshift clothing, since she wasn't sure what had happened to her old dress after her bath yesterday. She went downstairs and all was still and quiet, but someone had built a fire in the kitchen fireplace, so she set about mixing up the dough for a loaf of flatbread. While it was baking, she cooked some apples with some spices she found on a shelf and made several pie crusts. She began frying apple pies in a pot, then used lots of cream and dried plums to make a plum custard. Then she fried a large stack of ham.

She'd had to shoo the occasional curious man out of the kitchen while she worked, but now she invited everyone to the table.

"This is quite good, Sophie," Dominyk exclaimed.

"V-v-v-very g-good."

Vincz laughed. "Much better than what Gotfrid made last week. He tends to mix the salt up with the sugar."

Gotfrid scowled even deeper than usual and suddenly made a rough grab for Vincz's shirt. Sophie didn't dare breathe until Dominyk sat them both down with a stern look.

Walther looked over at Sophie and winked. "Maybe you can make some labels for the jars."

The rest of breakfast continued on peacefully, though by the end of the meal Sophie was anxious to leave the table. She had gone to check on Gabe earlier, but Bartel wouldn't let her in Gabe's room, claiming Gabe wasn't yet dressed. As the eight men promised to clean up after breakfast, Sophie put some food on a wooden tray and hurried up the stairs to see Gabe.

Gabe felt as weak as a kitten, but at least his fever seemed to have lessened and his head no longer felt like a horse was kicking him in the back of his skull. His shoulder still hurt but not as sharply. He might actually live.

Now that he felt better, he realized he was hungry. Bartel, the monk caring for him, had been giving him watered-down wine with herbs, and Gabe hoped his next course of treatment was food. Whatever was cooking downstairs smelled wonderful.

Sophie had knocked on the door earlier, but Bartel was just helping him get up and dressed, meaning she needed to stay in the hallway. He hoped she would come back soon. He had a fuzzy memory of her sitting beside him the day before and telling him they were safe, and he was eager to see how she was doing now. He had been crazy with worry when he was too weak to go look for her, and he had called for her numerous times without her appearing. He kept remembering a room full of nothing but men when they'd arrived.

Now, alone again, Gabe was tired of lying in bed. Bartel's orders or not, he would go look for Sophie himself.

As he sat on the edge of the mattress, the room began to spin. He blinked several times to clear his vision and stood up—and immediately had to brace himself with a hand on the wall, which caused a sharp pain to shoot through his shoulder.

Clenching his teeth, he put one foot in front of the other, taking miniscule steps toward the door. He was almost to the threshold when a knock sounded.

"Gabe?" Sophie's voice came from the other side of the door. "Come in."

Sophie's face peered in. When she saw him, a smile spread over her face. He'd never seen a more welcome sight.

"Gabe! Should you be up? Are you feeling better?" She swept in wearing an oversized robe, her hair pulled back in a thick braid that hung over her shoulder. She was carrying a whole tray of baked delights.

She set the tray down and came toward him, her brows slightly knotted. "Where were you going?"

"I was coming to find you, to make sure you were all right."

She stood next to him and pulled his right hand over her shoulder, wrapping her arm around his back. "While I appreciate your worry, let's get you back to bed."

He let her lead him. He sat down, and she swooped his legs up and onto the bed, surprising him with her strength.

"I'm not helpless, Sophie," he teased, still happy to see her smiling. As she bent over him to pull up the covers, he caught a whiff of a different smell, like flowers, as if she'd taken a bath with the petals from a sun-kissed meadow.

His head began to spin again, this time for a different reason.

"So you're better?" She was still bending over him, and she laid her small hand on his forehead. "Your fever is gone! Praise God." She clasped her hand reverently to her chest as she gazed into his eyes.

She abruptly straightened and went to fetch the tray of food.

Bartel had propped Gabe's pillows so he could sit up in bed. Sophie set the tray across his lap. "I made it all myself," she said proudly, affecting a breezy, informal air.

"You're saving my life," Gabe said, picking up a piece of bread and taking a bite. "I was about to starve to death."

She giggled. "Don't talk with your mouth full. Our hosts downstairs have very good manners and will insist you not gobble your food."

"Well, they're not here now, and this is the best food I've tasted ... ever." He took a huge bite of fried apple pie. The filling was just the perfect balance of tart and sweet, wonderful spices melding with the apple flavor.

"Sophie, you are a wonderful cook," he said between bites.

She beamed at him, so he continued complimenting her.

"Is this Lombardy custard?"

She nodded.

"It's so much better than our cook's at home that I almost didn't recognize it."

She smiled more and even blushed, making her perfect, pale complexion light up with pink. She was so pretty he stopped eating to stare at her.

She looked around, as though looking for something to do, but there was little of anything in the bare room. Finally, she started straightening the covers at the foot of his bed.

He finished eating. She filled his cup from the flask on the small table beside him.

"Thank you." His fingers brushed hers as he took it from her, making his heart quicken.

He drank the wine even as his eyes drank the sight of her in from over the rim of the cup. He had been telling himself that she would be better off marrying Valten, that Valten was the blessed one, the one with the wealth and the power. But Valten had not seen where she came from, the abuse she had endured, the sweetness in the way she treated other people. Would Valten treat her as well as she deserved? Love her the way he should?

Gabe was wrong to think this way. He felt as though he

were on the edge of a cliff and about to jump off. If he made the wrong choice, not only would his life be ruined, but a lot of other lives as well. Especially Sophie's.

"I'm so happy you're better." She knew she'd already told him that, but relief was washing over her at seeing him eat so heartily, his color coming back into his face.

"Like I said, you saved my life with this food. Mm-mm."

"Hardly." She laughed. She had wanted to run up the stairs last night to thank him for saving her life, and now he was teasing her about saving his. "How is your shoulder?"

"Practically back to normal." He winked, and Sophie felt happy to see him in such a jovial mood. She remembered how much pain he had been in, how sick he was, how she had supported his weight in the saddle. Was that only yesterday? *Thank you, God, for healing him so quickly.* She would have to thank Bartel too.

What should she say to him now? She wanted to see his shoulder, to examine his wound and see for herself if it looked better. But she was afraid to ask. It shouldn't be awkward for a sister to examine her brother's wound ... but it would be.

Finally, she hit upon a safe topic of conversation. "Have you met all the men yet?"

"No, only Bartel, although I believe there were two others who helped me to bed yesterday."

"One of them plays the lute, like you. His name is Siggy. He has a bit of a problem speaking, but he seems very kind. And Dominyk plays the drum—he appears to be their leader. And there's Vincz, who has trouble staying awake, and Gotfrid, who is rather grumpy, and Dolf, I believe, is deaf, and Heinric ... Heinric is very happy. Except when he's ... not happy. You will meet them all in due time, I'm sure."

Gabe began to look a little grumpy himself. "I'm sure these seven men are all quite taken with you."

Sophie laughed. "They do seem to enjoy my cooking. I don't think they enjoy doing that task themselves much." She smirked and avoided looking at him. But from the corner of her eye she saw his unhappy look.

"I have no doubt they enjoy your cooking."

"Now you rest. You shouldn't strain yourself. You have to get well."

She straightened his blanket and had just picked up the now-empty tray when Walther knocked and entered the room.

"Looking much better today, my lord," Walther said, fixing his eyes on Gabe.

Sophie wondered at Walther calling him "my lord," then realized they should all call him that. He was the son of a duke. She blushed at the familiarity of her calling him by his given name all this time.

"Thank you, I am," Gabe said. "And I want to thank you for saving Sophie and me from the duchess's guard. We would not be here if it weren't for you. I am very grateful, and if there's anything I can do for you—"

"As it happens, my lord, there is something ..."

"Of course. Go on."

Walther scratched the back of his neck, hesitating for a moment. "I cannot go back to Hohendorf now, and my wife and children are dependent on me ... I was hoping your father—"

"Of course. He always needs capable, loyal guards like you. I shall write a missive to him now and you can take it to him. Sophie, can you find me some paper or parchment, a quill, and ink?"

Sophie hurried from the room and found Bartel nearby. At her request, he fetched the writing implements and then Sophie brought them to Gabe.

"I should like to leave today," Walther was saying.

What would this mean for Sophie and Gabe? Walther would take his family and go to Hagenheim. He would certainly tell Gabe's family about his injury, as well as their whereabouts. Gabe's father would send men to bring them back to Hagenheim, and Sophie would have to marry Valten.

Gabe was busy writing a message to his father, no doubt telling him what Walther had done for them and recommending that his father hire him. She was happy Walther would have a position and would be able to provide for his family. There was nothing she wouldn't do for him after what he had done for them. Perhaps she should go with Walther to Hagenheim. After all, what excuse did she have for staying here with Gabe?

"Thank you, my lord." Walther bowed to Gabe as he took the paper from his hand.

"Godspeed."

Gabe did indeed look the part of the wealthy duke's son, sitting in bed and writing letters, bidding a giant, burly man "Godspeed." She glanced down at herself—too thin, dressed in strange garb, her only skills cooking and cleaning—although she could also read. Gabe would be happy to hand her over to his brother and then marry Brittola, the well-bred daughter of a count.

Walther left the room. When Sophie looked up from noticing her worn shoes, Gabe was staring at her. Sophie hurried over to clear away the writing implements from the bed so Gabe could sleep.

"Sophie?"

"Can I get you something?" She turned to go. "I'll take these things back to—"

"Wait." Gabe grabbed her wrist, startling her. His warm brown eyes locked on hers, stealing her breath away. He was so handsome. The stubble on his face and chin only made him more appealing. She longed to reach out and rub her hand along his jaw. But that would only embarrass them both.

"Sophie, tell me the truth. Now that Walther is leaving, are you truly safe with all those men around?"

Even more appealing than his appearance was his concern for her. It made her heart constrict almost painfully.

"I feel safe enough, but perhaps I should go with Walther to Hagenheim." She turned away from Gabe so he wouldn't see how she was trying to get control of herself. He continued to hold her wrist and she didn't try to pull away.

"Walther isn't going straight to Hagenheim."

"Oh. He's not?"

"No. He's going back to collect his wife and children. While you were out of the room he told me he'd sent them to stay with relatives in a village not far from Hohendorf while he came to save you from Malger. He'll take them back with him to Hagenheim."

"Will he come back here, to the Cottage of the Seven, on his way to Hagenheim?"

"I don't know, but if he does, it will take him at least six days to get back here. Will you be all right?"

"I am safe, Gabe. These men are kind and honorable. They will not harm me, so you can rest and not worry."

He relaxed his hold on her wrist and she pulled away.

"But thank you," she whispered, "for caring."

"I do. Very much."

Sophie straightened, holding the tray between them. When the door opened and Bartel came inside, Sophie hurried away.

⁂

Sophie and the seven men loaded packs and bundles of food and supplies on Walther's saddle in such abundance he claimed his horse would never be able to carry both him and the supplies. Then they bid him farewell and watched him ride away.

That afternoon it was raining too hard for the seven to do their usual work of cutting down trees, so Sophie discovered she had lots of help in performing several apparently overdue cleaning tasks around the cottage. She put Heinric and Vincz to work scrubbing the plaster walls, which were painted with brightly colored scenes of flowering meadows and trees and small animals—rabbits, birds, squirrels, fawns. A little soap and water uncovered the true beauty of the murals, eliminating layers of gray caused by years of dirt and soot. And as she scrubbed, she wondered who had painted the murals, and why. So she asked Vincz.

"It was Dolf and Siggy. See the animals? Siggy does those, and Dolf paints the background—the flowers, trees, and clouds."

Sophie did notice a difference in style, now that he mentioned it, between the animals and the other elements of the murals.

"It is very beautiful. I should think everyone would want their houses decorated in such a way."

"Dolf and Siggy spent a year in foreign lands east of here, painting these sorts of murals for people. Everyone there loves them, and it is very fashionable, Siggy says."

"How did they end up here, at the Cottage of the Seven?"

Vincz shrugged. "The same way we all did. People become frightened of people who are different and then start rumors, accuse us of being demon-possessed or cursed." He turned a sheepish smile on Sophie and shrugged again. "It doesn't matter. We are happy here."

Sophie smiled back. "No one who knows you could say such things. And I am happy that you're here too."

All the men were eager to help, so she put Siggy and Gotfrid to work mopping the floors. And Dolf and Dominyk were soon clearing the cobwebs from the massive wooden rafters. Dolf would pick up Dominyk, holding him over his head, and Dominyk would sweep the ceiling with his broom.

Bartel was out in a nearby chapel—his usual place, she was told—praying and meditating. She didn't want to disturb him, but she thought it was a shame she didn't have his help when Dolf's arms got tired.

Sophie, in the meantime, began preparing their midday meal. She washed and peeled what fruit she could find—apples, plums, pears, and grapes—for custard, and used what was left of some recently harvested venison for mince pies. She chopped the meat until her hand was numb and her arm was aching. Then she added egg, lots of spices, a little red wine, cider vinegar, some currants, and dried grapes. She mixed it up with her hands, squishing it between her fingers like she'd seen Petra do, and placed it in stiff pastry shells. Then she covered it with another pastry and rubbed egg whites over it before putting it in the oven with some loaves of bread that had been rising all morning.

When Sophie came out of the kitchen to check on the men and their cleaning, they seemed to be making great progress. Most of the walls were clean and Heinric's sleeves were soaked all the way up to his armpits. But he was smiling, and he waved at Sophie. Dolf and Dominyk were cleaning the thick glass window in the front of the cottage. Outside, the rain was still coming down, lending a pleasant, drowsy hum to the day.

The house was nothing like Hohendorf Castle. The cottage was snug and cozy and warm, while the castle had been drafty and cold and unwelcoming. And no one there had ever let her boss them around. Most of the servants liked her and were kind to her, but they also knew the duchess hated Sophie, so they treated her cautiously. She was just another servant.

But Gabe didn't treat her that way. Although he had seen how she lived, seen how the duchess treated her, he treated her well. He treated her with kindness and respect, as if she were a member of his family. Which she nearly was.

She realized she was staring out the window at nothing, not even seeing the rain dripping down the pane. She hurried back into the kitchen to make sure nothing had burned and to finish her fruit custards.

Gabe joined them for their midday meal. Bartel didn't even have to help him down the steps. He'd also shaved and looked more like the fresh-faced man she'd first met. Well, almost. When he looked at Sophie, there was a strange expression on his face, almost a look of sad longing or uncomfortable awareness. It made her feel ... unsettled and confused. But she concentrated on how happy she was that he was strong enough to come downstairs.

All eight men sat around the table, with Dominyk at the head, leaving the opposite end for Sophie. For the first few minutes, after Bartel said a prayer thanking God for the food, no one spoke as they were too busy eating. Sophie glanced around the table, surprised at how much she enjoyed watching the men enjoy the food she had cooked. But after a few moments, the compliments began, just as they had at breakfast, each man complimenting her in his own way.

"It's wonderful, Sophie," Gabe said. He looked clean and well-rested now, and yet, the first thought that came to her as she looked down the long table to where he sat at the end next to Dominyk was that she wished they were alone again on horseback, running from the duchess and her evil guard.

*What an irrational thought.*

The men all agreed Sophie's mince pie was the best they'd ever tasted. She smiled graciously at them, but the bleakness of the gray day, which earlier made the cottage seem so cozy, now seemed to weigh on her like the dreary, unrelenting rain beating down on the thatch roof of the cottage. Now that Gabe was better, would he leave her to go visit his betrothed, Brittola? And Walther, if he traveled hard and didn't stop back by the Cottage of the Seven, could arrive in Hagenheim in ten days, where he would tell Gabe's brother Valten where they were. Then Valten might send men to fetch her immediately. Or he might come for her himself. Instead of giving her a feeling of anticipation, as it had when she first left the duchess, the thought of marrying Valten filled her with dread.

Valten might not even believe she was the duke's daughter and his betrothed, and therefore might never send for her. Perhaps then she could stay here and take care of the Seven's house and cook for them. And Gabe would marry Brittola.

She was so engrossed in her thoughts she hadn't noticed everyone had finished eating and was now beginning to stand and clear off the table. She stood too quickly and knocked her small bench to the floor behind her with a crash, drawing every eye to her. Ducking her head, she righted her chair, then picked up the pitcher of milk, along with the leftover custard, and carried them to the counter. She knew, without looking, that all eyes were still on her as tears pricked her eyelids.

As she set the pitcher and pie down, a tear tracked down first one cheek, then the other. She didn't even know why she was crying. She should be happy. Gabe was better, his fever was gone, and he looked like himself again. The seven men were happy with her cooking and treated her well. She was safe from the duchess. She was free. She may soon be getting married to her betrothed, the oldest son of a duke ...

Her tears came faster. She placed her hands on the edge of the rough wooden counter, leaned over, and stifled a sob, glad the others had left the kitchen.

Sophie brushed the tears away with the back of her hands. She hated crying. It did absolutely no good and was embarrassing. *Stupid.* That was what the duchess called her sometimes.

Now, she wondered if perhaps the duchess was right. She was stupid, too stupid to force herself to stop loving—

"Sophie?" Gabe's voice came from behind her.

Quickly, she rubbed her face to get rid of the tears.

"Do you need something?" Her voice shook. She cleared her throat and kept her back to him.

"Are you all right?" He laid his hand on her shoulder and she jerked away instinctively. But she regretted her reaction when Gabe took his hand away.

But she had to protect her heart.

"Are you all right?" he asked again. "Did one of the men say something wrong?"

"Of course not. They are nothing but kind." Sophie still refused to turn around and face him. She continued trying to look busy, stacking dirty dishes and putting away spices. She wondered what he was doing behind her, what he was thinking . . . if he had left. But then his hand touched her shoulder again. She didn't flinch this time, but stopped what she was doing.

Gently, he placed both hands on her shoulders and turned her around to face him. She looked up into his eyes. He wore a strangely intense, pleading expression in his brown eyes. His gaze traveled down to her lips, causing her to shiver inside. Terrified he would kiss her—and wanting him to anyway—she slipped her arms around him and buried her face in his chest, realizing too late that doing so only made her heart ache more.

His arms immediately wrapped around her and pulled her close. He laid his cheek against the top of her head, bringing back memories of their riding together, the three days they'd spent in the same saddle.

He felt so solid, so strong, warm, and wonderful. Was he thinking of her as a sister? Because she certainly wasn't thinking of him as a brother, and feared she might never be able to again. She could feel him taking a deep breath as he hugged her more tightly, could hear his heart beating, pounding almost as hard as her own.

Chair legs began scraping across the floor of the front room. Were the Seven coming to check on her? Of course they were. They always did. Just as the footfalls reached the door, Sophie broke away from Gabe and spun around to the counter.

"Help Sophie," Heinric said in his usual loud voice, as they surveyed the dirty dishes and few leavings from their meal.

"That's all right," Sophie said, "I can clean up today. You go—"

"You and Gabe need to rest," Dominyk said firmly. "Now go."

Before she could say another word, Gabe was untying the strings of her apron and pulling it off of her. He placed his hand on her back and guided her from the kitchen into the large main room at the front of the cottage. He led her to a chair and sat beside her.

They sat in silence. Then Gabe reached over and took her hand in his. She pulled it away. Why was he doing this to her?

"What's wrong, Sophie?"

She might have been imagining it, but she thought she heard pain in his voice.

"Nothing's wrong." She angled her body away from him so that he couldn't see her face.

"Talk to me," he pleaded.

Why did he have to make this so hard? She fidgeted, toying with the edge of the sash she had tied around her waist. Such ugly clothes. She was ashamed for Gabe to see her in this. How she wished she had something pretty to wear. But what did it matter? She shouldn't be trying to look pretty for Gabe.

"I suppose your father will come to escort us back when Walther tells him where we are. Or perhaps Walther will stop here on his way to Hagenheim and I can go back with him." She held her breath as she waited to see how he would respond.

Gabe was silent so long she took a peek at him. He looked a bit pale. "I didn't even think of that." He closed his eyes for a moment, and she wondered if his fever was coming back. "Of course Walther will tell Father about us being here. He could be here to fetch us in two weeks."

He snatched her hands out of her lap, and this time he gripped them so tightly she didn't bother trying to pull away. He stared hard into her eyes. Gabe's throat bobbed as he swallowed. "Almost dying makes a man think about what's important. My family is important to me. But Sophie—"

"I know, Gabe. Your family is important to me too. I'm glad you mentioned them, because I want you to know that I'm so happy you will be my brother after Valten and I are married." She spoke quickly and didn't look up at him, unable to meet his eye. "And if Walther comes back to the Cottage of the Seven on his way to Hagenheim, I will go with him. You can stay here with the Seven as long as you need to. You should be completely well before—"

"Sophie, wait." She gazed up at him. He was looking at her intently, his brows drawn together in almost a pained expression. "That wasn't what I wanted to ... what I mean is ..."

Heinric burst into the room from the kitchen. "Sophie, Sophie, Sophie." Siggy and Vincz came in behind him, and Gabe let go of her hands, looking frustrated.

"Gabe," Vincz said, "Dolf just saw a man lurking at the edge of the woods."

"Do you know him?"

"Dolf had never seen him before," Dominyk replied, having followed Vincz and the other men into the room. "No one else lives around here."

"It could be someone the duchess has sent to ferret us out."

"The rain has stopped," Vincz said, grabbing a cloak and

hood that hung from a peg on the wall. "Siggy and I will go search for him and force him to tell us what he's doing here."

Gabe stood. "I'll go with you."

Gabe glanced back at Sophie, his forehead creased in thought. He said softly, for her ears only, "We need to talk when I get back."

Sophie was too numb to speak.

He turned back to Vincz and Siggy. "I'll go get my crossbow."

When Gabe started up the steps, Dominyk told Siggy and Vincz, "Don't be gone long. He is still weak."

# Chapter
## 17

*Soon they were gone and Sophie was left to* wonder if the duchess had sent another man after them, someone who had tracked them to the Cottage of the Seven.

But mostly she wondered what Gabe had meant when he'd said, "Almost dying makes a man think about what's important. My family is important to me." What had he been about to say? That he couldn't jeopardize his relationship with his brother? That he loved his family too much to fall in love with her? Then why had he grabbed hold of her hands? Why had he stayed in the kitchen and said kind words to her, held her in his arms, made her want him so much her heart felt as though it were breaking in two? But she had done the right thing by saying what she did. She just wasn't sure she could say it again and mean it.

Feeling very restless, she sat back down. She could still feel his hands, so warm and strong, holding hers, his rough callouses reminding her how he had held the horse's reins the last three days, riding hard to save her.

*He probably has no idea the effect he has on me.*

Perhaps rich nobles behaved this way all the time. Men kissed women's hands in greeting, Petra had once told her. Gabe had probably held a hundred ladies' hands, held his sisters in his arms to comfort them. It meant nothing to him. She was only another woman to him.

Either way, she could never let him know how his holding her hands and embracing her made her feel. It was her duty to her dead father to honor his agreement with Gabe's father. But more than that, she didn't want to hurt Valten or his family.

Sophie jumped up to go start making some more pies, to take her mind off all these tumultuous thoughts, when she saw Dominyk come into the room carrying something across his arms. He brought it to her.

"I have here an underdress that belonged to my sister, one she left here many years ago," Dominyk said. "I had forgotten about it, but you are welcome to have it."

The long-sleeved white dress lay on top of Dominyk's outstretched arms. Sophie picked it up and saw red underneath.

"I also have this red fabric. It's too fine for us but it would make a lovely dress for you. Please take it as well."

The fabric was a beautiful shade of red and very soft. Sophie had never seen such exquisite fabric, except on Duchess Ermengard. "It is more beautiful than any I've ever seen."

Sophie held out her arms. Dominyk draped the cloth and dress over them. "At the fair, Siggy and Vincz traded our wood for it, but we never knew what to do with it."

"It will make the finest dress I've ever worn. Thank you." *Ask and you shall receive.* Jesus had said that. She hadn't actually asked, only thought what she'd needed, and God had provided it. *Thank you, God.* If only he could give her direction, peace of mind, and a mended heart so easily.

⁂

Sophie went to work on the dress right away. Dominyk told her she didn't have to cook, that the men could take over while she sewed her dress.

Sophie had often been praised for being good with a needle and thread, and had often been chosen to sew the other servants' clothing. She had an idea of how she wanted to make this dress, patterning it after one of the duchess's recent dresses, and she set to work with single-minded energy.

Gabe, Vincz, and Siggy returned saying they found tracks from a man and his horse. They'd tried to track him but finally had to come back when it started raining again. Sophie only got a glimpse of Gabe, but he looked tired and pale, sending a tremor of worry through her. He certainly wasn't recovered from his wound yet, but she trusted Bartel and the other men to make sure he rested while Sophie went to her room and sewed—and prayed, asking God to tell her what to do about her feelings for Gabe. The only solution she could think of was to avoid him until his father's men came to take her back to Hagenheim. *God, I wish you would tell me what to do.* Sometimes God gave her answers to questions she put to him in prayer. But this time, she heard only silence.

Sophie was summoned to supper. When she sat down at the table, she noticed a missing chair. "Where is Gabe?"

The men glanced up at her, then nervously looked away, their eyes coming to rest on Bartel.

Sophie instantly felt sick. Was he hurt? What had happened?

Finally, Bartel cleared his throat. "He was tired."

"Is he all right?"

"His fever has returned."

"Oh." She felt the blood drain from her face, but she didn't want anyone to think she blamed them for letting Gabe go with them. Nevertheless, Siggy and Vincz looked sheepish.

"Does he need anything? Can I take him something?"

"It is best to let him sleep," Bartel said. "He asked me to tell you to stay inside the cottage until they find the man who was lurking about the woods. We all think it best." He was speaking kindly to her. Did that mean her life was in danger? That Gabe's life was in danger?

"Of course." Several pairs of eyes were on her now, and she looked down to keep them from seeing how concerned she was for Gabe. *God, please help him get better.*

After supper, Sophie watched Bartel go upstairs. She prayed silently, then followed him so she could retrieve the material for her dress. While sewing downstairs, she imagined how beautiful the dress would be when it was finished. But mostly her mind was on Gabe. What had he been trying to tell her this morning? The more she thought about it, the more she was afraid she didn't want to know. Either he loved her, which was a terrible, unsolvable problem, or he was going to tell her that his family was too important to him and that she could never be more to him than a sister. That they needed to stay away from each other from now on.

That would be best, she told herself. It wasn't what she wanted, but since when did she get what she wanted? Just as a servant had few rights, a girl born to a duke quite possibly had even fewer. She must marry whomever her parents chose. Even if the man they chose never came to love her. Even if she loved someone else.

Siggy began to play his lute again after supper. Vincz, who usually fell asleep within moments of sitting down, walked over to Sophie.

"Would you dance with me, my lady?" His brown eyes reminded her of a dog that belonged to the village baker. Droopy and sad, but sweet. He smiled and held out his hand.

"Oh no, thank you. I don't know how to dance."

He tried to persuade her but she shook her head and smiled apologetically. Her unfinished dress was still in her lap, and she wanted to finish it tonight. Besides, she would likely mess up every step. So she worked her needle in and out of the fabric while she listened to the songs.

It should have been a very pleasant evening. She wasn't accustomed to the pleasure of listening to music, not to mention the pleasure of creating a new dress from beautiful fabric for herself, but she couldn't stop thinking about what Bartel was doing to Gabe in the room upstairs and why he lingered there so long.

Finally, the men started yawning—Vincz had long since fallen asleep in his chair—and they all started getting ready to go upstairs. Sophie gathered up her dress, since she needed to try it on before finishing it, and headed back upstairs as well.

Bartel was coming out of Gabe's room as she was walking down the corridor. "How is he? Is it bad?" She surprised herself by sounding breathless and scared.

"I think he only made himself too tired. He needs to stay in bed for a few days."

"How is his fever?"

"I hope it will be gone again by morning."

"And his wound? Does it look all right?"

"It has been oozing a lot of water and blood, but I think that is normal."

Her heart was in her throat as she told Bartel thank you. She wanted to see Gabe, to feel his forehead to see how bad his fever was, but she was afraid. What if he told her to leave him in peace?

Besides, Bartel was taking good care of him. Gabe didn't need her constantly running in.

At least she could finish her dress tonight.

Sophie got up early and pulled on the white chemise Dominyk had given her, followed by the new red overdress, tying the laces under her arms and down the front of the bodice. She had also made a matching red sash to wear in her hair; after weaving the sash into her two braids, she wrapped each plait so they rested atop her head, tied in place by the end of the sash. She liked the effect of the crimson against the black of her hair, which she could see in a small looking glass in her room.

She longed to knock on Gabe's door and ask how he was feeling and see if he'd notice her new dress, but that was foolishness. Besides, he was probably still asleep. She continued down the corridor and down the stairs to make breakfast for everyone, carefully putting on the largest apron to protect her new dress from stains.

When the seven men came for their morning meal, she had already taken off her apron. The men stared at her, and she realized they were looking at her gown.

"Do you like it?" she asked them, glancing down at it.

"You look as b-b-beautiful as a s-s-s-s-sunrise," Siggy said.

Dolf pointed to her dress, smiling and nodding. The others all complimented her as well. It *had* turned out quite lovely. The bodice was fitted to her waist and the full skirt flowed all the way to the floor. Perhaps it was almost as fine as the dresses Gabe's mother and sisters wore. She wished he were here to see it.

But Gabe did not come downstairs for breakfast. Sophie was disappointed, even though Bartel had warned he needed to stay in bed for a few days. She asked the stoic monk how Gabe was doing, but his reply was vague, saying Gabe was about the same and just needed rest. At midday it was the same response. When she went upstairs to get something out of her room, she told herself if no one was around, she would knock on Gabe's door. But Bartel was just coming out when she entered the corridor. He stood with his arms folded across his chest as she approached.

"How is he?"

"The same."

It was on the tip of her tongue to ask to see him, but Bartel's serious, rather disapproving look stopped her and she moved on. It was for the best, anyway. She needed to keep her distance.

That night, Gabe didn't join them for supper.

After the meal they sat down to listen to Siggy and Dominyk play, as usual. This time Dominyk also sang, revealing a wonderful baritone voice that woke up Vincz, who added his deep bass.

Sophie had offered to do some mending for the men, partly to keep her mind busy. Between the rhythm of the stitches and the melodies the men created, her mind was fairly occupied, until she heard a dull thump from upstairs followed by another, louder one. She looked around the room to gauge the others' reactions, but they were all occupied with the music. She stood up, laid her work in her chair, and hurried out of the room and up the stairs, no longer caring how Bartel would react to her going to Gabe's room. She hadn't seen Gabe for more than an entire day and she couldn't bear it any longer. Besides, she reasoned, he may need help.

Her heart was in her throat as she reached the top of the stairs. She stared at his door. Her hand shook as she reached out to knock.

The door opened just as her knuckles were about to touch the wood. Gabe stood there, his face troubled.

"Gabe. What are you doing up?" Her voice sounded breathless. She made an effort to calm her breathing. She couldn't tell if the look on his face was anger ... or hurt.

# *Chapter*
## 18

*Gabe stared down at Sophie, propping him-*self against the door frame. How good it was to see her face. He reached out and touched her arm. From the look in Sophie's eyes, she was glad to see him too.

"Where have you been?" he asked softly. "Why did you stay away?" He tried not to let her hear the emotion in his voice.

"Bartel said you needed rest."

"He's worse than a prison guard."

"Are you all right? Is your fever gone?" She stood on tiptoe and touched his forehead, bringing her face very close to his.

As her hand lingered on his forehead, their eyes met. He tried to read what was hidden there. Her hand was so cool and pleasant on his forehead.

"You still feel warm," she whispered.

He leaned closer. Her deep blue eyes, which appeared almost black in the dark corridor, held a little bit of fear. Her thick eyelashes curled delicately against her skin. A strand of black hair had worked loose and lay against her cheek. He was tempted to brush it back just to see if her hair was as silky and her skin as soft as it looked now.

Hair and skin that only Valten should ever be allowed to touch.

He stifled a groan and clenched his jaw instead. *Why do I have to have such a loud conscience, God?* It was beyond frustrating.

Sophie took a step back.

He pulled on her arm. "Come inside for a moment. Before Bartel comes back." *I only want to talk to her, God. Can't I just talk to her?* He effectually ignored his conscience's answer.

She flinched and he let go, staring down at her arm. He had forgotten all about the long arrow wound. She followed him inside, and he shut the door behind them.

"I want to see how your arm is doing. Have you let Bartel look at it again?"

"My arm is well. You're supposed to be resting." She nodded toward the bed. "Bartel would not be happy if he knew you were out of bed, would he?"

"No, probably not." Gabe knelt in front of the fireplace and stirred up the smoldering fire.

"You should let me do that."

He added more wood. She pulled on his arm, trying to make him stand up. When he finished, he straightened, then stumbled and almost fell, propping himself against the wall. Sophie put her arm around him and helped him to the bed.

He hated letting her see him this way. He wanted to be strong, to take care of her as he had when they'd been running from the duchess's guards. He wanted to find the man who might be stalking them, trying to hurt Sophie. And he wanted her to trust him.

*If it wasn't for this cursed fever . . .*

She started to pull the blanket up to his chin, but he held out his hand to stop her. "I want to see your arm."

"As you wish."

"Will you light the candles?"

She lit the pillars on the table by the bed, and he was finally able to see her better. He noticed she was no longer wearing her old servant's garb or the men's clothes Dominyk had provided. Instead, she wore a beautiful red dress.

"Sophie," he breathed, looking her up and down. He pulled himself into a sitting position. "You're beautiful." He had never seen her wearing anything so exquisite. Her clothes hadn't detracted from her natural beauty, but he'd always had to imagine what she'd look like in the clothes of the nobility. Now, in the elegant gown that, with its perfect shade of red that accentuated her flawless skin and ebony hair ... she took his breath away. Before him stood a woman who could grace any dance floor in the Holy Roman Empire and make all the other women look plain.

She blushed as she glanced down at her dress. "The men gave me the fabric."

"So that's why you didn't come to see me. You were busy."

"Gabe, I — " She hesitated, using her finger to smear a dribble of hot wax on the side of a candle.

He held his breath, waiting for what she would say, wondering why she was so hesitant.

"I wasn't that busy," she said, still picking at the candle. "I was afraid to disturb you and afraid of ..." She bit her lip, her brows drawing together.

"Afraid of what?"

She pulled her hand away from the candle and started rubbing her finger, shifting her weight from one foot to the other, and refusing to look him in the eye. "I don't know. It doesn't matter."

"Tell me, Sophie." She had avoided him and now refused to tell him why. He leaned forward and took her hand, wondering if she would pull away from him again.

But she didn't offer any resistance. Her small hand fit perfectly in his, and she clasped her fingers around his. She faced him, searching his eyes, as if she was trying to read his thoughts.

"I was afraid of what you were about to tell me when we

were interrupted yesterday." She sat down on the stool beside his bed, then swallowed, her eyes still fastened to his face, still searching intently.

"But you're not afraid now?" He spoke softly, as if she were a skittish foal he was trying not to spook.

"I'm just as afraid, if not more." Her lips trembled as if she were trying to smile but was too nervous. "But I had to see you, to see how you were." She took a shaky breath, as if her next words were difficult to say. "And now I am ready to hear what you have to say."

Now he wasn't sure he should say it. They had been through a lot together, but they had only known each other a few days. She probably wanted to forget him so she could have the life she deserved. After all, she would gain so much more by marrying Valten.

It would be for the best if they could forget about each other. If he and Sophie tried to break their betrothals, many people would be hurt, including Valten. And though he and Valten had often fought and been angry with each other, Gabe realized, maybe more than ever before, that he loved his brother and desired his respect.

But looking into her earnest face, feeling her hand clasped to his ... he wasn't sure he could ever let her go. Not if she felt the same way he did.

"I was about to say ..." He swallowed, afraid of saying too much and afraid of saying too little. "My family is important to me, but you are very important to me too. Truthfully, I don't know if I could bear to ... I don't want to let you go."

He held her hand tight and gazed into her blue eyes, the light of the candles dancing inside them. Her lips were parted and her eyes were wide, almost childlike.

He loved his brother, but he couldn't let Sophie marry Valten if she didn't want to. *Please say something, Sophie.*

She whispered, "I know." Bowing her head, she squeezed his hand with both of hers.

They were quiet for several moments. Gabe soaked up her presence and the fragile touch of her hands.

"Let me see your arm," he said softly.

She let go of his hand, reluctantly it seemed, and slowly inched up her fitted sleeve to reveal the bandage that stretched from her wrist to her elbow. Sophie unwrapped it. He took her arm in his hands and leaned over to examine it closer to the light. The wound was starting to close up as it should, but it was important that it be properly cleaned and wrapped.

"I think Bartel needs to look at it."

"What do I need to look at?" Bartel stood in the doorway, his arms hidden under the folds of his brown robe.

He let go of Sophie as Bartel drew nearer.

"Sophie was wounded by an arrow."

"I know. I have been bandaging it every night."

"Thank you."

"She didn't want me to stitch it closed, but it is healing." Bartel began rewrapping her bandage and tied it snugly in place.

Gabe perceived by his expression that Bartel didn't approve of Sophie being in his room. All the more reason for Gabe to get well so he didn't have to stay cloistered. If it killed him, and even if he had to defy Bartel, he would go downstairs tomorrow instead of letting Bartel force him to stay in bed.

"How is Lord Gabe faring?" Sophie asked Bartel.

Her calling him "Lord Gabe" reminded him that they would have to conform again to society's rules. The other people around them would dictate how they addressed each other, and every other behavior. And once again, everyone would say how irresponsible Gabe was.

"He is improving," Bartel said. "But I do not want him leaving his bed until I'm sure the fever is gone and he is stronger. And then he isn't to leave this house or do any work."

"Of course," Sophie mumbled.

"You may go now."

"Of course, Herr Bartel." Sophie dropped a quick curtsy and started to leave.

Gabe wanted to call her back, but with Bartel standing there, he simply said, "Good night, Sophie."

"Good night, Gabe. Good night, Herr Bartel."

As soon as Sophie finished making breakfast the next morning, Bartel appeared at her side. He quickly took the tray she prepared for Gabe. She had hoped to take him the food herself.

"Come upstairs when you finish breakfast so I can change your bandage," he ordered before he left.

She hurried through the meal and left the seven men to clean up. Her thin shoes swished up the steps, and she had to pause at Gabe's door to catch her breath, even though running up one flight of steps had never made her lose her breath before.

She knocked on the door and Gabe's rich voice bid her come in.

Sophie hurried in, her heart pounding at seeing Gabe alone. "*Guten Morgen.* How are you feeling?"

"Much better," he said, pushing himself into a sitting position. "Will you open the shutters to let some more light in?"

Sophie turned to the window, hoping she didn't have any smudges of flour on her face and that her hair wasn't falling down. She opened the shutters and a flash of movement at the edge of the trees caught her eye. A man stared straight back at her, his face partially covered by a thick beard. There was something about his eyes that sent a shiver through her, and Sophie gasped. The man turned and disappeared into the trees.

"What? What is it?" Gabe sat up straighter, pushing the blanket back.

"Nothing, nothing. I just need to go tell Dominyk something." Hurrying out the door, she said quickly, "Stay in bed. I'll be right back."

Sophie closed the door behind her and raced down the steps. She ran into Dominyk coming out of the kitchen.

"I saw a man."

"Where?"

"In the edge of the forest, behind the house. He was slender and had a thick brown beard. He saw me."

"Stay in the house. We'll deal with him." Dominyk disappeared back into the kitchen.

Sophie hurried back up to Gabe's chamber, her hands shaking a bit as she remembered the malevolent look in the prowler's eyes. But she had to appear calm when she faced Gabe. She didn't want him to know about the man. He would only be upset that he couldn't go out and search for him.

Sophie slipped back into the room and smiled at him. A day's worth of hair growth on his face and chin gave him back that rugged, masculine look, the one that had made her heart skip a few beats the first time she saw him unshaven. Her smile faltered, and she swallowed the rock in her throat.

"What happened? Did you see something outside?"

"I just had to tell Dominyk something. Now tell me how you are feeling this morning." Her hand shook a bit as she passed the open window and bent to blow out a candle on the bedside table.

"I am much better now." Gabe smiled at her, making her heart flutter. His sun-darkened skin was a nice contrast to his white teeth. His russet-brown hair waved across his forehead and his dark eyes fixed on hers, drawing her closer.

"You're beautiful, Sophie. I suppose you've heard that all your life."

The duchess had always told her she was ugly. Sophie had always struggled to not believe the duchess, especially after her hair had been cut off a few years ago.

"Not everyone says I'm beautiful."

"The duchess? She doesn't count."

He had read her mind. Or maybe he just knew her, knew her better than anyone ever could without seeing where she'd come from and knowing her mistress ... or, rather, her stepmother. How could anyone really know Sophie without knowing what the duchess had done to her? But Gabe knew. He knew everything and still cared about her.

She rewarded him with a bigger smile. For now she would push back the worry. She simply wanted to enjoy whatever time she had with him and pretend she had all the time in the world to enjoy his company, his conversation ... to enjoy looking at him.

"Have you come to get your bandage changed?"

She nodded, taking the tray from his lap and setting it on the table.

The door opened and Bartel walked in. Gabe looked on as the monk repeated what he had done the night before, wrapping her arm tightly with a clean, new bandage.

Bartel, who rarely ever looked her in the eye and never for more than a moment, looked at the floor and said, "I will change Gabe's bandage now," as if to dismiss her.

"Oh, good." Sophie tried to sound innocent. "I would like to see his wound to know how well it is healing."

Bartel looked at her with a suspicious glint in his eye. Sophie smiled at him. He finally turned away from her, a disgruntled look on his face, as he focused on Gabe.

He opened Gabe's shirt down the front and pushed the material off his shoulder.

Her face grew warm and she wondered if this had been a bad

idea. But when Bartel took off Gabe's bandage, exposing the raw, open wound, she stepped closer and cringed.

"Does it look all right? Is it healing the way it's supposed to?"

Bartel didn't pause or look back at her as he studied the wound and then started applying a green paste to it. "Yes."

She waited for him to say more, but he didn't.

Bartel rewrapped the bandage around Gabe's shoulder. "He needs to rest now," Bartel said.

She nodded and hurried out the door.

When Gabe woke again, the sun was high. Bartel had closed the shutters, but Gabe could still see the bright rays of light through the cracks. *What has Bartel been giving me to drink?* Every time he drank Bartel's herbed wine, he lost hours to sleep. Gabe threw back the covers and got fully dressed, noting his fever was gone. From now on, he wasn't drinking anything Bartel gave him. From now on he would spend his days downstairs ... with Sophie. After all, he had less than two weeks to find out just how she truly felt about him.

And what to do about it.

Gabe slipped on his boots, reveling in feeling strong again. His shoulder was still extremely sore, but that wasn't enough reason for Bartel to give him something to make him sleep, just to keep him cloistered upstairs.

As he descended the stairs, the wonderful smell of fresh bread and warm spices filled him with anticipation.

Sophie was setting the dishes on the table. She saw him and her face lit up. "You look ... good." She smiled.

"You look better than good."

She blushed. "I meant that you look rested and strong. You have your color back. Are you feeling better?"

He moved close to her. "Do you think I still have a fever?" He hoped she would press her soft hand to his forehead.

"I'm sure your fever must be gone"—she gave him a saucy smirk, seeing right through him—"or Bartel never would have let you come downstairs."

"Bartel doesn't know." He smirked right back, leaning dangerously close.

# Chapter
## 19

*She stared into his eyes like a deer in that* instant it sees the arrow coming straight for its heart. Her deep-blue eyes were wide, her pink lips slightly parted. His heart pounded against his chest. He bent his head closer.

"Sophie, Sophie, Sophie."

Sophie stepped away from him with a startled jerk of her head, and Gabe's soaring heart dropped like a rock.

Siggy stood in the door, his ears red, the bright color spreading up his neck and into his cheeks. Heinric was just behind him, grinning ecstatically, drool at the corners of his mouth, as he repeated Sophie's name.

Siggy couldn't meet their eyes. "W-w-we rang the bell. The others sh-should be c-c-coming."

"Thank you, Siggy." Sophie glanced at Gabe and then turned back toward the counter.

Gabe followed her and helped take the food out to the table. Every shy peek from under her eyelashes was worth gold.

As they waited for the rest of the men, Gabe asked Siggy, "Where are they?"

"Dominyk and Dolf are w-w-working the mines. Vincz-z-z-z and Gotfrid are w-w-working in the forest, cutting trees. We are miners and w-w-woodsmen. Bartel p-p-prays in the chapel out back."

"Heinric help too."

"Heinric, you are a g-g-good helper." Siggy patted Heinric on the shoulder. "Heinric and I are s-s-staying near to make sure S-s-s-sophie is safe."

"Heinric good helper," Heinric said. "I protect Sophie."

"Thank you," Gabe said. "I am glad you are here to take care of Sophie, Heinric." Heinric was almost as large as Walther. Anyone who threatened Sophie, with Heinric nearby, would likely regret it.

Soon the rest of the men trooped in and sat down on the benches at the trestle table. Gabe managed to get a spot next to Sophie. She seemed at ease with the Seven. They looked at her with respect and kindness in their eyes, and she in turn looked at them with an almost familial air. She cared about them. But the look she gave Gabe was unmistakably different.

Valten was going to kill him. He shouldn't be encouraging Sophie's attention. If he wasn't mistaken, she would have let him kiss her a few moments ago. *I'm sorry, God, but she never promised to marry Valten, and for that matter, Valten never promised to marry her. The agreement was made by their parents, not them.* But he and Brittola *had* agreed to marry. Perhaps there was a way to break the betrothals, a way that wouldn't anger their families or the king, bringing down his wrath on them. The king had approved the original betrothal, but he could change his mind, couldn't he? He'd done it before.

If Sophie loved Gabe, he would make a way.

Sophie noticed that Gabe wasn't using his left hand. She wanted to ask him if his shoulder still hurt, but she was afraid to even speak to him in front of the men, especially after Siggy and Heinric had come into the room just when it looked as if Gabe was about to kiss her. She didn't know if he would have, but it must have looked that way to Siggy. What would the men think of her? Especially if they knew she was betrothed to Gabe's brother?

Earlier, while Sophie had been preparing the meal, Dominyk told her that Vincz and Dolf had gone to look for the man she'd seen, but they had only found a few tracks before quickly losing his trail. They believed it was the same man they had seen before.

"He could be the duchess's henchman, so stay inside at all times. We will watch out for him."

"Thank you." The thought of another one of Duchess Ermengard's men spying on her made a chill snake down Sophie's back, but she pushed the thought from her mind. Besides, neither the Seven nor Gabe would let anything harm her.

When the meal was over, the seven men began to disperse to their jobs. Dominyk said, "Siggy, you stay near the house and Heinric can come with me. I want you to watch the woods for any sign of" — he glanced at Gabe — "trouble. Sophie has you, Gabe, and Bartel. I know the three of you will keep her safe."

Siggy nodded, and the rest of the men left.

Sophie and Gabe gathered the dishes and took them to the washbasin while Siggy went outside to look around. Gabe brought her the tankards, and she poured some warm water from a large, beaten copper pan into the basin to wash them. As he set the dishes down on the wood shelf beside her, his shoulder and upper arm brushed hers. Her arm tingled as she stared into the pan. She rinsed the cups and then began washing the bowls. He put his hands into the water and helped, their hands colliding under the water.

She couldn't tear her eyes away from the way he held each item with his left hand and scrubbed with his right. She kept working, pretending not to notice him, but her breath seemed to have caught in her throat. Finally, when she was washing the very last bowl, Gabe placed his hands over hers, following along with her movements as she rubbed the dish clean and placed it on the cloth next to the washbasin. With one hand holding hers, he picked up a towel with the other and began to dry her hands.

His upper arm was rock solid against her shoulder. His face hovered just above hers and his warm breath brushed her temple. Her knees were like pottage. His nearness made her want to press in closer, but if Bartel were to walk in now, she'd be even more embarrassed than she had when Siggy and Heinric had walked in on them before the midday meal. But Gabe's arm pressing against hers was so exhilarating, and the gentleness of his hands sent pleasant shivers all through her, and when he started rubbing her fingertips inside the cocoon of the towel ...

His warm breath loosed a strand of her hair and it brushed her cheek. She desperately wanted him to kiss her.

"Someone needs to take out the dishwater." Sophie's voice sounded strained and breathless, betraying just how much his touch was affecting her. She stood still as a stone, afraid to move, her head bent, as he took the towel off her hands and threw it on the counter.

"I'll take it outside in a moment." His voice sounded gruff.

She waited for him to move away. Instead, with slow and deliberate movements, he placed one hand on her shoulder and he cupped her cheek with the other as he turned her body to face him.

She placed her palms against his chest, feeling as if she were in a slow-moving dream. She couldn't avoid looking up at him any longer. She met his smoldering eyes, the golden flecks all but swallowed up in the dark brown irises. In their depths, there was only a solemn tenderness as he drew her nearer. He bent his head and pressed his lips to hers.

The world vanished. She was engulfed in warmth and exhilaration and strength—and guilt. But she pushed the guilt away.

Her hands slid up his chest and around his neck. He pulled away slightly, then kissed her again. *Oh, Gabe.*

The events of the last few days flitted through her mind. Gabe, looking so noble and sure of himself when he'd lifted her onto his horse the day they left Hohendorf. Gabe, so sweet and vulnerable when he'd stared into her eyes after taking the arrow in his shoulder to save her. Now he was kissing her.

Her life had been tragic before Gabe, and it would be tragic again if he left. She held on to him as if she could keep this moment from ending.

Gabe gently ended the kiss, and she buried her face in his chest. Trying to quiet her breathing, to get back some control over her emotions, she breathed in the scent of him, a warm, comforting, masculine smell of outdoors and clean skin. Memories rushed over her, of riding with him on Gingerbread through the woods and beside the river, her head against his chest.

"Sophie." His deep voice caressed her ears. He held her close, stroking her braid, then her shoulder. She was afraid to move, afraid to loosen her hold around his neck for fear he would pull away.

*What are we going to do now?* The words were on the tip of her tongue, but she bit them back. She didn't want to ruin the moment, especially if Gabe had no lasting intentions beyond this kiss. It was too good, this feeling of being loved and wanted.

She would pretend it would last forever, pretend no one would ever find them. They would hide forever right here at the Cottage of the Seven, happily ever after.

*Thank you for this moment, even if it doesn't last.*

"I'll be right back." Gabe's deep voice rumbled through her, his stubbly chin rubbing her temple.

Sophie let her hands slide away from him as he kept one arm around her shoulder, pressing his lips to her forehead before turning away to pour the water from the pan into a bucket. He hefted the bucket with one hand and carried it outside.

She watched him go, her heart thumping happily in her throat as she admired the breadth of his shoulders and their obvious strength. Even with an injury, he was capable of taking care of her.

He came back inside and set down the bucket, then held out his hand to her.

She couldn't wipe the smile off her face. Just the act of reaching out and taking his hand, that tiny act of trust, made her heart trip. Her hand shook slightly as she let him enclose her small fingers in his larger, more powerful hand. She gazed at his gently smiling face, his eyes sparkling as they stood in the kitchen together.

Gabe felt as if he were dreaming when Sophie squeezed his hand and let her cheek brush against his sleeve as they walked to the front room. The beautiful spring day, visible through the windows, smelled of flowers and sunshine and wet grass. He would always love this smell, from this day on, and it would remind him of Sophie ...

He was in love. What he had felt for Brittola was nothing compared to this. He had kissed Brittola once, the day they had parted over a year ago now, but he'd felt none of the overwhelming emotions that were going through his mind and heart at this moment. Sophie filled his senses.

The urgency to break both their betrothals pulsed through his brain. There had to be a way, and he had to find it.

He pulled Sophie to him, inhaling her scent as she threw her arms around him, pressing her face against his good shoulder. They were alone. There was no sound in the house except their own breathing—and the pounding of his heart. Sophie seemed shy, not wanting to look up at him. He pulled her to a bench against the wall and they both sat down, her back resting against his chest. He wrapped his arm around her waist and played with the wisps of hair that had broken free from her thick braid. If they were married, he would have the right to pull her black hair from its braid and run his fingers through it . . .

He had to do this the right way, to find a way to annul their betrothals, to show he was responsible and honorable, and to preserve Sophie's reputation and dignity, not to mention his family's good name. Valten would be incensed, but if Gabe handled this correctly, he could stave off any lasting consequences, to his family's name, and to Sophie's.

Sophie took his hand from her waist and began stroking his fingers in a way that was too stimulating for comfort. She lifted his hand to her lips and kissed it.

She didn't realize how beguiling she was in her innocent gestures.

Perhaps he was selfish to want her for himself. But he could love her, and somehow, Gabe would create a decent—a more than decent—life for his wife and children. Somehow he would make sure Sophie was never without anything she needed or wanted. He swore to himself that he would never be irresponsible again.

He stroked her rose-petal-soft cheek with a fingertip, marveling at the feel of her skin, and laid his cheek on the top of her head. He couldn't stop thinking about their kiss and wanted to kiss her again.

"Are you happy?"

She hugged his arm and leaned her head back against his good shoulder. "Yes . . . but what are we going to do?"

He sighed. His father would come and find them. "I'll figure out something, I promise."

"You will?" she asked in a tremulous voice.

"You want me to, don't you?"

"More than anything in the world. But . . . do you love me?"

"More than anything."

She pulled his hand to her lips and kissed his palm, then his fingers. His chest ached with the desire to turn her around and kiss her again, but he forced himself not to.

"What if your family is angry and never accepts me?"

"My family is not like that. I'll tell them it was my fault, and they'll believe me. I will find a way. Trust me, Sophie."

She kissed his hand again and he twined her fingers through his.

For the first time, he noticed a pale brown mark on her neck below her ear. The mark was about the size of his thumbnail and was in the shape of a flower with five rounded petals. Some day he would have the right to kiss that spot on her neck. But in the meantime, he would figure out a way to make her his.

"I'll make a way." *Somehow.*

# Chapter
## 20

*Gabe stayed in bed a couple of hours that* afternoon because Bartel ordered him to and Sophie begged him to do as Bartel asked. He pretended to drink the wine Bartel gave him, but when Bartel left the room, he poured it out the window.

At supper he tried to concentrate on what Siggy was saying to him but found his mind wandering to Sophie and the wonderful hour they had spent alone together, how sweet it had been to kiss her … He forced himself to look at his food, at Siggy, at the other men, but it was difficult when she was sitting on his other side looking like perfection from heaven and everything he wanted on this earth.

After supper the men cleaned up the dishes while Sophie collected the mending and sat in a corner. Heinric captured Gabe and all but dragged him outside to look at a root he had found that was shaped like the crescent moon. Heinric had been talking about it all through supper. Gabe clapped him on the back and assured him it was the most wonderful root he had ever seen.

"Thank you, Gabe. I let you touch it."

"Thank you, Heinric. You're a good man."

Heinric grinned his impossibly wide grin.

When they came back inside, Siggy and Dominyk were getting their instruments and everyone was settling down to listen.

"Gabe, Sophie told us you had to leave your lute in Hohendorf. Can I go upstairs and get another lute for you?" Vincz asked.

Gabe nodded. Vincz leaped up the steps two at a time.

Sophie was smiling at him, but when his eye caught hers, she looked down.

Gabe was glad to be invited to play. He'd been mentally rehearsing the song he'd written in Hohendorf, the song that was supposedly for the duchess but that he'd actually written with Sophie in mind. Now he could sing it just for her and tell her how beautiful he thought she was.

When Vincz got back with the instruments, Gabe and Siggy discovered a couple of songs they both knew, and they began to play.

There was something about music, the way it flowed through his body and mind and spirit all at the same time, that felt like an intimacy between him and the person listening to it. Never had that feeling been so strong in Gabe as now, when he was staring straight into Sophie's eyes and playing for her. It was almost as if they were one, the same thoughts flowing from him to her and back, as the music filled the space between them.

Sophie tried to concentrate on her mending, but her stitches were going all awry. Finally, she simply gave up and watched Gabe play the lute with Siggy and Dominyk. He played as if he was born with the instrument in his hands. And his look of absorption made him even more handsome. She didn't want to miss a single moment of his playing.

During the next song, he sang with Siggy, their voices blending harmoniously.

He kept his gaze on her while he sang, and her heart lodged

in her throat, his warm brown eyes trapping hers. No one else seemed to exist, and he seemed to be singing the words directly to her. It was a song about a hunter in love with a dove who changed into a woman when the moon was full. It was as if they were the only two people in the room, as if he was strumming her soul, seeing straight into her heart with his penetrating brown eyes.

She couldn't tear her gaze away until he finished the song and looked at Siggy. They spoke quietly. Then Gabe looked around at all the men who were sitting around the room.

"This next song I wrote a few days ago. For Sophie." His gaze found her and he winked, his lopsided grin stealing her breath.

He started playing, looking down at his lute as he found the right notes. His head was bent, but she could see his concentration in the pursing of his lips and the slight crease of his forehead. When he began to sing, he looked up at her. His deep, clear voice was more beautiful than anything she'd ever heard before, so real and true, and the words of his song made her wish she could keep this moment in front of her forever.

Gabe's eyes stayed locked on hers as he sang about her blue eyes and her heart of love, her grace and innocence. He compared her hair to ebony, her skin to a dove's white feathers, and her lips to a rose.

Her face grew hot with self-consciousness at the words of his song, and tears welled in her eyes to think that he had written these verses about her. He couldn't have meant them, because she was sure he hadn't loved her when he'd written it. He'd surely been writing it for the duchess. But the look in his eyes as he sang the words told her that he meant them for her.

How was it possible for her to experience so much happiness? Her heart swelled inside her until she could barely breathe. Gabe loved her. Or at least he seemed to. He went on to sing more words of adoration, flowery declarations of her beauty and his helplessness to stop loving her.

When the song was over, Sophie's face was still burning. She wanted to place her hands over her cheeks, but her hands were shaking and she didn't want anyone to notice. She stared into her lap and took up her mending, trying to get her breathing under control. But she only pretended to sew. Her hands were too shaky to make a stitch.

Gabe and Siggy played more songs, but Sophie kept her eyes down as much as possible.

When the music was over, the men began clapping Gabe on the back and talking. Bartel came over to her to rewrap her bandage.

"Your arm is healing quickly," Bartel said, "but it needs a bandage for a while longer." She felt his eyes boring into her, staring at her face like he'd never done before. What was he thinking?

The men were going their separate ways and Sophie lost sight of Gabe. Would she see him again before she went to her room? Nervously, she gathered up her mending, put it away, and hurried upstairs. Bartel was right behind her. She wasn't sure if she was relieved or disappointed that he would prevent her from having a private word with Gabe.

When she reached the top of the stairs, Gabe was coming out of his chamber. His eyes met hers in the dark corridor, then he saw Bartel over her shoulder. He stepped forward and took Sophie's hand. He kissed it reverently, his eyes closed. He held on as she moved past him, his fingers caressing hers as long as possible.

"Good night, Gabe."

"Good night, Sophie."

Gabe squatted next to Dolf as they pulled weeds from the large vegetable and herb garden behind the cottage while Sophie cooked in the kitchen. Every now and then he couldn't resist looking through the window to catch glimpses of Sophie. Sometimes she was sneaking looks at him too.

Bartel stalked up to him. "You shouldn't be working at this."

Dolf continued to work, glancing up at Bartel, while Gabe stood. "I'm only using my right hand."

"You've done enough for today. You must rest and get well." He started walking toward the tiny chapel a few feet away before saying over his shoulder, "You can come with me. I have some easier work for you."

Gabe looked down at Dolf, pointed to his wounded shoulder, frowned, and pointed over his shoulder at Bartel, rolling his eyes to the sky.

Dolf chuckled, then shooed Gabe away, nodding and smiling. Gabe followed the monk.

Inside the stone chapel, an altar glowed with several lit candles in front of a picture of Mary and baby Jesus. Both men looked up at the portrait of Jesus on the cross on the wall behind the altar and genuflected, crossing themselves and bowing to say a quick prayer.

"I am trimming candlewicks," Bartel pointed to two large spools of string. He sat on the hard floor, folding his legs and malformed feet underneath him before covering them with the hem of his robe.

Gabe sat in front of him and watched as Bartel measured a length of string about two feet long, then cut the piece from the spool. Gabe did the same thing with the other spool. In a few minutes, they each had a stack of wicks by their sides.

"We've all become quite fond of Sophie, as you can see. Walther said she is rumored to be the daughter of Duke Baldewin, alive and well. Is this true?"

Gabe shifted slightly. What was Bartel aiming at? "That's true. Sophie didn't even know she was the duke's daughter until a few days ago, when I arrived to rescue her."

"I must thank you for your heroics in saving her. Though the men and I have been wondering what your intentions are toward Sophie. A few of us recall hearing, years ago, that as a baby, Sophie was betrothed to a duke's son—Duke Wilhelm's oldest son, Valten." Bartel didn't look at Gabe as he spoke, but his voice was unyielding and purposeful. "Are you her betrothed?"

Gabe's face flooded with heat. "No, I'm not. But I intend to find a way to marry her."

Bartel sat stone-faced, cutting wick after wick. Finally, without looking up from his task, he said, "Betrothals are legally binding. Her betrothed may not like you trifling with his future wife."

"I am not *trifling* with her." Gabe wanted to tell Bartel it was none of his business. He wanted to argue that she belonged to him because he had risked his life for her, taken an arrow for her. He was the one who loved her. Valten didn't love her, could never love her the way he did.

But he stopped himself. He had to handle this responsibly.

"I never intended to fall in love with Sophie." He took a deep breath and let it out slowly. "She is betrothed to my brother Valten, the future duke of Hagenheim."

Saying the words aloud seemed to have a dampening effect on Gabe's spirits. When he looked at the facts, they were stark indeed.

"I even tried not to fall in love with Sophie." He squeezed his eyes shut. *Please help me, God.* "But I believe it was God's will that I be the one to rescue her from Duchess Ermengard. Valten had broken his leg and was unable to go to her when we found out she was still alive. If I hadn't gone when I did, Sophie might be dead now."

Truthfully, he thought his presence at Hohendorf had probably hastened the duchess's deciding to kill her. But hadn't he felt a supernatural urgency to go and rescue her? He'd sensed the danger she was in and had felt compelled to go and save her. Perhaps she *would* be dead now if it hadn't been for Gabe.

"If God had wanted Valten to rescue her, would he have allowed Valten to break his leg?" Gabe asked, turning to face Bartel. "It was God's will. He knew Sophie and I would fall in love, that we were meant to be together."

"If God intended you two to be together, then why did he allow her to be betrothed to your brother?" Bartel fixed a hard eye on Gabe.

"Maybe God wanted to show his power by making a way for us to now break our betrothals."

"Betrothals? You mean you are also betrothed?"

Gabe winced. It sounded bad when Bartel said it in such a shocked and appalled tone.

"So you are betraying not only your brother but your own betrothed as well?"

Gabe's heart sank. This conversation was not going well. He continued to measure out the string and cut it, the pile of wicks growing.

"How do you know Sophie loves you? She is very young. As are you, and it appears you have not known each other long. Perhaps you will both change your minds."

Was Bartel right? Didn't she deserve to marry the good brother? The one who always did everything right, who was admired and respected, who would inherit wealth and power? The one she was supposed to marry?

Gabe stopped his work and stared at Bartel. What could he say? The more he defended himself, the more foolish he would appear. But two things he knew: Sophie was not married, and his love for her was real. It would not die no matter how long he lived.

"You may ask her yourself," he said softly.

"Have you asked her? Have you asked her if she prefers to marry you and not your brother?"

"Not in so many words." He wasn't sure how much longer his patience and self-control would hold out. He felt like hitting this cold, self-righteous monk.

Not a very Christian thought.

"How do you plan to break your betrothals? Will you tell your betrothed, 'I'm sorry, but I fell in love with someone else. Can you and your father kindly let me out of our agreement, on which I and my parents staked our good name?'"

Actually, that was very close to his plan. "There will be a way. Sophie's parents are dead so they can't complain. My parents and brother will agree." *They won't like it, but they'll eventually agree when they see that Sophie loves me and that I love her, and how she has changed me.* Sophie had done what all his parents' cajoling and his older brother's goading had been unable to do. She had made him want to be responsible, made him want to make his own way in the world and have a family.

"My betrothal was not written down or blessed by a priest," he added.

Bartel gave him another hard, long look. "So you feel comfortable breaking it for that reason?"

Gabe glared back at him, then looked away, not wanting to have hatred of a monk on his conscience—along with all his other sins.

"I am not trying to anger you, Gabe. I only want to make sure you've thought these things through and asked God what he would want you to do. You must think about whether you are doing the right thing for Sophie."

A physical pang went through his chest as Bartel continued

cutting the string into the correct length, looking as tranquil as a woodland pond.

Was Gabe doing the right thing for Sophie? How could Bartel know this was the very thing that plagued him, that stirred guilt inside him?

Perhaps he was being selfish, but he simply could not bear to lose her.

Gabe continued working, pretending to ignore Bartel's words.

"You say Sophie's parents are dead." Bartel cut two more strings before continuing. "But her father is not dead. He is alive."

Gabe laid down the string. "What did you say?"

"Sophie's father lives."

# *Chapter*
## 21

"*Where? How?*" Gabe stared at the monk sitting cross-legged on the floor in front of him. "Her father is Duke Baldewin. Are you telling me Duke Baldewin is alive?"

"I am."

Gabe clenched his teeth again at the monk's reticence. "How do you know this? And where is he?"

"I know it because he lives at Gemeinhart Monastery, where I lived for ten years before I came here."

"If Sophie's father is alive, then why did he leave her all alone with the evil duchess? No father could be that cruel."

"He thought she was dead. Everyone believed she was dead, including me. In fact, how do you know this woman, Sophie, is his daughter? I admit she looks like she could be his daughter, but do you have proof?" Bartel unraveled the spool a bit more and snipped off another wick.

"Well, no. Though Petra the cook, who was there when Duke Baldewin was still there, says she is. The duchess also told me Sophie was the duke's daughter."

"Duke Baldewin told me he came home from a trip to find his daughter lying dead in a casket. Supposedly dead of a fever at two years old. He left without a word to anyone and came to the monastery. The duchess then told everybody he was dead as well."

Gabe stared at the flickering candles that were casting light and shadow on the picture of Mary and Jesus. He wasn't even seeing the candles or the picture when Bartel spoke again.

"If she is Duke Baldewin's daughter, he needs to know that she's alive and try to validate her parentage himself. The duchess may have lied about this scullery maid being the duke's daughter as part of a sick ruse. His daughter may truly be dead."

If that were true, they wouldn't have to break her betrothal to Valten. Because if she wasn't Duke Baldewin's daughter, she wouldn't be betrothed to Valten. Gabe would only need to find a way to break his betrothal to Brittola. And Brittola might not even want to marry him anymore. He hadn't heard from her in months.

His spirits lifted considerably as he continued the monotonous task of cutting candlewicks. He began planning what he needed to do. He would have to go talk to this man at Gemeinhart Monastery and determine if he truly was Duke Baldewin. If Sophie found out about him, she would want to go too. But that wouldn't be wise.

He remembered how much she had enjoyed hearing about Gabe's family. She'd wanted to hear story after story about what it was like to belong to a loving family. He didn't want her to be disappointed if this man at Gemeinhart turned out to not be her father, or if he had died or didn't care about her. Gabe didn't want her heart to be broken.

"Don't tell Sophie about this."

"Don't even think about riding out yet. Your shoulder isn't healed enough."

Bartel had read his thoughts again. But Gabe would only wait a day or two, no matter what Bartel said. Then he'd go find Duke Baldewin himself.

Duchess Ermengard paid her new huntsman and watched out of the window as he left the castle and headed toward the stable—and reminded herself to tell him to shave that bushy beard. Then she stepped to her mirror to gaze at herself.

Sometimes it seemed as if the mirror was her only friend. It always told her the truth, comforting her by showing her that her nose was still perfect and straight, her teeth were still pearly white, and her lips were still plump and red.

But Sophie was still alive and living with Gabe and seven men—seven misshapen and abnormal men. At the thought of these seven, the duchess shuddered delicately, then smiled at her reflection. The men were misfits who needed to hide away in order to keep the superstitious rabble from persecuting them as men accursed and afflicted by the devil. And now they were harboring Sophie, as well as that foolish boy, Gabe, who appeared to be injured.

If her guards had done their job, he'd be dead.

Her lip curled as she thought about how she would make those seven men sorry for helping the little twit and her foolish savior. But she corrected the scowl and turned it into a smile. *There, that's better.* The mirror smiled back at her, revealing the demure expression of an enchanting duchess, beautiful and desirable.

She could contemplate her revenge without ruining the fairness of her face or creating scowl lines on her lovely skin, couldn't she?

She could not have Sophie and Gabe running around telling people that she had mistreated the *lovely* daughter of Duke Baldewin, that she, the duchess of Hohendorf, had faked the *poor* girl's death. They would speculate that she had murdered Duke Baldewin. Sophie and Gabe must die—*keep smiling*—and so must their new friends, the seven who lived in the cottage in the woods. Yes, once she disposed of Sophie, she would have them all killed. And she would have to accomplish the task herself, naturally. If a beautiful duchess wanted something done, especially revenge, then that clever, beautiful duchess must do it herself.

Yes, she still had a lovely smile. Much fairer than the smile of a dead girl. Much fairer than the grinning skull of a poisoned ... rotting ... miserable dead girl.

*Keep smiling.*

Sophie kept busy cooking and cleaning for the Seven and enjoyed the sense of family around her.

But Sophie thought about Gabe almost every moment, wondering where he was and what he was doing. It seemed that Dominyk and Bartel had conspired to keep him busy. For two days she and Gabe hadn't spent any time alone, and she had only seen him at meals and after supper, when he played with Siggy and Dominyk. Sophie found herself looking forward to that time when she could sit in the corner and watch Gabe play and listen to him sing. She loved music, but she loved his voice even more.

Gabe's skin seemed to glow tonight. He had worked outdoors quite a bit in the garden lately, giving him a healthy complexion, and he seemed at ease and happy with the other men. They all seemed to like him too. Sophie sighed happily as she settled into her corner, Gabe's gaze frequently finding her there.

Gabe didn't pick up his lute. Instead, he walked over and whispered something to Siggy, who winked at him and started playing. Then he turned and strode purposefully toward Sophie.

She held her sewing in her lap, her heart thumping hard against her chest. He looked so handsome, with the cocky half grin. Yet there was a vulnerability in his warm brown eyes that twisted her stomach. She longed to throw her arms around him and be embraced by his warmth and his scent, but she was much too aware of the seven pairs of eyes watching them.

Gabe held his hand out to her as he approached. "Dance with me."

Sophie shook her head. "I don't know how." It would have been embarrassing in itself if she hadn't been afraid of embarrassing herself worse by being in Gabe's arms in front of the seven men.

"Don't worry. I'll show you."

She placed her hand in his, and he pulled her to her feet. Grabbing her sewing as it slipped from her lap, she laid it on the chair.

"Gabe, I can't. We really shouldn't." Her face grew hot.

But he was smirking, pulling her toward the middle of the floor. He took her other hand, and with their arms tucked to their waists, holding hands side by side, he stepped in a circle. Sophie followed his lead, her eyes captured by his.

They stepped in time to the lively music, then Gabe reversed their direction by pulling her arm over her head and spinning her around. Sophie let her limbs stay loose as she tried to anticipate his next move. They moved fluidly over the floor, as if they had planned every step. She concentrated on looking him in the eye and following his lead. Her thin leather shoes glided over the smooth wood floor. What did the Seven think of the intimate way Gabe was looking at her? Her face burned, but she was afraid to look away from him.

Soon it would become obvious that she had no idea what she was doing and did not know how to dance. But Gabe continued to spin her around the floor. He made her feel pretty, like she truly was the daughter of a duke.

Questions swirled inside her head the way her skirt was swirling around her ankles, but she smiled at Gabe anyway. It was impossible not to.

The music stopped. Gabe and Sophie stopped a few moments later. They both looked over at Siggy, who gave them a sheepish glance before looking at Bartel.

Bartel stood, his arms folded underneath his robe, and stared at them from beneath lowered brows. He did not look happy.

Silence reigned. Sophie made two attempts to swallow the lump in her throat.

"Men," Bartel said, glancing around the room, "it is time for bed. Gabe and Sophie need to talk."

What was Bartel implying? Gabe did not look happy either. His expression mirrored the one on Bartel's face. She tried to pull her hand free of Gabe's, but he held on and squeezed, as if to reassure her.

The rest of the seven men were already hurrying up the stairs. When they were gone, Gabe said, "Thank you for giving us a few moments of privacy, Bartel."

"You know why I'm giving you this time. You and Sophie must talk, to ask the hard questions and be honest with each other. I will be back in a few minutes."

Without another word, he turned and stumped out of the room with his slightly lame gait.

*Ask the hard questions? Be honest with each other?* Suddenly the room seemed devoid of air.

Gabe turned to her, taking her other hand and bringing them both to his lips, looking as though he was still struggling to replace his scowl with a happier expression. "Come, we'll sit." He led her back to her chair. She set aside her sewing while he pulled another chair up next to hers.

"Bartel wanted to know what my intentions were toward you, Sophie." His thumb caressed her knuckles in a way that sent shivers across her shoulders. She tried to concentrate on his words. What would he say? That he loved Brittola more than her? That he couldn't betray his brother?

"I told him my intention is to marry you, as soon as possible, if you will have me."

His words stopped her breath as she gazed into the overwhelming intensity of his eyes.

"Will you marry me, Sophie? Give up the rank and status and wealth of marrying Valten, a man who will someday be a duke?"

She opened her mouth to say yes, but he pressed a finger over her lips.

"Don't say anything yet. I have to get this all out." He paused, as though forgetting what he was about to say as he stared at her lips. "I love you, Sophie. Bartel thinks I should unselfishly let you marry my brother, that I'm wrong to try to break the betrothal. Perhaps I am wrong. I know I'm selfish. I want you for myself. Say you love me. That you don't want my brother and don't care about his money and power and prestige."

His tone was fierce, but by the time he finished, his brown eyes were pleading. Before she could answer him, he grabbed her shoulders and drew her to him, kissing her. Sophie's arms went around his waist, almost by themselves. His kisses made the whole world disappear until she felt as though she'd stepped into a cocoon of warmth and love.

He loved her. He wanted to marry her. She was surely dreaming.

His lips moved to her cheek. She couldn't bear any more happiness or pleasure, it was too wonderful. Sophie buried her face in his shoulder.

"I love you, Gabe. I love you so much."

"If I find a way to break our betrothals, do you truly want to marry me?"

"Oh yes."

"I will marry you, Sophie. I will find a way." He stroked her hair, then her back. "Please forgive me for wanting you for myself—"

"Oh, Gabe, thank you for not giving me over to Valten. I love you, and I can't imagine feeling the same way about him. Please don't ever leave me." She squeezed him tighter, pressing her cheek against his good shoulder. Why did the pressure in her chest feel so intense, even painful? This love was wonderful and frightening at the same time. She'd never felt so vulnerable, never laid her heart bare this way, and it was exhilarating.

"I won't give you over to Valten. I'm just not that good." He pulled away and she saw the tender smile on his lips. He stroked her cheek with his fingers, sending tingles of pleasure through her. "I am selfish, but you make me want to be a better man. You make me want to be married, to have children, and to be responsible for your well-being and theirs. I want to make you happy."

He bent and pressed a soft kiss to her temple. "But we must wait a little while," he said, his warm breath caressing her forehead. "I have to work things out so that I don't disgrace you."

"Do you think your family will forgive us?"

"Of course."

"Won't Valten be angry with you?"

"Let Valten save his own damsel in distress. I'm sure there are other maidens he can fall in love with."

"What about Brittola?" She felt a pang of pity for the girl who had lost Gabe and didn't even know it yet. "Won't she be heartbroken?"

The smile disappeared from his face. "She couldn't have loved me much. She rarely wrote to me, and we had hardly spent any time together. Now stop worrying. All will be well."

He tucked her head under his chin and squeezed her tight. She could have remained there all night.

But Bartel had only promised them a short time. He would be back at any moment.

"What will you do now?"

"I have to leave in a day or two, to try to work some things out."

"Can I go with you?"

He sighed, then pulled away and pressed his palm against her cheek. "It will be best if you stay here with the Seven. They will take care of you and keep you safe."

"Why can't I go? Please take me." How could she bear to watch him leave?

"I need to do this alone. Besides, it isn't proper for us to be traveling alone together."

"You will be safe, won't you?"

"Of course. But I may not be able to be back before my father, or at least his men, come looking for you." He began to pull away from her slowly, as if reluctant to let her go. "If they insist on you going with them, go ahead and go, and I will follow you to Hagenheim Castle as soon as I can."

"You will make me face your family . . . alone?"

He gently squeezed her shoulder. "You are a brave girl. My family is not frightening. They will love you, just as I do."

Facing his family alone would not be as difficult as other things she'd done in life. After facing the wrath of Duchess Ermengard, she could surely face Gabe's family.

"He's coming." He kissed her hand just as Bartel came through the kitchen door.

"I trust you have admitted the truth between you." Bartel still had the somber look on his face, as though he was admonishing criminals.

"Yes, we have." Gabe stood but kept his hold on her hand.

"Sophie?" Bartel pinned her with a serious stare, eyebrows raised in question.

"Gabe and I are going to be married." Sophie glanced up at Gabe. The look that passed between her and Gabe made her blush. Poor Bartel, having to see them like this. She felt a little sorry for him, for anyone in the world who wasn't as happy as she was, and she figured that was everyone.

Gabe headed for the stairs, still holding her hand, and they walked up together. Surprisingly, Bartel didn't follow them, and they were able to share a kiss before Gabe whispered, "Good night, Sophie."

"Good night, Gabe."

The next two days, Bartel didn't watch them as closely as he had previously. Gabe was grateful for every minute with her. His shoulder was healing, and it was almost time for him to leave. His time was running out, as his father—and maybe even Valten—would be coming for Sophie as soon as Walther told them where they were.

The Seven had left Sophie and Gabe to clean up the breakfast dishes while they went about their various jobs. As he stood beside her at the sink, smelling the flowery soap she used, the memories of their first kiss washed over him. She had been so sweet and warm and ... he had better keep his mind on the dishes.

While he was finishing the last dish, a wet sensation on the back of his neck made him spin around, slinging water in a wide arc. Sophie squealed and laughed as the water droplets sprayed her face, and he realized she'd put a wet cloth down his shirt. He wriggled until he was able to extricate the cloth from his shirt.

His hands were dripping water onto the floor. Instead of drying them on a towel, he held them up threateningly and backed her against the wall. She was still laughing, her blue eyes dancing in the rays of light coming through the kitchen window. He placed his wet hands on her face and she giggled hysterically, holding her hands up in an ineffectual attempt to keep him away.

Staring her in the eyes, he lifted the apron and wiped her cheeks. Her radiant blue eyes focused on his lips. Dropping the apron, he pulled her close. She came willingly, pressing her lips to his.

Cleaning up after meals was his new favorite activity.

She ended the kiss and she pressed her face into his shoulder. "How is your wound?" she whispered.

"It's getting better. I can lift my arm without pain."

"Does that mean you'll be leaving soon?"

"Yes."

"Tomorrow?"

"Unfortunately."

"Won't you tell me where you're going?"

He shook his head. "I won't be away from you a moment longer than I have to. I can promise you that."

Her brows came together, forming a slight crease of worry above the bridge of her nose. He reached up and smoothed it with his finger. She wanted to know more, but if she would just be patient, he was sure it would all work out. The only problem was, he couldn't tell her *how* it was going to work out yet. Because he didn't know.

Bartel came to the back door, and Gabe and Sophie broke apart and pretended to be cleaning.

Tomorrow he'd be gone. But Sophie would be safe, and God would help him discover the truth about Sophie's identity.

*Please, God, help me work things out for Sophie and me to be together.* He hadn't wanted to seek God's will, had been afraid that God truly didn't intend for them to be together. But now he knew he needed God's favor. *You said all things work together for the good of those who love you. I wasn't listening to you before, but I know I need you now. Please let it work out, God, for me to marry Sophie. God, I will follow you, no matter what you ask me to do.*

# *Chapter*
## 22

*Sophie went about her work, and though she* had been happier last night than she had ever been, a heaviness filled her today—worry, even fear, that things would not turn out as wonderfully as Gabe believed they would. There were so many things that could go wrong. And the fact that Gabe wouldn't tell her where he was going hovered over her like a black cloud.

Was he going to see Brittola? She couldn't think where else he could be going. What if he arrived and decided he wanted to marry Brittola after all? What if he couldn't break their betrothal without angering the girl's father and placing himself in danger? When he saw Brittola, the privileged daughter of a count who had been raised knowing how to handle herself in Gabe's privledged world, he wouldn't be able to help comparing her to Sophie. After all, she was little more than a scullery maid. Her skills were limited to making meat pies and fruit custards and knowing how to scrub wood tables and stone floors. The duchess had always told her she would never marry, that all she was good for was scrubbing floors.

Perhaps her romance with Gabe had been doomed from the start.

The thought of Gabe leaving her to go to Brittola, even if he intended only to tell her he wanted to break their betrothal, filled her with pain so intense she had to stop chopping leeks and wrap her arm around her middle. "God, please help me." *Help me to bear whatever pain is in my future.*

*Don't borrow trouble*, Petra had once told her. Sophie rarely had to borrow trouble, because it was always with her, but Jesus had also said in the book of Luke, "Who of you by worrying can add a single hour to your life?" And Gabe had told her that Jesus had also said, "Don't worry about tomorrow, for each day has enough trouble of its own." Still, Sophie couldn't seem to shake this feeling of foreboding, that a wonderful future of love and marriage to Gabe was too good to be true.

Sophie had told herself she didn't believe what the duchess said about her being unlovable, but the words were like burrs, stuck in the corners of her mind, so embedded that she didn't know how to get them out. How could Gabe, who was so handsome and desirable and kind, who had grown up with loving parents, ever love someone like her? Of course he would choose Brittola over her.

Tears sprang to her eyes. She tried to blink them away, but one fell on her arm, and soon they were dripping down her face.

Gabe walked through the door at that moment and the air rushed out of her. How could she let him see her like this? How could she explain these tears? She tried to turn away from him.

"*Liebling,*" he said, using a term of endearment she'd rarely ever heard.

He pulled her into his arms while she tried to wipe away the tears that were still streaming down her face. He took the knife she'd been holding in her other hand and laid it on the table while she struggled to control herself.

He nestled her against his chest and murmured against her head, "Why are you crying? Please tell me. Did something happen?"

"I'm sorry." Sophie was ashamed of her tears, but at the same time, a warmth having more kinship with anger than anything else, welled up inside her.

"You can tell me," Gabe crooned, stroking her back.

"It is nothing. I am well."

"Please tell me."

"Nothing! It is nothing!" She pulled away from him, wiping her face with her apron. She turned her back on him.

There was only silence behind her. What was he thinking? That she was not worth his trouble?

"Are you angry with me for leaving?"

"Yes. I mean, no." She shook her head. "I'm not angry." What reason did she have to be angry? Could she be more un-dignified? More unreasonable?

He pulled her back against the hardness of his chest.

"You're leaving me." *Shut up, Sophie. Don't say any more.* "You won't tell me where you're going."

"Sophie, please. I —"

"Go back to your Brittola! Marry her! Why would you marry me when you have her?" She threw the words at him like she was hurling rocks. She knew she should stop but the words continued to flow from her mouth. "You don't deserve to have a scullery maid for a wife. Go on."

Gabe let go of her shoulders. She didn't dare turn around. Had he left? Had he gotten sick of her crying and her cruel words and walked out the door? She wouldn't blame him. She was an imbecile, a lackwit. How could she say those things to him? The pain inside her grew until it had overwhelmed all rea-son and restraint.

She wiped her face. Turning, she found Gabe still standing behind her, leaning against the kitchen table. He pulled out a chair and sat down, resting his elbows on the wood and leaning his face in his hands.

*What have I done?* Her stomach twisted at the obvious

anguish he was feeling. He probably *would* decide to go see Brittola now, even if he wasn't before. She *was* a lackwit.

He looked up at her, dropping his hands from his face. He gazed at her sadly, his brown eyes tearing at her heart. She had thought herself all cried out, but she had to bite her lip to keep from crying again. If she couldn't control herself, she'd never find out what he was thinking. Why didn't he say something? She couldn't look him in the eye after all the stupid things she'd said. *Why must I always doubt him? Doubt myself?*

Instead of speaking, Gabe simply stretched out his hand toward her.

She stared at his hand, held out to her, waiting. She moved toward him and he slipped his arm around her waist. He drew her down on his lap and buried his face in her hair.

Sophie wrapped her arms around his neck. Listening to his breathing, feeling the slight rise and fall of his shoulders, her heart gradually slowed to normal. She breathed him in.

He was leaving.

She couldn't let him leave without apologizing for her ridiculous outburst. "Forgive me, Gabe. I'm sorry for what I said." Still, he didn't move. "I'm afraid you'll marry Brittola instead of me. Please say something."

With a deep sigh, he pulled away and loosened his hold on her. "Sophie, I love you. I don't love anyone but you, and you will marry me, if I have anything to say about it. So stop trying to get rid of me." He dropped his head so their foreheads were touching. His expression was serious. "But I do expect you to trust me."

"You're right. I should trust you. I'm sorry. I know I behaved badly. I let my fear take control, and what I said was ridic—"

He stopped her with a kiss, pressing his lips firmly to hers. Then he pulled back and captured her gaze with a penetrating and somber look. "I know your stepmother did some bad things to you. She said things to you that weren't true." He spoke quietly, but unwaveringly. "My mother once told my sister, 'You must let God's love heal you.'"

Sophie touched his cheek, and he reached up and cradled her face in his hands. "You must let God's love and the blood of Jesus heal you of all those things the duchess said and did to you."

Sophie swallowed. "I will."

"My mother's childhood was a little bit like yours. She had to let God heal her, and you have to do the same. You don't have to believe those lies. You can give them to God."

Give them to God? "How do I do that?"

"God says we should cast our burdens on him and give him our cares. And you have some heavy burdens you need to give to God." He sighed. "And so do I."

"You do? What?" They were both whispering, and Sophie didn't want to break this magical moment, feeling as if Gabe was not only revealing God to her, but he was about to reveal himself to her.

He seemed to think about that, staring past her for a moment. She held her breath while she waited for him to speak.

"I should have let God heal me of the pain of being compared to my brother. Others said Valten was stronger, more of a warrior, and more responsible than I was. And I let that affect me more than I should have."

She caressed his cheek with her fingertips.

"And I think I let my guilt over my sister's death make me do stupid things and give up on myself instead of trying to be everything I should have been."

"Oh. Why would you feel guilty?"

"I was there when she died. I could have saved her if I'd only known she was drowning. I was six years old and I didn't realize what was happening until it was too late. But I so wished I had saved her. I felt responsible for her. I wished I could have spared my mother the pain of my sister's death."

Sophie's stomach twisted at the pain he must have felt, at the pain she could see in his eyes now as he was looking away from her. She hugged him close, pressing her cheek against his neck and whispering, "It wasn't your fault." His arms tightened around her, and they sat like that for a long moment.

She pulled away and looked him in the eye. "You must let God heal you of this guilt. Because I think you're very strong and capable and *very* responsible."

He gave her a tiny half smile. "And I think you're beautiful. Everything the duchess said was a lie. You are clever and resilient, yet so sweet, it makes my heart ache just to look at you."

"Then we shall both give our pain to God and let him heal us." She hugged him again. "Thank you telling me all that." As she hugged Gabe tighter, she wasn't thinking. She was only feeling . . . floating . . . sealing up the broken places of her heart with God's love . . . and Gabe's.

⋘ ⋙

Sophie held the bag of food she had packed for him—nuts, apples, cheese, bread, dried fruit, and dried strips of venison— while Gabe made sure Gingerbread's saddle was tight. He took it from her with a murmured, "Thank you," and tied it to his saddle. Then he mounted his horse. He'd hugged her and kissed her, but her heart had been so heavy, it was hard to enjoy it, especially when she knew the Seven were watching them out the kitchen window.

"Don't go anywhere without one of the men," Gabe told her for the fifth time. "The duchess might still be looking for you."

"I know. I won't."

"I'll be back for you as soon as I can, or I'll follow you to

Hagenheim." He stared hard at her. "You must trust me. I need you to trust me."

"I know. I will, Gabe." She reached up to him and he clasped her hand in his. "I think you're one of the most responsible people I know. And the bravest."

He leaned down and kissed her.

Then he left, urging his eager horse forward, disappearing through the trees.

The days seemed to stretch out long before her. But she had promised herself she wouldn't be sad. She would hold on to her happy memories of Gabe, and she would trust him to work things out and come back for her.

She sighed and went back into the kitchen, deciding to bake several fruit pies and custards and perhaps some extra bread. If she kept busy, she wouldn't have time to cry.

The men seemed to be making an effort to be cheerful that night. Siggy played only fast-paced music, and some of the men danced a jig, making Sophie laugh at their antics. She was so tired that night, after keeping herself busy all day, she fell asleep while praying for Gabe and his safety and success.

Two days after Gabe left, the sky was overcast and dreary, but as Sophie worked in the kitchen, preparing food for their night's dinner, she concentrated on remembering every conversation she'd ever had with Gabe, starting with the first day he had arrived at Hohendorf Castle. She was thinking of the day he'd gotten shot protecting her, when she saw an old woman approaching the back of the cottage. The woman was bent over, hugging a basket to her middle, a hump protruding from the place where her right shoulder blade should have been.

How odd to see another human being of any kind, but especially a woman. Sophie hurried to the back door and opened it.

"*Guten Morgen,*" Sophie called.

The old woman barely raised her head, as though her neck didn't work correctly. Something about her reminded Sophie of Pinnosa, the old woman who used to help Petra with the baking at the castle. She immediately felt a pang of sympathy for the poor woman, remembering how kind Pinnosa had been to her.

"Good mother, won't you come in?"

The seven had warned her not to let anyone in the house, but Dolf was somewhere nearby, and Bartel was in the chapel praying, or doing whatever he did in there. Surely she could not be in danger from an old woman.

The woman ambled slowly toward her, and as she drew closer, Sophie still couldn't see her face. She wore a headscarf of brightly colored cloth, and from underneath it peeked strands of white hair. Her hands appeared crippled and gnarled, and the handle of her basket hung on her wrist.

"May I help you inside?" Sophie moved forward to take the old woman's arm so she could help her the rest of the way, but the woman seemed to bristle when Sophie touched her, as though her help was unwanted. But surely Sophie imagined it.

"You mustn't mind an old woman." The woman's voice squeaked as though rusty from disuse. "I can manage. But I would like to come inside and rest a moment."

"I should think so. Did you walk far? I wasn't aware there were any other houses around here."

"Oh, I am on my way to visit my sister. She lives in a village over that way." She moved her head to indicate the direction she was heading, but Sophie hadn't heard about a village, there or anywhere else nearby. She must still have a long way to go.

Sophie helped her inside the kitchen and led her to a wooden chair. The old woman sank down heavily on it and groaned. *Poor thing.* She shouldn't be walking so far on such a warm day.

"Let me get you some cool water."

Sophie filled a clean tankard from the bucket of water she'd just brought back from the well.

"Here you are." Sophie tried to see underneath the woman's scarf, but the old woman reached up to pull it lower over her forehead. Sophie noticed that her hand wasn't nearly as wrinkled as she had initially thought. Perhaps the woman wasn't as old as her hunched back would indicate.

The woman shook her head and refused to take the water. "I have something to give you, since you are so kind to allow an old granny to rest in your kitchen." She uncovered her basket and showed Sophie a single red apple resting inside.

The hair on the back of Sophie's neck prickled, she wasn't sure why.

"Thank you." Sophie held out her hand for the gift.

The abbot took the letter Gabe handed him, the letter Bartel had written, and read it. Then the abbot stared.

"So you are Gabehart Gerstenberg, second son of Duke Wilhelm of Hagenheim."

Gabe nodded respectfully.

"I had the pleasure of meeting Duke Wilhelm once. He is a fine man and great leader."

"Thank you for saying so. He is indeed."

Gabe waited. The man stared down at the letter again. Finally, he rang a bell and a young monk entered the room through a side door.

"Go to Brother Baldewin and ask him to come. Have him wait in the anteroom."

The young man bowed and walked away.

"You may wait here." The abbot rose and left the room.

Gabe sat in the only chair available and waited. The monks had welcomed him and let him share their food. They had shown him to a room with a small cot where he had stowed his things, assuring him he was welcome to rest after his long trek. But he could not sleep until he found Duke Baldewin.

Was Sophie the duke's daughter? He found himself wishing more and more she wasn't, not only to lessen his guilt, but also the number of other meetings he would need to orchestrate to make Sophie his bride.

He should soon find out. Unless the duke refused to see him.

Gabe tapped on the arm of his chair, humming a song and thinking the words in his head. He got up and paced around the bare room, counting the cracks in the walls. The floors were very clean, but a spider with furry legs was busily building a web in the corner. Gabe watched it, impressed with the creature's structural techniques. Finally, he walked back to his chair and stared up at the ceiling. "How much longer, O Lord?" he asked aloud, just as the door opened.

"Brother Baldewin will see you now." The abbot's assistant stood in the door, his hands hidden in his robe.

Gabe crossed the room and followed the monk down a long corridor to a small chamber. Once he was inside, the abbot's assistant closed the door, leaving Gabe alone with a still form. As his eyes adjusted to the light, or lack thereof, he saw the form was actually a man wearing the same brown robe as the monk who had brought him here. The man was kneeling at the back of the room facing a small crucifix on the wall, his head bowed over his clasped hands.

Was Duke Baldewin praying? Gabe wasn't sure if he should interrupt, so he stood and waited, staring at the kneeling figure, willing him to look up and acknowledge his presence.

"You wished to speak to me?" The figure didn't move.

"Yes, Your Grace."

"Don't call me 'Your Grace.' I have not been that person for fifteen years now. You may simply call me Brother Baldewin."

The man still had not moved. His face and head were hidden by the cowl of his robe.

"Thank you for agreeing to see me, Brother Baldewin." Speaking to a person's back was a little uncomfortable, especially when what Gabe had to say was already difficult. But he was too anxious to have his questions answered to spend much time dwelling on how to broach the subject.

"I have come seeking information, and I believe I may have information of great interest to you as well." Gabe hoped Baldewin would say something to make this easier. But there was only silence.

"My name is Gabehart Gerstenberg. Many years ago my brother, Valten, was betrothed to your only daughter, whom we believed to be dead. We were recently told by a servant woman named Pinnosa that your daughter was still alive and living at Hohendorf castle."

Gabe wasn't sure if it was his imagination, but the man's body seemed to become more and more tense and rigid the more Gabe talked. His head had inched up and his back had straightened ever so slightly.

"My daughter," he rasped, his voice vastly changed, "is dead. I saw her body lying in a casket when she was but two years old. She died while I was away, but I saw her—" His voice cracked.

"Forgive me for bringing to mind such a painful memory." Gabe shifted from one foot to the other, then rubbed his stubbly chin and cheek. He couldn't stop now. He had to find out for sure, for everyone's sake.

Gabe waited, and Baldewin finally sat back on his heels and rubbed his face with both hands. He lowered the cowl from his head, letting it lay in folds around his neck, and looked over his shoulder at Gabe.

"Pray, go on." His voice was steadier.

Baldewin's hair was a mix of gray and white; he had strong

features, but nothing that particularly reminded Gabe of Sophie. Perhaps Sophie wasn't Baldewin's daughter. Perhaps she truly was an orphan from nobody-knew-where.

But he had to find out for sure. Sophie—and Duke Baldewin—deserved to know the truth.

"Two or three weeks ago, I decided to go to Hohendorf Castle to investigate whether this story was true, whether Sophia, your daughter, was still alive. The old woman who told us this wild tale had said that the girl was in danger from Duchess Ermengard. When I arrived, I found that there was a young woman matching the old woman's description—black hair, pale skin, blue eyes, and great beauty—serving at the castle as a scullery maid. This young woman knew nothing of her parents and had been told by the duchess that she was a poor orphan. The duchess kept her in servitude in the castle."

The man turned and fixed his deep blue eyes on Gabe. Those eyes. They were quite similar in shape and color to Sophie's.

"What you say rings somewhat true." Baldewin stood slowly to his feet and faced Gabe. "I can easily imagine Duchess Ermengard doing such a thing to my daughter. But I saw Sophie's body myself, laid out in her favorite dress, lying as still as a stone." He turned away, staring back at the crucifix. "I had just returned from a trip to some holdings several miles to the east. I was only gone for a few days, but how I wish I had never gone ... wish I'd done anything but left my little Sophie."

The duke seemed overcome with grief and said no more. Gabe spoke softly.

"Pinnosa said that the child had been given a sleeping potion. Apparently, the duchess wanted everyone to think your daughter was dead."

Slowly, slightly, Baldewin nodded his head. "I left as soon as I saw her lifeless body. I wanted nothing more to do with Hohendorf. I had lost my gentle wife and had married a fiend in her place. Losing my little Sophie broke something inside me. I didn't want to live, didn't want my responsibilities. I simply left and never went back."

"Are you aware," Gabe said, feeling that he was closing in on the truth, "that the duchess has told everyone that you are dead as well? My father, Duke Wilhelm, believed you died with your daughter of the same fever that supposedly killed her fifteen years ago."

His shoulders stooped, Baldewin stood still and silent. Finally, he shook his head. "I didn't know. I didn't care about anything when I came here, and I haven't communicated with anyone since coming here. Here I'm known only as Brother Baldewin. Only a few brothers, including the abbot, know who I am or that I am even here.

"But it's also possible," Baldewin went on, "that Ermengard let poor, old Pinnosa believe a lie and that this Sophie isn't my daughter at all. Ermengard enjoys"—he paused as he seemed to be searching for the right word—"twisting other people's lives with her deceptions, so I can imagine her perpetrating a trick of that kind."

"I thought of that as well." Gabe took a step toward the duke. "But there is one thing that might prove, or disprove, that she is your daughter." Gabe took a deep breath, concentrating on Baldewin's reaction as he said the next words. "Was your daughter born with a small brown mark somewhere on her body?"

Baldewin got a faraway look in his eyes. Finally, he spoke, his voice cracking again. "On her neck, below her right ear. It looked like a five-petal flower."

Gabe swallowed. "The very same as my Sophie."

# Chapter
## 23

*The apple is quite unnaturally red. The thought* seemed to drift through Sophie's mind as though seeking somewhere to land. Why did this make her pull her hand away? It was only an apple. If it was redder than usual, what did that matter?

"Go on. Take it." The old woman picked up the apple and held it out to Sophie. "An apple from my orchard. They're the sweetest apples in the Empire."

Sophie reached out her hand again and took the fruit, noticing again that the old woman's hands didn't look like the hands of an old woman. In fact, the hands looked familiar.

The old woman hid her hands in the folds of her shawl, as if she realized Sophie was staring at them. Sophie was frustrated about being unable to see her face, which was still mostly hidden underneath the cowl of her shawl.

"Go on. Take a bite," the old woman encouraged.

Sophie stared at the fruit. It did look good. But something continued to nag at her. There was something almost sinister about the way the woman seemed so eager to give her the fruit. But sometimes people became addled in their old age. Sophie should humor her.

"What is your name, good mother? Perhaps I've heard of your orchard."

The woman jerked her basket impatiently. "Oh, I don't think so. I only share my fruit with a small number of people."

Sophie waited for the woman to reveal her name. She was fidgeting with the basket, and Sophie had the urge to punch her hump to see if it was real. A strange thought. But Sophie was more determined than ever to find out the woman's name and why she was so eager for Sophie to eat the apple. It reminded her of the story the priest often told from Scripture, of the serpent who tempted Eve to eat the forbidden fruit.

"My name? You want to know my name?" The old woman sounded agitated. Her voice wasn't as raspy now as it had been before, and suddenly Sophie knew. This was no old woman. This was Duchess Ermengard.

Sophie's hand began to tremble. Her knees went weak, and she took a step back. "I-I think I w-will eat the apple later." She carefully set it down on the table beside her.

"Eat it now!" The woman stood to her feet, stood tall, no longer bent over, and allowed the shawl to fall from her head. The duchess's face was without its white powder and was quickly turning red. Her lips twitched, and her eyes were wide and gleamed dangerously down at Sophie from her great height.

"Eat the apple," she hissed. "I didn't come all this way to fail now. Eat it, I say." She picked up the apple and shoved it in Sophie's face.

"No." Sophie clenched her teeth and pursed her lips tightly, afraid the duchess would try to force it into her mouth. She backed up another step and the duchess followed her until Sophie's back was pressed against the wooden counter.

"Stay away from me." Sophie tried to think how she could defend herself against the duchess. Her stomach clenched in fear, but then anger arose inside her. "You have no right to hurt me. Get out of here." Her legs trembled, but she would fight this woman if she had to. She couldn't allow her and Gabe's efforts to escape the duchess end in tragedy. She had too much to live for. *I will not let you harm me.* Heat rose inside her as she stared at the duchess, rage so strong Sophie could barely focus her eyes.

But getting angry wouldn't help her. She had to think clearly, to get the attention of Bartel and Dolf. She could scream, but Bartel probably wouldn't hear her from inside the chapel, and Dolf couldn't hear her at all, even though he was most likely nearby.

"I came all this way to get rid of you," the duchess rasped, leaning closer, still holding the apple in Sophie's face. "And I will not be denied."

Sophie cast her gaze over the room. She would have to knock the duchess down, somehow get past her and to the door. She glanced at the counter but it was cleared off and there was nothing she could use as a weapon.

"Why do you hate me so much?" She would stall the duchess with talking. Meanwhile she hoped Dolf or Bartel would come into the kitchen, as unlikely as that seemed. *God, please help me! Send someone or something to help me or show me what to do.*

"You think you're clever, trying to distract me." The duchess's lips curled into a sneer. "But I will tell you anyway. I hate you because you are younger, and everyone thinks you are more beautiful. I hate you most of all because your father loved you more than he loved me. He didn't love me the way he loved you and your precious mother, no matter how I tried to gain his attention. I hate your dead mother, I hate you, and I hate Duke Baldewin. I drove him to despair by making him think you were dead, and it was one of the greatest moments of my life." She smiled maliciously, her gaze unflinching as she stared into Sophie's eyes.

Sophie thought again about trying to push the duchess down, about kicking her, fighting her, but the duchess was bigger and taller. How could she overpower her?

"I thought about poisoning you as I had been poisoning him, but I had to plan my greatest revenge out carefully." Her lips puckered in a moue of pity. "I couldn't allow the king to put me in his dungeon, could I?"

"Isn't the apple poisoned?"

"Of course. But how will anyone prove I did it? You are so far away from Hohendorf, and everyone in the surrounding villages knows I never leave the castle. No one knows I am here now. I have new guards, you see, ones who will not become deserters and fail me, and they are under orders to tell anyone who comes to my chambers that I am ill. And I shall kill anyone who dares say I left Hohendorf's grounds."

"You don't have to do this." Sophie's back ached from pressing against the counter behind her. "I won't return to Hohendorf. You never have to see me again." The duchess had no reason to know where she was planning to go or the life that awaited her in Hagenheim with Gabe.

"I can't risk letting you live." The duchess's eyes were cold and black, and from the way the strands of white hair at her temple were trembling, her whole body must have been shaking. "I shouldn't have kept you alive as long as I did. I simply enjoyed tormenting you too much and imagining how bad Baldewin would feel if he knew." She cackled, a cruel laugh.

"I won't tell anyone you were here if you go now." Sophie kept her voice calm. Perhaps she could soothe the duchess into letting down her guard.

"I'm not leaving until you're dead. Lorencz failed me, but I will see this through."

She pushed the apple against Sophie's lips so hard Sophie felt her teeth cut her lip, tasted blood as she turned her head. Sophie grabbed the apple, wrenched it out of the duchess's hand, and threw it across the room.

A sharp slap resounded through the room. Sophie lifted her

arms to protect herself, her cheek stinging where the duchess had struck her. When she opened her eyes and focused, the duchess was smiling. In her hand, poised above her shoulder, gleaming in the room's meager light, was a knife.

It was true, Gabe realized. Sophie was the duke's daughter. Gabe was in love with Valten's betrothed.

Duke Baldewin covered his face and fell to his knees, moaning. "I should have stayed instead of running away like a coward. I should have gone back. I should have protected my little girl." He began weeping, his shoulders shaking.

Gabe ran his hand over his stubbly jaw. *Perhaps I should have broken the news to him more gently.*

The duke lifted his tear-stained face. "Is she safe? Is she well? Where is she?"

"Yes, she's safe and well. I left her with Bartel at the Cottage of the Seven, two days' ride west of here. I will take you to her as soon as you're ready to leave." The sooner the better, since his father would be arriving at the cottage any day now to take her to Hagenheim.

Baldewin groaned piteously, bowing his head to the stone floor. "How will she stand the sight of me after I left her with that witch?"

Gabe had never seen a grown man in such anguish of spirit — nor any man with more cause.

"It's not your fault, Your Gra — Brother Baldewin. You couldn't have known. You thought your daughter was dead." Gabe stared down at him, wondering what else he could do or say to comfort the duke. "The duchess did this, not you. You mustn't blame yourself."

"I should have known. I should have felt in my spirit that she was still alive." He groaned again.

This hadn't been what Gabe had expected. He'd thought the duke would be happy that his daughter was alive, would joyfully grasp Gabe's hand and grant his permission for Gabe to marry Sophie after learning how he'd saved her from the duchess. Gabe had imagined the duke being more than glad to go to Duke Wilhelm and Valten to ask them to break the betrothal so Gabe could marry the daughter Baldewin long thought dead but who was now alive. And perhaps she would be dead, if not for Gabe. Gabe would be sure to mention that.

But now ... Gabe's grand plans for a joyous reunion seemed to be dashed, or at least delayed. What could he say that would bring the duke to a point of action? Perhaps he should allow the duke some time to grieve. If only it wasn't so urgent that they hurry.

Gabe sat on the floor a few feet away, leaning against the wall. *God, help Duke Baldewin forgive himself. Help him to know you forgive him as well.*

Gabe wasn't sure how much time had gone by, maybe half an hour, when the duke lifted his head and said, "Can you leave me alone for a while? I need to pray."

"Of course." Gabe got up and went to the small cell where he would be staying. The sun would be setting soon, and he was tired. He hated to go to bed with things so unsettled, especially since he'd hoped the duke would agree to leave with him early in the morning to go back to Sophie. Suddenly, he was filled with uneasiness about leaving her and felt an urge to go back. But it was probably only because he'd seen Baldewin's great regret at leaving her all those years ago, the great price Baldewin was paying for not realizing she was still alive. He'd missed his only child's entire life.

Gabe lay down on his thin mattress. No use staying awake. He closed his eyes and allowed himself a needed nap.

Sophie screamed as she grabbed the duchess's wrist. She forced the knife back as she squeezed the center of the duchess's wrist in desperation, knowing she was sending sharp pain through the duchess's hand. The duchess dropped the knife but yanked Sophie's hair with her other hand, yanked it so hard Sophie screamed again. Then the duchess, still holding her hair, threw her down forcefully. Sophie's head hit the edge of the kitchen table.

Everything went black. Sophie blinked hard, trying to ignore the pain in her head. When her eyes focused again, the duchess was again holding the knife. She plunged it toward Sophie.

Before Sophie could react, she felt the knife strike her chest hard.

She was surprised to find the pain in her head was actually worse than the pain in her chest. But she could not deny the knife was lodged in the middle of her chest. *I am going to die.* "Lord Jesus, receive my spirit," Sophie whispered, then closed her eyes.

Duchess Ermengard had done it. She'd finally killed her.

She stared down at the blood that was pooling at the side of Sophie's head and the knife sticking out of the girl's chest. Then she leaned her head back and laughed hard and long, sucking in great draughts of air between the peals of laughter. "That will teach you to run away from me, you selfish, little ungrateful twit."

Now to show those seven misfits and the rest of the world that they couldn't defeat Ermengard, Duchess of Hohendorf. She stuck her hand in the kitchen fireplace and grabbed the unburned end of a piece of wood. Holding the burning end out in front of her, she carried it into the main part of the house. She looked around until she spied a basket with several articles of clothing—obviously someone's mending. She stuck the burning end of the wood into the basket. The fire caught the fabric and blazed up.

She turned to leave and found herself staring at a man, quite tall, with brown hair and a shocked expression on his sun-tanned face.

"Out of my way or I'll kill you too."

The man merely stared at her, a perplexed look coming over his face.

She pushed past him and hurried toward the door, the heavy peasant-style skirts slowing her down.

Suddenly, the man let out an animal-like sound that sent ice through the duchess's veins. She didn't turn around but ran out the door, hoping he was occupied with putting out the fire.

*Sophie is dead. Sophie is dead.* The thought was so wonderful, she let it pound through her head over and over as she ran toward the river. If she could reach the bridge over the river, she could get to her horse on the other side and then Sophie's little men would never catch her.

A bell started ringing loud and sharp behind her. She turned her head. The tall man was yanking on the string of a large bell at the side of the house, then he started running after her.

The duchess picked up her skirts and ran faster. A shout came from behind her, then another. It seemed all seven men must have been alerted and were shouting and getting closer to her. She kept running, laughing because Sophie was dead. But she couldn't let them catch her. She couldn't let them take her to the king. If King Sigismund found out what she'd done, he would certainly have her hanged.

She jumped over a dead tree trunk, surprised at her own speed and agility. Crouching to avoid a low tree branch, she glanced over her shoulder and saw that the men were getting closer, the tall brown-haired man closest.

No. She was so near the river now. But she would never make it to the bridge. The man was too fast. She was not a very good swimmer, but she had no choice. She ran to the bank and jumped into the rushing stream.

She sank, the coldness of it taking her breath away. Fighting her way to the surface was hard, too hard. She flung about, trying to loosen herself from whatever was dragging her to the bottom. Until she realized her impediment was her clothes. They were saturated with water and pulling her down.

She grabbed a root that was sticking out of the side of the bank and pulled with all her strength, drawing herself above the surface. Gasping for breath, she clung to the bank, mud sinking under her now broken fingernails.

Her clothes were so, so heavy.

The brown-haired man was beside her. He grabbed her arm and started to pull her up, but she slapped his hand away. She couldn't let him capture her. They would all despise her for killing Sophie. They would turn her over to the king.

She let go of the bank and the man's grip on her wet arm slipped as he lost his hold on her. She was free of him but had to fight to keep her head above water. The river's current pulled her downstream even as her heavy garments pulled her under.

Desperation gripped her as her chest began to ache from lack of air. She fought to get herself back to the surface, but the current was pulling her downstream too quickly. Finally she began to rise to the top again. She gasped, then choked, flailing her arms and splashing water. Again, the brown-haired man leaned over the edge of the bank and grabbed her, getting purchase on both of her arms this time and holding her up. He began to drag her out, but when she stopped sputtering and got a good deep breath into her lungs, she saw several other men's faces, all staring down at her in horror and anger.

No. They would capture her. She couldn't let them, especially not them. "Let me go!" she screamed at the man, but he only looked at her as if she hadn't said anything, still pulling her farther onto the bank. Two more men stepped forward and reached for her. "No! Let go!" She lifted her hands to the tall man's face and dragged her broken, ragged fingernails down his cheeks.

He cried out and let her go. She fell backward into the river with a splash.

The current grabbed her again, readily embracing her even as her cloak weighed her down. The shouts from the men seemed to come from far away, muffled and gurgled. Fighting to get back to the surface, she also tried to propel herself to the opposite side of the river, away from the men. But suddenly she wasn't moving at all. Something was holding her in place. Frantically she flailed her arms under the water but she wasn't heading upward or downstream. Then she saw that the skirt of her dress was caught on a root at the bottom of the river. She tugged at her skirt, trying to rip it, but it wouldn't give.

She was going to die. Her strength was ebbing. Her chest was burning almost unbearably, causing her to swallow mouthfuls of water.

After all the things she had done, she couldn't ask God for help or mercy. She would soon face the consequences.

But at least Sophie was dead.

# Chapter
## 24

*Gabe lay on the cot, unable to fall to sleep,* even though he'd spent two days of riding hard and a night sleeping in the forest. He found himself listening for the sound of someone coming to fetch him, or for the duke himself. The longer he lay there, the more anxious he became about getting back to Sophie. When he could lie still no longer, he got up and went to ask for some water so he could clean himself up.

Was the duke still lying on the floor after hearing his daughter was alive? Surely he had come to his senses and was happy about the news Gabe had brought. Or was he still wracked with guilt, knowing that the duchess had treated his daughter horribly?

After washing himself up a bit, Gabe pulled on his boots, left his chamber, and went in search of the duke. A young boy scurried up to him and offered to take him to dinner.

"Can you take me to the du—I mean, Brother Baldewin?"

"He said to tell you he is still praying and can't be disturbed."

Gabe blew out a frustrated breath and agreed to follow the boy to the dining hall.

The boy led him to the abbot's table, where they feasted on roast beef, eel soup, fresh bread, and stewed fruit. But he could hardly enjoy it, eager as he was to get back to Sophie. What was she doing now? Cleaning up the supper dishes? Spending time with the Seven as they played their musical instruments and sang for her? They adored her, but who wouldn't? She was sweetness and beauty personified. And she was his. He wouldn't give her up to Valten, not now, not ever.

*She deserves to be Valten's wife, to be privileged and pampered.*

Gabe shifted uncomfortably in his chair. He wouldn't listen to that voice.

But it came again. *Wouldn't she be happier with Valten? After all, he is the responsible one, the one who can give her everything.*

Sweat broke out on Gabe's forehead and trickled down his temple. *She doesn't love Valten,* Gabe answered the voice defiantly. *She loves me. She wants me.*

*How do you know?* the voice argued. *Instead of giving her a chance to choose, you tried to confuse her with kisses and premature declarations of love.*

Gabe stared down at his food, his appetite lost.

Sophie blinked and realized she was lying on the floor. The second thing she realized was that her head hurt, and the third thing was that the seven men were hovering over her, and most of them had tears running down their cheeks.

"Just lie still, Sophie," Bartel said.

She had never thought she would ever see the calm and impassive Bartel looking so pale and horror-stricken. "What is it? Is my head bleeding?"

They bent closer. Their eyes were all moving from her face to her chest, back and forth, with horror and curiosity. Sophie looked down and gasped. The knife was still sticking out of her chest. She cried out, then gasped again, surprised she didn't feel great pain.

Bartel glanced around at the men hovering about. "Someone bring me some clean cloths and bandages."

A few of the men went scrambling around and quickly brought two stacks of cloths. Bartel pressed two of the cloths against the side of Sophie's head, making her wince at the sharp pain. Bartel motioned for Vincz to come over and continue holding the fabric to her head. "Hold it firmly so it will stop bleeding."

Next, Bartel focused on the knife that was sticking out of her chest. Indeed, it looked gruesome, and there was a sting in her chest, but she didn't feel as if she was dying. Even though she surely must be. A person didn't survive a knife wound like this, did they?

"Just hold still," Bartel said again as he reached down and took hold of the knife's handle, his gaze flicking to her eyes, then down to the knife again. Bartel gave a short tug and the knife easily came up — along with the wooden cross she wore around her neck.

Sophie grabbed hold of the necklace still underneath her dress, and Bartel yanked on the knife, pulling it out of the pendant. Then Sophie lifted the necklace over her head and held it up.

Looking down, she saw the blood soaking through her clothing where the knife point had gone all the way through the wooden cross and into her skin. Bartel leaned over and pulled her neckline down just enough to see where she was bleeding and probed the wound with his finger.

He looked around at the men. "It isn't serious." He reached for another cloth and pressed it to her chest. "She will survive."

She looked at each of the seven faces huddled around her, whose expressions were rapidly changing from abject grief, to joy and relief.

"She stabbed my cross." Sophie's voice revealed the wonder she was feeling, and she laughed.

Vincz started laughing too. Bartel said, "The cross must have stopped the blade from penetrating her breastbone. The duchess thought she had killed you, but the cross took the brunt of her blow."

Dolf sank to the floor beside her, smiling and taking over holding the cloths to Sophie's head for Vincz, who started wiping his tears on his sleeve.

A spontaneous whoop went up from Siggy, Dominyk, and Gotfrid.

Heinric, however, burst in loud sobs and cried, "Sophie hurt! Sophie hurt!" His sobs were so loud they vibrated the floor and reminded Sophie of the pain in her head and of how her head had struck the edge of the table in her struggle with the duchess.

Siggy went to try to comfort Heinric and distract him while the other men asked her how she was feeling and told her not to get up just yet.

She noticed Dolf kneeling beside her. "Oh! What happened to your face?" Red scratches, three on both sides of his face, were oozing blood. "She did this to you, didn't she?" Pity rose up inside her for her friend. "Does it hurt very much?"

Vincz signed her words to him, and Dolf shook his head, making a quick gesture with his hand.

"Nothing. It's nothing," Vincz interpreted for Dolf.

"Nonsense. We must wash those scratches with clean water." Sophie clicked her tongue against her teeth.

"I'll take care of it," Bartel said, letting Gotfrid hold the cloth to her chest.

Sudden fear gripped her. "Where is she now?" Sophie whispered. She made the sign for *where* to Dolf, one of the signs the men had taught her.

Dolf shook his head. He closed his own eyes, pushing his eyelids down with his fingers.

"She's dead," Dominyk explained.

"You're safe from her now," Gotfrid said, scowling. "She won't harm you again."

"What happened?"

"She drowned," Dominyk said. "Dolf tried to pull her out of the river several times, and she scratched him. By the time we fished her out, she had drowned."

"Oh." Sophie felt numb as Bartel washed the blood off her head and bandaged it. Then she insisted he wash Dolf's scratches. Dolf let Bartel wash his scratches, but when he wanted to apply some of his green paste to the scratches, Dolf pulled away and grunted and gestured no.

"Dolf, you must," Sophie said. "I insist you let him do it."

The other men signed to Dolf what Sophie said and he instantly sat back down and didn't move while Bartel applied his green salve to Dolf's face.

After the men helped her up and into a chair, Dolf made some signs to her.

"Dolf wants to know what happened to you, what the duchess did to you," Vincz said.

Sophie's voice shook as she told of the duchess appearing as an old, crippled woman, how she'd offered Sophie a poisoned apple and then come after her with the knife, and how Sophie had tried to fight her off. She shuddered, remembering the hatred in the duchess's eyes.

After she finished the tale, Dominyk handed her necklace back to her, its face now marred by a hole shaped like a knife blade. Several of the men crossed themselves when they got a better look at the necklace, their faces pale. Heinric began crying again, tears streaming down his face until Bartel went to get him a cloth to wipe his face and blow his nose.

A strange feeling came over Sophie as she thought about the duchess drowning, refusing help, dying at the bottom of the river. The thought of her having to face God made her feel sick. But now Sophie was truly safe. Wasn't she? Somehow it still didn't feel real.

Gabe spent the rest of the evening waiting for Duke Baldewin to send for him. He prayed for a while in his room, then went out to the stable to groom his horse, making sure Gingerbread hadn't suffered any bad effects from their hard ride to the monastery.

His feeling of uneasiness about being away from Sophie had increased. If the duke wasn't going to talk to him today, perhaps Gabe should go back to the Cottage of the Seven and bring Sophie here to see her father. But that might not be a good idea. With Sophie riding along, he didn't think they could make the trip as quickly, which would put him alone with her for too long … No, if he went to fetch Sophie, he'd have to bring Bartel and at least one of the other men with them.

The same little boy who'd greeted him two hours ago came running into the stable. "Sir, Brother Baldewin wishes to speak with you now."

Gabe left his horse, who looked well taken care of, and hurried to the monastery's main building.

The boy led him to Baldewin's own small cell, the gray walls bare, with no furnishings except a narrow bed, a stool, and a bench. His face and hair looked newly scrubbed and clean and his expression was blank as he nodded at the bench in front of him.

Gabe sat. He waited for the duke to break the silence and start the conversation, but after several minutes, Gabe decided to broach the subject that had been on his mind since he'd arrived.

"Brother Baldewin, I know the news I gave you yesterday was unexpected, but I urge you to let me escort you to your daughter right away. We could leave now and be there in two days." *Please, God, let him say yes.*

The duke's hands were hidden inside the sleeves of his coarse woolen robe. He lifted his head, and his bloodshot eyes met

Gabe's. "Tell me everything. I'm ready to hear it now. How did you come to find her?"

Gabe took a deep breath. Not what he wanted to hear, but he had no choice but to be patient with Sophie's father.

He told him of Pinnosa's tale and her death, how he'd felt compelled to go find and rescue Sophie, and the fact that his brother Valten, Sophie's betrothed, had a broken leg and couldn't travel. He told of how he and Sophie escaped the duchess and how he had been shot by their pursuer, one of the duchess's guards.

"So my daughter is with Bartel — with the Seven?"

Gabe nodded.

Baldewin seemed to hug his arms closer to his chest and stared down at the floor.

Just as Gabe was about to again suggest they leave to go to her, Baldewin spoke.

"So you've spent time alone with my daughter. What are your intentions? Do you love her?"

"Yes, Your Grace — Brother Baldewin. I have come to love her deeply, and I believe Valten will give his assent to allow me to marry her, if you will also give your permission."

The duke gave Gabe a sharp look, then stared at the floor again. "What does Sophie want? Does she love you?"

"Yes." He swallowed hard, his mouth suddenly dry. "She wants to marry me."

"Even though she's betrothed to your brother, the future Duke of Hagenheim?"

"Yes, Your Grace." Gabe stared back defiantly while quaking inside.

"Do you think it is God's will that she marry you and not Valten? Do you think your brother is so unworthy?"

Gabe's breath shallowed as he fought to think of an appropriate response to questions he'd not yet been able to answer.

What was the truth? He was in a monastery with a man of God and prayer. He felt the pressure to be as truthful as possible.

"Valten is not unworthy." He took a deep breath and let it out slowly. "Valten is ... a good man. But perhaps there was a purpose in Valten breaking his leg when he did, and Pinnosa arriving while my brother was unable to travel. God knew what he was doing, surely. He put the urgency in *my* spirit to send me to Sophie. Perhaps it was His will for us to be together." *And the strange thing is, I believe that. Please let Baldewin believe as well.*

But Baldewin didn't seem moved by Gabe's impassioned speech. He frowned. "Or perhaps you only want it to be so."

Gabe felt anger rise inside him, but he pushed it down. He had to keep a steady head. He needed Sophie's father as an ally, not an enemy.

"I know it sounds bad. It sounds as if I am taking advantage of an opportunity to get myself a duke's daughter to wed, as if I'm stealing her away from her rightful betrothed." Gabe swallowed past the scratchiness in his throat, wishing he hadn't said the words. They sounded much too damning. He wasn't sure he even liked himself anymore. "But I set out with a noble cause, with noble intentions. I intended to bring her back safely to Valten. I never wished to betray my brother or take away what is rightfully Sophie's. But I fell in love with her in spite of myself. I love her and she loves me, and now I can't imagine living without her."

Baldewin softened his features with a partial smile. "But perhaps you are right. God can do anything. Perhaps he wanted you to find my daughter and save her. But you know and admit that I could see it otherwise. A less sincere man than yourself, for example, could see this as an opportunity to raise his own position in the world. The second son of a duke has fewer prospects for wealth and authority. But ... if he should convince the daughter of a duke to fall in love with him ... to break her betrothal ..."

Gabe's stomach sank, but he wasn't about to give up.

"What you say, sir, is true. But I am not that avaricious person. I had no thoughts of betrayal or advancement when I set out." Would Baldewin believe him? "I fought each feeling I encountered. I thought of her only as my brother's betrothed—"

"So you went to her rescue because your brother asked you to?"

It was very hot in the tiny cell, and stuffy. "I went to her rescue because I—I wanted to help her, a lady in need. Her situation sounded dire ... and I wanted to prove I could save her myself."

"So you didn't go because God urged you to."

Gabe took a deep breath to calm himself. "I'm being completely honest with you." Couldn't the man appreciate that? "If I hadn't come when I did, Sophie might be dead now." He flung the words at the duke, but regretted them when Brother Baldewin pressed his lips together. A flicker of pain crossed his features just before he closed his eyes.

"Forgive me," Gabe said. "The truth is, I love your daughter with my very soul, and I beg you to allow me to marry her. I promise to provide for her, to give her everything she needs, everything she wants. I'll treat her like a princess, for to me she is a princess."

"And if your brother were not betrothed to her, are you free from any obligations? Have your parents not betrothed you to a local nobleman's daughter?"

Gabe tried not to choke. "I agreed to marry a count's daughter a year ago."

Baldewin was quiet. Gabe bowed his head and waited. He must seem like a man who didn't keep his promises and wouldn't be faithful. A bead of sweat ran down Gabe's back as Baldewin remained silent. The duke would never help him now.

"I know how it must appear to you, but I love Sophie,"

Gabe said. "And she loves me and we want to be married. Please help us."

Baldewin slid to his knees on the stone floor and turned to face a small crucifix on the wall beside him. "Come. Come and pray with me. We shall ask God his will. You must pray sincerely, from your heart, to know God's will for you ... whether or not you and Sophie should marry."

Gabe got on his knees beside the duke and clasped his hands in front of him, staring at the small statue of Jesus dying on the cross. He closed his eyes against the picture of his Savior's suffering, but the image was imprinted inside his eyelids, it seemed.

He willed his mind to concentrate, to focus on asking God what he wanted for him, but he found himself begging God to let him marry Sophie, to influence the duke to agree.

He shook himself mentally. *God, if it is best for Sophie to marry Valten, please tell me so now.*

He waited, emptying his mind of all thought.

Gabe bent lower, still listening. *God, you sent me to Sophie. I know you did.* He clasped his hands tighter. *If it be your will that we marry, I promise I will protect and love her and be the best husband I can be. I'll love her till I die. Please speak to Baldewin and myself and make your desires known, make it known that you want Sophie to marry me and not Valten.*

Gabe continued to kneel silently. *God, I need your approval, as well as Baldewin's, Valten's, and ... Brittola's.* How could he marry Sophie without hurting Brittola? No doubt it was inevitable, but it would be for the best for everyone ... somehow.

Gabe's knees were aching and his thighs were starting to cramp. Finally, Baldewin sat back on his heels and sighed audibly. His eyes were still closed, and his lips continued to move silently, but then he crossed himself and fixed Gabe with a blue-eyed stare.

"If Sophie loves you and wants to marry you, then you

have my blessing. But you still have to convince your father and Valten to release Sophie from the betrothal, and your betrothed's father to release you as well."

Gabe let out the breath he'd been holding and had an almost irresistible urge to clap the man on the back. But he thought better of it and managed to contain his joy. "Thank you, sir. You shall not regret it, I promise you. I'll make Sophie the happiest woman on earth."

"Yes. You will. Or you'll have to answer to me." Baldewin glared, then allowed himself a slight smile. "Now help me up. It's time I ate."

# *Chapter*
## 25

*As Sophie and the seven men sat down to* breakfast, she thought about the way Gabe used to finagle in order to be able to sit beside her. She missed his smile and the look in his eyes whenever she glanced his way. *Hurry back to me, Gabe.*

*What if he never comes back?*

The worrisome thought haunted her. Being able to marry him still seemed too good to be true.

But she mustn't think this way. Gabe had asked her for one thing, and that was her trust. *I need you to trust me*, he'd said. And she'd promised to do that. Didn't that trust include believing that he would come back for her?

Once she finished eating her breakfast of eggs and fruit pasty, the Seven helped her clear away their dishes, carrying it all to the sink before the men headed outside. Today they would bury the duchess.

A numbness seeped into Sophie's bones as she stared at her stepmother, laid out on the dirt beside the root cellar, where they had kept her overnight.

Perhaps Sophie should have been relieved that her stepmother would never hurt her again. But mostly she just felt ... numb. Speechless. Cold and dull. She touched the bandage on her chest.

The duchess had directed so much evil at Sophie, and now she was dead.

Sophie shivered and wrapped her hands around her arms, wishing Gabe would come back. She longed for his warmth, for his confident brown eyes that always made her feel safe and loved and wanted.

But Sophie now realized God was capable of keeping her safe. He'd protected her with her own wooden cross. And God loved her, she knew, from what the Bible and the priest and Gabe said. And because she knew God wanted to heal Gabe of his past hurts, she knew he wanted to heal her too. She just had to let him.

She turned and went back into the kitchen to start the midday meal.

She refused to look out the window while she threw herself into her task, baking extra bread and pies and starting a stew for the evening meal. When she finished, she went outside to call the men.

Apparently the Seven had removed the body—Sophie didn't care where as long as she didn't have to see it—and none of them were in sight. But two figures on horseback emerged from the trees near the river. Sophie recognized them at once.

"Petra! Roslind!" Sophie ran to meet them, almost tripping over her dress in her headlong rush.

"Sophie!" Roslind cried as she dismounted. "You're safe. We snuck away as soon as we realized the duchess was truly gone."

Petra, who'd begun dismounting as soon as Sophie had come outside, reached Sophie first and threw her arms around her, laughing and crying at the same time.

Roslind continued. "We prayed for you, and Petra said you would be well, that God would take care of you. Is Gabe here? Did Walther find you? We are quite famished. Do you have any food?"

Sophie laughed at Roslind's childlike speech. She hugged both women together, then each of them separately.

"It's so wonderful to see you! However did you make it here by yourselves? No, don't tell me yet. Let me get you inside and feed you!"

Sophie was already anticipating having her "sister" and her "mother" to confide in. She could hardly wait to get them alone to tell them all that had happened between her and Gabe, and let them know they never had to worry about the duchess's cruelty again.

Petra and Roslind helped Sophie carry the food to the table. Before they were finished, Dominyk entered the room, his gaze immediately settling on Petra, and big tears welled up in his eyes.

Petra stopped what she was doing, a pitcher of milk in her hand, as a smile spread across her face. With a quiet giggle, she set down the pitcher and she and Dominyk met in the middle of the room. Petra leaned over to accomodate Dominyk's smaller stature and embraced him.

When they pulled apart, they were both wiping their eyes.

Numerous questions rushed through Sophie's head, but it seemed irreverent to break into their private moment.

Dolf, Bartel, Siggy, Vincz, Gotfrid, and Heinric burst into the room, crowding behind Dominyk as they stopped and stared, open-mouthed, at the spectacle of two additional strange women in their house, one of whom was hugging their indomitable leader.

Dominyk blew his nose, rather noisily, into a handkerchief and then turned to his men. "What?" he asked. "Haven't you ever seen a man hug his sister?"

The men all coughed and shuffled their feet, but instead of averting their eyes, they continued to stare at the two women.

"All these years of peace and quiet. Now this." Gotfrid's lip curled in disgust, but Sophie saw a glimmer of interest in his eyes.

Heinric let out a bellow and started toward Roslind, who was standing just behind the table. His eyes remained fixed on Roslind as his grin widened and his arms stretched wide.

Sophie stepped forward, but she would never be able to intercept him before he reached Roslind. She knew from experience how determined Heinric could be. How would Roslind react to such a welcome? Sophie had known her to dissolve into tears with much less provocation.

When Heinric had almost reached Roslind, Siggy managed to intercept him, stepping in front of him and locking him in a bear hug.

Sophie breathed a sigh of relief as Siggy forcefully nudged Heinric away from Roslind, and Vincz and Dolf quickly stepped in to assist and help calm Heinric, speaking to him in placating tones.

"Gentlemen," Sophie said, "these are my friends from Hohendorf Castle. This is Roslind."

Sophie didn't miss the look of shy but ardent admiration in Siggy's eyes as he nodded politely to Roslind, who smiled at the men. Her gaze seemed to lock on Siggy as well. An expression of shy confusion came over her face and she looked down.

"And this—"

Sophie was cut off by Dominyk. "This is my sister, Lady Petra Kukelbrecht."

Sophie tried to take in his words. Petra was a "lady"? How could that be? She was a cook at the castle.

From the look on Petra's face, she was quite uncomfortable with the sudden attention, so Sophie invited everyone to come to the table and partake of the midday meal.

The table was quieter than usual. Sophie longed to talk to Petra, but she was all the way at the other end of the table sitting by her brother. Together they spoke in hushed tones between bites. Roslind sat to Sophie's right, but she was unusually silent. Siggy sat across from her, and their eyes met many times—Roslind's eyes wide, Siggy's serious and intense.

Then Dominyk cleared his throat. "Sophie, have you told Petra and Roslind what happened to the duchess?"

When Sophie shook her head, the table became quite lively as the men explained what had happened—the duchess showing up in disguise, trying to kill Sophie, and then drowning in the river.

Sophie allowed the men to tell it all. She was glad she no longer had to fear the duchess—that Petra and Roslind no longer had to fear her—but the subject brought up painful memories. Gabe's words kept going through her mind: *Let God heal you.*

Petra, Roslind, and the Seven all speculated what would happen to the village of Hohendorf and the servants who were left at the castle.

Dominyk said, "King Sigismund will have to be notified. I suppose I should write the letter myself, informing him that Duchess Ermengard has died. And there is the matter of who will inherit the duchy of Hohendorf."

Everyone turned to look at Sophie.

"Me?"

"You are Duke Baldewin's only heir," Petra said gently.

"But there is no proof that I am she."

"He has only my word, then." Petra sat very straight, holding her head at a regal angle, and she did not look anything like a cook.

Monks—or men who dwelled in monasteries—were not to be rushed, apparently.

Gabe prayed for the strength not to strangle his future father-in-law for the fiftieth time. It seemed Baldewin was determined to take his time in quitting his home of fifteen years.

After he'd supped the night before, he'd insisted they sleep before departing, and had spent the morning saying formal farewells to every man at the monastery. The process was interrupted many times so the duke could spend several minutes to an hour praying in various alcoves, or at certain graves and tombs. Only after every inch of the grounds had been visited would he even consider the gathering of his belongings. Gabe was exhausted from the waiting.

*How much longer is the man going to take? Doesn't he want to see his daughter?*

The duke seemed to be stalling. Perhaps he was afraid of what he'd encounter at the cottage.

Gabe confronted the former duke as they sat down at the long trestle table to break their fast. "Are you afraid your daughter won't forgive you? Or is there another reason for all these delays?"

Baldewin gave him a long, unblinking stare. Standing, he was a few inches shorter than Gabe, a rather small man, but he had a stare that would wilt flowers. Gabe began to wish he had prayed for more patience about the man's slowness rather than goading him.

"The work of God cannot be rushed. The young are impulsive, eager to take action, but the wise man waits for God's direction." The duke turned and stared out the open window behind them.

He was right, of course. But if they didn't get back soon, Gabe's father and brother might reach Sophie before they did and carry her off to Hagenheim. Would his faither insist Sophie marry Valten soon after they arrived? Would she be too intimidated by them to protest?

Gabe could hardly bear the thought of such a thing. To see Sophie married to his brother, to know he could never have her . . .

"I understand how you must feel, sir, but a man sometimes feels a call to action, to act on behalf of those unable to act on their own. Surely you can understand—"

"I understand. We shall leave directly after breakfast."

"Oh, thank you, sir." Gabe felt such a surge of relief, he almost hugged the man.

Baldwin frowned. "But not all your urges are from God." His eyebrows lowered sternly.

"Yes, sir. Of course not."

The man would be as uncomfortable a companion as one might expect his future father-in-law to be.

That night Sophie, Petra, and Roslind took turns brushing each other's hair. The two women would bed down in Sophie's room in the two empty beds, which would be more comfortable than the cots they had slept on at Hohendorf Castle, and much more comfortable than the nights they had slept on the ground as they had made their way to the Cottage of the Seven.

Sophie had already told the two women about falling in love with Gabe and their plans to marry. "I just don't know how things will work out."

Petra was in the middle of brushing Roslind's hair when she looked over her shoulder at Sophie. "You must not worry. Gabe is the sort of man who will do anything for the woman he loves."

"I know you're right, Mama Petra. I just wish we could be wedded tomorrow."

Roslind sighed. "Wouldn't it be wonderful to have a wedding at this cottage? Everything is much nicer here compared to the castle."

Both Sophie and Petra nodded, and Sophie prodded them to tell her about their journey from Hohendorf.

Roslind, with her usual forthrightness, told of all their

hardships and the amazing ways God had provided for them. They hadn't even seen a wolf the entire time they journeyed, which was quite fortunate. But they had had a close call with a bear, one cold night when they hadn't been able to find even rudimentary shelter, and the second night, they'd had to go to sleep hungry, but in the end, they arrived at the Cottage of the Seven unscathed.

The three sat together, their knees touching, on Sophie's bed.

Sophie finally asked Petra, "If you are a lady, then who were your parents? And how did you come to be at Hohendorf Castle?"

"I am Baron Kukelbrecht's daughter. And I came to Hohendorf Castle because I loved your father."

Sophie tried not to show too much shock and amazement. When Petra simply stared down at her hands in her lap, Sophie gently said, "Go on."

"I knew your father, Duke Baldewin, when we were children. I was always a bit in love with him. He had blue eyes, just like yours." She smiled at Sophie, finally looking at her. "He was gentle and kind but also very intense and serious. After his first wife, your mother, died, I met him again at a ball given at Hagenheim Castle. But he was so grief-stricken, he couldn't talk about anything but her — and you."

"My father spoke of me?" Sophie's voice trembled, and she cleared her throat.

Petra reached out and stroked Sophie's cheek. "Yes, of course. He loved you very much."

As the pause became longer, Sophie urged, "Go on. You saw him at Hagenheim."

"I saw him that one night, and then he left. I couldn't get him out of my thoughts. Foolishly, I traveled to Hohendorf, just to see him. I hoped ... well, I hoped I could get him to fall in love with me." She stared down at her lap, her head bowed low. "It was an ill-conceived, impulsive plan. No plan at all, when I think about it. I … I had always loved him, and I didn't want to lose him if there was a chance he might marry me now that his wife had died." She shook her head. "He was not there when I arrived, and I did not reveal my identity to anyone. I managed to get hired as a cook, even though I knew nothing about preparing a meal. Pinnosa taught me everything I knew after I told her who I was and confided in her I was in love with Duke Baldewin.

"She and I often took turns helping your nurse take care of you, allowing her to visit her family in the village from time to time. And I loved you, hoping that one day" — her voice became a whisper as her breath caught in her throat — "I might call you my own daughter." A tear dripped from her eye and fell onto her hand. "But when your father returned a few months later, he had already remarried. Married that fiend, Ermengard."

Petra began to sob softly into her hands. "Forgive me," she said, between sobs, "I am sorry."

When Petra's sobs had subsided and she'd wiped her face with the handkerchief Sophie gave her, Sophie asked, "Why did you stay?"

"Because I loved him. And I loved you. I was afraid for you both when I realized how insane and cruel your stepmother was. Your father rarely saw me, as I stayed in the kitchen, and I was often so shy around him I averted my face. But when I saw him, I noticed he began to look even more haggard than he had when he'd been grieving your mother. That witch, Ermengard, was killing him, probably poisoning him, or at the very least torturing him with her evil nature. I wanted so much to help him, to help you, but what could I do, short of killing her? Perhaps that would have been the kindest thing I could have done, but I didn't have the courage." Petra buried her face in the handkerchief.

Sophie patted her shoulder. Roslind had lain down on her bed and fallen asleep. No doubt they were both exhausted from their long, hard trip. But Sophie had to hear the rest of the story.

"Pinnosa and I believed Ermengard must have given you a sleeping potion, hoping to convince Baldewin you were dead. You were only two years old ... They went through the entire funeral rites. The priest assumed you were dead too. And immediately following the funeral, Baldewin ... disappeared. No one knows what happened to him. I believe Ermengard poisoned him as well.

"Ermengard must have recovered your body, however, because the next morning, you were found in your bed. That's when a few of the household servants, including myself, realized you were alive. Ermengard got rid of all of them except Pinnosa and me. I don't know why she kept us on. Maybe she thought because we worked in the kitchen we wouldn't realize who you were. But the fact that you were alive never made it beyond the castle."

"Until Pinnosa told Gabe and his father." Sophie's heart was pounding.

"Yes."

"But what happened to my father? How did she kill him so quickly?"

"I don't know. Ermengard told everyone he was dead, but there was no funeral, no body. I used to believe he was alive, but I didn't know where he would have gone, and I didn't know where to search for him, so I stayed at Hohendorf to protect you. With your father gone, you became my reason to stay."

"Do you think my father could still be alive?"

"I don't want to get your hopes up, Sophie ... It's been so long. I don't think he is."

"But he *could* be," Sophie said. *And he thinks I'm dead.*

Petra touched her arm. "Perhaps I should have waited to tell you."

A heavy weight settled over Sophie, but she didn't want Petra to see how sad her story had made her feel. "I am well.

Thank you for telling me the truth." She forced a smile. Petra, a lady, and in love with Sophie's father. Somehow it didn't seem so strange. It was almost as if she had always known.

Petra settled down on her own bed and was soon asleep. Sophie lay awake, praying, "Please bring Gabe back tomorrow. And please let my father be alive."

Valten kept his head up and his eyes alert, scanning the surrounding forest while the horses drank from the slow-moving river.

As soon as Walther had arrived in Hagenheim with Gabe's letter, confirming that Walther had helped Gabe and would make an excellent addition to Duke Wilhelm's guard, Valten and his father had extracted from him the entire story of how Gabe had escaped from Duchess Ermengard with a scullery maid named Sophie who was believed to be Duke Baldewin's daughter. Since then Valten had only been able to think about one thing, and that was getting to Sophie and bringing her back to Hagenheim where she would be safe.

Of course, Valten couldn't be certain that this scullery maid was Sophia Breitenbach, the daughter of Duke Baldewin Breitenbach, but it seemed very likely.

Father was concerned about Gabe. Walther had informed them that Gabe had been injured and was unable to ride, though he was being tended by a monk at a cottage of seven ... rather uncommon men. But Valten believed that Gabe would be well. He was strong and young and should mend quickly. At least he had kept Sophie safe and unharmed. Valten wouldn't admit it to his father, but he was impressed Gabe hadn't gotten both himself and the girl killed. He should never have attempted such a dangerous rescue by himself, against their father's advice. Sophie wasn't his betrothed, after all. She belonged to Valten. And he would have gone after her in due time.

He glanced down at his leg. The healer said the break wasn't completely healed, but it seemed perfectly sound to him. He wore a splint because otherwise his father, on advice of the healer, would not have let him come on this errand to fetch Sophie and Gabe.

It had become much too dark to ride, so tomorrow, Valten, his father, and six of their strongest knights would let Walther resume his lead as they rode at a hurried pace through the trees, continuing to follow a small path south.

South to find the Cottage of the Seven, his reckless little brother, and his own betrothed—the beautiful Sophia.

Tomorrow he would meet his bride.

# *Chapter*
# 26

Sophie, Petra, and Roslind were washing clothes together behind the cottage. Birds were singing and the sun was shining warmly on their shoulders. Sophie and her two companions had risen early to make breakfast for everyone and had spent the time discussing the duchess and what had happened to her. The three of them spoke in hushed tones as they prepared the food. Petra told Sophie what had happened at the castle after Sophie had escaped — the duchess had locked herself in her chamber and screamed at anyone who tried to bring her food or clean her room.

But during breakfast, they threw off the pall that had fallen over them from talking about the duchess, and now they laughed as they talked and stirred the clothes in the large black pot over the outdoor fire pit. They took some out to cool and to scrub some more before hanging them on the line.

Petra lifted her head, as though to listen, and then Sophie heard it too. Was that thunder? But then Sophie realized it was not thunder, but horses' hooves.

*Gabe!*

But as the sound drew nearer she realized it was a lot more than one or two horses. It sounded like a small army. She waited, her heart thumping inside her.

Bartel came out of his chapel to stand beside the women

as the riders broke through the dense wood and headed toward them, horses snorting and shifting their feet as they came to a halt a few feet away.

Sophie immediately recognized Walther, and she knew. Gabe had not made it back before his father had come for her. She grabbed Petra's arm for support.

"Good day to you," Bartel said, calmly nodding at the men.

"Good day," said a man with dark brown hair that was sprinkled with a small amount of gray. He sat straight and regal on his large black horse. From his familiar features, Sophie realized he must be Gabe's father.

"I am Duke Wilhelm of Hagenheim, and these are my men. We come in search of Gabehart Gerstenberg and a young lady, called Sophie, who was with him. We were told they were being sheltered in the Cottage of the Seven."

"Your Grace, you have come to the Cottage of the Seven. You are very welcome here," Bartel said solemnly, then nodded his head at her. "This is Lady Sophia, daughter of Duke Baldewin. But your son, Lord Gabehart, is not here."

"Not here?" Duke Wilhelm sounded annoyed. The duke fixed Bartel with a fierce gaze.

"No, Your Grace. He left for Gemeinhart Monastery several days ago and has not returned."

Gabe's father seemed to control himself with effort as he gripped his saddle horn. "What business did he have at Gemeinhart Monastery?"

"He—" Bartel looked at Sophie and hesitated.

"Yes?"

Bartel gave Sophie an apologetic look, then turned back to Duke Wilhelm. "He went there to find Duke Baldewin."

Sophie felt her knees go weak, and she held tighter to Petra's arm. Then she noticed all the blood had drained from Petra's face and she was swaying slightly. Sophie steadied Petra as best she could while trying not to let her own knees buckle. Why hadn't Gabe told her?

"Duke Baldewin is dead," Duke Wilhelm said, but his tone sounded uncertain.

"He was alive, Your Grace, when I left the monastery seven years ago."

Duke Wilhelm's eyes conveyed calm acceptance as he nodded. Sophie thought she heard him murmur, "Praise God," echoing her own thought.

The duke dismounted, and the young man behind him followed his lead. Duke Wilhelm stepped toward her and sank to one knee. He grasped her hand and said, "My Lady Sophia, I am honored." He bowed over her hand, then abruptly stood and backed away.

The young man behind him immediately took his place in front of her. He also knelt before her and took her hand, and then he kissed it.

His voice was gruff and his expression seemed carved from stone, and the several small scars on his face were like careless nicks from the sculptor's chisel. "Lady Sophia," he said. "I am Valten, your betrothed."

---

Gabe chafed at Duke Baldewin's slowness. The man hadn't been on a horse in fifteen years, but it seemed as though he would remember how to ride at some point on this supposed-to-be-two-days trip that threatened to stretch into a multiple-night journey. Gabe reminded himself, for the hundredth time since midday, that he couldn't afford to lose his temper with Sophie's father. He tried to distract himself with thoughts of how happy she would be to learn her father was alive and how she would react when he told her that her father had promised to help them to wed.

As twilight began to set in, Gabe began worrying that he might go off the trail in the dark woods and get lost. He forced himself to slow his pace so as not to leave Duke Baldewin behind. Gingerbread picked his way through the dense trees and undergrowth until Gabe saw the cottage in the waning glow of the sky. He heaved a sigh of relief. "Thank you, God."

As his heart quickened, he couldn't help urging his horse to walk faster. A woman came out the kitchen door and dumped a pan of dishwater on the ground, but her form wasn't quite right to be Sophie. She was a little heavier and her hair was lighter. Had he come to the wrong house? But no, he was sure this was the cottage.

The woman looked up and saw them coming. She stood perfectly still as she watched them draw closer. Finally, Gabe realized her gaze was focused not on him, but behind him, on Duke Baldewin. He turned in his saddle and saw that Baldewin's eyes were wide as he stared back at her.

The duke halted his horse, got off, and walked toward her, obviously forgetting his saddle sores. He strode toward her as if striding toward home.

Such a strange thought. Duke Baldewin had never been to the Cottage of the Seven before, so it certainly wasn't his home. And how could he know this woman? Who was she?

The woman waited. She looked like Petra, the cook from Hohendorf, and it looked as if she was crying. When Baldewin had come within two feet of her, he stopped.

Curious, Gabe nevertheless turned away from the pair and led his and Baldewin's horses to the stable. He unsaddled them himself, anxious to see Sophie and tell her the good news, to see the reunion between father and daughter. He forked some hay to the animals in their stalls and then latched the barn door before hurrying to the house.

Not bothering to knock, he burst into the large front room and found all seven of the men gathered around.

Siggy, instead of playing his lute, sat smiling at a young woman about Sophie's age who was smiling back at him, and for a moment it was as if Gabe were watching himself and Sophie. But this girl was not Sophie; Gabe recognized her from his first day at Hohendorf as Roslind.

Where was Sophie? A quick glance around the room told him she wasn't there.

The men quickly noticed him standing there and jumped up to greet him.

"Gabe!" Several of them came and grasped his shoulder or his hand, welcoming him back.

"Is Sophie upstairs?"

The men's expressions immediately changed and their smiles fled. Only Bartel could look him in the eye. "She's gone. Your father and Valten came earlier today. They set out immediately for Hagenheim Castle."

Gabe's stomach sank to his toes. He'd missed them, missed being there to explain things to his brother and father. Sophie had had to face them alone. And now they were a full day ahead of him.

Or, he should say, *them*—he and Baldewin. He couldn't go to Hagenheim Castle without Duke Baldewin. More's the pity. The man's slowness would try the patience of Job.

Where was Duke Baldewin anyway? If he didn't know better, he'd say the man was trysting with that woman behind the kitchen.

He rebuked himself for having such a thought about a monk.

"Can I help you with your horse?" Vincz asked.

"Thank you, but I already stabled them." He looked back

toward the kitchen. "I arrived here with Duke Baldewin. Have any of you seen him?"

The men muttered, asking each other if they'd encountered the duke, already deciding to search for him and who should go where, when Baldewin and the woman entered the door from the kitchen.

For a moment, no one said anything as they all stared at Baldewin and the woman, and the woman stared at the floor, her cheeks pink. Baldewin returned each stare with a leveled one of his own.

"Everyone," Gabe spoke up. "This is Duke Baldewin of Hohendorf. He is Sophie's father."

They all bowed—all except Heinric, who grinned.

Duke Baldewin nodded—Gabe had been half afraid he would take issue with being called a duke, as he had when Gabe had addressed him as such at the monastery. But instead, he stood to his full height, seeming to throw off the humble demeanor of a monk. He looked as majestic as any nobleman, though without a nobleman's attire.

"And this," Baldewin said in his most kingly tone, "is Lady Petra, daughter of Baron Otto Kukelbrecht, a woman I've been wishing to talk with again for many years."

Valten was almost home; his bride was riding her own horse—the horse he had personally selected for her—safely in the center of his father's knights. And he had hardly said two words to her. But the important thing was that she was safe. And it didn't hurt that she was quite beautiful.

He hoped Gabe wasn't too disappointed that the attractive girl he had risked his life to rescue was marrying Valten, her rightful betrothed. He was surprised his brother wasn't even there. Walther had made it sound as if his injury had been life-threatening, but when they'd arrived at the Cottage of the Seven, Gabe had apparently recovered and flitted off on a quest to find Duke Baldewin at the Gemeinhart Abbey. Which was fine; Gabe could do all the gallivanting he wanted while Valten escorted his betrothed back to Hagenheim.

The problem was that Sophie, as they all called her, was lovely to look upon, but she didn't seem the least interested in even acknowledging his presence. But to be honest, he'd only tried to converse with her once or twice. He would never admit it to anyone, but he was a bit intimidated by the cold look on her face and the way she seemed determined to avoid him, staying as far away from him as possible. Valten reassured himself there would be plenty of time for talking and courting before they wed. After they arrived home, they'd likely wait at least three weeks while they cried the banns before the wedding.

Plenty of time.

Still, he should probably start to at least greet her every day, make sure she wasn't afraid of him.

Many maidens seemed to react with fear to him. He was much larger than most men, true, and usually wore some armor and carried at least two weapons at all times. And he did have a few scars on his face that women seemed to have an aversion to, though he didn't understand why. His scars were all small. It wasn't as if he had a big, jagged scar all the way across his face or was missing an eye or anything like that.

Perhaps his bride-to-be was simply timid around men. And she hadn't known until recently that she was even betrothed. Though surely she must have been pleased to find out her betrothed was the future duke of Hagenheim and a tournament champion known all over the Holy Roman Empire and beyond. He straightened in his saddle and looked over at Sophie. She met him with the same cold stare she'd been giving him the entire time.

He would make an effort to speak to her tonight. It would be the last night before they arrived in Hagenheim, after all.

Sophie was so exhausted when they stopped at the inn—the first inn they'd stopped at since they left the Cottage of the Seven—that she sighed with relief. It would feel good to sleep on an actual mattress and with a roof over her head.

*Does Gabe have a roof over his head? Does he know I am on my way to Hagenheim with his brother and father? Does he even care?*

No, she wasn't going to think like that. Gabe had asked her to trust him and she would. He had never given her a reason not to. Well, until he'd left without telling her where he was going, without telling her her father was still alive.

*Trust, trust, trust.*

*But I need you now, Gabe. I don't know what to say, what to do. You've abandoned me with a very off-putting man, to whom I happen to be betrothed.*

Who had dismounted and was coming toward her that very minute.

"Lady Sophia," he said, reaching up to help her down off her horse.

She accepted his help, as there was no way to refuse. His big hands reached around her waist and lifted her with apparent ease. His shoulders were as broad as Walther's, and she felt small as he set her down beside him. *Oh, Gabe, where are you?*

"We shall stay at this inn tonight." His eyes stared into hers with complete openness, but without any affection. He didn't even give her a slight smile.

She supposed she should feel bad for him, as he thought she was to become his wife, when in fact she was in love with his brother. Somehow, though, the only emotion she could feel for him was aversion.

He wasn't Gabe.

Sooner or later she would need to tell him that she couldn't marry him. What would he say? Would he become angry?

"You will have your own room, of course, and I will sleep outside your door."

"Oh." He looked fierce, as if contemplating the ruffians he would relish defending her from. "Thank you, but that isn't necessary. I can bar the door."

"It is my duty to protect you from anyone who may wish you harm. I take my duty seriously."

She could certainly believe that, if the look on his face was any indication. But she couldn't help contrasting ... Gabe protected her just as fiercely, and he did it with a cute smile and a wink, not to mention doing it out of love instead of duty.

Valten turned and seemed to be waiting for her to pass in front of him. She did so, hoping he didn't expect her to take his arm.

Inside, Valten and his father spoke with the innkeeper and ordered dinner and bedchambers. There weren't enough rooms for all the knights who traveled with them, so Duke Wilhelm's men arranged to stay in the stable with the horses. She wasn't sure which was worse: sleeping in the stable with smelly horses or sleeping on the hard wood floor in front of the door of a girl whom you thought you were going to marry—but weren't.

At least, she hoped he wasn't going to marry her. But if Gabe couldn't make the arrangements ...

*No, I will trust Gabe.*

The inn's stew tasted good, especially after eating nothing but jerky, apples, and stale bread for three days. She sat between Valten and Duke Wilhelm. The duke was a good conversationalist, asking her, gently, about her childhood. She told him and Valten that she didn't remember her parents, and she hadn't known that Duchess Ermengard was her stepmother or that she was the daughter of the duke of Hohendorf until Gabe came and told her.

"I am glad my son found you when he did."

Sophie smiled. "As am I." She felt Valten stiffen beside her, but she couldn't stop herself from speaking the words rushing through her head. "He was so well-mannered and chivalrous, and very brave—even after he was struck by the arrow that was meant for me."

Valten stared at her, unblinking, his jaw clenched, as if her words didn't exactly please him. But she refused to be intimidated by him.

"I am very thankful to the men at the Cottage of the Seven. When we arrived at the Cottage, Gabe was so ill. I was terrified for him, but Bartel, one of the seven, was very knowlegable in the healing arts, and was able to save him, and all the men there were so gracious to us. They all came to love Gabe—it would be impossible not to."

Duke Wilhelm's eyes remained kind, but Valten was scowling at her so darkly, she wondered if she'd gone too far.

"Do you think Gabe will follow immediately to Hagenheim?" Duke Wilhelm asked. She was suddenly very grateful that he had accompanied Valten on this trip.

"He said he hoped he would only be gone for a few days, and he would follow us to Hagenheim if you and Valten had already come to fetch me when he got back."

"Had it all planned out," Valten muttered. "He would." He crossed his arms, bulging with muscles, and glared at the wall.

"Brothers," Duke Wilhelm said, smiling a lopsided grin that very much reminded her of Gabe. "Always a bit of rivalry there."

*Yes, especially if the older one is a bully.* But she smiled back at Gabe's father. He was a handsome man, and her heart swelled at the thought that he would one day be her father-in-law.

Valten continued to scowl. He had spoken very few thoughtful words during the meal. In fact, he had hardly spoken at all during the three days she'd known him. But now he looked at her and said, with his usual, serious expression, "I'm glad you *and Gabe* are well and safe after your escape from the duchess."

She searched his eyes for sarcasm but saw only sincerity. Maybe he wasn't so bad after all. Gabe seemed to love him, even if they had not always been kind to each other while growing up. *Not that I want to marry Valten.*

She held his gaze and allowed her eyes to soften slightly. "Thank you."

"It is growing late," Valten said. "If you are tired, I will accompany you to your room."

They all stood up and made their way upstairs. Both Duke Wilhelm and Valten inspected her room, looking under the bed and combing every foot of the room, as if someone could be lurking. They tested the lock on the door, and then Duke Wilhelm sprinkled dried pennyroyal on the bed "to keep away fleas."

"Thank you," Sophie said as they left her room. She had no doubt that Valten truly would sleep outside her door on the hard wood floor.

Unfortunately, he was doing it because he thought she was soon to be his wife.

# *Chapter*
## 27

*Gabe had known Duke Baldewin would slow* him down, but it couldn't be helped. Without the duke's blessing, there was little chance he would ever be allowed to marry Sophie. At least the duke had been willing to set out for Hagenheim the day after they arrived at the Cottage. Although he had seemed a bit reluctant to leave Petra behind. Twice before they left, Gabe had walked into a room and found the two of them speaking to each other, their heads together as if they were whispering. When Gabe asked the duke if Petra would be accompanying them, he said no. Petra and Roslind would stay with the Seven and help the men with the cooking. But something about his manner gave Gabe the impression that there was something unsettled between him and Petra. There had been plenty of opportunity to ask the duke about it during their slow trip to Hagenheim, but he decided to let the duke have his privacy.

Gabe was just happy to be on his way back to Sophie. And happy he had her father with him to grant permission for her and Valten's betrothal to be broken.

*Thank you, God.*

Arriving in Hagenheim early in the afternoon after their night at the inn, Sophie tried to take in everything her eyes landed upon—the buildings, the streets, the people. Did Gabe know this person? Had he ever been inside that building? Was that young man a friend of his? She could see the towers of the castle rising above the rest of the town at the far end. Was his bed-chamber behind one of those windows? Where was his mother? Would she be happy to meet Sophie?

Her heart gave a little lurch at the thought of meeting Gabe's mother for the first time. Would she be as warm and welcoming as Gabe promised?

Valten brought his horse alongside hers, startling her. He kept his gaze straight ahead. The townspeople lined the streets, staring at them, some of them waving, others shouting "*Willkommen!*" An older woman called out, "Good health and long life to our young lord and his new bride!" More shouts rang out and people came running to join in the celebration.

Feeling like she was betraying them all, Sophie smiled sheepishly and waved back to the children who were calling after her, "*Schönesjunges Fräulein!* Lovely Lady Sophia! Lovely! Lovely!"

Valten kept his gaze straight ahead while his father nodded to acknowledge those welcoming them home. The people seemed to adore their duke and his son. Sophie couldn't imagine the people of Hohendorf reacting in such a way toward Duchess Ermengard.

Although they'd probably react in just this way when they learned she was dead.

Their entourage of knights soon traversed the length of the city, crossed the *Marktplatz* with its impressive buildings that surrounded the cobblestone square, and entered the castle court-yard. Before she knew it, she and all the knights were dismounting their horses, and groomsmen were leading the animals away.

Someone was taking her hand. She turned to see Valten placing her hand on his arm. *Will he actually speak?* No. Instead he silently led her to a huge wooden door in the side of the gray stone castle.

They entered, and as her eyes grew accustomed to the dark interior, she heard a gasp, then quick footsteps coming toward her. She focused on a woman just moments before that woman took both her hands and said, "You must be Sophie. I am Rose, Valten's mother. Welcome to Hagenheim, my dear. I hope you will be very happy here."

Sophie smiled. Gabe had been right. His mother was just as he'd said.

Gabe's mother ordered a bath be drawn for her, reminding Sophie of the seven men's kindness. She bathed in a large tub, with warm water and scented soap and a wonderfully fragrant liquid soap for her hair. She almost began to feel like a lady.

Every time guilt rose up to scold her for deceiving her new family-to-be, Sophie let the warm water distract her. After all, when Gabe arrived, he would make everything right. He would convince his family to let the two of them marry, and Valten could find himself his own wife. They would understand.

But without Gabe here to attest to their love, how could she tell them? Surely she could put it off until Gabe arrived.

*Make haste, Gabe.*

After her bath, Sophie received what she had been longing for—hours of talking to Gabe's mother, who insisted she be called Rose. Lady Rose hinted that her own upbringing hadn't been so different from Sophie's. She'd grown up the daughter of a woodcutter outside the town walls, before the town healer befriended her and made her a healer's apprentice. The healer had been kind to her and had taught her many things, including how to read. Sophie hoped to hear the rest of that story in the days to come, hoped to learn how she ended up marrying a duke when she was only a woodcutter's daughter. But Lady Rose wanted to know about Sophie.

Sophie told Rose that she'd had to leave her most prized possession, her pages from the Gospel of St. Luke, in Hohendorf. She confessed she wanted to be able to not only read in Latin, but also in other languages, and to speak and write them as well.

"And so you shall," Lady Rose said with a smile. Then she introduced Sophie to Gabe's sisters, and the five of them talked and giggled until it was time to go to the Great Hall for supper.

Sophie had the urge to stay very near Lady Rose as they entered the Great Hall. Would she be expected to sit near Valten and make conversation with him? *Please, let us be placed as far apart as possible.*

Lady Rose sat at the end of the long trestle table and motioned for Sophie to sit beside her. Sophie sank down on the bench and Rose's oldest daughter, Margaretha, sat on her other side. Sophie sighed in gratitude.

Soon the men entered the room, all impeccably dressed, their hair looking damp and clean. Valten had changed clothes and was wearing a rich-green doublet and a crisp white shirt. Somehow he looked even more forbidding, even more like a warrior, than he had in his rough traveling clothes, so sharp was the contrast of his lordly clothing to his muscular size and rough demeanor. The scars on his cheeks and chin were more noticeable without the dust of the road to obscure them, and he seemed to overwhelm the sophisticated clothing with his broad shoulders.

He sat on the other side of the table, opposite his mother. He looked at Sophie and seemed ill at ease, glancing away and then back again. Then he was staring at his mother, as though studying her face.

Sophie glanced over at Lady Rose, who was pursing her lips and giving Valten a strange look, lowering her brows and nodding at him.

Valten cleared his throat and asked, "Are you well tonight, Lady Sophia?"

"Yes, I am quite well, I thank you."

"Good." Food was placed in front of him and then he only had eyes for the roast pheasant.

They all began to eat, and Sophie relaxed a bit. She was hungry after her long trip, and she ate heartily of the rich venison and pheasant, the puddings and fried pasties. Valten hadn't said a word to her since the food arrived, and Sophie made small talk with Margaretha and Lady Rose, feeling happier than she had since Gabe had gone to Gemeinhart Monastery and left her with the Seven.

Duke Wilhelm leaned over to Lady Rose and whispered something, then nodded and stood up. Sophie began feeling sick to her stomach as she waited for his announcement.

As soon as he began to speak, the entire hall, which was full of people — perhaps sixty or seventy in all — fell silent.

"Friends and family, I would like you to welcome the newest member of the Gerstenberg family, the betrothed of our eldest, Valten, Earl of Hamlin. Until recently, we thought she was lost to us, but now she is here, alive and well. Please welcome Sophia Breitenbach, only daughter of Duke Baldewin of Hohendorf."

"Stand up, my dear," Lady Rose whispered, touching her elbow.

Duke Wilhelm also motioned for her to stand. As she did so, the entire assembly clapped their hands and stomped their feet, cheering so loudly she wondered if the roof would lift. Sophie waved in a way she hoped looked graceful and sat down, her face heating.

Valten was looking at her with the closest thing to a smile that she had seen on his face.

*I am a fraud.*

The cheers and clamor continued for quite a while, long enough for Sophie to imagine how shocked and hurt her new family would be when she told them she was in love with her rescuer, not her betrothed.

*Gabe, why aren't you here?*

Sophie went to bed on the softest, most-comfortable bed she'd ever slept on, and when she woke up, was surprised to see the sun already rather high in the sky. She was sure she had never slept so late in her life.

A servant was standing by to help her dress in a lovely blue-green gown, loaned to her by Margaretha, who happened to be Sophie's size. When she emerged from her room, Margaretha and Kirstyn, who was carrying Adela, escorted her to the kitchen to get her some food, giggling all the way.

Sophie ate her breakfast, sighing in between bites, as her new sisters—for that is what they declared themselves to be—alternately hugged her arm, patted her shoulder, and bantered playfully with each other. Gabe's brothers, meanwhile, occasionally piped in with a story about the time they almost got a bull's eye in archery, or a unique frog they had found once in the pond. To belong to such a family—it was all she had ever wanted, ever dreamed about. She only hoped they wouldn't hate her in the days to come.

She longed to tell Lady Rose her secret. She would understand, wouldn't she? She was obviously in love with Duke Wilhelm. Sophie could see it in her face every time she looked at him. She would understand how Sophie had fallen in love with Gabe. After all, Sophie hadn't meant for those feelings to develop. But Gabe was so loveable, so kind and gentle and charming and handsome ... Gabe was Lady Rose's son too, so perhaps she would understand.

"Sophie! What's wrong?" Margaretha asked, wrapping her arm around Sophie's shoulders and looking at her with warm brown eyes. Sophie marveled at how Gabe's sister could look at her with such love after only just meeting her. The girl had no doubt lived a sheltered existence, but there was no selfishness in her expression.

Sophie took a deep breath to absorb the tears, smiled, and shook her head. "Nothing, nothing."

"Aren't you happy to be here with us?"

"Of course! I am very happy," Sophie said, but her words only made her remember how much she wished Gabe were there.

"You *are* sad! What is it? Do you miss your home? I would be terribly sad to leave my home, which is why I am determined to never get married. I've already told Mother and Father I plan to stay here with them for the rest of my life."

"No, no. I don't miss my home." Sophie shook her head again and looked down, afraid to look anyone in the eye.

"Do you not want to marry Valten? Is that it?" Kirstyn, the second oldest, asked, bending low to see into Sophie's face. Her light brown hair hung in perfect ringlets by her cheeks. There was a serious but kind look about her light blue eyes.

Sophie couldn't speak as she tried to blink back the silly tears. Was her distress that obvious?

"I know he looks quite scary," Kirstyn went on. "I've always been a little afraid of him myself, but he is a good brother, and I'm sure he'll be a good husband."

"Tears work quite well with him too!" Margaretha exclaimed. "If I want something from him, all I have to do is cry and he gives it to me. He can't resist tears. He doesn't talk much, but Mother says men don't always want to waste their words, while women sometimes have enough to spare. Mother is very wise, don't you think?"

"Yes, she is," Sophie agreed, hoping the conversation would be steered away from Valten.

Adela, the youngest at only two years old, said, "Valten carry me!"

Margaretha smiled at her little sister indulgently. "She's talking about the time she scraped her knee and Valten carried her all the way home."

"Don't worry about Valten, Sophie," Kirstyn said. "I saw him smile at you last night. I think he likes you already, and before you know it, you two will be looking at each other the way Mother and Father do."

Sophie didn't know what to say to that.

Soon it was clear that Sophie couldn't eat anymore, so the sisters showed her around the castle, promising to also show her around the courtyard and, if they could find Valten to escort them, to show her around the *Marktplatz* and the main sections of town. Sophie enjoyed being with them, so she went along, vowing to confess the truth of her feelings for Gabe—and her lack thereof for Valten—as soon as she was able.

They showed her every part of the castle, pointing out the various family members' bedchambers, including Gabe's room, which Sophie paid extra attention to. As they wandered around the courtyard, the sisters telling Sophie various stories of their adventures growing up, they turned and there was Valten, standing with his usual stern expression.

The three sisters greeted him and, with a slight softening of his expression, he bent down to receive a kiss on the cheek from each of them. He cleared his throat and said, "I came to ask Lady Sophia to go on a picnic with me."

If Sophie hadn't been sure he was incapable of such things, she would have believed he was blushing.

What was it with unwanted men and picnics? Unlike her first few requests from Lorencz, she couldn't think of a single excuse to turn Valten away. "Can Margaretha, Kirstyn, and Adela come with us?" At least she wouldn't have to be alone with him.

"As you wish."

Valten led them out of the town gate after collecting a basket of food from the kitchen and a blanket for them to sit on. The three sisters skipped arm in arm across the meadow, leaving Sophie and Valten behind, no doubt on purpose.

"Have my sisters talked you to death yet?" Valten asked, breaking the uncomfortable silence.

"Oh no." Sophie smiled. "I'm enjoying them very much. They are very sweet girls. You're very fortunate to have such a wonderful family."

He was looking at her strangely, as if he didn't understand her words. He probably took them all for granted, probably wasn't even worried about Gabe, his brother, who could be in danger or hurt or lost.

*Trust . . .*

Sophie took a deep breath.

The sisters exclaimed at a baby rabbit they had found hiding in the tall grass and called Sophie and Valten over to look at it. It didn't hop away, but its nose twitched and its heart was beating so hard Sophie could see its brown fur vibrating.

Valten took a brief look, then walked on, so they turned and followed him.

The picnic was rather awkward, with Valten's presence dampening Sophie's spirits. The outing would have been so much more fun if he weren't there. But at least he carried their heavy picnic basket. *God, forgive me for being ungracious.*

After they finished eating, Margaretha and Kirstyn took Adela to see if the rabbit was where they had left it while Sophie and Valten packed up the basket. Just when Sophie was sure she had survived the picnic without having to say more than a few words to the man she hopefully wouldn't marry, Valten asked, "So did my little brother really rescue you, or did you have to rescue him?"

Valten's look of disdain made Sophie want to punch him in the face. "Gabe was very brave, as a matter of fact. He saved me not only from Duchess Ermengard, but also from a wolf that was about to attack me, and as I mentioned at the inn, he took an arrow that was meant for me." She crossed her arms and glared at him. "I doubt anyone could have done any better, even a man who's won every tournament he's ever entered but who has never faced a true life-and-death situation."

Valten stared at her, his jaw as hard as stone. His face turned red, but he never took his eyes off her. Finally, as though it was difficult to unclench his teeth, he opened his mouth and spoke. "So Gabe is your hero then?"

Sophie wasn't going to keep quiet any longer. If he wanted to know the truth, she might as well tell him now instead of waiting. "He is." She stared back at him.

"Is there something between you and Gabe that I should know about?"

She tried to think of the best way to say this, but before she could speak, his sisters ran toward them, squealing.

"We saw two more babies! And the mama! When we tried to pet her babies, she hopped up to us and tried to scratch us."

The girls continued squealing and giggling. Valten turned and picked up the basket with far more force than was necessary, and they all headed back toward the castle. And Sophie determined to go straight to Lady Rose to tell her the truth.

# Chapter
## 28

*Sophie returned from the picnic, only to discover*
Lady Rose had gone to visit an orphanage and wouldn't be back
before supper. Sophie spent anxious hours in her room, and attempted to remain calm during her periodic visits from Gabe's
sisters.

Sophie chafed through supper, which offered no moments
to tell Lady Rose even part of what now weighed upon her.
Instead, she picked at her food while suffering Valten's glares,
until she decided to glare right back at him. But that only made
her feel guilty, so she returned to ignoring him for the rest of the
meal. The moment the last dish was cleared, she begged Lady
Rose to allow her to speak to her alone.

Lady Rose ushered her to her sitting room while the rest of
the family stayed in the Great Hall to hear music and talk.

"What is it, my dear?" Lady Rose asked. "Did you and
Valten not have a good time on your picnic?"

"The truth is ..." Sophie had thought this moment would
be a relief, but now, as she looked into Lady Rose's kind face,
she was terrified that what she had to say would anger her future
mother-in-law. What if Lady Rose hated her for falling in love
with Gabe? What if Lady Rose told her she had to forget about
Gabe and marry Valten? But she couldn't hold the words back
any longer.

"I am in love with Gabe," she blurted. "I didn't mean to fall in love with him. He immediately told me I was betrothed to his brother, so I tried to think of him only as a brother, always as a brother, but I ... I failed." Sophie blinked back tears.

"Oh, my dear." Lady Rose held out her arms and enfolded Sophie. "Oh."

At least she didn't seem angry.

"I'm so, so sorry," Sophie said. "I would never want to upset you or your family, but I love Gabe so much, I can't imagine loving anyone else. When he left me at the Cottage of the Seven, he said he had to do something important, and I know now that he went to find my father. But I've been so terrified that something has happened to him, that he won't be able to come back to me, or that he won't be able to make a way for us to marry."

"Oh, Sophie." Lady Rose continued to hug her, then she pulled back and looked her in the eye. "I'm so glad you told me. And I'm sure Gabe will return for you, if he said he will. But perhaps we should wait for him to come before we tell anyone else about this."

"I think Valten already knows I love Gabe. Or at least suspects I do. But he doesn't love me, doesn't even know me, so he won't be too hurt, will he?"

Lady Rose smiled, but it was a sad smile. "I don't think his heart will be broken, but his pride may be bruised. And sometimes, it's worse to hurt a man's pride than to break his heart."

Sophie couldn't see why Valten should be offended. He hadn't even known she was alive until a few weeks ago.

"Valten is a very ... determined man," Lady Rose continued. "It will be hard for him to think of his little brother winning the love of the woman he should have rescued, the woman he should have married and protected."

Sophie was being heartless not to feel any sympathy for Valten. Of course it would be hard for him.

"He will recover." Lady Rose squeezed Sophie's shoulder. "And you will be good for Gabehart, I have no doubt. He was always a rather thoughtless, though good-hearted, boy. I'm glad you've won his heart."

Sophie looked at this amazing woman in wonder. "I'd hoped you would listen, but I never imagined you would be so understanding. I was afraid you would be angry at me."

Lady Rose shook her head. "I know a thing or two about falling in love with someone while trying not to." She gave Sophie a mysterious smirk. "And in the meantime, I'll stop insisting that Valten spend time with you."

Sophie's eyes went wide, her groan turning into a muffled laugh.

There was a twinkle in Lady Rose's eye, but she sounded rather sober. "Duke Wilhelm may be upset, however, and Valten certainly will. But don't worry. If you and Gabehart are meant to wed, I'm sure there is a way to work this all out. We will wait for Gabe to come, and we'll hope he is able to break his betrothal to Brittola in a way that is satisfactory for all."

Thinking of both Brittola and Valten made Sophie sad. Her happiness would bring them ... heartbreak. Or at least bruised pride. Must her happiness cause them pain?

The next day, Sophie and Margaretha walked down the long corridor near the Great Hall. The mid-afternoon sun was shining through the narrow windows that looked out at the inner courtyard as they went inside the library. Margaretha wanted to show her a book.

The library was a large room, though less than half the size of the Great Hall. The fireplace connecting the library to the hall was ablaze, and candles were burning on the tables even though the room appeared to be empty. Sophie had already discovered that the family often retired to the library after supper to enjoy music and each other's company. It was a cozy room, with plenty of chairs and rugs for sitting.

Before Margaretha could find the book she was looking for, Sophie heard a shout, muffled through thick stone walls.

Margaretha grabbed Sophie's hand and hurried toward the door that led to the corridor. "Let's go see who's here."

Someone burst into the corridor from the courtyard. By his clothing, he looked to be a groomsman from the stable. The young man looked left, then right, where he spied Margaretha and Sophie as they exited the library. "Good ladies, I wish to tell his grace, Duke Wilhelm, that his son, Lord Gabehart, is just arriving with a visitor."

Margaretha turned and screamed, "Mother! Father! Gabe is home!"

Sophie stood still, but only for a moment. She gathered her skirt and ran out into the courtyard, Gabe's sister at her heels.

They made it as far as the well in the center of the courtyard before the steward came toward them. "Ladies," he said, bowing to them. "I have a message from Lord Gabehart for Lady Sophia."

Margaretha's eyes were as round as her open mouth.

"Yes?" Sophie rasped.

"He wishes you, along with Duke Wilhelm, Lady Rose, and Lord Valten, to meet him in the library."

Sophie and Margaretha clung to each other's arms, while Margaretha searched Sophie's face. "You should go. I will find Mother and Father and Valten."

They dashed off in the direction they had come, entering the main corridor of the castle. While Sophie waited nervously in the library, stifling a giggle at having to go back to the place she had just run so vigorously from, Margaretha located both the duke and duchess and brought them in. She then left to go find

Valten, and Sophie glanced at Gabe's parents. Duke Wilhelm wore a somber expression, but Lady Rose gave her an encouraging smile.

Valten entered the room. She doubted he looked any fiercer on the tournament field wielding a sword and lance. He avoided looking at her at all, instead turning his back on them all and staring at a tapestry on the wall.

Sophie clasped her hands to keep them from shaking. Lady Rose threw open some shutters, letting in more light.

Then Gabe walked into the room. She wanted so much to run to him and throw her arms around him. She'd missed him so much. Had he missed her? She searched his face, desperate to read his thoughts, wondering if he'd found her father. He looked at her too. Was that a smile? More of a lopsided grin. But it quickly disappeared as he looked away from her and acknowledged his parents.

His mother hugged him and his father did as well, clapping him on the back. Valten turned halfway around and gave him a curt nod.

*Is my father here as well? Isn't Gabe excited to see me? Why doesn't he come and embrace me?* But of course, he couldn't do that. She wasn't his to embrace.

She devoured him with her eyes, taking in his disheveled hair and the travel dust still on his clothes. The four or five days' growth on his face made her breath hitch in her throat.

Then she saw another shorter man enter behind Gabe. Could he be her father?

"Mother, Father, Valten, and Sophie, I have someone I want you to meet." Gabe turned to the man standing behind him and motioned him forward. The man had blue eyes that almost looked familiar, though she was certain she didn't know him. He looked to be about Duke Wilhelm's age. *Could he be ... ?*

"Is that you?" Duke Wilhelm stepped toward him and Lady Rose covered her mouth with her hands.

"Yes, I have returned to my rightful place, old friend."

Sophie held her breath as those blue eyes turned her way. Gabe also turned to Sophie and said, "This ... is your father, Duke Baldewin."

# Chapter
## 29

*A buzzing sound filled her ears. My father?* Sophie couldn't move. She'd been thinking about him since Bartel had told Duke Wilhelm about Gabe's quest, but she'd never quite believed Gabe would find him. She stared at the man, who stared back at her with tears in his eyes. He tentatively took a couple of steps toward her, then stopped.

"Can you ever forgive me for not knowing you were still alive? For not coming back to find you?" He held out his hands in supplication.

Her mind was churning.

"The last time I saw you, your eyes were closed, you … you were laid out as though dead. I couldn't bear the thought of life without you and your mother, and so I went to the monastery and shut myself away. I never imagined Ermengard could have faked your death. Can you forgive me?"

"Of course." Sophie could barely breathe. Her father crossed the room and put his arms around her. She buried her face in his shoulder and put her arms around him, too stunned to think. "I have a father."

"I will never leave you again," he said softly against her ear. "I will follow you around like a lost puppy if you let me. I love you, Sophie. God has given me back my little girl."

Sophie became aware of Gabe and his parents talking in one corner while Valten stood by himself in another. She broke away from her father and looked into his face.

He wiped at a tear in the corner of his eye. "You are so beautiful, just like your mother."

She half laughed while choking on her own tears. She had a father. Gabe must not have wanted to tell her about his mission because he'd been afraid that the man he sought wouldn't be Duke Baldewin after all. But he was, if Duke Wilhelm and Lady Rose's reaction was any proof.

Gabe stepped away from his parents toward the center of the room. "The real purpose of me bringing Duke Baldewin here, aside from introducing him to his daughter, is . . ." He glanced at Valten, who was scowling at him, his arms crossed.

Gabe cleared his throat. "I want to apologize to you now, Valten. I should have never gone off, alone, to rescue your betrothed. It was foolish of me—thoughtless, even. And when I arrived in Hohendorf, I never intended to fall in love with Sophie, but I did. I assure you, I tried not to, and I never wanted to grieve you or anyone else. Yes, I was irresponsible, and I wanted to get glory for myself, and for that I am sorry. I never wanted to hurt anyone, but I love Sophie. I want to marry her, and I'm asking you, Valten, and you, Father and Mother, to give your consent to breaking your betrothal to Sophie."

Valten uncrossed his arms and balled his hands into fists as he stared at Gabe.

"I'm sorry too." Sophie spoke before she had time to get nervous. "After he told me I was betrothed to you, I wanted to love and marry you, Valten, and even imagined what our life together could be, but . . . I fell in love with Gabe. I am so sorry as well." Her face must have been glowing red, but she didn't care. It was a relief to finally tell him the truth. Her father squeezed her shoulder encouragingly.

Valten stared at her, then at Gabe, then he turned and faced the window. He seemed to be breathing hard, his shoulders rising and falling rapidly.

Duke Wilhelm stepped forward. "What do you have to say about breaking the betrothal, Duke Baldewin?"

Sophie's father pressed his hands to his chest. "Since the betrothal was made when Sophie was only a baby and Valten a child, they had no say in the matter. And circumstances being what they are, I don't believe they should be bound to that agreement. I believe Gabe and Sophie are in love, and I, for one, will not prevent them from marrying. I am willing to write the king to explain the situation, if you are also willing, Duke Wilhelm."

"What about Brittola?" Valten turned to face them, gesturing with his hand.

Duke Wilhelm took a deep breath before speaking to Duke Baldewin. "Gabe made an agreement with Brittola and her father, and he was no child when he made that alliance. Our family's honor is at stake in the matter. Gabe, you must break the betrothal honorably."

"I don't yet know how, but I will," Gabe said, looking more contrite than Sophie had ever seen him. "I am sorry to cause pain to anyone, but Brittola is young and I believe she will forget me. She will no doubt get a better offer."

Valten snorted contemptuously. After crossing, then uncrossing his arms, he declared, "I release Sophie from the betrothal. I could never marry a woman who is in love with my brother." He bowed curtly to them all, then stalked out of the room and was gone.

A pang of guilt sliced through her, and Gabe looked uncomfortable.

Duke Wilhelm stepped closer to Gabe. "Gabe, falling in love with your brother's betrothed shows an irresponsibility and lack of self-control that is not pleasing, as does the fact that you decided to save her yourself after we had forbidden it."

Sophie's heart sank. She knew how hurt Gabe must feel to hear his father call him irresponsible. She searched Duke Wilhelm's face, praying, *God, please let him not forbid our marriage. Please let him understand. Make him say he forgives us.*

"But you also showed fortitude and bravery in saving her from her enemies, and in being truthful about your love for Sophie." He paused as he looked Gabe in the eye. "When I consider what could have happened and the alternatives, falling in love and being determined to marry is not the worst thing you could have done. In fact" — his voice softened — "it shows that you have returned to us as a responsible man, Gabe. Taking all the circumstances into consideration, I'm proud of you." He was almost smiling as he gazed tenderly at his son.

"Thank you, Father."

"So what do you propose to do about Brittola?"

"I shall write her and her father a letter begging to be released from our marriage agreement."

Duke Baldewin, who still stood at Sophie's side, spoke up. "And I shall offer them an inducement if they will break the agreement."

Duke Wilhelm nodded. "I see you have thought this through and acquired an ally."

Gabe gave a hint of a smile.

"Have you thought about what you will do if Brittola's father refuses your offer?"

"I have. But perhaps it is best you do not know."

Duke Wilhelm gave his son a very stern look. "I wouldn't have asked if I didn't want to know."

"I shall marry Sophie anyway."

"Are you prepared to deal with the consequences?"

"I am."

"The count could make a complaint to the king against you, even though no formal papers were signed. The king could punish you in any way he chooses."

"I am aware of that, Father."

"Very well."

Gabe's mother and father began talking to him in hushed tones again.

Sophie wanted to go to Gabe, to talk with him, touch him. It was painful to stay away from him, to see him staying away from her, but she admonished herself to be patient. He probably wanted to talk to her as much as she wanted to talk to him, but he was being discreet and self-controlled.

Her father turned to her and began speaking. He told her what little he knew of her escape from the duchess. Forcing herself to look away from Gabe, she began regaling her father with the stories of Gabe's bravery and strength.

"I am so sorry I wasn't there to protect you," her father said with pain in his eyes, "from all the terrible things Ermengard must have said and done to you."

Sophie put her arms around her father, hugging him tight. "Don't be sad, Father. God is healing me ... God is healing me. And He will heal you too."

They held each other for a long time, and she knew from a few sniffs that her father was most likely crying, or at least holding back tears. She and her father broke away from each other, her father drawing out a handkerchief and dabbing the corners of his eyes.

Just then, Sophie noticed a messenger enter the room and hand a sealed piece of parchment to Gabe. Gabe broke the wax seal, then clutched the parchment with both hands, his eyes quickly scanning the text. Sophie watched Gabe's throat bob as he swallowed, still staring at the letter.

When he tore his eyes from the piece of parchment, his gaze went straight to Sophie, a strange look on his face.

He tossed the letter over his shoulder, strode across the room toward her, his eyes alight with triumph. He grabbed Sophie around the waist, tilted her backward, and kissed her passionately on the lips.

Finding herself off balance, Sophie held onto his shoulders. Her heart soared at his sudden display of affection.

When he stopped kissing her and let her stand a little straighter, she stared into his eyes for a clue as to what had come over him. Gabe smiled at her as if they were the only two people in the room. His gaze shifted to her lips.

"God worked it out for you, son. And the timing could not have been more serendipitous."

Sophie peeked around Gabe's shoulder and saw Duke Wilhelm handing the letter to his wife while he grinned and shook his head. "Valten always did say you were the luckiest boy alive."

Lady Rose scanned the letter then looked up, smiling at Sophie. "This is from Brittola's father. He is offering remuneration to Gabe because Brittola has married someone else. The betrothal is broken!"

Before Sophie could say anything, Gabe dipped her backward and kissed her again. And she kissed him back.

That night, at supper in the Great Hall, Sophie felt bad enough for Valten that she asked Gabe to not touch her hair or shoulder or arm in front of everyone, to behave himself and eat his dinner without staring at her every moment. She couldn't keep him from sitting beside her and decided not to begrudge him holding her hand under the table. And if his knee happened to brush against hers, well, he was her fiancé and they would be married in a few weeks.

Seeing her father alive and well across the table from her, talking companionably with Gabe's father, Sophie marveled at how God had given him back to her after all these years. It was a miracle.

Gabe squeezed her hand and she blinked up at him. She read the love in his eyes and felt her own love for him spilling out in a contented sigh. The man she loved, loved her too, and love was the greatest miracle of all.

# Epilogue

*Gabe's entire family waited outside Hohendorf* Castle in the place where the burned-out chapel once stood. A priest stood with them, waiting for the bride to emerge from the castle so the wedding could begin.

"I wish you well, little brother." Valten embraced Gabe, clapping him on the back.

"So you forgive me?" For once, Gabe couldn't make a joke out of the situation. He met Valten's eye, praying for mercy.

"Of course I forgive you. I would have done the same thing had I been in your place." But Valten looked a bit rueful.

Gabe let out the breath he was holding and laughed.

"I can't let you best me, though," his giant brother said. "I'll just have to rescue my own damsel in distress."

"You will, big brother. You will."

Gabe truly did have a wonderful family, as Sophie daily reminded him. And though things had been very tense between the two brothers these past several weeks, Valten had forgiven him for stealing his betrothed. *Thank you, God.*

Duke Baldewin joined them on the grassy knoll, standing before the priest, and then the bride made her appearance. Even though her face was veiled, Gabe had no trouble recognizing his beautiful Sophie. She took his hand as they faced the priest, all of Gabe's family behind them, along with the servants who'd stayed at the castle and all the villagers of Hohendorf. Gabe tried to force himself to listen to and comprehend the priest's words, but it was difficult, as Sophie's beauty kept distracting him.

Sophie and some other women had planted flowers in a circle, outlining the smoke-stained stones of the chapel that had been demolished. Sophie seemed to have an obsession with flowers. All he had to do to make her happy was bring her an armful, or even a handful, of colorful blooms. Ah, but she was sweet when she was happy.

The priest was still talking about God's plan for man and woman, and Gabe figured he had a few minutes before he would have to pay attention.

Duke Baldewin had hired a master mason to come to Hohendorf and build not only a new chapel, but also a new castle, as he claimed the old castle held too many bad memories to be allowed to stand. Gabe was to be the mason's apprentice, to learn all about designing and planning and building. Sophie's father had promised to make Gabe his heir, but it made Gabe feel better to think of having his own work, his own purpose, and Sophie said she didn't need to stay in Hohendorf. She wanted to go with him wherever his work led. Besides, based on the way he looked at Lady Petra, Duke Baldewin would be marrying again soon and would have more children of his own. Gabe wanted to make his own way in life.

"... Do you take this woman, Sophia Auriana Gersenda Breitenbach, to be your wife ..."

*Time to pay attention.* "I do."

"I'm not finished," the priest whispered.

"Sorry," Gabe whispered back.

Sophie pressed a hand over her mouth.

"To have and to hold, from this day forward, for better, for worse, for richer, for poorer, in sickness and in health, to love and to cherish, till death you do part, according to God's holy ordinance, and thereto plight her your troth."

"I do." *Oh yes. Most definitely.*

He breathed in deeply, squeezing Sophie's hand.

She had her turn, listening to the words of the priest, and then saying, "I do."

"You may kiss the bride."

Gabe lifted Sophie's veil. She was beautiful, with a little extra glow about her, but he didn't take time to stare at her. He'd have the rest of his life to look at her. Instead, he kissed her, not holding back anything.

If Gabe's life were a book, it was time for the next chapter. And he was ready.

# Acknowledgments

*I want to thank my wonderful editor, Jacque* Alberta, whose constructive advice and way of looking at the overall story is sheer genius. (And thank you, Jacque, for your easy-going, positive vibe! I need it!)

I also want to thank my agent, Rachel Kent, for being so supportive, kind, caring, and great at her job—an all-around nice person. Thanks so much for everything.

I want to thank Sue Williams for always being there for me, and for being a wonderful friend, a great writer, and a really fun traveling buddy. Keep writing!

Thanks to Regina Carbulon for always being willing to pray for me and for being such a great example of faith. You taught me how to start my sentences with, "I'm believing for ..."

Thanks to Denita Black and Sherry Slaughter for praying for me and for listening.

Thanks to Caren Fullerton, Jamie Driggers, and April Erwin for critiquing and encouraging. I love you girls.

Thanks to Linore Burkard and Debbie Lynne Costello for being such great friends. A three-strand cord is not easily broken.

Special thanks to Carol Moncado for always being ready to brainstorm with me, read my stories and critique, or just listen. You are the hardest-working writer I know! It's only a matter of time, girl.

And another special thanks to Cory Kohl for her great horse sense, and for answering so many of my questions, especially with my next book. Thank you!

Thanks to Chriscynethia Floyd, Sara Merritt, Jonathan Michael, Gwen Hendrickson, and all the wonderful people in the Zondervan marketing department. You go above and beyond, and I'm so thankful for you. Thanks to everyone at Zondervan, in all departments, who work hard to make my books look good and sell well. I am forever grateful for your vision.

And thanks once again to Mike Heath of Magnus Creative, the genius who creates my book covers and trailers. I love them so much!

I want to thank all my writer friends in ACFW who are quick to help in every way possible; quick to encourage, quick to give a hug, and really quick to take up for me. You make me laugh and lift my spirits, and you're a big part of the reason I am where I am.

And to all my friends in Seekerville ... thanks for all the cyber hugs, and for chastising me when I want to be lazy or whiny. Your love is a lifeline!

I have to say that I'm very grateful to Taylor Swift, who writes such great songs. I plotted this entire novel, over many months, while listening to "Love Story" and "Enchanted."

Thanks most of all to my readers, and especially those who take time to send encouraging Facebook messages and emails through my website. I couldn't keep doing this if it wasn't for you. You readers are the most important links in the process, the beginning and the end.

And to God who sustains and blesses me. Thank you for helping me keep it all in perspective. I can't live or move or breathe without you.

# *Chapter*

# 1

*Spring, 1386. Hagenheim. The Harz Mountains, Lower Saxony.*

*The townspeople of Hagenheim craned their* necks as they peered down the cobblestone street, hoping to catch a glimpse of the Duke of Hagenheim's two handsome sons. The top-heavy, half-timbered houses hovered above the crowd as if they too were eager to get a peek at Lord Hamlin and Lord Rupert.

Rose shifted her basket from her left hip to her right and wrinkled her nose at the stale smell of sweat from the many bodies pressed close, mingled with the pungent scent of animal dung. Chickens and children skittered about, the clucking and squealing adding to the excited murmurs.

"I'll wait with you to the count of one hundred, Hildy, then I'm leaving." Rose couldn't let Frau Geruscha think her apprentice was a lazy dawdler.

"Are you not curious to see if they've changed?" Hildy asked, her green eyes glinting in the sun.

"No doubt the duke's sons have developed into humble scholars after two years at Heidelberg's university." Even as she spoke, she glanced up the street. In spite of wanting Hildy to think her indifferent to the young noblemen, Rose was glad she had a good view.

Rose's dog, Wolfie, began barking so zealously his front paws lifted off the ground.

"*Hist.* No barking." Rose leaned down and rubbed the ruff of fur at the back of his neck.

"Rose!"

Her heart leapt at the horrified tone in Hildy's voice, and she stood and faced her friend.

"You didn't even wear your best dress!"

Rose glanced down at her green woolen kirtle. "Oh, Hildy. As if it matters."

"At least your hair looks beautiful." Hildy ran her hand down Rose's loose mane of brown curls, only partially hidden by her linen coif. "How do you ever hope to get a husband if you don't pay more attention to your clothing?"

Rose scowled. "I don't hope."

How many times would she have to explain this to Hildy? When Rose was a little child, Frau Geruscha had taken a liking to her. Now that Rose was grown up, the town healer had chosen Rose to be her apprentice—an honorable life's work that would prevent Rose from being forced to marry. Frau Geruscha, having grown up in a convent, had not only taught Rose about medicinal herbs, but also how to read Latin—a skill Rose was very proud of. But it was a skill most men would hardly value in a wife.

"You don't fool me, Rose Roemer. Every girl wants to be married. Besides, look across the street at Mathias." Hildy pointed with her eyes. "He speaks to you every chance he gets, and he's quite handsome."

Rose harrumphed at Hildy's dreamy tone. "The blacksmith's son?" *With his lecherous grin?* "He only wants one thing from me, and it isn't marriage."

"How can you be so sure ..."

Hildy's voice trailed off at the crowd's whispered exclamations as six men on horseback came into view around the bend in the narrow street.

Hildy grabbed her thick blonde braid and draped it over her shoulder then chewed on her lips to redden them. "You should at least try to catch their eye."

Rose shook her head at Hildy. "You know Lord Hamlin is betrothed—as good as married—and Lord Rupert must marry an heiress." Rose took hold of her friend's arm. Someone had to be the voice of reason. "I hate to dampen your excitement, Hildy, but if either of the noble sons takes a single look at us, I'll be vastly astonished."

Hildy smirked. "I won't be."

The approaching clop-clop of hooves drew Hildy's gaze back to the street. "Shh. Here they come." She set her basket of beans, leeks, and onions on the ground behind her and smoothed her skirt.

The throng of people fell silent out of respect for their young lords.

The duke's elder son, Wilhelm, Earl of Hamlin, led the way down the street on his black horse. His younger brother, Lord Rupert, rode beside him. Two bearded knights on cinnamon-colored horses followed three lengths behind the young men, with two more bringing up the rear.

The knights were simply dressed, but the noble sons were covered from neck to toe in flowing robes. Rose stifled a snort. They were only returning home. Did they think they were on their way to the king's court?

Yet as he drew nearer, she saw that Lord Hamlin wore not a robe after all, but a plain cloak of dark wool. His bearing and the proud tilt of his head were what made him look so regal.

In contrast to his brother's outerwear, a fur-trimmed surcoat of lustrous sapphire silk hung over Lord Rupert's lean frame, with only the toes of his leather boots peeking out. The disparity between the brothers went beyond their clothing. Lord Rupert's light brown hair was long and curled at the ends, and a blue ribbon gathered it at the nape of his neck. A jaunty glint shone from his pale eyes. Lord Hamlin's black hair hung over his forehead, and he seemed oblivious to the crowd. He focused his gaze straight ahead, toward Hagenheim Castle, whose towers were visible over the tops of the town's tallest buildings.

No, she'd say they hadn't changed at all.

"*Willkommen!*" Hildy called out. "Welcome back, my lords!" She waved her hand high, as though hailing a messenger.

All eyes turned to Rose and Hildy. A spear of panic went through Rose. She wanted to hide, but it was too late. Lord Hamlin's eyes darted in their direction, alighted on Rose, and held. His expression changed and his features softened as he looked at her. Then his gaze swept down, taking in her basket and her dress. He quickly faced forward again.

*He realizes I'm nobody, a peasant girl.* Heat spread up Rose's neck and burned her cheeks.

Lord Rupert's huge blond warhorse walked toward Rose and Hildy as the crowd suddenly took up Hildy's cheer. "*Willkommen!* Welcome back!" The horse came within three feet of the girls and stopped, stamping his hooves on the cobblestone street and sending Wolfie into a wild fit of barking.

Rose threw her arms around Wolfie's neck to hold him back. Her temples pounded at the sight of the warhorse's powerful legs.

The younger nobleman swept off his plumed hat, bowing from his saddle. His eyes roved from Hildy to Rose, then he winked. "I thank you, ladies, for your kind welcome." He grinned and swung his hat back on his head, then spurred his horse into a trot and caught up with the others.

"Did you see that? Did you see it?" Hildy pounded on Rose's shoulder.

Wolfie calmed as the men rode into the distance. Rose let go of him and stood up, glaring at Hildy. "I can't believe you called out to them."

"Lord Rupert actually spoke to us. *To us.* And did you see how Lord Hamlin looked at you?" Hildy clutched her hands to her heart, gazing at the clouds. "Are they not the most handsome men you've ever seen? I could hardly breathe!" She turned and smiled at Rose. "I knew they'd like what they saw once they caught sight of you."

"Would you keep your voice down?" Rose urged Hildy to start walking toward the *Marktplatz*. She glanced around, afraid the townspeople would overhear their embarrassing conversation. She imagined the miller's skinny wife, who walked ahead of them, snorting in derision at Hildy's compliment. The shoemaker's buxom daughter, striding down the other side of the street, would laugh out loud.

Hildy and her romantic notions of love. She was a candlemaker's daughter, dreaming about the local nobility as if she had any chance of inspiring a serious thought in them. As a woodcutter's daughter, Rose held no grand illusions about her own prospects.

Hildy's chatter faded into the background as Rose wondered at Lord Rupert's flirtatious wink. But what stuck in her mind was the way Lord Hamlin had looked at her. Thinking of that, her face began to burn once again. She'd encountered her share of leering men and their crude comments, but Lord Hamlin's look was different. It had made her feel pretty—until he noticed her clothing.

She should have worn her good dress, the crimson one with the bit of white silk at the neck and wrists that Frau Geruscha had given her. Hildy said it brought out the red tint in her chestnut hair. But how could she have known Hildy would draw the attention of both Lord Hamlin and Lord Rupert and that they would look straight at her?

Realizing her train of thought, she snorted. What difference did it make which dress she wore? Everyone knew Lord Hamlin was betrothed to the daughter of the Duke of Marienberg. But betrothed or not, he'd hardly be interested in her. And Lord Rupert, as the younger son, would inherit none of the family's wealth and so would need to find a rich heiress to marry.

If, as an apprentice, Rose could impress Frau Geruscha

with her skill, she would become the next healer—needed, respected. She could avoid the indignity of marrying someone out of desperation.

So she'd never experience love. Most married people didn't, either.

Rose dipped her quill in the pot of ink and concentrated on scratching out the next sentence of the tale she was writing. Frau Geruscha encouraged her to write her stories, although she said it was probably best if she didn't tell anyone about them.

Shouts drifted through the open window of the healer's chambers. From her vantage point in the southwest tower of Hagenheim Castle, Rose peered out, seeking the source of the commotion.

"Make way!"

Two men hastened across the courtyard. They carried a boy between them, using their arms for a seat. A woman ran behind them.

Rose scrambled to hide her parchment, pen, and ink in the small trunk beside her desk. "Frau Geruscha! Someone's coming!" She snatched up a gray apron that lay nearby and slipped it over her head.

Wolfie adjusted his grip on his bone and growled low in his throat.

"Wolfie, stay."

The dog's lips came together, sheathing his fangs, but he focused his eyes on the door.

Frau Geruscha entered the chamber from the storage room, her wimple bobbing like the wings of a great white bird.

The two men carrying the boy burst through the door, the woman following close behind. Rose recognized one man as a farmer who lived near her parents' home. The boy was his son, perhaps eight years old. He wore ragged brown hose and his torn shirt drooped on his thin frame. Bright red blood covered one of his sleeves. His lips were white, as if all the blood had drained out of his body.

Here was her chance to show Frau Geruscha she was a competent apprentice. She would strive to appear calm and ready to help. She was thankful she had already braided her hair that morning and covered it with a linen cloth, as her mistress had instructed her.

"Frau Geruscha!" Fear and panic lent a high pitch to the woman's voice. "Our son fell on the plow blade."

The healer's wise face wrinkled in concentration as her gaze swept the boy from head to toe. She pointed to a low straw bed against the wall, and the men laid the child on it.

Pain drew the boy's features tight. Rose longed to comfort him, but she didn't want to get in Frau Geruscha's way.

Frau Geruscha sat on the edge of the bed. She showed no emotion as she pulled back his sleeve, revealing the gaping wound.

"No!" The boy screamed and shrank away from her. He held his arm against his chest and drew his knees up like a shield.

Rose turned her head. *O God, don't let me get sick.* She had to prove herself.

Frau Geruscha glanced back at Rose. "Fetch me some water from the kettle and a roll of bandages."

Rose scurried to the fireplace and grabbed a pottery bowl. Using a cloth to hold the lip of the iron kettle, she tipped it to one side and poured hot water into the shallow vessel. She carried it back to Frau Geruscha then dashed to the storage room to get the bandages.

"Don't touch it!"

Rose tried to force the boy's terrified voice from her mind. When she returned, Frau Geruscha was washing the blood from the wound. Rose held out the roll of fabric.

Her hand shook. She had to get control of herself before her mistress noticed.

Frau Geruscha took a section of the clean linen and used it

to soak up the blood and water around the wound. "Rose, get him some henbane and wormwood tea." She turned to the parents. "The herbs will help ease his pain."

Biting her lip, Rose ran into the adjoining storage room again. She should have guessed Frau Geruscha would want that tea. She should have already gone for it instead of standing there with her mouth open. So far she wasn't proving herself very competent.

Shelves of dried herbs lined the walls. She grabbed the flasks labeled *henbane* and *wormwood* and scooped a spoonful of each into a metal cup, then used a dipper to ladle in steaming water from the kettle.

She hurried back and placed the cup in the mother's outstretched hands. The woman held it to her son's lips.

Frau Geruscha made the sign of the cross and laid her hand on the boy's arm. She then closed her eyes. "In the name of the Father and of the Son and of the Holy Ghost, we ask you, God, to heal this boy's wound in the name of Jesus and by the power of his blood. Amen."

The smell of blood, warm and stifling, mingled with the odor of sweat. The bowl of water was now bright red, and Rose caught another whiff of the familiar, sickening smell.

Frau Geruscha opened her eyes and crossed herself again. She reached into her box of supplies and held up a needle. The tiny metal object glinted in the morning light.

The boy locked wide eyes on the needle and screamed, "No! No! No!" His father moved to hold him down.

Rose fled into the storeroom, her bare feet noiseless on the stone floor. She leaned against the wall and sucked in deep breaths. Her head seemed to float off her shoulders, as light as a fluff of wool, while her face tingled and spots danced before her eyes.

How childish. Rose pressed her face into her hands and stifled a groan. Had Frau Geruscha seen her flee the room? She must get back in there and overcome this squeamishness.

She drew in another deep breath. The earthy odor of the herbs that hung from the rafters was stuffy, but at least it didn't trouble her stomach like the smell of blood. Rose focused on the sights around her—the rushes strewn over the stone floor … low shelves packed with flasks of dried herbs … the rough stone wall poking her back. The screaming drifted away.

The tingling sensation gradually left her face and she breathed more normally.

She entered the room again, stepping carefully so as not to rustle the rushes on the floor and draw attention to herself. The boy's eyes were closed and his lips were the same ash gray as his face. He must have lost consciousness, since he didn't even wince as the needle pierced his skin.

Frau Geruscha quickly finished stitching the wound. After she tied the last knot and clipped the string of catgut, she wound the remainder of the bandage around his arm and tied a thin strip of cloth around it to hold it in place.

Finally, the people left, carrying the limp boy with them.

Rose hurried to clean up the water spills and the bloody linen. Her stomach lurched at every whiff of the metallic odor, but she had to pretend it didn't bother her, to hope her mistress didn't notice how it affected her.

"Are you well?" Frau Geruscha's gray eyes narrowed, studying Rose. "You looked pale when you ran into the storage room."

So her mistress had noticed. "I am very well."

How could she be so pathetic? She had to find a way to prepare herself for the next time she must face the blood, screams, and smells.

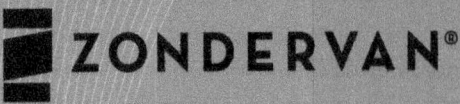

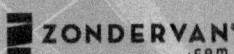